The Rabbi of Resurrection Bay

The Rabbi of Resurrection Bay

A Novel

SETH B GOLDSMITH

ISBN: 1515094340
ISBN 13: 9781515094340
Library of Congress Control Number: 2015911640
CreateSpace Independent Publishing Platform
North Charleston, South Carolina

Dedicated to the memory of my grandparents who had the courage and foresight to come to the United States and my parents for their unwavering support and love

Acknowlegments

Many people have provided encouragement, assistance and guidance during the course of my writing this book. To all of these individuals, particularly the ones who I have inadvertently failed to mention, I am grateful and to them I am appreciative.

First, I want to thank my wife, Wendy Benjamin Goldsmith, who was a source of constant encouragement and periodic useful criticism based on listening to me read various chapters and revisions. Her support was immensely important.

Special thanks goes to Barry Alter, MD who read the completed manuscript with a fine toothcomb and offered invaluable observations and suggestions that I believe strengthened the final version of this book. Thanks also to Bernie Greenspan, MD and Carol Sassoon who served as additional "beta" readers and provided me with important recommendations for the final manuscript.

I also wish to acknowledge numerous other people who at various points in my writing shared their technical expertise and experiences with me. These people, who were kind enough to assist me are: Lowell Goldsmith, MD; Rabbi Gideon Goldenholz; Rabbi James Kahn; Barry Nathanson, MD; Steven Schultz, MD; David Berkhower, MD; Jeremy White, MD; Tim Coons, Stefan Nilsson, Cindy Clock, Robert Tell, the late Dario Martinez, David Owens, Andy Cagnetta, Attorney Jeffrey Robinson, Attorney Andy Pevehouse, Attorney Benjamin Goldsmith,

Dr. Rafael Medoff, Dr. Jonas Goldsmith, Sam and Audrey Meline, Leslie Fried, Amy Benjamin, Brian Perry, Attorney Debra Benjamin, Evan Benjamin, Wendell Gray, MD., Ph.D.; and Attorney Marc Raspanti.

Special thanks to Rabbi Jack Reimer for granting me permission to publish the poem, "We Remember Them," that was authored by Rabbi Reimer and Rabbi Sylvan Kamens. The poem "Kol Nidre" is from a book authored by my late wife Sandra Brooks Goldsmith.

Part One
In The Beginning

One

BAL HARBOUR, FLORIDA

Despite the enormous competition for the honor, Marc Cohn, MD, President and CEO of THE FIVE-STAR INTERNATIONAL INSTITUTE FOR COSMETIC SURGERY, was known as the most arrogant and egocentric physician in South Florida—a reputation easily earned by his well-known narcissism, a complete lack of empathy toward the impoverished, and incessant TV and web advertisements promising male and female *mieskeits* that Cohn and his staff could perform miracles. Even though most people still thought he was a *putz*, they didn't talk much about it because they felt sorry for him after his wife's recent death.

In fact, other physicians and most of his patients recognized Cohn as a talented plastic surgeon. The physician-rating websites invariably were filled with glowing client testimonials about their experiences undergoing Brazilian butt lifts, breast enhancements, Botox treatments and facelifts at the Institute.

Cohn's medical practice, as well as careful investments, had made him a wealthy man (only dealing in cash—no Obamacare for him). His money though had turned him into a voracious consumer without a charitable bone in his body. For example, when a homeless guy at the Aventura exit off Interstate 95 would ask him for spare change, the poor person was not only met with a refusal, but he also received a derisive lecture about taking handouts, getting a job, and the importance of "making it on your own." As far as Cohn was concerned, welfare and charity made people lazy. He similarly refused appeals from Miami's elite representing the American Cancer Society, Multiple Sclerosis Foundation, The Jewish Federation or a range of other worthwhile causes. Normally, in those instances he either avoided the fundraiser or offered a lame excuse for not giving a donation.

But, when it came to Cohn's toys—his Bentley Continental GT Speed Convertible or his 47-foot Intrepid Sport Yacht with its four 350-horsepower Yamaha V8 engines—money was not an issue. In Marc Cohn's mind he worked hard and was now reaping the benefits of that labor.

On Christmas Day, six months after his forty-third birthday, Cohn woke shivering and desperately needing to urinate. But first he wanted to remember his dream about walking barefooted in a snow-covered field while searching for a toilet. As hard as he tried to recall the details, they eluded him. But he still had to pee. Rolling onto his left side, he glanced at the green glow of the digital clock on his nightstand, which displayed 5:00 AM. His brain processed the information: time to start the day. He reached blindly for his glasses, trying to remember where he had left them when he had dozed off reading the latest Carl Hiaasen book comically disparaging life in South Florida. Hiaasen was his favorite author, particularly after he had read *Skin Tight* with its incredibly incompetent Bal Harbour–based plastic surgeon, Rudy Graveline. He hoped Hiaasen fans did not think that he was the model for Graveline.

As he had done for more than sixteen years, he carefully and slowly lifted the covers and slipped out of bed. He did not want to disturb his wife Cathy's sleep. Then he remembered. Cathy was dead. Her funeral was scheduled for later that afternoon. Cohn thought for a moment that it was a distressing way to start his winter vacation, which typically meant a week at their condo at the Ritz-Carlton in Dorado, Puerto Rico.

It had all happened so suddenly. Three days earlier Cathy had awakened in the middle of the night with what she had described as the worst headache of her life. She got out of bed, made her way to the kitchen for three ibuprofens, and went back to sleep. She woke up again at 6 AM and told Cohn she felt nauseous. He asked her if she had experienced any popping sensation in her head. When she answered "yes," he immediately called 9-1-1 and went in the ambulance with her to the emergency room. The diagnosis was subarachnoid hemorrhage—she was bleeding in her brain. The hospital team tried its best, but eighteen hours later she was dead.

Cathy's death shook Cohn to the core. He kept obsessing over what he should or could have done, always reaching the same conclusion: he was a failure, a physician who couldn't save his own wife. He hadn't been alert enough in the middle of the night to realize that Cathy's headache was a signal for him to act. Instead, after hearing her complain at 3 AM, he went back to sleep till 5 o'clock, got up, went downstairs to the gym for fifty minutes of cardio on the elliptical, and only when he came back upstairs at 6 o'clock did he ask her the key question. At that moment, hours after her initial symptoms, Cohn recognized the seriousness of the situation and called for help. By the time Miami-Dade Fire Rescue arrived, Marc Cohn already feared that the golden hour, that precious time period when a person's chances of survival are at their highest, had slipped away because of his lack of attention.

Cohn was thinking about Cathy as well as the fragments of his dream as he walked slowly through his $3 million condominium to stand on the living room balcony overlooking the Atlantic Ocean. He loved to watch the morning sunrise, particularly the mix of colors and the moment of the fireball sun rising on the eastern horizon. As he stood there that morning gazing over the Atlantic he started thinking about his eulogy for Cathy, and about Max, their fourteen year-old son. Max was a good kid, but he certainly had a basketful of challenges. Dealing with him had been Cathy's full-time job. Now it was his and he was sad and maybe even resentful. He knew his life had changed, forever altered, and it was definitely for the worse.

Cohn turned around, came back through the sliding door, and walked to his front entrance to pick up his two newspapers: *The Wall Street Journal*, his financial bible, and the *Miami Herald*, the hometown gossip sheet. He took the papers into the kitchen, placed them on the counter, got out one of his many "Institute" mugs that prominently featured his picture, and popped a hazelnut K-Cup into his coffee maker.

For the next few hours he appeared dazed as he tried to focus on reading the papers while his mind wandered back to thoughts of Cathy. He couldn't believe she was dead. They had been together since his fifth day of medical school at Columbia when he had spotted her sitting alone studying at a table in the Augustus Long Health Sciences Library. She was a senior nursing student with dark hair, sky blue eyes, and a flawless complexion. His first thought was that she wasn't Jewish and his parents would kill him—a thought that passed quickly as he remembered that he was free to do what he wanted; his parents were dead.

Now sitting in the kitchen with its expansive views of the Atlantic Ocean he was sad and lost thinking about a eulogy for the wife he would never touch again. Cohn's morose thoughts were interrupted by a yell from across the apartment, "Dad, what should I wear?" Cohn wasn't ready for any of this.

"Max, stop yelling and wear your blue suit. Uncle Norman, Aunt Blake, and your cousins will be here in a few minutes for breakfast and we will be picked up at 1 o'clock." It was also time for him to get into gear.

He drank his coffee, rinsed out the mug, and headed for the en suite bathroom with its faux gold faucets, two-person Jacuzzi, and the bidet that Cathy and he used as one of the world's most expensive magazine and newspaper racks. The Travertine marble was cold to his feet as he made his way to the section of the toilet room where he had what he called his single greatest and silliest extravagance: an almost $14,000 custom-made urinal shaped like a conch shell. But it always made him smile. Turning on the TV that was embedded in the mirror above the sink, Marc started to get ready for what he thought was going to be the worst day of his life.

Maria-Sofia Gonzales-O'Brien, the local station's weather "girl" came on to present her forecast: the temperature in Miami was 73 degrees, going up to 82, no rain, one to three foot chop in the ocean. He remembered Maria-Sofia from her recent breast enhancement surgery. It had clearly done wonders for her career. His mind returned to the weather. *Too bad,* he thought, today would be a good day to take out the boat, but a funeral trumps all plans.

Two

SEWARD, ALASKA

A week after moving from Boston to the Seward subdivision of Resurrection Bay, Hannah (Chani) Weissfogel Kahn found her dream house—a three-bedroom Cape Cod with gray weathered cedar shake siding and a high-pitched slate roof. She was initially drawn to the modest house by its expansion possibilities as well as the views of Resurrection Bay, nearby Mount Marathon, and the peaks of the 587,000-acre Kenai Fjords National Park. Location was also of paramount importance for her work life. The house had the benefit of being close to the highway that linked Seward to Anchorage with spur roads to the rest of the Kenai Peninsula and, more importantly, the Seward Municipal Airport where Chani kept her plane.

Immediately after purchasing the house Chani began the process of adding an 800 square foot room that would serve as the Jewish community's library, meeting area, and synagogue. The new space was constructed as a two-story Alaskan timber frame room with floor to ceiling windows and exposed spruce trusses and beams. Dominating the southern end of the room was a stone fireplace with a granite slab hearth decorated with cushions. This nook was designed as a place to sit and warm-up during the myriad cold winter evenings on the Kenai Peninsula.

The northern end of the room was designated as the synagogue. It had an eight inch raised platform known as a *bima*, and hugging the back wall of the bima was a wooden cabinet that held two large parchment scrolls called *Torahs*, a custom-designed table for resting the Torahs when they are being read, and a few chairs. Functional, clean, and elegant in their simplicity—just the way Chani designed it.

As a child growing up in a Fort Lauderdale Modern Orthodox Jewish community Chani only knew about two places: her home in Florida and a summer cottage her family owned in New York's Adirondack Mountains.

Alaska first entered her consciousness when she was in the sixth grade and learned that it had become part of the United States in a purchase negotiated in 1867 by Abraham Lincoln's Secretary of State William Seward for an amount of $7.2 million—or two cents per acre for a land area twice the size of Texas. Since she had never been to Texas she dug through her geography books and figured out that the 663,267 square miles of Alaska was greater than the total land area of every state on the eastern coast of the United States from Maine right to the tip of Florida.

Chani was intrigued to learn that Alaska was known as "Seward's Folly" because many Americans thought that the U.S. government official had made a bad deal. That changed when gold was discovered near Juneau in 1880, and Nome became another center of gold exploration in the 1890s. Then in 1896 the gold rush went into high gear with discoveries in the Klondike that propelled several Alaskan towns into staging, supply and recreation areas for the fortune seekers. Typical of those making their way to the last frontier was Wyatt Earp and his Jewish wife Josephine Marcus who came to Nome in 1897, and cashed in on the gold rush by running a saloon (some say a brothel) for prospectors.

When her parents asked her what she wanted for a bat-mitzvah gift she answered, "A trip to Alaska." The trip began the day after Chani completed the 8th grade with an evening flight to Vancouver, British Columbia. The following afternoon they boarded a cruise ship heading north along the Inside Passage with initial stops at Ketchikan, Juneau, and Skagway. All of the sights along the way were awe-inspiring, but nothing caught her attention more than the final stop in Seward. The joy Chani experienced in the Alaskan outdoors by fishing on Resurrection Bay, hiking the area around Exit Glacier, and watching bears catch salmon on a nearby river, lead her to tell her parents that her dream was to someday live near Resurrection Bay.

Growing up Chani always looked forward to the last few weeks of July and the month of August. That was the time when she and her parents would escape Florida's heat and humidity by staying at their cottage near Tupper Lake. The vacation home was an isolated three-bedroom log cabin set on ten acres. The property had its own a small private lake complete with two vintage wooden canoes, several hiking trails, and countless Great Northern Loons. Each evening these birds with their checkered black and white summer plumage would usher in the dusk with their assorted trills. There was even a family or two of bears that roamed their property.

For Chani this was paradise. But her most soul satisfying adventures started when she was a teenager. Two or three times each August she would bike twelve miles along the quiet country roads from her cottage to Mount Arab, hike up to the mountain's 2,450-foot summit, climb the abandoned fire tower, and then take a seat on the wooden floor. After a few minutes of looking down at Eagle Crag Lake and across the woods at the Adirondack Mountains in the distance, Chani would close her eyes and quietly begin singing and praying. These were her most precious private spiritual moments of the summer.

As important as the outdoors were for her, she also always looked forward to Friday evenings when the family would make the fifteen minute walk into Tupper Lake and attend services at the hundred-year-old Beth Joseph Synagogue. She knew that the house of worship was often called The Peddlers' Synagogue because of the work-life of the thirty or so original families who in 1905 built the Italianate style *shul*. The building, which was closed from 1954 through 1988 and then restored to its original architectural elegance, was now primarily a tourist attraction with summer concerts and lectures—except for services on Friday nights in July and August.

Chani enjoyed being in that restored wooden synagogue and inhaling the still lingering scent of the pine wood paneled walls. She would sometimes close her eyes and imagine that she was in a small shul in Eastern Europe, where he great-grandparents may have prayed. For her, going to Friday night services in that remote village in upstate New York, and listening to the chanting of the prayer leader and congregation, connected her with something unfathomable—warm and full of contentment.

In stark contrast to her Adirondack experiences, shortly after her eleventh birthday a friend invited her "up north" to Easthampton, Long Island for the fourth of July weekend. She went and found herself bored by the barbeques, overpriced shopping, and restaurants. The worst part was being dragged to a birthday party on July 5th for her friend's pet golden retriever. As she was being driven back to Manhattan to meet her parents for a few days of vacation in the city, she came to the conclusion, even at that young age, that the playgrounds for the rich and famous were too ostentatious and vapid for her. She simply loved the solitude and beauty of nature that she felt was best found in rural America.

At the age of seventeen Chani graduated from high school as valedictorian of her class. After applying to the three top small liberal arts colleges in the country, she selected Amherst College. As she explained her decision to family and friends, she said that her brain told her that either Amherst, Williams, or Swarthmore would provide the intellectual challenge which she needed, but her heart whispered that she would most enjoy the ambiance of Amherst and its sister town of Northampton—and she tried hard to listen to her heart. With a smile on her face she would also say that she definitely looked forward to hiking in the nearby Holyoke Mountain Range and kayaking on the waters of the Connecticut River.

At five foot seven inches, with a slender yet muscular build, she was an extremely attractive young woman. She had a smooth skinned face accentuated by high cheekbones, wide set gray-blue eyes, a narrow slightly turned up nose covered with a light sprinkling of freckles, and a wide mouth that seemed to be in a perpetual smile—perhaps a reflection of her generous spirit and overall optimism about life.

When not studying or outdoors she was a committed fitness buff. Her days at Amherst began at 6:00 AM with five-mile runs followed by a regimen of weights and stretching. During her freshman year she joined the track and field team and in the spring started rowing with the crew club and found pickup ice hockey games at Orr rink several evenings a week. Eating was also passion. Fortunately, from her mother, she had inherited the genetic blessing of a supercharged metabolism that allowed Chani to maintain her slim body despite her absolute love of the food for which the Pioneer Valley had become justly famous.

Nowadays her hikes in Alaska, while less frequent because of her professional obligations, still offered the solitude she needed to handle the everyday challenges of life. Her continuing passion for sports and the outdoors were evidenced by what she called the "junk" she stowed in her plane's luggage compartment and the backseat of her SUV. This junk included running shoes, hiking boots, hockey skates, a helmet and stick, plus a hamper full of clothing for each sport. *Someday*, she vowed, *this mess will be cleaned up.*

A year after she moved to Resurrection Bay she began training for one of Alaska's most famous human races: the annual Fourth of July Mount Marathon Race in nearby Seward. Through her training she developed a group of running buddies. The simple but demanding goal of completing the 3.1-mile race up the 3,022-foot Mount Marathon and back downtown was amongst the pleasures of her summers.

The challenges Chani liked least were the grueling winter drives through Alaska. When the weather was cooperative, typically in the late spring through the early fall, her trips away from home meant flying her five-passenger twenty-three year-old Cessna 206. Ever since she received her initial certification as a pilot during her college years she had wanted to someday own a plane.

With the move to Alaska that dream became a reality and a serious responsibility. Although by the time Chani arrived in Alaska she had been a licensed pilot for almost a decade with more than 2,500 hours of flying experience, she enrolled in an eight-day bush pilot training program that was given in Talkeetna, Alaska, a small town south of Denali National Park. Even though she did not intend to fly to the remote and rugged areas of Alaska, her research led Chani to the conclusion that bush pilot training would best equip her with the skills necessary to handle emergencies. Her friends often marveled at her dedication to improving her flying skills. A few wondered if her real goal was to become a commercial bush pilot, but most thought that this was just another example of Chani's commitment to her craft, in this case flying.

If you asked her about her favorite book the answer was, without hesitation, The Bible. She particularly loved the proverbs and one she frequently quoted was 16:18, "Pride goes before destruction and arrogance before failure." She felt this proverb particularly applied to flying in Alaska.

She knew she was a good pilot who took meticulous care of her plane, but to be on the safe side she carved out several days each summer for a refresher flight-training course back in Talkeetna. Although she enjoyed the hours of flight instruction, as well as the interactions with the staff and other pilots, the best part of that trip were the views from the air of Denali National Park and the 20,322-foot Mt. McKinley, the highest and perhaps most majestic mountain in North America. At the end of the course, as she headed home with the images of Mt. McKinley in her mind her ritual had become the singing of the Hebrew *Shehecheyanu* prayer, a blessing of praise: "Blessed are You, Lord our God, Ruler of the Universe, who has granted us life, sustained us and enabled us to reach this day."

Chani's typical work related flights were either down the Kenai Peninsula to Homer or across the Kenai Mountains. Her mission was always the same: to visit and teach congregants in the towns of Kenai, Sterling, and Soldotna.

On those rare occasions when her work required her to be away for the weekend the return flight was invariably filled with joy. For her the sight of the small Seward airport and the surrounding mountains meant home. She particularly loved the landings in the late spring through the fall. Coming in over Resurrection Bay, and lining up on 'Runway 31', she could see snow on the mountains ahead as well as the radiance of the setting sun. Those were the moments when Rabbi Chani Kahn felt she was one with the Lord.

But, for the Rabbi of Resurrection Bay, life's bounty and the apparent fulfillment of her dreams had come at the cost of three lives.

Three

Seward, Alaska

A few minutes after Cathy Cohn died Dr. Marc Cohn dialed a cell phone number in Alaska that was routed to voicemail. His next call was to the central number of the Office of the Alaska Public Defender in Seward. He identified himself to the operator and told her it that he needed to speak with Norman Cohn, his older brother. Dr. Cohn was politely informed that Attorney Cohn was in a meeting at the Kenai Peninsula Maximum Security Prison with two inmates and would be available in an hour. In a trembling voice Marc emphasized that the call was about urgent family business and requested that Norman be located and interrupted.

Six minutes later Norman was on the phone and seconds after that he learned of his sister-in-law's death, listening patiently and quietly as his younger brother tearfully shared with him the details of Cathy's last hours. When the call was over he went back to the inmates he was meeting with, told them he had a family emergency and would see them after the New Year. He then called his supervisor in Anchorage, explained the situation, and arranged to begin his Christmas break early. Next he left the prison and on the way home telephoned his secretary and told her of his changed plans. He decided that his wife Blake should learn of this tragedy in person. Fifteen minutes later he was home. As he was sitting on the bench in the mudroom tugging off his snow boots, Blake walked over to greet him.

Sensing a problem she looked at Norman quizzically and asked, "What's up, sweetie; how come you're home early?"

"Bad news. Marc called. Cathy died. I need to skip the Aleyeska ski trip and go to Florida for the funeral."

Tears suddenly filled Blake's eyes and she walked over to Norman and hugged him. "Oh my God, what happened? I am so sorry."

Norman, fighting back tears answered, "I don't really know, some kind of brain aneurysm. It was quick and totally unexpected. I really can't believe this is happening. Look, I have to go to Florida, but if you guys want to stay home or go skiing that's OK with me."

"No, we're all going," Blake answered firmly. "Frankly, Cathy was a good sister-in-law and a wonderful lady. Why she was with Marc is beyond me. She was a kind and gentle soul with a genuine spiritual orientation and a real giving nature. I remember talking to her a few years ago about her volunteer work at the Jewish Home for the Aged in Miami, and it was truly beautiful."

Perhaps because of his background in mental health law, or maybe some thread of familial loyalty, Norman would always end these discussions about his brother by defending Marc's behavior. He invariably argued that it was an understandable response to the stress of their mom being ill for years with cancer, and then the murder of their parents. That afternoon he kept quiet.

By 4:30 PM (Alaska time) Blake and Norman Cohn and their twin twelve-year-old daughters Rachel and Rebecca had repacked, pulled the ski equipment out of their four-year-old Chevy Suburban, booked flights to Fort Lauderdale, arranged for the feeding and exercise of their two Alaskan Malamutes, and were off on their trip from Seward to Anchorage.

They reached downtown Anchorage by 7:30 PM with more than five hours to spare before their 1:35 AM flight to Seattle. Since this was the Christmas season, all the stores were opened late so the family went on a mini-shopping spree for some lightweight clothing before checking in at the airport.

At 10:00 PM they arrived at the Ted Stevens International Airport and rapidly went through the check in and security procedures. Once inside the secured gate area, they headed over to the Norton Sound Seafood House for a dinner of fish and chips. After placing their order, Norman excused himself to make a call on his cell phone. Blake asked whom he was calling and when he replied she smiled approvingly.

Norman dialed the number and a familiar voice answered, "Hi, Norman, what's up?"

"Chani, I'm sorry to bother you so late but I need your advice on a couple of matters. First of all, we had a tragedy in our family—my sister-in-law unexpectedly died in Florida—so all of us are going to the funeral, and we will be staying there for a few days. Actually, we are already in Anchorage at the airport waiting for the flight to Seattle. So I need to ask you to do me a favor and also tell me what to do about a few things."

Norman was interrupted with a whispered, "I am so sorry."

"Chani as you know Christmas Eve and Christmas Day are a big deal at the prison. I saw that you pulled the chaplain's duty for those days and the weekend, and I was going to talk to you about it today. Obviously my sister-in-law's death prevented that conversation. Anyhow, the holidays are a challenging time for lots of the inmates so you'll probably be quite busy. But I would appreciate it if you would keep an eye on two of my clients who seem to be having a rough time of it. Both of these guys have appeals that are coming up for hearings the end of January and they are extremely anxious. Wendell Amaz is the first one, and I am working on the appeal of a life sentence without parole. When I saw him yesterday he was particularly distraught. The other person you already know—our favorite Russian prisoner—Gregory Vishinski. Frankly, the case against him for fraud is so airtight that it will be a miracle if I can win an appeal. And Gregory is smart enough to know that he is probably going to have to do fifteen years. I saw him this morning, before the call from my brother, and he is really very depressed."

She answered, "I understand. Thanks for the heads up. What else did you want to ask?"

Norman replied, "Simply, what am I supposed to do? I knew my sister-in-law and she was a decent lady. As I've probably told you before, my brother is an arrogant jerk and I really have little to do with him. But I am his only family."

She thought for a few seconds and then said, "Norman, being there with Blake and the girls is the biggest statement of support you can make. Listen to your brother, don't give any advice, and follow his lead. Does he have any children?"

"Yes, a son about fourteen. To be honest, I hardly know my nephew. I think he is just a spoiled brat. But, I don't really know much more."

"Just be a good uncle to the boy and try to help him and your brother get through the *Shiva*. I don't know what your brother is going to do about Shiva, but as we once discussed in our class, it's essentially a week when the family stays home and mourns while friends and family visit. Frankly, I most appreciate the approach in Orthodox circles where visitors to a Shiva are told to sit quietly with the mourners and not come in being champion chatterboxes. And certainly they should not ask painful questions. Sometimes people act really stupidly at a Shiva house. So let me suggest that you do whatever is needed, including policing the behavior of the people who visit. You'll see it will all work out. Maybe later on there will be more you can do but one thing at a time. And give Blake and the kids a hug for me. Call me when you are settled and give me your brother's address. I would like to send him a Shiva tray of some food from our congregation."

Norman replied, "Thanks. You're a lifesaver! I am so happy God brought you to Seward. We'll see you when we get back."

When the conversation was over Blake looked at her husband and asked, "Was she helpful?"

Norman replied, "Definitely!"

The flight from Anchorage to Seattle arrived at 5:50 AM and less than three hours later they boarded the nonstop flight to Ft. Lauderdale that, thanks to strong tailwinds, landed at 4:40 PM, twenty-five minutes ahead of schedule.

By the time the Cohns of Alaska had collected their luggage and taken a taxi to the Seaview Hotel in Bal Harbour, just down the street from Marc's condo, they were exhausted. Norman spoke to his brother on the phone and made a plan to see him the next morning for breakfast. They would then all go to the funeral together.

The family ordered hamburgers from room service and by 7:30 PM had placed the trays outside the door for collection, hung the "do not disturb" sign on the outside knob, and were sound asleep.

Four

FORT LAUDERDALE AND NORTH
MIAMI BEACH, FLORIDA

After Marc Cohn spoke with his brother he scrolled through his wife's phone and found the number for his next call: Rabbi Yitzchak Friedman of Fort Lauderdale. He explained to the rabbi's assistant who he was and why he was calling. A minute later the rabbi picked up. "Dr. Cohn, I am so sorry for your loss. I just saw Cathy a week ago and she seemed fine. Do you mind sharing with me what happened?" Cohn went on to explain to the rabbi, whom he had never met, the events that led to his wife's death.

The rabbi responded, "Doctor, I had great admiration for your wife. She was an extraordinary person. You know her work at the Jewish Home deserves a medal. I first met her when my own mother was on the dementia unit and Cathy would come by and sing to her, do magic tricks, and kibitz. My mother loved her. In fact, because of your wife, I became a more frequent visitor to the home."

The rabbi then asked about the funeral arrangements. Cohn gave him the details. "As you know we are not Orthodox and in fact we don't even belong to a synagogue. But, Cathy admired you a great deal, and I also know that if she had a choice, she would want you to officiate at her funeral. Is that possible?" Without a moment's hesitation Rabbi Friedman agreed and they made a plan to meet at the funeral home prior to the service.

The Greenberg Funeral Home on Dixie Highway near Miami Gardens Drive was a nondescript one-story building with a hearse and one Cadillac limousine parked in front. Several men stood in the street directing traffic to a rear parking lot. Cohn didn't expect many people at the funeral since their circle of friends was quite limited and, despite living in a large condo building, Cathy and Marc kept pretty much to themselves. Like many of their neighbors it oftentimes seemed that their closest relationships in the building were with the concierge, doormen, and car valets.

When Cohn, his son, brother, and brother's family arrived at Greenberg's the place was totally quiet. It had already emptied out from the funeral that began at noon. Marc was greeted by the funeral director and quietly asked to accompany him to a room in order to identify Cathy's remains. Marc told Max to wait with his Uncle Norman, and then he dutifully walked into the room with the mortician, stared at Cathy one last time, nodded his head, and then the lid was closed. Marc Cohn sat down, placed his head between his legs, and waited for the wave of nausea to end. Several minutes passed before he felt strong enough to rejoin his family in a private sitting room.

A short while later a tall slender man walked into the room and his eyes swept across the Cohn family trying to pick out Marc. The man, Rabbi Friedman, was wearing a black suit, white shirt, dark blue tie, and a wide-brimmed black Borsalino hat. His outfit was in sharp contrast to piercing green eyes and a face that was largely covered with a flaming red and gray-speckled beard. Marc looked up and could only imagine what the rabbi saw: two men who were the most unlikely looking brothers. Norman was tall, just over six feet in height, and looked like he was a lumberjack in an ill-fitting suit. His 220 pounds, barrel chest, and dark, wild full beard suggested he wasn't a typical Floridian. Marc was slightly shorter, but trim, neatly groomed, and well-tailored—something that tipped people off, including Rabbi Friedman, to his profession of plastic surgery.

Marc Cohn walked over to the rabbi with an outstretched hand. Rabbi Friedman ignored the hand and instead embraced Marc in a bear hug followed by a kiss on the cheek. With tears in his eyes the rabbi whispered words of sympathy into Marc's ear. Marc's eyes also teared up as the two men stood in an embrace for what seemed like minutes.

After being introduced to Max and the rest of the family, Rabbi Friedman went on to outline the funeral service that they were about to experience. He then performed the *K'reah* rite where he tore a portion of Marc and Max's shirt pockets and gave Norman and Blake a black ribbon to wear that he cut with a knife. This he explained was an outward manifestation of mourning and symbolic of how the heart is torn by the loss of Cathy. Rabbi Friedman next asked the family to join with him in a prayer. He handed each of them a card with all the words in Hebrew, English, and transliteration and slowly began: "*Baruckh ata adonai eloheinu melekh haolam, dayan haemet*" [The Lord has given and the Lord has taken, blessed is the name of the Lord. Blessed is the Judge of Truth].

The rabbi then sat with Marc for a few minutes to discuss the remainder of the service. Initially Marc had planned on giving the eulogy. However, by the time he arrived at the funeral home, he felt too emotionally fragile to say even a few words in front of the handful of people he was expecting. After speaking with Friedman, he asked if the rabbi would offer the eulogy. The rabbi said he would be honored to do it. They next discussed the burial and the traditional weeklong Shiva period. Marc said he was reluctant to observe the Shiva, but the rabbi explained that, in his experience, it was an important way for people to show their respect for Cathy as well as support for the family. Marc also said that he wasn't at all prepared to have people visiting in his condo.

After a few more minutes of conversation Marc agreed to a limited Shiva and called his building to alert the front desk that visitors might be coming. While Marc was on the phone with the condo staff, Rabbi Friedman called a nearby kosher market on Harding Avenue to have trays of food sent to Cohn's apartment. The rabbi then suggested that this was a good time to take a few minutes to rest and have some water.

Marc excused himself and went with the funeral director to a small room where he quietly sat with his own sadness and tried to prepare himself for the service. He was feeling numb and lost.

Rabbi Friedman turned to Norman and asked where he lived and what type of work he did.

"I am a public defender doing appellate criminal defense work and we live in Seward, Alaska, which is a small town about three hours south of Anchorage."

Friedman was intrigued and followed up by asking, "How does a nice Jewish boy from New York wind up doing that in Alaska?"

Norman answered, "Happenstance. Basically, my wife is from Anchorage and after we had kids she wanted to go home so we moved from Massachusetts where I had been working to Alaska. Up there I was able to get a public defender job and eventually I was promoted and joined the appellate division. It turned out that most of my clients were doing hard time at the maximum-security prison in Seward, so after two years of commuting we decided to leave Anchorage and move to Seward. For Blake, it was almost like going home because as a kid she had spent summers on her parent's boat in Resurrection Bay."

Rabbi Friedman was fascinated; "Sorry to play a little Jewish geography but I think one of my congregants lives somewhere out there. Her name is Hannah Weissfogel. I lost touch with her a while ago but I recall that last summer someone from my shul was on an Alaskan cruise and said that had run into her in Seward and that she was a rabbi."

Blake smiled. "We sure do know her—you're talking about Chani Kahn, our rabbi. She is one of our closest friends and a fabulous rabbi. Now that I think about it she grew up somewhere down here."

Rabbi Friedman smiled and said, "Right. She was married for a short time to a very nice young man who died rather tragically and I think his name was Kahn. Please send her my warmest regards and tell her I am very proud of her."

Blake relied, "We certainly will say hello to her for you." Then remembering the tragedy that eventually brought their friend to Alaska Blake wanted to change the subject when the funeral director appeared and told them that it was time for the family to enter the chapel. Marc, dragging his feet and on the verge of tears, looked around and was stunned. He expected fifteen to twenty people, mainly his office staff. But the chapel was filled with close to 200 people—most of whom he didn't know. Later, he learned that the strangers to him were all people who respected and admired his wife and, like the Cohn family, they were also devastated by her loss. Many were the residents and staff at the Miami Jewish Home, where she had volunteered in a variety of ways twice each week for over a decade.

The funeral director stood by the microphone and said, "Ladies and gentlemen, please be seated. The funeral will be presided over by Rabbi Yitzchak Friedman of The Cambridge Community Synagogue of Fort Lauderdale. Following the service the internment will take place at the Montefiore Cemetery in North Miami Beach. Shiva will be observed at the Cohn Residence on 10701 Collins Avenue, Bal Harbour. Thank you. Rabbi Friedman?"

The rabbi approached the lectern and began, "We start today's memorial service for Catherine Feldman Cohn, Rivka Bat Avraham, with the 23rd Psalm. 'The Lord is my Shepherd . . . .'"

He read several other psalms and finally came to the Book of Proverbs 31:10—which is thought to be authored by King Solomon and describes an *Eishes Chayil,* a woman of valor, the ultimate good wife. After this reading, he looked at the Cohns and began his eulogy.

"Marc, Max, Norman, Blake, Rachel, and Rebecca, we are all gathered here this afternoon to mourn the loss of an extraordinary woman— a wife, a mother, a sister-in-law, an aunt. Nothing will ever replace her but of the many people I have known in my life, she is someone who deserves the respect and honors normally reserved for royalty. Why? Because in my book she was royalty.

"There is a story in the Talmud about Elijah the prophet walking through a marketplace and someone asks him who gets to go to *Olam Haba.* This is the term we use for the world to come, or as some people think of it – heaven. Elijah points to two people sitting in a corner and says that they will go to Olam Haba. The questioner is stunned by Elijah's response and says 'But who are those people, they are not scholars or rabbis.' And Elijah responds, 'Yes, that is correct but they make people smile.'

"No one I ever met made more people smile than Cathy Cohn, Rivka Bat Avraham. Twice a week her charm, her magic, her juggling, and her beautiful singing would ring through the halls of the home for our Jewish seniors. I first met Cathy almost a decade ago when my own mother of blessed memory was on the dementia unit at the home. I walked into her room and rather than what I had seen in the past—my mom sitting and staring vacantly at the TV—she was holding hands with this beautiful volunteer and they were singing Yiddish songs together.

"After her visit with mom I chatted with Cathy for a few minutes and casually mentioned that mom had grown up in Newfoundland where I was born. The next week when I came around the corner there was my mom and Cathy singing together 'Jack Was Every Inch a Sailor'—an old Newfoundland folk song that my mom used to sing to me. Frankly, I was in tears to see my mother back with us even for a minute.

"Over the years, since my mom passed away, I would visit congregants and their families at the Home and invariably roaming the halls and spreading her special blend of joy was Catherine Feldman Cohn, Rivka Bat Avraham.

"We have lost a jewel. But, she will always be in our hearts and minds. You all honor her and her family by being here today. And all of us can honor her by learning the lessons of her life—that is, being an outstanding parent, dedicated spouse, and committed member of our community. Cathy understood that to live a good life requires the hard work of giving of yourself and your talents to your family as well as the most needy amongst us. Rivka has left us, but in her leaving there is a message and a challenge. Our job is simply to follow her example of chesed, kindness, and love for one another.

The rabbi then looked directly at Marc and Max and said, "May Rivka's memory be a blessing for all of us. *Hamakon yenachem etchem b'toch she'ar aveiki tzion v'yerushlayim*—May God comfort you together with all the mourners of Zion and Jerusalem."

Rabbi Friedman concluded the memorial service with the *El Maleh Rachamin* prayer asking for God's protection of Catherine Feldman Cohn's soul as it ascends to His embrace.

The burial and days after the funeral were a blur for everyone. Max spent most of the time in his room playing video games and coming out for meals. Twice he agreed to take his cousins to the pool where he sat and stared out at the ocean. One afternoon Blake took Max and the girls on a field trip to the Everglades. Rachel and Rebecca thoroughly enjoyed their experience with nature in Florida. The airboat ride through the "River of Grass" and spotting a variety of birds as well as seeing an alligator close up were simply thrilling. Max was bored and said almost nothing.

Marc felt that he needed to be a host during the Shiva and he would greet visitors and listen to their stories about Cathy. Sometimes the conversation would turn to innocuous subjects such as the future of the Dolphins—Miami's professional football team—and whether the Marlins or Heat (baseball and basketball, respectively) would have another disastrous season. By the week's end Marc couldn't wait to get back to work.

The Shiva ended on December 31st. The rabbi had told Marc that the traditional way of ending Shiva was a walk around the block. When Norman arrived at 8:30 AM with fresh bagels and cream cheese, Marc asked his brother to take a walk with him to formally conclude the Shiva. The brothers slowly strolled south on Collins Avenue to 96th street, east a block to the ocean, and up the ocean walkway to the Haulover Cut, one of the channels built by the Army Corp of Engineers in the 1940s that allows boaters to transit between the Atlantic Ocean and the Intracoastal Waterway. Before heading back to the apartment they walked out on the Haulover pier and spent a few minutes watching a handful of fishermen trying to catch lunch and dinner. On the elevator ride back up to the penthouse Marc looked at his older brother and said, "Thank you. I couldn't have done this without you, Blake, and the girls."

Then in a totally uncharacteristic move he hugged Norman and said, "I love you guys." While they were sitting down for a second cup of coffee Marc asked about Norman for the first time in a week. He wanted to know how life was for him in Alaska. Norman replied that he loved it up there. The job was good, the pay and benefits were reasonable, and the girls enjoyed the outdoor life—particularly their summer jobs at a kennel and the fishing on the used boat they had recently purchased. He went on to tell Marc that there was a small but very special Jewish community and, finally, he hoped that Marc and Max would come up for the Memorial Day weekend when Rachel and Rebecca were scheduled to have a joint bat-mitzvah. Marc, in an atypically exuberant moment said, "Count on it!"

At 2:00 PM on New Year's Eve there were kisses and embraces all around in front of the condo as the two Cohn families separated—one heading back to Alaska and the other heading back inside a beautiful and now lonely condominium.

Part Two
The Provenance of Chani

Five

Fort Lauderdale, Florida

Chani's initial feelings of isolation from her Jewish community began during grade school. Of all the children whose families were members of Fort Lauderdale's largest Modern Orthodox congregation, the Cambridge Community Synagogue (CCS), she was one of the two girls who did not go to any of the Hebrew day schools in Broward County. The only other student was Yossi and Carlotta Greenblatt's daughter Tamara. Instead, the two young girls attended the Academy of Broward Country, one of the finest prep schools in the United States. Both the lower and higher division of the Academy occupied the same eighty-five acre campus with small man-made hills, a four hole par 3 golf course, a pond, a field house, indoor and outdoor pools, a baseball field, outstanding classrooms and science laboratories, an ice rink, and a library better than many of the County's branch facilities.

The Weissfogels and Greenblatts had a nodding acquaintance. Yossi and Carlotta were both "Jewbans" (Cuban Jews), who often attended different *minyans* than their non-Latin fellow congregants. The "Jewbans" typically socialized with one another and as a group looked down on their less glamorous and "frumpy" fellow CCS members. Despite the lack of a relationship between their parents, Chani and Tamara became close friends from their first day together in grade one.

Although there were numerous Jewish students at the Academy, Chani and Tamara were the lone members of the Orthodox community. Chani felt uncomfortable with many of the nonacademic aspects of school from the food in the cafeteria to the Saturday sports activities. A major issue almost every year was the need to miss classes on Jewish holidays that did not fall on weekends. Tamara and her parents were "Florida flexible." If an activity had important social or academic interests for Tamara they put the Sabbath or *Yontifs* aside.

The relationship between the two girls started to develop fault lines when they were ten years old. More than anything Tamara wanted a horse for a birthday present. So her father bought her a one, along with riding and dressage lessons, and countless outfits. Almost every weekend was spent riding, competing and developing a new group of acquaintances. The final straw in their unraveling relationship came a few years later. The day after Tamara's bat-mitzvah Chani announced to her family that she wanted nothing to do with her oldest and only close friend at the synagogue.

What precipitated this decision was Tamara's Sunday bat-mitzvah where she gave a speech talking about her love of Blackie (her horse), and how much the horse had taught her about life. She then went on to thank her father for giving her Blackie and making the summers so special with four weeks of snowboard and ski and camp in Chile. Next Tamara thanked her mother as the "greatest mother who ever existed." She concluded her talk, which was supposed to be a commentary of the Torah portion of the week, by sharing with the hundred women at the bat-mitzvah that her favorite times were when she and her mother took their monthly all-day shopping trips to The Town Center Mall in Boca Raton. Her final words were: "I hope someday I too can share with my own children the joy of shopping that I have with my mom."

Chani was incensed. She felt that Tamara was shallow and missed the whole point of the bat-mitzvah. She made a decision to distance herself from her neighbor and friend. In that decision she sent the earliest of signals of the type of people with whom she wished to associate. Years later while recalling that incident, she used it to illustrate the words of one her favorite Talmudic writings from the *Pirkei Avot,* The Ethics of the Father, which said, "*Keep far from an evil neighbor and do not associate with the wicked.*" Chani knew that Tamara was neither evil or wicked, but merely lacked spiritual depth and was self-absorbed. But, for Chani, that was enough reason for her decision.

As an adolescent Chani tried to blend in with the other teenagers during the Sabbath and holiday services by dressing modestly with a long skirt and blouse that hid her blossoming womanhood. But on typical school days she was often seen in jeans, shorts, T-shirts, and tank tops. After Chani started high school a number of the braver upper grade CCS boys took a particular interest in her. These young men were often seen *schmoozing* with her at the Shabbat Kiddush table and when they had the courage, calling her up for a date that she always refused.

Chani's social life primarily revolved around the activities at the Academy. Her infrequent dating was usually with Jewish boys from the Academy but mostly she went to parties with the other kids in her grade. Her athletic prowess brought her attention both at the Academy and in the local area through several *Sun-Sentinel* newspaper articles. By the time she was a junior she had become a star cross-county runner (and holder of several school records), and number one player on the tennis team. Her racing record landed her an invitation to the Junior Olympic Cross Country meet in New Mexico where she placed second in her age division. At that point she seemed to have a lock on a training position on the U.S. Olympic Team. However, for Chani, issues at home and her own intellectual and emotional ambitions were of greater importance to her than spending years training in hopes of fleeting moments of glory.

All of these experiences and feelings of isolation in the CCS community, and to some extent Judaism, changed for her during a two-week period toward the end of her junior year at the Academy. The change began on April 19th, the day after the conclusion of Passover. Although a secular school, for more than four decades the Academy had encouraged the Jewish high school students to go on a two-week trip known as "The March of the Living." That year Chani, and twenty-seven other students from the Academy, joined up with close to 14,000 high school students from around the world. The trip leader was Rabbi Joel Rodman, a bear of a man with a long black beard who was the senior rabbi of a conservative congregation in Miami Beach. His imposing physical presence was matched with a deep knowledge of Jewish history and a passion for teaching teenagers about the Holocaust from both an intellectual and emotional perspective. By the end of the trip Chani and all her classmates simply loved Rabbi Rodman.

Chani knew that her mother's side of the family had lost relatives in the Holocaust who had lived for generations in the Polish city of Krakow as well as in smaller neighboring towns. But she was not truly ready for the emotional upheaval she experienced in Poland. The trip started immediately after their arrival in Warsaw when the teens, exhausted from a 5,269-mile fourteen-hour flight from Miami, boarded a modern tour bus for the fifty-six mile drive to Treblinka, the death camp located between the large cities of Warsaw and Bialystok. The starkness of the large empty space with its stone monuments to destroyed Jewish communities was very upsetting to Chani. Later she was totally heartsick when Rabbi Rodman told the teenagers of the million Jews who were cremated on that site in full view of nearby villages.

The next few days were equally troubling and horrible as the kids from the Academy traveled the roads of Poland to learn firsthand about the atrocities of the Holocaust. The final day in Poland was, for Chani and thousands of others, the most powerful. They arrived in the 40,000-person town of Oswiecim, once a place popularly known by its Yiddish name of Ospitzin and with a fifty percent Jewish population before World War II. Now it was just known as Auschwitz because of the death camp located within its borders.

The weather that day was cold with a light snow falling. As the students were getting ready to leave the comfort of their bus by zipping up their blue nylon March of the Living parkas and putting on gloves and hats, Rabbi Rodman stood up and said, "If you really want to experience what our grandparents, aunts, uncles, and cousins had to deal with I suggest you leave your parkas, gloves, hats, shoes, boots, and socks on the bus and walk on the frozen wet ground . . . think about it . . . but don't do it! I do not want to hear from your headmaster or parents. But do think about what your own families actually experienced at the hands of the Nazis and the Polish collaborators." And Chani and the others did think and talk about it from that day through the remainder of their days at the Academy.

The March of the Living itself was a three-kilometer walk, often eight abreast, from Auschwitz to the killing fields of Birkenau, directly through the village of Oswiecim. Almost all the talk amongst Chani and her classmates was about the closeness of the houses to the route they were taking, and astonishment about how the Polish people could plead ignorance of the destruction of the Jews.

At one point in the March, Chani and her classmates crossed a small bridge, and at its' crest they turned around to look at the sea of young Jews behind them wrapped in Israeli flags and waving the flags of their home countries: Brazil, Mexico, Argentina, Panama, Britain, Australia, New Zealand, Taiwan, Poland, South Africa, France, Germany, Holland, Canada, the United States and more than fifty other countries. A chill went through Chani's body and soul when the rabbi said, "Just remember, that at this very site within two to three days every single person you see all around us, all 14,000, would have been murdered and cremated."

Later the sadness of the day gave way to a renewed strength and resolve when they reached the end of the killing fields where a ceremony was being held. Here the thousands of marchers participated in a Yom HaShoah, Holocaust Memorial Day program. When the final speaker concluded his remarks, the teenagers joined by thousands of adults from numerous countries, stood on the sacred ground when millions had died, and joined together in the singing of Hatikvah, the national anthem of Israel. At that moment Chani felt an enormous renewed pride in her personal Judaism and the Jewish people.

Ten hours after the March she and her group were back at Warsaw's Chopin Airport en route to Israel. This was Chani's fourth trip to Israel and she often said it was her best except for the time when she met Nathaniel. The week in Israel was spent touring, visiting the Old City, dancing in the streets, and then celebrating Yom Ha-Atzmaut, Israeli Independence Day. When she finally got home she was exhilarated, exhausted, and ready for a vacation that she knew would come after her final exams forty days later.

She also knew that the time had come to discuss two touchy subjects with her parents. First, Chani, like many of her classmates and others she had met on the March, had started seriously thinking of making *aliya,* that is, moving to Israel after high school. When she broached the idea to her parents Chani was surprised by her mother's reaction.

"Darling, if you want to make aliya we will definitely be supportive. But, it's important to understand that Israel is a tough place to make a living. It's not Disney World; it's a real place where rent is expensive, food is expensive, and good jobs are scarce. On several occasions we've also thought about moving there but decided all in all we were better off here and that living in the States was better for you. So our advice is plan to make aliya, but do it after college, after you have more education and the ability to support yourself.

"Do you remember Dr. Bob Silverman and his wife Linda who used to live here? He gave up a very good medical practice and she gave up a good job as a school psychologist to move to Jerusalem with their five kids. For a long time we kept in touch with them and I think it took him close to six years to build a practice in Israel. Before he was able to build that practice though he was running around the country like a chicken without a head working in a few different practices, two hospitals, and one nursing home. And Linda never did find as good a job as she had here. So we are not discouraging you but saying go there with the best skills you can get here, and then we'll support you. Who knows maybe if you make aliya we'll move there."

Several years later as she was sitting in a graduate class on clinical practice and the instructor was emphasizing the importance of "validating the client's words" the conversation with her mother came back to her mind. She thought about it and smiled to herself. She had been 'validated' and was then ready to let the idea go.

The second question on her mind was, "How come if we're Orthodox Jews, and all of this is so important to us, did you decide to send me to the secular Academy and not a Hebrew day school?"

Shimon and Devora Weissfogel looked at each other; Shimon nodded to Devora as if to say, "I've got this" and began.

"Chani, it was an extremely difficult decision. We knew from the beginning that sending you to the Academy would isolate you from some of the kids in the community and that there would be scheduling conflicts around the holidays and social activities. Also, we realized that we would be putting many temptations in front of you, from *treife* food to non-observant friends. But we also felt that the two of us had the time and spiritual resources to give you what you weren't getting at the day schools. Then there was also the educational piece. Frankly, when you were starting school, the day schools were not nearly as good as they are today. They were full of all kinds of faculty and parent conflicts. There were teachers coming and going all the time and big arguments over the curriculum. Your mother and I felt we owed you the best secular education that we could afford, and the Academy offered that.

"Finally, both of us came from New Orleans, where although there were 10,000 Jews, we were still very much a minority. When we grew up there was a small Orthodox Jewish community down by Lake Pontchartrain, but we both lived uptown near Tulane. In our neighborhood there was a Conservative shul in an old public school, the JCC on St. Charles, and big Reform temples where both of us belonged. Also, as you know, we both went to the same private school and despite, or perhaps because of, our upbringing, we both decided to become Orthodox and live our lives inside an Orthodox community. Our goal for you is simple. We want you to have a strong secular education, which you are getting at the Academy, and a strong Jewish identity, which you are getting from our home and our Modern Orthodox community. Does that answer your question?"

Chani nodded, stood up, and said, "Thanks. I've got homework to do." She started to leave when her father called her back.

"Sweetheart, there is one more thing we need to talk to you about. And frankly for us to share this family secret with you is a quite painful. As you already know your Mom's family came from Poland and my parents came from Neustadt, Germany. What I don't think you understand is that the grandfather you knew, Zeyde Manny, the man I treated as my father was not in fact not my biological father. This was Bubbe Bryna's deepest secret; in fact, she didn't tell me about it until just before you were born. I guess she was either embarrassed or it was just another Holocaust secret they chose not to discuss. My mother married grandpa after she was already pregnant with me."

Suddenly Chani's attention was piqued and she thought, *Oh my God, a scandal in the family.* Shimon added to the story. "You see, after Kristallnacht things were very bad for Jews in Germany and my biological father, Herman Weissfogel, was a doctor in Neustadt. He started to see the handwriting on the wall when the Nazis came to power in 1933 and the discriminatory Nuremberg laws were passed in 1935. Then Kristallnacht happened in November 1938, when the Nazis and their sympathizers burned the synagogues in Neustadt and destroyed most of the Jewish businesses. Herman's medical practice was pretty much ransacked.

"After that he and about two dozen other Jews from his town desperately tried to get out of Germany through a program to resettle German Jews in Alaska that was being promoted by the U.S. Secretary of Interior Harold Ickes. Unfortunately, nothing happened. When my biological father couldn't get a visa despite letters to Ickes, various U.S. State Department officials, and bribes to Germans including Nazis, he decided that he needed to protect his wife and unborn child. To do this, my father chose to divorce my mother so that his older brother, the man you knew as Zeyde Manny, could leave with her as his wife. Manny was really my uncle as well as stepfather.

"This crazy but heroic contrived divorce and marriage was only possible because before Zeyde Manny married my mother he was a confirmed bachelor, and he was already a professor of psychiatry at the medical school in Heidelberg. In January of 1939, he had been invited to teach at Tulane in New Orleans and the German government had granted him a visa. So, that's what happened. Zeyde and he married and were able to leave for America. My father and the others were left behind in Germany. They never made it to Alaska and probably died in some camp. Unfortunately, we'll never know."

Chani listened and didn't react. She just went to her room, perhaps a bit overwhelmed with all this family history.

That summer followed its usual pattern, working part-time in her father's business, the trip to the Adirondacks, and then, finally, her senior year. Back at the Academy everyone was buzzing about college. Most of her school friends were either aiming for the Ivy League schools up north or the southern Ivies like Tulane, Emory, Vanderbilt, and Duke. A few were planning on Gainesville, and fewer still were thinking about the local schools such as the University of Miami, Florida International, or Florida Atlantic Universities.

On Saturday, the casual conversations among the girls at synagogue were also about colleges but focused instead on a different group of schools with large populations of Orthodox Jewish students such as Stern, Penn, Maryland, or Barnard. However, almost all of her peers at CCS were first going to Israel for a year of study at a women's yeshiva.

But, for Chani, life would go in a different direction.

Six

Fort Lauderdale, Florida

B efore the scandal, the Cambridge Community Synagogue (CCS) was known as one of the most successful Modern Orthodox congregations in the United States. What started out as a *shtibl*, literally small house of prayer, had grown to a vibrant synagogue with a wood and glass 500-seat sanctuary overlooking an inlet of the Intracoastal Waterway, a library whose holdings were similar to those of a yeshiva or a small college, countless adult education programs, numerous classrooms, and five chapels for separate groups and those who wished to pray in smaller and more intimate spaces. On any given Sabbath or holiday there were prayer services starting at 7, 8, or 9 o'clock in the morning; separate services for those members from Sephardic backgrounds; and a service for young professionals, teenagers, and families with young children.

The community's phenomenal growth began when Avi Klein arrived on the scene. Klein was a CCS member and a visionary developer. After making his first fortune developing strip malls in nearby Hollywood and Hallandale, Florida, he bought up all the property on a run-down Isle off Las Olas Boulevard that was entirely made up of two-story walk-up seasonal rental residential buildings. Within a year of owning the entire Isle, he had demolished all the buildings, gated the area, and renamed it the Isle of Cambridge. Klein went on to make his next fortune building luxury condos and homes all designed with the Modern Orthodox family in mind.

Every house or apartment had a kosher kitchen, equipped with two of every appliance—sinks, ovens, stoves, and dishwashers. In the largest and most luxurious properties he even built separate kitchens for Passover. Subsequently, other areas off Las Olas started filling up with Modern Orthodox families and then a day school was built several blocks away on the east side of US 1 and north of Broward Boulevard. Within five years the entire area was a popular destination for Orthodox Jews from Miami to Palm Beach for its array of good kosher restaurants, Judaic bookshops, and two kosher supermarkets.

The synagogue was also known for its affluence, particularly its roster of members who were billionaires and multimillionaires. In addition to Klein, who had gone on to become one of the wealthiest and most philanthropic men in South Florida, there was Jacobo Meirwicz, a billionaire from Brazil whose worldwide sneaker empire had company owned stores in forty-one countries and manufacturing facilities throughout Asia; Yossi Greenblatt, the Cuban-born sportswear manufacturer whose various labels could be found in stores ranging from Neiman-Marcus to Costco and whose factories in Bangladesh were the single largest employer in East Asia; and then there was the infamous Ozzie Wolfe, the billionaire investment guru, author, advisor to the governor, and philanthropist.

Thanks to Ozzie's charisma and apparent piety, close to twenty percent of the CCS's membership were invested in securities with Wolfe's firm. All of this came to a shocking end the day the FBI arrested Ozzie and seized his financial and personal records.

Ozzie did not start out to dupe friends and strangers. In fact, his first fortune was built on hard work, attention to the details of the stock market, and a belief that God had a special mission for him that included his being very rich. As his affluence grew so did his circle of friends who wanted to hitch their own financial future to Wolfe's apparent success. Because of this interest Ozzie eventually established his own boutique wealth management firm with many of the first investors being fellow congregants in the CCS community.

Initially the returns they received were similar to those from other investment firms. Then as the stock market took a nosedive, Wolfe doubled down on his bets and within a year the market started recovering. Ozzie and his staff were viewed as geniuses for the returns they garnered from their big bets on Apple and other high tech companies. The money from the outside poured in.

Unfortunately, Ozzie and the others never heard the words of the Microsoft billionaire Bill Gates: "Success is a lousy teacher. It seduces smart people into thinking they can't lose." Just one year later the bets Ozzie Wolfe made did not materialize, but Wolfe's investors still craved their returns. So, Wolfe started paying off old money with new money and doubling down even more on his bets. Eventually some young analyst at the Securities and Exchange Commission took a deep dive into Wolfe's financial records and came up with fraud.

For reasons that no one could explain Wolfe limited his clients from the CCS to investments that were no more than $3.6 million. Such an investment provided the "lucky few" with a return of close to $400,000 per year, most of it tax-free thanks to the creative accounting of Wolfe's affiliated and essentially in-house CPA firm. When the Ponzi scheme imploded, thirty-one members of the CCS community were forced to sell their million dollar homes, nineteen others declared bankruptcy, and numerous members were in financial trouble. Many of the physicians, dentists, and attorneys in the community were forced to reexamine their retirement plans and, in most cases, they decided to continue working for another five to ten years in order to rebuild their nest eggs.

The years after the Wolfe scheme imploded proved to be enormously challenging to the CCS. The initial problem was money. The year prior to the financial mess the annual *Kol Nidre* appeal had garnered close to $2 million in pledges. The following year there was barely $350,000 in pledges. It then dropped to $300,000 before finally stabilizing four years later at almost $250,000 per year. Another problem for the community was the loss of donations for the day school and a number of families moving away from the community—those who simply couldn't afford to live any longer in the Isle of Cambridge community.

Throughout this trying time the community was blessed with the steady leadership of Rabbi Yitzchak Friedman who was born in St. John's, Newfoundland, and educated at Yeshiva University. His gentleness, wit, and wisdom is often credited with leading the community through it darkest days. What perhaps is most often remembered is his *Kol Nidre* talk a few months after the disaster. He approached the lectern slowly and, with a palpable sadness on his face, he took a moment to look out at his congregation making brief eye contact with the many people he had known for decades. Then he began.

"While it is for the courts to decide in our civil society who is guilty and who is innocent, and it is for God to make the final judgment, it is for each of us to look inside our own hearts and to assess our own complicity in the economic and I daresay spiritual tragedy that has enmeshed many in this congregation.

"Dear friends, let's try to be painfully honest on this Kol Nidre night. Let's not confess in a rote manner. Let's really confess to ourselves as well as those around us. Let's confess that we can be greedy and haughty. And, worst of all, we are, with all our successes, our fine educations, our wealth, our sophistication about food, wine, and definitely single malt scotch, and most significantly, our *halacha* based lifestyles, we can also be smug and arrogant.

"We have forgotten who and what we are and what our path should be. And because we have lost our way we have lost our homes, our marriages, our fortunes, our dignity, our privacy, but most importantly our self-esteem and sense of direction. Kol Nidre is the beginning of our new lives; the beginning of our claim to a better future. But to have that future we must grow and change.

"Let me tell you a story about the Trocme family. Ever heard of them? I'm not surprised. They lived in a village on a 3,000-foot high plateau in the South-Eastern France. The village is named Le Chambon sur Lignon. Ever been there? Not likely. Andre Trocme was the family patriarch and the community's Protestant Huguenot minister. Along with his wife Magda, as well as the entire village, close to 5,000 Jews were rescued and sheltered during World War II. All of this was taking place in Vichy, France, an area of the country that was closely aligned with the Nazis. How did this all happen?

"Basically the Trocme family created a community of goodness within a sea of hate. They created a force field of goodness to rescue their Jewish brethren. Their guide was Torah, specifically Deuteronomy: 19, which teaches us that: 'Innocent blood shall not be shed in the midst of your land that the Lord your God gives you as an inheritance.' As Elizabeth Koenig-Kaufman, a young girl who survived the war because of the goodness of the people of Le Chambon testified, 'Nobody asked who was Jewish and who was not. Nobody asked where you were from. Nobody asked who your father was or if he could pay. They just accepted each of us, taking us in with warmth, sheltering children, often without their parents—children who cried at night from nightmares.'

"Tonight, dear friends, we are dressed in our *kittels*, our white robes that will someday in the distant future be our burial shrouds. A little while ago we began our twenty-six hour fast, and as many rabbis in the past have noted, we are, in a sense, rehearsing our own death. And, if today is indeed our last day on this earth, what shall we worry about? Money, interest rates, *halacha*? Or family and love? Remember whether you believe in *Olam Habah*, the world to come, or not, there is absolutely an afterlife and people will speak of you and me for generations to come, often in the present tense—so what you do today, and how you resolve to live tomorrow, will be the measure of your life and the life of this community. I wish each of you a meaningful fast."

The congregation sat and listened politely. Some congregants were moved, others stunned and angered. For Chani, the message of personal responsibility and the power of both individuals and a community to stand up to evil through their own profound goodness struck a chord that would guide her future academic pursuits at Amherst College and her later career decisions.

Seven

Fort Lauderdale, Florida

Amongst those in financial trouble was Chani's father, Shimon
Weissfogel, a synagogue vice president and certified public accountant. Shimon's day-to-day financial well being was, in large measure, related
to the steady flow of primarily tax-free income from his $3.6 million invest-
ment with Wolfe's firm. In Shimon's opinion, his multimillion-dollar equity
investment with Wolfe was both secure and highly liquid. This deal with
Wolfe he felt gave him the freedom to speculate on other riskier projects
that had the potential for even bigger returns. One of those projects, in
fact, his largest, was a highly leveraged purchase of five nursing homes that
served a Medicaid population in the northern section of Broward County.

For the first several years of Shimon's nursing home ownership the
business was quite profitable. Then a downturn in the Florida economy
that translated into lower Medicaid reimbursement rates for long-term
care, as well as generally poor management of each of his five facilities,
resulted in a reversal of Shimon's fortunes. Within months of the nursing homes starting to hemorrhage money, the Wolfe scheme also col-
lapsed, and Weissfogel found himself in a cash crisis.

Shimon's solution to his economic problems was to develop a plan
that started with his taking over the financial management of the resident

trust funds, those monies belonging to nursing home patients, but held in trust by each of his five long-term care facilities. He then systematically borrowed money from the accounts in a slow and orderly manner. Additionally, Shimon kept careful records of the money on a ledger he titled "Trust Account Loans." During the 23 months he engaged in this activity he managed to "borrow" in excess of $390,000.

His behavior came to light after the death of a resident whose daughter was a partner in a large public accounting firm. An audit of her mother's accounts led the daughter to the conclusion that the nursing home had misappropriated thousands of dollars. Once the local district attorney got involved the system was quickly uncovered and Weissfogel was arrested.

After six months of negotiations, Shimon's attorneys were able to reach an agreement on a plea bargain that included a forced sale of his nursing homes, the provision of restitution to the injured residents, a fine of $475,000, a suspended sentence of six months, and 500 hours of community service. The Florida Board of Accountancy also fined him $5,000 and revoked his license as a CPA. Within a period of twelve months Weissfogel had lost his business, his $3.6 million investments through Ozzie Wolfe, and most significantly for Shimon, his *shem tov,* good name.

All of this became irrelevant when, while Chani was heading home from Massachusetts for winter break during her senior year, Shimon Weissfogel died from a massive stroke. He left behind his wife Devora, their daughter Chani, and an estate worth over $5 million dollars.

The *Shiva* for Shimon Weissfogel began immediately after his funeral. For the first few days the house was inundated with neighbors, fellow congregants from CCS as well as several distant cousins who lived in South Florida.

By the third afternoon the house had become quiet. Trying to make some sense out of all that had transpired Chani was reading Rabbi Harold Kushner's book, *When Bad Things Happen to Good People.* She felt that her father had made mistakes, was prepared to do *teshuvah,* that is, repentance, and take his punishment like a man. She also thought that he was a caring person who had done much good in his life while asking for nothing in return. As she was brooding about all of this, Rabbi Friedman walked into the house of mourning, sat down, and following the Orthodox custom, remained quiet waiting for Chani to speak. From the low stool on which she was sitting she looked up at Friedman and finally said, "Rabbi, I am glad you are here. My mom is napping and I know that she would like to see you. Will you stay for a few minutes? I'd also like to talk with you about a couple of personal things."

Rabbi Friedman answered, "Certainly I'll stay. Also, let me tell you that I meant every word I said at the funeral. Your dad was a pillar of this community. He was kind and charitable, a true mensch. He was one of those people who would be the first to volunteer and the last to seek recognition and praise. I shall miss him very much."

Fighting back tears Chani said, "Thanks, rabbi. I appreciate your saying that. I loved my father very much and realize that what he did was wrong. Yet I am proud of his admitting his error and owning up to his responsibility to the nursing home residents and the community. I'm just sorry that *Hashem* didn't give him more time to do his teshuvah. Would you mind if I changed the subject ? I'd like to ask your advice about my own future."

The rabbi nodded and in a weary voice Chani continued, "First let me tell you I thought your Kol Nidre talk a few years ago was amazing. I was so inspired by what you said that I undertook a project to learn as much as I could about Le Chambon and the Trocmes. Frankly, I think they are my role models. They were not only good people, they inspired others to be good. And they motivated others by their hard work and example, not by lectures and threats, but through love."

The rabbi was uncertain about where this conversation was going. So he simply nodded and said, "That's wonderful. I agree. They were truly amazing. But, how is this about your future?"

"Rabbi, I am considering one of two career paths, and I'm interested in your advice. Initially I was thinking of becoming a social worker. I have already applied to Miller College School for Social Work and feel pretty confident about being accepted. If I go that route, I'll start this coming summer, a few weeks after I graduate from college. What I like about their program is that it has a fair amount of hands-on training and it's oriented around both case management and therapy. I think I could probably be a pretty good therapist."

The rabbi again nodded and simply said, "Sounds good to me."

Chani hesitated, then slowly spoke while looking down and averting her eyes from Rabbi Friedman's steady gaze, "But there is another field that interests me quite a bit more Now I know neither you nor my parents, or perhaps anyone in our shul would approve, but I am considering the option of studying for the rabbinate. What do you think about that idea?"

Rabbi Friedman just stared straight ahead, thought for a minute as he stroked his beard, and then turned to Chani and quietly asked, "Will you allow me to give a somewhat long response?"

"Of course, I very much want to know what you think about my becoming a rabbi."

"Before I respond to your idea I trust that you understand that I'm certainly in the progressive or liberal wing of Modern Orthodoxy. I am a strong supporter of gender equality including women studying all aspects of Torah alongside men, and women playing a leadership role in the synagogue. For example, here at CCS women have served on the board of directors for decades and last year Miriam Moss was elected president of the board. And, I think our shul is doing an outstanding job of Tikkun Olam, repairing our little corner of the world. As you know we have one of the most active "feeding the homeless" programs in the county. And, I'm sure you remember that it seems as if a contingent from our shul is involved on dozens of Sundays each year with one or another of the charity walk-a-thons. And I'm very proud of our *bikkur cholim* committee that makes very meaningful visits to the sick at the hospital and shut-ins at home. My favorite program though was the one that you were part of, the teen clown troupe that also visited the sick and elderly. And, from my perspective, I am quite proud of the fact that most members in the community do not isolate themselves from either the gentile or nonorthodox Jewish community. In fact I count several of the Conservative, Reform, and Reconstructionist rabbis here in Broward and Dade as my friends.

"But Chani, there are some lines that are not crossed. And one of them is the Orthodox rabbinate. Simply put, Modern Orthodoxy does not ordain women as rabbis. Maybe someday it will happen, but not now, or in the foreseeable future.

"On the other hand, if what you're saying is that you want a career as a Jewish educator or scholar in Judaic studies, why not go down the path of a MA or PhD? Alternatively, if your interest is Jewish communal services, pursuing social work is a great choice. But, I would suggest going to the Wurzweiler School at Yeshiva University rather than Miller."

Chani hesitated, took a deep breath, and then said, "Rabbi I have a confession. I do not consider myself Orthodox. I am not sure what I am, other than a committed and confused Jewish woman. But I do know that at some level I want to help people learn more Torah, conduct services, prepare and deliver Torah discussions on Shabbat, teach, and maybe, if I'm lucky, inspire Jewish kids to be active Jews, participate in the life cycle events of a congregation, and be at the heart of a Jewish community. I realize that if I pursue the dream of becoming a rabbi I will have to go to a Conservative, Reform, or Reconstructionist rabbinical seminary. My next question, though, is if I did become a rabbi would I be ostracized in this community?"

Rabbi Friedman thought for a minute, looked directly at Chani Weissfogel and said, "Please don't interpret what I am about to say as patronizing but here is my take on your question. First, if you truly want to be a rabbi, clearly you have no choice but going to a seminary outside of the Orthodox movement. Second, no one in the Orthodox movement will recognize your ordination, including me. That means you will never have an Orthodox pulpit or even find a job in an Orthodox synagogue or day school. Would I address you as 'rabbi' and consider you a colleague? Definitely! But certainly there will be members of this community who think that your decision to pursue a rabbinical career is the moral equivalent of Darth Vader going to the dark side of the force. As we say here in South Florida, *Asi es la vida*—such is life."

The rabbi's last comment brought smiles to both their faces and diffused the tension for a moment. "Chani, please remember that I grew up in Newfoundland where my grandfather had settled in 1912. In our town we had a very tiny Jewish community, maybe less than a hundred. Today the Jewish population is even smaller, perhaps ten or fifteen families. But there was one lesson we all learned, and that was Klal Yisrael—that is, we are all one people, no matter how we *daven*, or even whether we daven. And through thick and thin, we all stick together.

"I like to quote the late Rebbe Menachem Mendel Schneerson, the distinguished seventh leader of the Chabad Lubavitch movement, who put it beautifully when he said, 'Labels are for clothes, not people.' Chani, no matter what you do, including becoming a rabbi, I will always be proud to say I was part of your life and count on me to always be available to help you out in any way that I can." To Chani, Rabbi Friedman's words felt like another inspiring sermon resonating within her soul.

At the conclusion of Shiva, Chani stayed around for another week to help her mother with the paper work, and drudgery of cleaning up the mess that most people leave behind.

Eight

The final semester of Chani's senior year turned into something between a disaster and a farce. At school she was taking three courses, none of which was particularly demanding. One class that she had signed up for had a reputation as a "gut course" but for Chani "The Sociology of Government Leadership" proved to be an important experience. Taught by an Amherst alumnus who had been a deputy assistant secretary of state, the first four weeks were focused on reading and discussing Doris Kerns Goodwin's *Lyndon Johnson and The American Dream*. The students in the class devoted the next nine weeks to research reports. Thanks to the professor's lack of creativity, or perhaps laziness, and her good fortune of having a last name at the end of the alphabet, she and Andrea Zweig were scheduled for their final project presentations on the last day of the term. The assignment was to write a research paper on "The response of U.S. government leaders to critical issues in foreign countries."

Recalling the conversation with her parents a few years earlier about the 1938 plan to save German Jews by resettling them in Alaska, Chani decided that this would be the focus of her paper that she titled, "The Holocaust: The Alaskan Proposal and Political Response."

Her research took her into the archives of the nearby National Yiddish Book Exchange located a few miles south of Amherst on the wooded campus of neighboring Hampshire College. As she explored her subject she learned of the Slattery Report, the actual plan proposed by the progressive Secretary of Interior Ickes, an appointee of President Franklin Delano Roosevelt. This plan, later introduced into Congress as the King-Havenner Bill, would have saved 50,000 German and Polish Jews who Ickes wanted to relocate to four communities in Alaska as part of an initiative to develop the nearly barren territory as well as save an imperiled population. It turned out that the report had fallen on deaf ears in Congress and at the White House.

Chani was particularly disturbed that the opposition to the plan came from many segments of Alaskan society, as well as Rabbi Stephen Wise, a leading reform rabbi of the era. Also, she was saddened to learn that another important opponent was Ernest Gruening, a Harvard educated physician and assimilated Jew, who in 1939 was appointed Governor of the Territory of Alaska and was later the state's U.S. senator. For Chani the only bright spot in her research was that there were some towns in Alaska that voted to support the relocation plan, including her favorite spot of Seward, a place that would later become her home.

During those final months at Amherst, Chani made two decisions. The first was that she would follow Rabbi Friedman's advice and pursue a career in social work. After reviewing the programs at Yeshiva University and Miller, she decided that her first impulse about Miller was correct. She liked the program's block plan course scheduling that alternated summer semesters of intense didactic study with fall, winter, and spring semesters of supervised fieldwork.

Throughout her last semester Chani was also spending many hours each week talking with her mother in Florida who she feared was seriously depressed over Shimon's death. At spring break she like tens of thousands of other college kids flew down to the warmer climes of the Sunshine State. However, her visit to Florida did not include beer, sand, and bikinis. Once back home Chani immediately saw that her mother was indeed sad and depressed, and almost unable to function. Her mom's days were spent in a darkened and disheveled house, with occasional breaks to speak on the phone with members of the synagogue or go food shopping. Dirty dishes were piled high in the sink and on the counters; expired food clogged the refrigerator. Her mother's room was a mess, and the house smelled musty. Chani immediately set about cleaning up and airing out their home. Hours later, totally exhausted from the physical labor, she finally sat down to talk with her mother. It didn't take but a few minutes to learn that Devora was feeling overwhelmed by the loss of Shimon along with the burden of managing the myriad activities related to settling her late husband's estate.

Chani worried about her mother's mental health and, when she let her mind wander, thought that her mom might even harm herself. By the time spring break was over it was clear that Devora Weissfogel required professional help but would not seek it on her own initiative. Chani was packing her luggage for her final trip back to school when Devora came into her room and informed her daughter that she was too tired to attend graduation. With a very heavy heart Chani returned to Amherst.

The last weeks of college seemed endless for Chani. Her anxiety over her mother's health weighed on her constantly. She couldn't get herself to do much beyond exercising and finishing all her required work. She avoided all the end of term celebrations, and decided to skip the graduation ceremonies in order to get some extra time at home before starting her MSW program.

A week before she flew back to Florida she called Rabbi Friedman and explained her mother's situation to him. He agreed to look in on her and to try to find her a psychiatrist. Then he startled Chani by saying, "I will try hard to identify an appropriate therapist for her but it won't be easy and it will probably not be someone affiliated with our synagogue. I hope you realize that mental health issues are rarely discussed in our community although many people here have serious emotional issues but are oftentimes ashamed to admit it.

"A few of these people get help but there are others who don't and really need it. In fact, I know people, including other rabbis, who think that if you have an emotional issue the only way to solve it is to study more Torah. I guess for some that may work. But, in my opinion, in this day and age, there are many people, including fellow Orthodox Jews, who need psychotropic medications as well as therapy to restore them to health.

"Years ago, the Rebbe said something to the effect that a hole in the body is a hole in the soul. I think what he meant is that when we have something wrong with us, whether it's a hangnail or depression, that pain becomes the entire focus of our life precluding us from getting to any higher emotional or spiritual level. I believe in psychiatry and therapy, and in fact I have a sister who is a geriatric psychiatrist in Toronto. If you don't object I'll call her for some advice after I talk to your mother."

Once again, a conversation with Rabbi Friedman encouraged her and affirmed what she had observed for so many years. She agreed to have the Rabbi visit her mother and consult with his sister. They also agreed to meet as soon as Chani returned from Amherst. A week later Chani was back in Fort Lauderdale and the following day she met Rabbi Friedman in his office.

"Chani, you are right. Your mom is seriously depressed. I spoke with my sister and she thinks your mom is a good candidate for medication and therapy. She checked with various colleagues and found an excellent psychiatrist at the University of Miami. Because time is of the essence, I took the liberty of setting up an appointment for her on Friday morning. I also talked to your mother and she has agreed to see this Dr. Appel. I assume you are OK with this?"

Chani nodded and when she looked up the rabbi could see that she was crying. He looked at her and optimistically said, "Don't worry, I think your mom will get into the right hands and before you know it she'll be back to her old self."

She looked up at him with her wet eyes and choked out through sobs, "I just want my mother back so badly . . . I really appreciate your help . . . sorry, I'm just overwhelmed."

Rabbi Friedman, stood up, walked over to her chair, lightly placed his hand on her shoulder, and quietly said, "Don't worry Chani, we will get through this. She'll be all right."

On Friday morning Devora and Chani drove south on Interstate 95 to the medical school campus of the University of Miami. As usual, traffic was horrendous. In a folder on the seat between them was the original seven page questionnaire that Dr. Appel's office had faxed them two days earlier and which they had completed and faxed back to Appel on Thursday evening. The form asked countless questions about Mrs. Weissfogel's physical and mental health. Devora's response to it was to say that she didn't have the strength to fill out the forms, so Chani agreed to ask her mother the questions and write in the answers.

The first page asked for basic demographic information. Pages two and three were the essence of the form where the patient was asked about dozens of symptoms. Her mother's answers indicated that she had experienced more than twenty symptoms ranging from difficulty getting out of bed to frequent feelings of guilt, worthlessness, sadness, hopelessness, and helplessness. By the time she had finished assisting her mother fill out the form Chani knew for certain how ill her mother was.

Dr. Saul Appel was a short rotund man slightly over five feet tall with white hair, a long white beard, dark brown eyes, a ruddy complexion, and an impish smile. When Chani first saw him her immediate thought was that if psychiatry dried up he could always work as Santa Claus. After greeting them pleasantly they were ushered into a comfortable office. The wall over his desk showed diplomas and certificates from Harvard, Yale, and the Columbia-Presbyterian Medical Center. He noticed Chani gazing at his degrees and said, "I believe in truth in advertising," and then let out a big belly laugh that instantly broke the tension in the room.

He began, "Mrs. Weissfogel, I've reviewed your paperwork and frankly, I am not surprised you are having some problems. We are all human and you have been through a great deal." He then asked if they were familiar with the Holmes-Rahe scale. Chani and Leah said they were not.

Appel went on to explain the scale. "This is a tool that those of us in the mental health field use to predict likelihood of people getting ill after various life events. The scale itself gives what is designated as 'life crisis units' for various events. For example, the worst thing that can happen to a person is the death of a spouse and that gets one hundred units. A lesser issue might be change in social activities and that gets eighteen units. Interestingly enough, sometimes events or activities that we think of as good things happening to us can also be stressful. A vacation, for example, gets thirteen units. Anyway, Mrs. Weissfogel, based on my analysis of the forms you submitted you are way passed the three hundred-unit measure. This means that from a predictive perspective, you are at a high risk for illness. So, your being here is not unexpected. But, most importantly I am pretty certain that if you'll comply with the plan we come up with, you will feel much better fairly soon."

With those last words both Devora and Chani started to feel a burden lift off their shoulders. The rest of the session was spent reviewing Devora's issues and halfway through Dr. Appel asked to speak to Devora privately. Devora appreciated this action by the doctor, and soon she was speaking candidly about her sadness, and frustration, even anger, at Shimon for how his greed had almost destroyed the family. At the end of the session Dr. Appel arranged for Devora to come back the following week. His plan was to meet with her to review the blood work and testing he wanted to do, and then provide her with a prescription that he felt certain would help.

The next weeks sped by. Mrs. Weissfogel was now under the care of a kindly doctor, and she had quickly shown obvious improvements in mood and functionality. On the day before Chani was due to leave for Northampton to begin her MSW program, Devora made one final request to her only child. She asked Chani to accompany her to a joint meeting with Jack Rabinowitz, her long time attorney, and Melanie Kensington her financial advisor. They decided to walk from their house to the office on the west side of Federal Highway and Las Olas Boulevard. It was a late morning in May, warm and humid, with a hint of rain in the air. Holding each other's hands the mother and daughter strolled down Las Olas stopping every few minutes to window shop. This was to be one of Chani's last, best memories of her mother.

Rabinowitz was a former varsity football, baseball, and basketball player at Tulane. He stood over six feet nine inches, but as he loved to say, "definitely shrinking," and weighed close to three hundred pounds. Although almost seventy-five years old he still practiced law full-time, worked out regularly, was a competitive sailor, as well as an excellent skier. Jack had been the family's lawyer and friend for as long as Chani could remember. Ten years earlier Shimon was considering switching to someone that Ozzie was recommending, but Devora insisted that they stick with Jack. It turned out to be an excellent decision since Ozzie's lawyer was indicted along with Ozzie and the investment firm's accountant.

Melanie, Jack's third wife, and twenty years his junior, was an insurance agent turned financial advisor and as petite as Jack was big. She had been handling the Weissfogel's portfolio and trusts for a decade and had consistently voiced concerns about Shimon's large investment with Ozzie Wolfe.

At the meeting Chani learned for the first time the family's financial situation. It turned out that subsequent to Shimon's death, Devora, on Melanie's advice and Rabinowtz's concurrence, invested half her money into an annuity that would ensure her an income that could support her lifestyle for the near term with the extra benefit of being judgment proof under Florida law. The annuity was established with Chani as the contingent beneficiary with a guaranteed 20-year payout. As the mother and daughter left the meeting and began the walk home Devora put her arm through Chani's and said, "You see, Chani, your dad was very smart and despite all the problems he really took care of us."

In a soft and tired voice Chani replied, "Yes, I think we are in good shape financially." But, in her heart she wished that she or her mother could have prevented her father's unethical and illegal business decisions. She wanted to scream, *Daddy, didn't you hear a word Rabbi Friedman said? He decried all this focus on materialism, he said we have to love and take care of one another—our mission is to be ethical, we are not chosen to be rich but we are chosen to be a light unto nations . . .*

It was too late for her father's decisions, but not her own.

Nine

NORTHAMPTON, MASSACHUSETTS

Like all first year students at the Miller College School for Social Work, the orientation program began on the last Friday in May and lasted through Sunday. The dorm assignments as well as a number of orientation lectures and social gatherings were designed to set the tone for the first summer of academic sessions.

Almost from the outset Chani felt comfortable with most aspects of the program, particularly its focus on therapy and its sensitivity to the lesbian, gay, bisexual, and transgender communities. She also appreciated its attention to the issues of sexism and racism. But she was quite bothered by a response to a question she asked during orientation about anti-Semitism.

Chani wanted to know why the curriculum appeared to ignore the issues surrounding anti-Semitism particularly since the Jews were an often discriminated against minority group. The answer she received was that while Jews may represent a minority from a demographic perspective, they were simply not discriminated against; and in fact, that they were an ultra-successful segment of the population. Chani found the answer to her question patronizing and factually incorrect.

She reacted by challenging the professor's assertion about success and boldly suggesting that it was a stereotypical answer. She continued by noting that there were close to half a million Jewish people living below the poverty line in New York City alone; particularly the elderly. Discrimination she stated still existed but it was subtle although equally hurtful. Chani was not interrupted as she then went on to say that no single act in contemporary history demonstrated discrimination and racism against Jews more than the Holocaust, a subject that appeared to be missing from the curriculum. Her final point was that the press was always vilifying Israelis as occupiers and Palestinians as victims while Jews in Argentina, France, Belgium and other countries lived under a cloud of anti-Semitic rhetoric and periodic physical harm yet received minimal newspaper or TV coverage in the United States.

When Chani had finished her remarks the professor quietly murmured a response that orientation was not the forum for this discussion. Listening intently to the give and take on anti-Semitism were two people. One was an adjunct faculty member and the other a field practice preceptor. They were both startled and pleased by Chani's intelligent and informed assertiveness.

At the lunch buffet that noontime they sought out Chani Weissfogel and asked to sit with her. The woman introduced herself as Blake Richards, a graduate of the Miller MSW program from several years earlier, and now the director of the Jewish Community Counseling Service in Springfield, Massachusetts. Her husband introduced himself as Norman Cohn, an adjunct faculty member who taught the first year mental health law course. Then after a hearty laugh he told Chani that his "real" job was running a mental health advocacy program in Northampton. Introductions completed they talked about Miller and the program for the next half hour. As they were getting ready to leave Blake looked squarely at Chani and said, "May I give you a piece of advice based on my experiences here at Miller?"

Chani nodded and Blake said, "This is a great school with an excellent faculty. The curriculum is solid but the best part of the program is the field training. By the time you finish you'll have a solid foundation for a career as a clinical therapist. But the keys are good field placements and finishing the academic portion of the MSW. Frankly, in my opinion, the school has some major weaknesses. It tries very hard to be politically correct and I don't think it means to ignore anti-Semitism but it is clearly more focused on sexism, racism and discrimination against gays and lesbians. My advice is ignoring it! It is not a fight worth fighting. Miller isn't changing and neither are you. Focus on your goal—getting an education, a degree, and a job. End of my advice."

Chani replied, "I shouldn't be too surprised. I've lived in the Valley for four years and am well aware of its PC-ness. I often thought it was all summed up in one line from Tracy Kidder's book *House* about some guy who built a house in the Amherst, I think the line was something like, 'Amherst has good public schools and its own foreign policy.' Blake, I appreciate your advice; my alternative was to go to Yeshiva University, but for me, I think that would have been too far on the other end of the spectrum. I guess I will have to learn to keep my mouth shut and endure the next two years."

The lunch period was over, they said their goodbyes, and Chani went back to her orientation. Blake and Norman returned to their work.

Then, on Saturday, almost as if it had been decreed by fate, the budding friendship was renewed and subsequently blossomed when Chani decided to start attending Shabbat services at Northampton's Congregation B'nai Israel. Her motivation to go to a synagogue was simply so that she could say the *Kaddish* prayer in memory of her father. The first people she saw when she walked in were Blake and Norman who beckoned to her to sit with them.

The service was both well attended with people of all ages and the recently ordained rabbi gave a fascinating Torah discussion. She was a bit surprised to see women reading from the Torah, being given the honors of blessing the Torah, and leading various parts of the service. Later she learned that this was originally an Orthodox synagogue that had morphed into one of the most successful conservative egalitarian shuls in the country. Months later as Chani became friendly with the rabbi he explained that the community's dream was a "big tent" synagogue and, through the efforts of many people over decades, that had come into being.

At the end of the service the shul's president made a few announcements and invited everyone to stay for *Kiddush*. Chani was surprised to find that the kiddush, which in Florida was wine, soda, and a few cookies, turned out to be more akin to a modest dairy luncheon with bagels, various cheeses, tuna and egg salads, cole slaw, potato salad, drinks, cookies, and some small cakes. While most of the people sat in the social hall Chani, Blake, and Norman found a bench outside near a children's play area where they could keep an eye on the Cohns' toddler twin daughters. Their conversation was lively. Chani told them about growing up in Florida and her love of the outdoors and many of the activities she was engaged in around the Pioneer Valley. Norm shared some of his story about growing up in New York. His embellishments almost made it sound like he was a New York tough guy when in fact it was clear that he had come from a middle-class background. Chani learned later about the murder of his parents.

Blake's story was the one that Chani found most surprising. Although she had been to Alaska on a cruise with her parents, this was the first person she knew who was a 'real' Alaskan. Soon she learned Blake shared her passion for sport fishing, hiking, and camping. As the luncheon waned Blake and Chani agreed that they needed to take a "ladies day" to go fishing on Martha's Vineyard. Chani suggested the following Sunday. Blake and Norman looked puzzled since the ride to the Vineyard was close to four hours plus a ferry ride. Now it was Blake's turn to be surprised when Chani said, "No worries, I have access to a plane, and I've been a pilot since my sophomore year in college." Blake looked at Norman whose shoulder shrug meant only one thing, 'it's up to you.'

"Okay," Blake said, "but on one condition: you come to our house next week for Friday night Shabbat dinner."

Within a week Chani had become Aunt Chani to the twins, Blake and Chani had caught their bluefish that Norm happily barbequed, and Blake and Chani had more plans for fishing trips.

With her new friends, and an attitude of acceptance about her MSW program, the first five-week quarter flew by. Before the second quarter began there was a one-week midsummer break and Chani went to Florida to spend the time with her mother.

Ten

Fort Lauderdale, Florida

Chani was looking forward to getting home and using her time there to be with her mother and chill out at the beach. She wanted to swim, surfboard, and try kite surfing. As it turned out, none of that happened.

On a telephone call the night before Chani left for Florida, her mom sounded upbeat and excited about her coming home. Like Jewish mothers throughout history, Devora was busy preparing Chani's favorite foods that she was certain were unavailable in the hinterlands of Northampton. Chani took an early morning flight and then caught a cab from the airport for the fifteen minute ride to her home. As she walked in the house, the smells of brisket and potatoes engulfed her. Devora ran to the door and greeted her daughter with a huge hug and smile. Tears of joy were running down her cheeks as if she hadn't seen her child for years rather than six weeks. Chani looked at her mother and immediately saw that she had lost a great deal of weight. "Mom. Are you on a diet?"

"No, why? Do I look thin?"

"Yes, are you eating OK?"

"Not really, I seem to have lost my appetite. I figure it's probably the antidepressant pills."

"Have you spoken to Dr. Appel?"

"No."

"Let's call him."

Dr. Appel confirmed that the prescribed pills had many side effects but appetite loss was not one of them. In fact, he said that most people gained weight on the medications. He suggested that something else was going on and that a visit to a primary care physician would be a good idea. Devora then called her doctor and arranged for an appointment the following afternoon. That business taken care of, Chani and Devora sat down to eat while Chani told her mother of her amazing new friends, the fishing trip to Martha's Vineyard, her new connection to the Jewish community in Northampton, and her classes at Miller. It was a lovely afternoon and evening. The next morning Chani awakened to the cries of her mother. As she ran into her mother's bedroom, she saw Devora mother standing in front of a long mirror crying.

"What's wrong?"

"Chani, look at me."

"What?"

"Don't you see? Look at my stomach."

"So you have a tummy."

"Chani, I'm losing weight and I look like I'm five months pregnant. I have no appetite. Something's very wrong. I'm scared."

"Mom, calm down, we'll take care of this today."

It wasn't taken care of that day. The physician ordered a series of blood tests, ultrasound examinations, and scans. By the end of the week, the diagnosis came back as ovarian cancer.

The diagnosis scared both Devora and Chani and, after thinking it over, Chani announced that she was taking a leave from Miller to help her mother. Devora rebelled and told Chani that she had plenty of friends and support in the community and it was important to her that Chani return to school.

Reluctantly, Chani agreed and on Sunday morning she flew back to Massachusetts. As soon as she in her dorm room she called Blake and asked to have coffee with her. Norman was out with the girls so Chani went over to the Cohn condo on Prospect Avenue near Childs Park. Chani explained the situation and Blake assured her it was the right decision to return for the second quarter. She also suggested that Chani might want to consider a field placement in South Florida even though she had already been assigned to an outstanding mental health center seventeen miles north of Miller in Greenfield, Massachusetts. With Blake's help and advice, she planned to request a meeting with the field training faculty director to discuss her transfer.

By the end of the first week of the second quarter the field placement office had handled Chani's request professionally and promptly. She was reassigned to a position with a foundation-funded program called the South Florida Jewish Outreach Center. Elsa Solomon, a vibrant seventy-nine year-old Holocaust survivor, who was a Miller School for Social Work graduate, directed the organization. The focus of the project was the provision of short-term counseling services to the large population of Holocaust survivors in South Florida, and Jewish inmates incarcerated throughout Dade and Broward Counties. Chani and her mother were thrilled with this placement. In September, a few days before Devora's first surgery, Chani was home to support her mother and begin her fieldwork. She would be in Florida until it was time to return to Miller in June.

The results of Devora's surgery were not encouraging. As anticipated by the gynecological-oncologist, she had stage IV ovarian epithelial cancer that had already metastasized to the liver and other organs. Devora agreed with her physicians to begin a course of chemotherapy. Unfortunately, the chemotherapy was quite exhausting often leaving Devora weak and nauseated. Both mother and daughter agreed that they needed additional daytime help to ensure Devora's safety and take her to doctors' appointments. With assistance from Elsa they found Dorothy Baldwin, a newly retired and widely experienced licensed practical nurse, who was willing to be Devora's companion ten hours each day. By the end of her first week of her work Dorothy was part of the family and Chani was able to focus more attention on her fieldwork.

Solomon turned out to be an outstanding mentor. She was patient in explaining the politics of her organization, and teaching Chani about the range of the techniques that could be utilized in order to reach therapeutic goals. As the weeks passed, Chani started seeing her mentor as a kindly new grandmother. Similarly, Elsa was quite pleased with Chani's intelligence, enthusiasm, and the quality of her therapy sessions as well as her case write-ups that were required by both Elsa and Miller College.

Unfortunately, by late January, Devora's health had deteriorated to the point where she had become totally bedridden. Her mornings and afternoons were spent with Dorothy Baldwin who ensured that she was clean, comfortable, and fed. Chani would get home by 4:00 PM and spend the rest of the day and evening hours sitting alongside her mother reading or talking to her while holding her hand. Over Devora's objections Chani moved a portable bed into her mom's room where she would sleep, listening to the sounds of her mother's labored breathing.

In mid-February, it became evident to Chani that her mother needed additional care that would best be provided by the local hospice organization. After a tearful discussion her mother consented to the new arrangement. Days after the first hospice visit Mrs. Weissfogel slipped in a deep sleep from which she never awakened. For those last few days Chani was by her side, talking to her, praying in Hebrew, singing, and telling her mother countless times how much she loved and admired her. During the last hours of her mother's life Chani listened to her tortuous breathing and the gurgling sounds of the 'death rattles.' She was grateful that the hospice workers were nearby to attend to her mother's needs and provide her with much welcomed support. When the hospice nurse told Chani that the end was near she called Rabbi Friedman who rushed over to both offer final prayers on behalf of Devora Weissfogel and comfort to her only child. Then for the second time in less than two years Chani was attending a parent's funeral and sitting Shiva. This time, her friend Blake was at her side.

The months after her mother's passing were a blur. Elsa's love and support, as well as the need to help others by providing therapy, saved

Chani's own mental health. The lesson that healing comes from giving proved to be a core value for Chani.

She also decided that she couldn't make any important decisions about the future under the time constraints she faced—including the field training she had to complete but also the need to return to Northampton for her last period of academic study before receiving her social work degree. Chani lived in the family home through May, and made arrangements through a realtor friend of her father's to rent the house to a young religious couple that were moving to Fort Lauderdale.

In June, the field training was completed and, with gratitude to Elsa for an outstanding professional experience and emotional support during her mother's sickness and death, Chani returned to Northampton for her next ten weeks of class. She was happy to see Blake, Norman, and the girls again and be in concert with the rhythms of the summer. Two weeks into the term she was informed that her second placement would be at the Greenfield Health Center, where she had been initially scheduled the previous year.

At the end of the summer Chani moved out of the dorm, rented an apartment in downtown Northampton, and began her second field placement. Her mentor was a seasoned therapist and outstanding teacher. The days passed rapidly and Chani, for the first time in many years, looked forward to the weekends when she would join Blake and her family for a Shabbat meal at their home or invite them to a Shabbat meal at her apartment. When the weather was nice on Sunday, Chani would frequently borrow or rent a plane at LaFleur Airport in Northampton and do some recreational flying. Occasionally Blake would join her for a quick fishing trip to the coast or an outlet-shopping trip in Vermont.

In mid-November Chani received an email from her academic counselor at Miller requesting an immediate meeting to discuss her master's thesis. The meeting was set for two days before Thanksgiving. Chani had been ignoring the thesis hoping it might disappear. But it wouldn't.

The professor explained that the thesis requirements would not be waived and that she needed a proposal by December 15th. As Chani sat in her apartment trying to think of a topic that might interest her, she was reminded of a lecture on the impact of naturally recurring events such as holidays on families, relationships, as well as emotional health. She recalled wondering whether Rosh Hashanah or Yom Kippur had a similar emotional impact on Jewish families as holidays such as Easter or Christmas might have on non-Jewish families. In thinking about this as a thesis topic she remembered the Rosh Hashanah tradition in her family of everyone asking each other for forgiveness for any wrong they may have committed during the past year. The concept was simple: Clean your slate before moving into the Jewish New Year.

After meeting with her advisor, she designed a study where she would interview a dozen orthodox Jewish families in Springfield about this pre-Rosh Hashanah practice. The results were surprising. She found that many Orthodox families used the holiday as a time to actually ask for forgiveness in a ritualized way. However, what she found most interesting was that others used the holidays to attempt to bridge difficult relationships in their family. For example, in one case she interviewed a woman who always made a point of sending flowers to her siblings and wishing them a 'Happy New Year.' She did this despite the fact that for decades she and her siblings had little in common and rarely talked to each other. The Springfield woman said she hoped the flowers "Keep the lines of communication opened."

The thesis was accepted and it, along with her myriad Shabbat experiences and time in the Northampton synagogue, was a powerful force bringing Chani to a new and unclear place in her personal Judaism. She wasn't certain what it all meant other than she needed to define herself as a Jewish woman with a mission. And that mission was not merely being a social work therapist in just any location.

As the August graduation neared, she made a radical decision, with ramifications she simply could not have foreseen. She decided that she needed to clear her mind and contemplate her spiritual and practical future by going to Israel for a few months.

Eleven

JERUSALEM, ISRAEL

Chani's impulsive decision to go to Israel was totally out of character. Typically, she would think through the costs and benefits as well as the implications of any major decision. In this instance she simply rented a storage locker, gave away most of her furniture, boxed up her clothes and books, and carted them to the unit. She then handed over her car keys to Blake and Norman and told them she would be back 'in a while.'

On the Tuesday after completing her program at Miller, with twenty-five inch roller bag and the large backpack that she had typically used for weeklong trips, she was off to Israel. The only thing she knew was that her first stop was Jerusalem where she had a reservation for a week at the Inbal Hotel. She left Kennedy Airport on an El Al flight that took off at 7:00 PM. After flying through seven time zones, the Boeing 747-400 landed almost eleven hours later at Ben Gurion International Airport, in the city of Lod, twelve miles southeast of Tel Aviv. It was Wednesday, 12:45 PM, Israeli time. After going through passport control, picking up her luggage, and clearing customs, Chani took a forty-five minute taxi ride to the historic city of Jerusalem.

Her future, indeed the very reason she was in Jerusalem, was unclear. She was exhausted and needed a more permanent place to stay than the hotel. After unpacking and for no particular reason other than feeling Israel under her feet, she went on a 'walkabout.' Her stroll took her up King George Street, past the Conservative Synagogue, the Orthodox Great Synagogue, a small park through which she could see the ramparts of the Old City, and when she reached Ben Yehuda Street she turned right. She always enjoyed Ben Yehuda Street not only because it was a pedestrian mall but she also loved its magnetic draw of energetic tourists and young Israelis. She turned again onto Jaffa Road and then again at Shlomo Hamelech walking through the Mamilla Mall (which reminded her of the Aventura Mall in Florida). Next she headed down King David Street, passing the various shops selling silver religious objects and Judaic oriented art to the hordes of tourists visiting the city, the Reform movement's campus with its various blend of new and older limestone buildings, gardens and courtyards, the historic pink limestone King David Hotel located at the nexus of Old and New Jerusalem—where every U.S. president since Nixon had stayed and virtually every celebrity from Elizabeth Taylor to Madonna had at one time or another been in residence. Then in a few more leafy blocks she was back at the Inbal. At that moment, although feeling disconnected and alone, she also sensed that she was finally at home.

On Thursday morning she awakened at 6:00 AM, slipped into exercise clothes, and went to the hotel's fitness center. After an hour-long workout Chani was back in her room in order to shower and dress before breakfast which at the Inbal was always a treat. It was a huge buffet with cold and hot foods. Most of the food was delicious and, for her, many of the items were rare indulgences. She piled her dishes high and found a table on the terrace overlooking the pool area. By 8:30 she had eaten, returned to her room for one more brushing of her teeth, and was then off to attend a lecture in the Old City. Dressed in a long black skirt, a cotton blouse that covered her arms, and a brown leather purse-backpack that contained a notebook, her wallet, hotel keycard, a beret, and a thin sweater she was heading down King David Street dressed in the uniform of a modest religious woman.

Her goal was to get to the Nay-Grodno Yeshiva before the start of a 10 o'clock public lecture to be given by Rabbi Velvel Benmoshe. For many years, she had been inspired by his writings and this was her opportunity to see and hear him in person.

The lecture hall was packed with people standing along the side and in the rear of the room. A few minutes after 10 o'clock, Rabbi Benmoshe walked in. A short man with white hair, a bushy white beard, and pink puffy cheeks, he closely resembled Dr. Appel; a dead ringer for Santa Claus. He looked over the audience, acknowledged some people with a nod and then began. "Shalom. Welcome everyone. And *Chag Sameach*. I can see that some of you know what I mean and are a bit confused by my saying Chag Sameach. For those who don't yet understand Hebrew, Chag Sameach means happy holiday. Why am I saying it now? Simply because I believe that every day we are alive and partaking of God's beautiful world we should also remind ourselves what a special day it is. In fact, it is an awesome day! So, dear friends, Chag Sameach.

"The teacher who was perhaps most influential in my life was the great sage, Rabbi Noach Weinberg—a leader in the Jewish outreach movement and founder of the Aish HaTorah organization as well as their beautiful Yeshiva that you can see from the Western Wall Plaza. Rabbi Weinberg wrote that one of the ways to wisdom is to be enthusiastic about each day. Let me quote from one of his writings, 'Human tendency is to take life for granted. Take five minutes and make list of the amazing aspects of creation.' One of the items on his list is a bird chirping while another is a child laughing."

To illustrate the value of this view of life, Rabbi Benmoshe told a story about the day he and his six year-old grandson visited the Jerusalem Zoo. His grandson was so obsessed with seeing the bears that were housed at the far end of the zoo that the boy ignored all of the active and interesting animals that they passed along the way to the bear habitat. And, when they finally reached the bears, they were sleeping.

The rabbi concluded his talk by saying, "Take the time to look around and see the abundant gifts that God has put before you. These gifts come in all colors, sizes, and, in fact, behaviors. Some gifts are furry; some have long necks, some fly, and some slither. And a lot of them walk around this earth on two legs. But they are the gifts that God created and we should respect each of them and always be grateful for these gifts."

Everyone was intrigued by Rabbi Benmoshe's message as well as his delivery. He then said he had a few minutes for questions or comments. The first question came from a tall, skinny young man with black curly hair, a dark bushy beard, and a knitted kippah held on to his head with two silver colored clips.

"Rabbi, thank you for your beautiful lecture. It will certainly make my visits to the zoo more meaningful. And your message about God creating these differences and our need to respect, perhaps even celebrate, these differences leads me to a question. Rabbi, how can you as an Orthodox rabbi, offering the message you just did, accept the discrimination that occurs in Orthodox Judaism against gays and women? For example, the only group in Judaism that won't ordain women rabbis is the Orthodox. Here in Israel there is even discrimination against Modern Orthodox by Ultra-Orthodox. Shouldn't we at least treat one another with the same level of respect and consideration that you have proposed for animals?"

Rabbi Benmoshe smiled, stroked his beard, and then answered, "So early in the day you have posed an unusually profound question! And, most importantly, you see the analogy between my trip to the zoo and people. You surely must be a rabbinical student."

Everyone laughed as the young man nodded. Rabbi Benmoshe continued, "I unfortunately do not have a good answer for you. There is no suggestion in the Torah that we as a people should be so fractionated. But, as we all know, our earliest history clearly tells us that we are tribal and more modern history tells us we are a people who follow different leaders with different interpretations and customs that become laws. Some Jews sit at Kiddush, some stand, Sephardic Jews eat rice during Pesach while Ashkenazi Jews do not eat rice. I can tell you with absolute certainly that, despite decades of study, I have never seen the word rice in the Torah. Clearly we do much post hoc reasoning and this gets us to where we want to go. In Orthodoxy we speak of clear roles for males and females. And in these roles people find comfort except for those people who don't. Fortunately, for those interested in egalitarianism there are other streams of Judaism. I do not believe that Judaism is a one-size-fits-all religion. Should these other groups be respected? Definitely, yes! Should everyone in a group have to do the same thing? Definitely, no! I hope I've answered your question. Next question."

At least two people were uneasy about Rabbi Benmoshe's response: the young man whose name was Nathaniel Kahn and Chani Weissfogel. When the seminar was over Chani walked over to Kahn and introduced herself. They rehashed the question and response and Chani learned that Nathaniel was from Dallas, Texas, a graduate of Swarthmore College, and now a fourth-year rabbinical student at the Klal Yisrael Yeshiva in Brookline, Massachusetts. Their meeting was cordial and Kahn asked nothing about Chani.

The jet lag hit Chani with full force on Friday morning. She could barely get out of bed. Her initial plan was to walk over to both the Conservative and Reform seminaries and see if there were any adult extension courses she might want to take. After those visits she intended to shop for some Shabbat clothes at the mall, take a nap, and walk to the Western Wall to welcome the Sabbath. She was hoping that at the Wall she would run into someone she knew, and perhaps be able to share a Sabbath meal with them. But, fatigue overwhelmed her. She decided to opt for 'plan B' and spend the day resting, reading, and sitting by the pool. She also made a dinner reservation at the hotel.

As sunset approached Chani returned to her room, showered, and dressed in a religiously modest outfit. She then headed to the hotel's Shabbat service which was crowded with men, poorly attended by women, and totally uninspiring. When the service was over she left the small stuffy room without speaking to anyone, walked up the curving staircase to the main floor, and over to the dining room hostess. As she was waiting for her table assignment a woman from across the room spotted her, started waving, and got up to greet her with an enthusiastic hug.

"Chani, it's so wonderful to see you particularly here and now. I thought you were up in New England."

Chani was also surprised and pleased to see the other woman. "Rebbetzin, it's so nice to see you too."

"Chani, please call me Leah. I hope you'll sit with us for dinner—unless you have other plans?"

"No, I don't have plans and I'd love to eat with you. Where is the rabbi and what brings you here?"

"He's still at shul. He should be here in about ten minutes. And, in answer to your question, we're here for our nephew Daniel's wedding on Monday. This is Yitz's oldest sister's son. So we just got here this morning, and tomorrow is the *auf ruf* at my sister-in-law's shul. The auf ruf is a real happening. Do you have shul plans tomorrow morning?"

"No."

"Great, you'll come with us. And, you'll definitely enjoy meeting Daniel and Malka, his *kallah*. "

Just then Rabbi Friedman appeared, greeted Chani amiably, and the three sat down for a Shabbat dinner. The Friedmans asked many questions and were quite intrigued by Chani's experience at Miller as well as her thesis topic and its conclusion. Finally, Rabbi Friedman asked the question that had been hanging in the air, "So, what brings you to Israel now?"

Chani was quiet for a minute and then answered, "Honestly, I am not sure. In my last months at Miller most of my classmates were looking for jobs. I wasn't because I'm not really certain about what I want to do. I am also uncertain about where I want to do whatever it is I do. I am truly confused! So, I decided Israel is as good a place as any, maybe even a better place than most, to sort out my thinking about my future. So here I am with no plans and no attachments."

Rabbi Friedman listened carefully and then replied, "What you say makes perfect sense. I pray you find what you are looking for. And now, dear ladies, the hour is late, I'm wiped; let's leave for shul at 8:30 AM."

They all agreed with the plan and said their goodnights. Chani went back to her room feeling less disconnected.

Right on time Chani was standing in the lobby as Rabbi and Mrs. Friedman appeared. Shabbat greetings were exchanged and the rabbi said, "A little truth in advertising. The shul we are going to is called Beth-El Yerushalayim and it's in a neighborhood called Katamon, near the German Colony. The place is really very interesting. My sister and her late husband were amongst the area people who founded the place. They use the Modern Orthodox Artscroll prayer book, their service is conceptually indistinguishable from ours, but they use the Etz Chaim Chumash for the Torah reading. Do you know that one? It's used mostly by the Conservatives." Chani nodded.

"They also have a very flexible, see-through *mechitza* separating men and women, and don't be shocked by women leading the service or getting called to the Torah. Having said that you'll also see it's a lively place, with great participation, and a knowledgeable and relatively young congregation. I think you'll enjoy it and I want to introduce you to my nephew and his kallah, a fine young woman who is in rabbinical school at the conservative seminary in New York. I guess in their religious world the bride and groom don't stay separated from each other as is customary in many Orthodox circles—although it's actually a custom, not halacha."

Chani's curiosity impelled her to ask the rabbi, "Does all this egalitarianism and participation make you uncomfortable?"

He laughed. "Chani, I am one of six siblings. My oldest brother is a dentist living in Tenafly, New Jersey, married to a lovely lady who is a convert, and they are active in a Reform Temple. Esther, my next oldest sibling you'll meet shortly. She is Daniel's mother, my nephew who is getting married Monday. Daniel went to college in New York and is a graduate of the School of Architecture at Columbia University. He was also an officer in the Israeli Navy. I love Daniel as if he were my own son. He's an adult and needs to find his own path, not mine. I respect that.

"I'm the next in line and I have a younger sister and a younger brother who also live in Israel. My sister lives in Haifa and she and her family are totally secular. My brother lives in Meah She'arim and is

Hasidic. Finally, my youngest sister is the psychiatrist who I contacted to help us with your mom. She and her family live in Toronto and are members of a Conservative synagogue. Am I uncomfortable? Chani, as I may have mentioned before, my background from Newfoundland makes me comfortable and uncomfortable anywhere and everywhere."

As they approached the synagogue Rabbi Friedman escorted Chani and Leah to the women's section entrance, then he hurried to find a seat in the crowded men's section. Chani kept her focus on the prayer book only occasionally looking up in order to see the face attached to the clear and emotion filled praying of the female cantor. The morning service completed, it was time to move into the Torah service. The Torah scroll was removed from the ark and paraded around both the men's and women's sections of the room. The congregation's singing was loud and enthusiastic as the Torah was marched to the table in the center of the room and preparations were made for it to be read.

Traditionally, the first person called to bless the Torah is a male descendant of Aaron the high priest, Moses's brother, and in Judaism these people are known as *Kohanim*. The second to bless the Torah are also from the same tribe as the Kohanim but are not the descendants of Aaron and are called the Leviim. The third grouping of people called up to the Torah include everyone else, and these people are the Yisraelites. It is a significant honor to be called first to the Torah and Chani was surprised to see that the man called for this first blessing was Nathaniel Kahn, the rabbinical student she had met at the yeshiva lecture. She leaned over to Leah and asked who he was, and Leah whispered, "The bride's brother."

The third person called up to the Torah was Daniel. When he completed the first part of the blessing, the reading of the next Torah section was chanted, and then Daniel read the second blessings. As he finished, wrapped candy showered him from every direction of the synagogue. The curtain separating the men and women was drawn back and enthusiastic dancing, singing and clapping began and continued for almost ten minutes as a way of celebrating Daniel's upcoming marriage. When the dancing was over children were invited to collect the candy and the curtain was then pulled back in place.

At the conclusion of the Torah reading, the Torah was dressed with its cover, silver crowns, and pointers and placed in the hands of a woman who held it (while seated) as another young women chanted a reading from the Book of Prophets known as the Haftorah. After she finished the Torah was again marched around through the synagogue and replaced in the ark.

Once again, the curtain separating the men's and women's section was drawn back and a young woman with long dark curly hair and deep green eyes walked to the front of the congregation to give a *D'var Torah* related to the week's reading.

She began: "Shabbat Shalom. Allow me to begin with a few announcements. First, welcome to all our family and friends from around the globe. Daniel and I are thrilled that you are here and you will add to our joy by being part of our wedding on Monday. Lest anyone here feel left out you are all invited to come back to the shul at 4 o'clock on Monday for the *badeken* and the *chuppah*. Then definitely stay for the party afterward. This is the Israeli way! Finally, in case there is any confusion about the extent of Israeli hospitality, you are definitely not invited on our honeymoon." The synagogue broke out in laughter and even a smattering of applause.

"This week's parsha is Bechukotai, which literally means 'by my decrees.' Oftentimes this parsha is read with the previous week's parsha Behar—but this is not the case this week. My *drash* will be short and perhaps not even profound since I am only a first year rabbinical student. If my brother Nathaniel who is about to be a fifth year rabbinical student was giving the drash it would be much more profound and three times longer. These are the tradeoffs."

More laughter rippled through the congregation. Leah leaned over to Chani and whispered, "Malka is a sweetheart, funny, and very bright. You'll enjoy talking to her." The bride continued with her talk.

"In the parsha we have one of the several times in the Torah where there is the admonition that if we follow God's ways we will be blessed but if don't we shall be cursed. This can be viewed as, either or both, a collective warning for all of Israel or personal advice for each of us. What strikes me is that this parsha is proof positive that we do have free will and the choices we make certainly have consequences. If we take the Torah literally we learn that following the laws will lead to rain in the proper season, plentiful harvests, and the vanquishing of enemies thanks to God's help and, most significantly, peace in the land.

"The question I must raise is: If we truly believe in the words of Torah why would we not follow every one of the 613 commandments? Allow me to suggest we aren't truly certain about what we really believe and our own cravings sometimes trump Torah. Finally, allow me a personal interpretation: What the Torah is offering us is aspirational goals. If you will, a plan to improve our world and ourselves. And, I can't think of a better parsha for Daniel's auf ruf and the days before our marriage. Marriage is in large measure improving your life with a person you love and who will be your lifelong helpmate. And thanks to Torah we have God's plan for a happy future. Our job is to implement that plan, particularly the words from this week's parsha: Be fruitful and multiply. Shabbat Shalom."

Once more, there was a ripple of laughter through the congregation. Malka sat down and another woman stood up and began leading the final sections of the Sabbath service.

At the conclusion of the service everyone went outside for the Kiddush, a casual gathering for some light refreshments. Chani walked over to Nathaniel Kahn, wished him "*mazel tov*" on his sister's wedding and began a conversation that almost never ended. They spent the afternoon together, later dinner, and, by Monday, Chani was his date to the wedding.

Twelve

JERUSALEM, ISRAEL

The following days were the best time Chani had ever experienced in Israel. Her hours together with Nathaniel were filled with hikes through the Judean hills, a visit to one of Nathaniel's classmates who had moved to the West Bank town of Efrat, a beach day in Haifa, and the almost obligatory stops at the *Kotel* and the *Mahane Yehuda* Market. During their days and evenings together they spoke of their families, college, and Nathaniel explained the nature of the nondenominational yeshiva he was attending. They shared their love of adventure and travel as well as their hope of building a life with roots in a community.

Nathaniel confided in Chani that his dream was to be a congregational rabbi in a small town. He told her that he had already tentatively lined up several interviews for positions in Northern California, Oregon, Vermont, and on the Olympic Peninsula of Washington.

On Wednesday evening, less than a week after they had met for the first time, Chani and Nathaniel were standing in the small circular driveway at the front of the Inbal Hotel when Nathaniel, in a quiet and remorseful tone, reminded Chani that he was leaving on Thursday night for Boston.

He asked, "What are your plans for the rest of the summer?"

"Nathaniel, I have no plans, that's why I'm here."

"May I make a suggestion? How would you feel about going to Boston with me?"

A bright smile crossed Chani's face when she replied, "I thought you would never ask. I'd love to be with you in Boston."

And, for the first time, Nathaniel reached over to hold Chani's hand, and she gently squeezed his hand with an inner joy flowing through her.

On Thursday evening Nathaniel Kahn left Israel to return to Boston for his last year of rabbinical school. Sitting next to him was Chani Weissfogel. Chani was not sure what she would do in Boston other than be with Nathaniel. What attracted this young rabbinical student to Chani was his obvious intelligence, his unequivocal devotion to a type of Judaism that Chani had barely experienced but found quite interesting, his love of the natural world, and something simply physical. "Chemistry" is how she explained it to Blake.

On the day they arrived in Boston, Nathaniel invited Chani to spend the night in his Brookline apartment. Despite their exhaustion from fifteen hours of traveling, the privacy of Nathaniel's apartment and the unburdening themselves of their luggage seemed to lead naturally to their being in each other's arms. Soon they were pulling off each other's clothes. It was as if a dam had broken. Their first round of lovemaking was hasty as well as clumsy. It was filled with deep kisses, touching, exploration, and swift penetration. Within minutes their relationship had moved from chaste handholding to total intimacy.

Exhaustion suddenly overtook them and moments later they were asleep. In the morning Nathaniel arose to see the eyes of Chani focused on his face. She raised her hand and lightly stroked his cheek. Nathaniel reached out to her and their two bodies moved slowly, and lovingly came together, followed by an hour of sweet snuggling. By the evening, they were discussing their future together.

Five weeks later, on the 6th of July, Chani and Nathaniel flew to Dallas. They were greeted at DFW airport by the newlyweds Daniel and Malka, and driven to the Kahn family's spacious ranch style home on

Drane Drive in Greenway Park, one of the older sections of the city. Chani had briefly met the Kahns in Israel and found them to be staunch Zionists who were quite proud of having both of their children studying for the Rabbinate.

The following morning a Ryder rental truck pulled up to the Kahn house and two men entered the living room. They proceeded to move most of the furniture into the family room and set up forty white folding chairs. In the front of the room a wedding canopy entwined with white roses was erected. At noon, the wedding ceremony of Nathaniel Kahn and Chani Weissfogel began. Theodore Rubin, an old family friend of the Kahns and now the Rabbi Emeritus of Temple Emanuel, the major Reform temple in Dallas, agreed to modify his typical ceremony into a more traditional one. Wearing a white lace dress, Chani circled Nathaniel seven times. For Chani this was a bittersweet moment. Of all the wedding guests only four were from her 'side': Blake, Norman, Rachel, and Rebecca Cohn. She was an orphan but she hoped her parents were smiling down on her at that moment. By 12:30 PM she was a married woman.

Thirteen

BROOKLINE, MASSACHUSETTS

Early in the morning on September 6th, just two months after they were married, Nathaniel Kahn took a nonstop flight from Boston to Seattle. As the Airbus A320 flew from the East to the West Coast, Nathaniel spent most of his time gazing out the window and thinking about his new bride and the life they might make together in the Pacific Northwest with his own congregation. Nathaniel loved the idea of Port Avis, an old fishing village that had recently developed into a tourist spot. The proximity of the Olympic National Park meant that in their free time Chani and he could hike and camp in the mountains, perhaps someday with their own children. His daydreaming was interrupted by an announcement that it was time to land. .

At Sea-Tac International Airport Nathaniel was met by Myles Dinnerstein the search committee chairman of a sixty-member synagogue in Port Avis, about seventy-five miles northwest of Seattle. The jobs in California and Oregon had already fallen through, so Chani was happy that Nathaniel still had the possibility of this position on the Olympic Peninsula in addition to the opportunity in Vermont. The plan was that if either the Port Avis community or the synagogue in Fisher, Vermont, was interested in hiring Nathaniel, both of them would make a second visit during the Succoth holiday. For Chani it was an exciting time because it meant a new start with her husband, and the chance to begin her own professional career as a social worker.

The trip to Washington State did not work out as Nathaniel and Chani had envisioned. The Jewish community did have sixty members, but that was down from over one hundred members eight years earlier. The membership was primarily comprised of senior citizens who had spent most of their lives in the local area and a small number of retirees from Tacoma and Seattle. The synagogue had only twelve children attending the makeshift Hebrew school. While the geography was very appealing, the job seemed to offer little promise of building a vibrant Jewish community. When Nathaniel reported back to Chani his disappointment, she offered her support although privately she was concerned that perhaps both of them might be engaged in a pipe dream.

The visit to Vermont, originally scheduled for the middle of September, was postponed until the first week of November. The plan was for Nathaniel and Chani to spend the weekend at the synagogue where he would lead services and then meet with the congregation. A week before the visit the synagogue's president had sent Nathaniel a two-inch-thick packet of material with photos of the new sanctuary and Hebrew school. To Chani and Nathaniel the job seemed to offer the kind of community and potential they had talked about. The possibility of living near the Green Mountains and its numerous hiking trails and ski resorts was an important extra bonus.

Founded fifteen years earlier by a group of young Jewish refugees from Boston and New York, the Har Yahrok Jewish Center (HYJC) in Fisher, Vermont had more than one hundred members, twenty-five children in the Hebrew school, and growing. It was in a beautiful part of the state with easy access to several lovely towns in Vermont, Western Massachusetts, and New York. As the time for the visit approached both Nathaniel and Chani became increasingly excited.

There was one problem. On the Wednesday before the weekend Chani awakened with a terrible sore throat and fever. In the afternoon she went to her primary care physician who took a throat culture, and recommended lots of fluids and bed rest. He gave her a prescription for a Z-pak but told her not to use it until after he got the culture back on Friday. He also advised her against traveling.

There was no easy way to get to Fisher so Nathaniel decided to drive. It took almost three hours on highways and secondary roads, but once he arrived the town and the Jewish community delighted him. Before services started he called Chani and learned that she indeed had a bacterial infection and had already started on the antibiotic. He was happy that she had chosen to stay home and rest.

The weekend went exceptionally well and on Sunday afternoon Nathaniel met with the board chairman who told him that they were quite pleased and would likely invite Nathaniel and Chani back sometime after Thanksgiving. Privately, the chairman told him not to be surprised if he received a formal offer sometime in the next two weeks. Nathaniel was thrilled and, when he called Chani before setting out on the return trip at 2 o'clock, they were both ecstatic about the next step in their life together. Chani, who had been lying in bed and watching television most of the day, urged Nathaniel to drive carefully because the first snow of the season was predicted for the northern tier of Massachusetts, which included the route that he was following for the trip home.

At 5:30 PM Sunday evening, Rabbi Bob Stevens' cell phone rang. He looked at the caller ID that said "MSP Holden." He immediately answered knowing that it was a call from the Massachusetts State Police where he served as a volunteer chaplain. The caller began: "Rabbi, this is Lieutenant Harry Morgan from the Troop C Headquarter Barracks. Unfortunately, we had a terrible five-car pile-up out here on Route 2 with four deaths. One of the victims has a Brookline address and I believe he's Jewish from his name and the fact he was wearing one of those skull-caps. First, do you happen to know him? His name is Nathaniel Kahn."

Stevens was quiet and then with a heavy heart he said, "Yes, I do. He lives in the area and is a rabbinical student. Has his wife been notified?"

The officer replied, "No, not yet. That's why I'm calling. Can you help us out and go over there as our representative?"

The rabbi replied, "OK, but can you give me any details and a number for Mrs. Kahn to call?"

"Certainly. The roadway was slick and visibility was less than a half-mile. We think the accident happened when a car went out of control pulling onto the roadway near Leominster and another car hit it and then a truck lost control. Mr. Kahn's car was just in the wrong place at the wrong time. Very sad." He then went on to provide the rabbi with a contact number.

Rabbi Stevens walked into the kitchen and told his wife about the accident. They had both spoken to Nathaniel often and knew him well. More recently Mrs. Stevens had gotten to know Chani and they were slowly becoming friends. She reminded her husband that Chani had lived in Northampton and suggested that he speak to his friend Rabbi Marvin Alexander who was the rabbi in that Western Massachusetts town. Stevens put a call into Alexander, who, knowing the relationship between Chani and the Cohn family, volunteered to call the Cohns about the accident. After being notified about the tragedy, Blake and Norman agreed that she would take the next bus to Boston and spend as much time with Chani as necessary.

At 6:00 PM the concierge on duty at the front desk of the Kahn's Beacon Street building rang Chani and said Rabbi and Mrs. Stevens were downstairs and wished to come up and see her. She said, "Send them up." She also wondered why in the world they were coming to visit her on a cold snowy Sunday night.

Part Three
The Cohn Brothers

Fourteen

ALASKA FLIGHT 27

The week in Florida had been sad and exhausting. Neither the girls nor Norman and Blake looked forward to the six-hour flight to Seattle, the hour layover, the three-hour flight back to Alaska and the final leg of their journey; a long drive home. Once they got settled on the plane Norman and Blake had a chance to review the week and do some reminiscing.

Blake began by asking Norman how he thought Marc was doing. Norman turned to his wife, slowly shook his head and, as if a dam had broken, a torrent of words flowed, "I think Marc acted as if this whole week was an incredible inconvenience. He seemed to spend as much time as possible watching the TV sports channel and talking on his cell phone. He was totally indifferent to the people who came to make the Shiva calls and he even told me that he wished that none of them had come.

"And I'm very upset about how he treats Max. Here, the kid's mother dies and Marc basically ignores him. And, he certainly also ignored our kids."

Norman then recalled an argument that he and Marc had had on the fourth evening of their visit. Norman had confronted Marc about his indifference to Max who was obviously hurting. Marc responded that

Norman lives halfway around the world and should mind his own business. The brothers didn't talk for the rest of the evening but the next day Marc offered a perfunctory apology and Norman decided to let the matter drop.

"I've often thought that Marc was a bit of a bastard and I hate to say it because he is my brother but this last week's experience with him only confirms my analysis that he is also a self-centered narcissist. He's smart, charming when he wants to be, but totally all about himself. Nothing changes. This is how he was as a kid and this is how he is now. Frankly, I wouldn't be surprised if he goes right back to his boob jobs and tummy tucks as if nothing happened. I suspect he'll have a girlfriend by the time we get unpacked! But, you realize, to my parents he was still the golden child "*Mein* son, the doctor.""

Blake already knew Norman's backstory that he was the brother who helped while Marc almost always found a way to avoid working in the family pharmacy. Norman was the one who started working in the store at the age of twelve doing the grunt work—stocking shelves and sweeping up. When he was fifteen his father began training him to be a pharmacy technician in the not so subtle expectation that his oldest son would become a pharmacist and take over the store. By the time he was sixteen Norman was experienced enough to fill prescriptions, attach the labels and after his father checked everything he would complete the process by handing the drugs over to a customer and collecting the money. Norman had told Blake that during his senior year in high school he realized that he already had enough of small-time retail pharmacy and wasn't interested in being a pharmacist. He saw the physical toll it took on his parents as well as the constant fear they lived with as they thought about how the big chains were killing the small independent drugstores.

When Norman told his parents of his decision they were both mildly disappointed but the following day Norman's father suggested a career in medicine. However, one semester of biology and chemistry at NYU was enough to cure Norman of that goal, so he switched out of his pre-med program and majored in political science with a minor in sociology.

By the beginning of his final year at NYU he was still undecided about a career until, halfway through sociology of law course, he read Anthony Lewis's book, *Gideon's Trumpet*. The book followed the case of fifty-one year-old Clarence Earl Gideon, a poverty stricken drifter with a string of petty crimes and multiple prison sentences to his name. Gideon was convicted in Florida of breaking and entering with intent to commit larceny that resulted in a five-year sentence. Norman learned that Gideon had asked for a court appointed lawyer, but his request was denied, and this likely illiterate man was forced to defend himself.

Subsequently, Gideon petitioned the Supreme Court for its review and they appointed a Washington lawyer Abe Fortas (later selected as a Supreme Court Justice) to represent him. The decision in *Gideon vs. Wainwright* established the principle that all criminal defendants are entitled to representation even if they can't afford it.

Norman Cohn was inspired. He decided that he wanted to be a lawyer—more specifically, a public defender. He also wanted to get out of New York. A partial scholarship to Boston University School of Law made Commonwealth Avenue his home for the next three years.

Blake then asked, "Do you think your parents would be proud of who Marc is today?"

Norman considered the question and then said, "They definitely would be proud that he's a plastic surgeon. I also think they would be okay with the fact that he is so wealthy. But my folks were also old-fashioned do-gooders and they wouldn't be happy at the way he spends his money on things like cars and boats. Additionally, they would be pissed that with all his money he is so unbelievably uncharitable. Finally, I think that they would also be upset with how unhappy Max seems to be and what a lousy job Marc is doing as a father."

Blake jumped on this comment, "What do you think Max's problem is?"

"Obviously the kid is depressed. But I don't know whether it's only because of Cathy's death or it's a longstanding problem. I have a hunch it has been going on for a long time. Also, he is quite isolated. That building they live in is beautiful, but if you didn't know better you'd think it was an assisted living facility for rich old people. I think Max is the only kid there and the average age must be close to ninety. I guess what I'm saying is that I have a feeling that Max is an outsider everywhere, and that Cathy was his anchor and now with her being gone I doubt if Marc can step up to the plate—whatever that means."

"But, why do you say that?"

"Because Marc is an indulged character and, when it comes to family, he's out to lunch. He never helped in the store, never helped at home, and in fact is all about himself. In this last week he asked about us just once when we halfway out the door. Did he ask you about the kids? Or how your practice was going? Did he ever ask you about your parents? Did he ever ask you about anything?"

Blake responded, "I think you already know the answer is no."

"That's right, no. For him, I'm sorry to say, this whole experience was an inconvenience. It took him away from his toys and work. Frankly, I am not sure why Cathy stayed with him."

"Wow, you're really hostile!"

"Come on, Blake, don't be my therapist. You asked me and I told you. I am glad we have each other and the girls. We own our life and Marc owns his; but I do feel badly for Max. After all he is my nephew. I do hope they show up for the kids' bat mitzvah, but frankly it wouldn't surprise me if he weaseled out."

Blake decided to calm the conversation by changing the subject. "Speaking of us, do you remember when we first met?"

"I certainly do. It was during orientation at Miller. I think I was the only straight guy around, at least the only non-swishy guy I saw. And there you were. Six feet tall with auburn hair that almost reached your tiny waist. And those green eyes, smooth olive skin, and high cheekbones. Initially you reminded me of a beautiful Indian squaw from a Western I might have seen at the movies. I had been teaching the mental health law course at Miller for a year so and I thought I knew all about the place. I was afraid you might be a lesbian, but I decided I still had to meet you. It took two cups of coffee for me to learn you graduated from

Bryn Mawr, and you knew my best friend from NYU who was a professor of chemistry there. I recall you telling me that you were a native of Anchorage, and your father was a surgeon who had come to Alaska as an Air Force Medical Officer at Elmendorf Air Force Base. How is that for remembering our first encounter?"

Blake's eyes were sparkling with teardrops as her husband retold the story of that initial encounter and how thrilled she was to see him again on Saturday of the first week at Miller. Norman recounted, "I received the greatest shock when I decided to go to on Shabbat to Northampton's synagogue and I discovered you joyfully participating in the service. Do you remember that I reintroduced myself and sat next to you? Then after services we chatted over the Kiddush with a few of your classmates and then we decided to explore the area with a walk through Childs Memorial Park. Who would have thought that less than a year later I would be proposing to you in the Rose Garden of that same park."

Blake looked at Norman and said, "You are such a blessing in my life. I love you. And now my darling, I'm taking a nap."

Fifteen

BAL HARBOUR, FLORIDA

On January 3rd life ostensibly returned to normal for Marc Cohn. He was up at 5:00 each morning and in the gym by 5:15. An hour later he was back in his condo for a quick shower and dressing for the office. His workplace outfit consisted of blue scrubs and black bull hide leather Dansko clogs, the only type of shoe he had worn since his days as an intern. By 6:45 he was on his way to the building's main entrance alternately munching on his whole-wheat bagel and sipping on a cup of hazelnut coffee.

As usual, his black Continental GT convertible Bentley was waiting for him at the front entrance. Just as he got into his car he waved at Clarita, his Honduran housekeeper, who was walking up the driveway from the Collins Avenue bus stop to begin her day of cleaning his penthouse, doing the laundry, making the beds, and getting Max up and out to school.

Marc Cohn loved the 6,000-square-foot Institute that his vision and success had built. It was fully accredited, had four state-of-the-art surgical suites, six recovery rooms, two overnight suites for his patients or family members, four consultation rooms, a large administrative suite, and a gracious entry way and waiting room. His inspiration for the "front end" of the facility was the Ritz-Carlton in Key Biscayne. He wanted his patients to feel as if they were in a five-star hotel with all the consideration and amenities that a guest of such a place would expect. When he first conceived of the Institute he made an initial business decision to go 'first cabin' and only market the practice on the basis of quality never price. In fact, the Institute's charges were typically the highest in Dade or Broward County. And, in spite of, or perhaps because of, their pricing structure, they operated at close to one hundred percent capacity.

For the past seven years Cohn had kept a rigid schedule of six or seven surgeries daily always beginning at 7:30 AM and ending no later than 3 PM. The hours from 3:00 PM till 7:00 PM were reserved for office consultations and minor procedures such as suture removal. This was the schedule that Cohn figured out was the most efficient and cost effective. He and his partner were able to gross close to $5 million per year, and despite the high overhead of his facility, such as the cost of the nurse anesthetists and other staff, the annual pretax income of the Institute was in excess of $2 million per year. Although he was a consummate consumer, he was also a shrewd investor. By his forty-second birthday, he had an extensive portfolio of stock, bonds, and real estate. Before Cathy's death he anticipated working another twenty years and then retiring to a leisurely life of fishing, golf, and travel. Now he wasn't sure about anything.

Five years earlier he had decided to hire an associate to handle some of the more routine procedures. The surgeon he hired was Alfredo Nussbaum, a Colombian by birth, whose family had brought him to the United States when he was three years old. He was a graduate of the University of Miami and went to medical school at the University of Rochester where he learned to hate the winter months of dreariness and Lake-effect snow. As a student he worked in the laboratory of Alan Lazar, the chair of dermatology. When it came time to apply for his postgraduate training, he talked for hours with Lazar who had become his mentor. Nussbaum was torn between plastic surgery and dermatology. While Lazar liked Nussbaum a great deal, he felt it was unlikely that he would match into a top-drawer program. So not so subtly, he pushed him into plastics where a good match was more probable.

For Nussbaum this truly worked out well. He applied to every program south of the Mason-Dixon Line and was fortunate enough to get selected for the six-year integrated plastic surgery residency program at the UT Southwestern Medical Center in Dallas. The years in Texas were great for Alfredo. He loved Dallas and slowly became a Texan, wearing his Lucchese cowboy boots to work each day and driving a red Ford pickup with a gun rack that usually held an umbrella.

All that changed for Alfredo when the residency was ending and it was time to find a job. His family wanted him back in Florida and the opportunities for him were limited in Dallas. When a search firm approached Alfredo about joining the Institute, Nussbaum flew to Miami for an interview. After spending three hours with Marc Cohn he felt it was the right place for him. He liked the physical setup of the office and operating suites, the clientele that Cohn had developed and the future that Marc had hinted at.

Now he was an associate partner; he performed the full range of plastic surgery procedures, paid his share of the overhead and kept the difference. He had no equity in the building or the goodwill of the practice. But his wealth was increasing rapidly and he was content. Marc was a good partner and friend. Indeed, when Alfredo got married two years earlier, Marc sponsored the bachelor party and was his best man at the wedding.

Marc Cohn's initial patient on his first day back was an attractive twenty-three year-old woman who wanted a breast enlargement because she thought it would enhance her career and increase her marital prospects. Cohn never argued or disagreed with any potential patients. He told himself that he was a repairman just fixing the broken mechanical parts or egos of his patients. In fact, he often spoke about one older patient who was placed on the schedule six weeks in the future and said that she would pay more money for an expedited surgery. When Cohn asked why, she replied, "If I wait too long something might happen to me and I want to be buried with my new boobs." When Cohn related this experience no one believed him—but it was true!

As Marc walked into the operating room the patient was conscious and awaiting sedation. He greeted her and the staff, reviewed the paperwork, particularly the consent forms, and then once again reviewed the procedure with the patient. A few minutes later he began the surgery, as he always did, by uttering the following words, "Ladies and gentlemen, now we begin. Let's do a perfect job."

Once a procedure had begun Cohn was all business. In his operating room there was no music, no jovial banter, and no kibitzing. That morning's surgery started with a 4.5-cm incision on the underside of the breast so that there would be minimal scarring. Ninety minutes later the procedure was complete, silicone implants had been inserted, and the woman's breasts had been enlarged. She was then sent to a recovery suite and by the late afternoon she was on her way home to Aventura in one of the Institute's Lincoln Town cars. The Institute also provided the patient with an aide who would stay with her for three additional hours. These were some of the concierge services that distinguished the Institute from other cosmetic surgical centers.

The next surgery was also a breast enlargement, followed by the newest rage in Florida: the Brazilian butt lift. By the time Cohn completed his surgeries at 2:30 PM, he had three urgent messages on his desk from the headmaster at Max's school.

Marc sat down and returned the headmaster's call. The secretary answered and asked him to hold. After having spent the previous six hours as commanding officer of his operating room where a word, gesture, or look from him made everyone jump, he was getting irritated waiting for the headmaster to pick up.

After thirty seconds the headmaster came on the line, "Dr. Cohn, this is Rod Bradford, the headmaster at Max's school. First, once again, I am extremely sorry for your loss. Cathy was a great person; we really enjoyed working with her. As you may remember from our conversation at the funeral she was an invaluable member of our school family and is truly missed. Frankly, I think your rabbi captured her spirit in his eulogy."

Cohn was stunned. He hadn't known anything about Cathy's involvement in the school and did not remember meeting Bradford who in a very formal manner quickly focused the conversation on Max. "I am sorry to bother you now, but we are having serious issues with your son. Since he returned to school this morning he has been in one fight with another boy who now at the ER at Aventura Hospital with what I suspect is a broken arm, he has verbally abused a teacher, and for the past three hours he has been sitting in my outer office crying and talking to himself. I think you need to get over here."

Cohn listened, thought for a moment about what the headmaster had said, and finally replied, "I'll have to cancel a few appointments but I should be there within an hour."

By the time Marc arrived Max was still sitting in the headmaster's outer office with his head down. He greeted Max and asked how he was doing. The quiet terse reply was, "OK."

Mr. Bradford then walked out of his office, greeted Marc, and escorted him into a private conference room where Roberta Annison, the school psychologist, joined them. Mr. Bradford began, "Dr. Cohn, Max is a good kid but obviously having a very hard time. What he did today is unacceptable."

Mrs. Annison added, "We recognize how stressful a mother's death can be for a child, but clearly Max is acting out beyond acceptable limits. We need to intervene quickly. Dr. Cohn can you tell me what Max's mood was when he went off to school this morning?"

Marc admitted he had no idea explaining that Max was sleeping when he left for the office and the housekeeper was told to awaken him and send him off to school. Bradford, a white haired, painfully thin man with pale skin and dark brown eyes, steepled his long boney fingers on the conference tabled and stared at Cohn who suddenly felt nine- years old and about to be spanked. Finally, Bradford spoke, "Unfortunately, this is a small school with a limited budget and this is not the kind of problem that Mrs. Annison or I can handle internally. Frankly Dr. Cohn, Max needs help! I assume you are a very busy man and your wife was the key person in caring for Max. Am I correct?" Cohn simply nodded. "As of today I am suspending Max for two weeks and will only allow him back if I am convinced that he is getting the proper help for his issues. If

I am not convinced he will be permanently suspended from the school and you will have the option of enrolling him in public school, finding another private school, or most likely home schooling him yourself. I suggest you take Max home and discuss with him what happened today."

Marc and Max left the headmaster's office and got into the Bentley. As soon as they pulled away from the curb Marc looked over at his son and asked him what was going on. Max shrugged and said nothing. They completed the ten-minute trip in silence. Marc dropped Max off at the front entrance and told him he was going back to the office and would be home at 7:00 PM at which time they were going to have a talk. Max went up to the condo, took a pizza from the freezer, and placed it in the oven. When it was ready he took it into his room, locked the door, and ate the pizza while playing video games on his computer. A few minutes past seven Marc came home, found Max's door locked with the light off. He went into his study and thought about the afternoon. He was at a loss. Although on the staff of two hospitals, he had almost no relationships with other physicians and, like many surgeons, held psychiatrists in low regard. Slightly below psychiatrists in Marc's book were psychologists and social workers.

Despite this attitude he figured the two people he could trust most were Norman and Blake so he placed a call to his older brother's cell phone. Norman looked at the caller ID and immediately answered.

"How are you doing, Marc?"

"I'm fine, just went back to work but I'm having trouble with Max and wanted to pick your brain."

"Marc, unless Max is a juvenile delinquent or an inmate I'm pretty useless. I can only share my experiences with the girls and truthfully they are easy and have a great mother. But what's the problem?"

Marc went on to relate the problems at school and Max's sullenness. He also said that he had no clue where to start to find resources in the community. Norman then suggested that he would talk to Blake who was the local Seward expert on problem children and that she might be able to find someone helpful in South Florida. Marc agreed to that idea and forty-five minutes later Blake returned her brother-in-law's call.

After listening to Marc, she said, "The kid is lost and needs help." She then went on to suggest that the first thing Marc should try is to spend much more time together even if it's only watching TV and not talking. "He needs to know that he is not alone in this world." Then she suggested that Marc rearrange his schedule so that he could have a few minutes with Max in the morning and perhaps take him to school. "The bitter truth, Marc, is that from now on your Max's father and mother!" Marc did not like hearing that from Blake, but he also knew it was true. Finally, Marc asked his sister-in-law if she knew any therapists who might help Max. She said she did not, but she would make some inquiries and get back to Marc in a few days. Blake also told him to expect that he too would be part of the therapy.

A day later Blake called her brother-in-law with a referral to a Dr. Reed White in Weston, a town that was about a thirty-minute drive northwest of Bal Harbour. According to Blake he was a psychologist who specialized in children who had experienced traumatic events. Before calling for an appointment Cohn went onto the Internet to examine White's background and credentials. He was overwhelmed: undergraduate degree from Yale in history, masters and PhD from Stanford in clinical psychology, postdoctoral training at Oxford, and former director of the child psychology unit at the Children's Hospital in Boston. Marc Cohn couldn't help but wonder why in the world a person with his resume would move to the Miami area. But, despite some misgivings, he made the call to Reed's office and set up an appointment for Friday afternoon.

By Friday, nothing had improved in the Cohn household. Marc hadn't rearranged his morning schedule because Max didn't need to attend school and was sleeping till noon, eating, and playing video games all afternoon. In the evenings he and Max would go out for dinner at one of the restaurants across Collins Avenue in the Bal Harbour Shops. Conversation between them was meager and for the most part they ate in silence each lost in their own thoughts. Marc was actually looking forward to Friday hoping that Dr. White could provide a fast solution to a troubling problem.

Sixteen

WESTON, FLORIDA

Although Marc Cohn loved many aspects of Florida living, especially the water and beaches, he also had a strong aversion to the inland suburbs—particularly Weston, a town that provided him with close to forty percent of his patients. Weston was an entirely new and affluent city built into the Everglades by a giant corporation. He thought the place was simply too clean, too quiet, and totally Disneyesque. He was surprised to find out that a person with Dr. White's background practiced there. But, then again, he thought it was probably a great place to practice because in his stereotypical view the "burbs" were full of rich kids with myriad real or imagined problems whose parents could afford private therapy.

And, as Cohn was to later learn, Weston was also home to the Miami Children's Hospital Dan Marino Outpatient Center, named for a popular retired Miami Dolphin quarterback, which was an outstanding facility for kids with neurological issues. Dr. White saw patients three mornings a week along with his Cuban-born wife who worked there as a full-time neurologist.

The practice had a three-room suite of offices on the second floor of a building in Town Center of Weston—a space that was designed to resemble the historic downtowns that were now boarded up throughout America. On Dr. White's floor were a host of other professionals including lawyers, a few CPAs, several dentists, and physicians, as well as a consulting firm. The office was identified simply as 'The White Center.' Marc and Max walked into a small, maroon-carpeted waiting room furnished along one wall with a chocolate-colored sofa big enough for three and two comfortable looking chairs separated by a table and lamp on the adjacent wall. Two other floor lamps augmented the natural light coming into the room from three high windows. Below those windows and directly opposite the large sofa was a seventy-five gallon aquarium sitting on a black stand.

Max walked directly over to the tank and stared. "Dad," he excitedly called out, "Come here quick. This is a great aquarium. See that fish over there. It's a royal angelfish and they can grow to over a foot but they almost never survive in aquariums. Amazing."

At that moment the interior door in the room opened and out stepped an athletic looking man, about five foot ten inches tall, totally bald, with a white, well-trimmed beard, and a smile that went from ear to ear. "Gentlemen, welcome. C'mon in. Marc, I recognize you from your ads, so you must be Max." As he ushered them into his neat office he asked them to sit down and said, "Max, you appear to be quite knowledgeable about my fish. I'm rather surprised—do you raise fish?"

Suddenly Max was engaged, "Not at home, but at school. I am one of the kids who take care of our class tank. Can I ask how long you've had that royal angelfish? It's beautiful."

White smiled, "Two weeks; I hope he lasts, my other one died after a month and they are not cheap to replace!" He then thought to himself, *the fish have done it again, instant rapport.*

When everyone was seated inside his office, Dr. White turned to Marc and began, "Gentlemen, I assume you are here because there are some problems and in a minute I would like to hear about them. Typically, I work with teens and their family for two to three months and, if we all cooperate, I can assure you that whatever the problem is it will get better, not necessarily totally solved, but definitely better. The way I work is we begin with a twenty to thirty minute session with all three of us talking about what's going on, followed by twenty minutes alone with Max, twenty alone with you Dr. Cohn, and the remaining time is a wrap-up for all of us. So, do you want to start?" Marc and Max nodded their assent.

For the next few minutes Marc filled White in on Max's trouble at school, Cathy's death, and the general lack of communication at home. Max sat silently, listening and looking around at photos of trees and the seashore that adorned the walls. When Cohn had finished and answered several questions, Dr. White ushered him through a different door into another waiting room. He explained to both of them that for the sake of privacy he used two waiting rooms—the second also exiting into the hallway through an unmarked door. He also scheduled patients far enough apart that the chance of running into another family was quite low.

With Marc out of the room, he turned his attention to Max, "What's bothering you?"

The question startled Max and he answered, "Nothing."

"How are you doing with your mother's death?"

"Okay."

"Why were you in a fight at school?"

"The other guy was giving me attitude and wouldn't stop."

"Does this have anything to do with your mother or father?"

"No."

"How do you get along with your father?"

"Okay."

"Do you guys talk much?"

"No."

"Play much?"

"Huh?"

"Play much; like, do fun things together."

"Not really."

White decided to shift the focus of the monosyllabic discussion, "Max, tell me about your mother."

"I miss her."

"Why?"

"I just do."

"If you could talk to her, what would you say?"

Max sat still looking at the wall. Then tears formed at the edge of his eyes. Dr. White reached for a tissue box and handed it to Max who wiped away his tears. White then quietly repeated, "Max, what would you like to say to your mother?"

Max whispered, "Mom, I miss you. Why did you die? I love you."

Dr. White suggested that Max take a break and opened the door to the second room where Marc was sitting. Marc got up glanced at his son and then sat down in the office. White began, "Obviously, Max is grieving a great deal, what about you?"

"I think I am more stunned than grieving and I think I deal with Cathy's death by working."

The next question threw Cohn for a loop, "Did you sit Shiva for Cathy?"

"Yes, but why do you ask?"

"Because these rituals, such as Shiva and the thirty-day period after it, and then the months of additional but less intense mourning are frequently very helpful. I urge my Jewish patients to follow the ritual and I certainly talk to my non-Jewish patients about it. In other words, I think that systematically dealing with a departed loved one's absence is the single best way of moving beyond the death. But we are really here to talk about Max. So, what is your diagnosis?"

"I'm a plastic surgeon, not a shrink."

"Come on Marc, you must have some ideas."

"Well, to begin with, I think he is lonely. His mother was not just a mother, but was pretty much his best friend, perhaps his only friend. I guess he was what's called a momma's boy."

"What do you mean?"

"Simply that he is a kid who was totally dependent on his mother from dawn to dusk. She would wake him up in the morning, cook his breakfast, drive him to school, pick him up and have a snack for him when he came home from school, make his dinner, buy his clothes. Frankly, I'm surprised that he is able to wipe his own ass."

"Marc, you seem angry about this."

"Look, honestly, maybe I'm selfish but I really did not want to have children. So when Cathy became pregnant we agreed that Max was primarily her responsibility. So, now she's gone and Max is lost. Totally! And, now it's all on my shoulders."

"Do you even care about your son?"

"What kind of question is that?"

"A tough and honest one."

"Yes, I care about him. But, I am also ready to have him be less dependent on me and I want him to grow up and be independent. . In my opinion, Max has no ambition and he waits for someone else to do everything for him. If I can be brutally honest, I want to see him standing on his own two feet. I don't want my son to be a loser."

"Dr. Cohn, now please allow me to be brutally honest. Both you and Max have suffered an enormous trauma. As an accomplished adult you are and will certainly deal with your loss in a mature and ultimately successful way. On the other hand, Max is suffering. Unless we intervene he will likely suffer for years, and there is a significant chance that he will never fully recover.

"My clinical approach to dealing with your situation is what is called trauma-focused cognitive behavioral therapy. Essentially, this is short-term treatment, typically two or three months, depending on how you and Max are progressing. In my treatment we examine the thoughts you and Max have about each other as well as Cathy and your situation. The goal is simply to get everything out on the table, examine it, clarify it, and try to get to some sense of reality and understanding. Next, we try to find helpful and nondestructive ways of coping. For example, we don't want Max to be punching another kid just because he feels the other person is giving him attitude. In high school, it might lead to suspension. As an adult, it could lead to prison. Finally, we need to provide assistance for you and Max to find a way to be in a kinder, gentler, more supportive, and loving relationship. Obviously, this is a tall order but perfectly workable if you, and of course Max, are willing."

Marc looked at Dr. White and asked if he could have a few minutes alone to think about the proposed therapy. White nodded his ascent and left the room to go downstairs for coffee. Marc sat alone in the office trying to sort out his feelings about the program that the psychologist had outlined. His initial thoughts were about how much he disliked therapists and what he as a surgeon considered to be their unscientific psychobabble. On the other hand, his instinctive reaction to White was positive. He found him warm and engaging. He liked the fact that he was well qualified and spoke to Max and him in a straightforward and approachable manner. He also reasoned that it was imperative for Max to get back into school and not cause problems. If that did not happen, Marc figured that his own life would become a living hell. When Dr. White returned he asked Marc if he needed any additional clarification.

Marc answered, "No. I think I understand what this is about. I'm ready. When do we begin?"

"Right now, let's get Max in here."

For the next three months, every Friday afternoon Marc and Max drove to Weston for their ninety-minute sessions with Dr. White. Typically, the weekly goal was for Marc and Max to increase the number of interactions they had each day with the objective of rediscovering each other, and to some extent reinventing their relationship. Dr. White's office was the safe place to talk about their feelings and plan for the following week.

By the end of the second month life had changed in the Cohn household. Marc had altered his schedule so that he could drop Max off at school every morning. Max had assumed responsibility for his schedule by getting up on his own each day and putting together his own breakfast and lunch. Marc was home most evenings by 6:30 and he started helping Max with some homework, particularly the science and math. Wednesday night was their "date night" when, after Max's homework was completed, they walked over to Harding Avenue or the Bal Harbour Shops for dinner. Saturday had become their day to play tennis, go fishing or just hangout. Sunday late afternoon had become movie time followed by pizza. Life had started to improve for both of them thanks to White and the weekly assignments.

Seventeen

SURFSIDE, FLORIDA

Three weeks before their planned trip to Alaska, Marc Cohn received a phone call from Rabbi Yitzchak Friedman suggesting that they get together for lunch; they chose a kosher restaurant on the ocean in Surfside, a ten minute walk from Cohn's office.

Marc, somewhat cynical about rabbis, had been expecting to hear from Rabbi Friedman and, as he hurried to the luncheon, he rehearsed his response to an anticipated request for a large donation. He knew that the Cambridge Community Shul (CCS) was in some financial difficulty but he simply was not about to start supporting an Orthodox synagogue, or any synagogue for that matter. He kept telling himself that money for his shul was Friedman's problem, and the fact that Cathy and the rabbi were friends was not his concern. Then he also reminded himself that he had already sent the rabbi $1,000 for doing the funeral. He was actually surprised when, in response to his "payment," he had received a thank you note back from the CCS saying the money had been placed in a charity fund.

While still mulling this over he realized he had reached the restaurant in time to see Rabbi Friedman stepping out of an older model dark blue Ford Crown Victoria. He chuckled to himself as he remembered one of his staff saying that the car was designed for senior citizens, detectives, and rabbis. He knew that the seniors had already switched to the Lexus 350 series, the police were in the Chevys, and now he wondered about the rabbis. Both men saw each other and once again Marc extended his hand to the rabbi only to be enveloped in a bear hug and kiss. Cohn's instant reaction was embarrassment but almost simultaneously he felt the genuine affection the rabbi had for him and he was transported back to the warmth he felt from his brother as they parted several months earlier. At that moment he also realized how comforting the rabbi's nonverbal affection felt and how much he actually craved it in his own life.

Friedman asked how Marc and Max were managing and Marc responded, "Okay; I'm usually very busy January through April and I guess in some ways that's a blessing. It's essentially my season because this is the time when a lot of the snowbirds arrive from the north as well as Latin America and they want their tune-ups, liposuction, Botox, and occasionally a repair job or new look with breast enlargement and other surgery. But, despite being busy, I miss Cathy— particularly when I get home. As I may have told you we were together practically from the day I started medical school. It's tough not having her around, especially for Max."

The rabbi nodded and again asked, "And how is Max doing?"

"Improving. Honestly, Cathy was in charge of Max and I was kind of in the background. Now I am the point guy and to be perfectly frank it's a hard transition for both of us. What I guess you saw at the funeral was a sullen and sad sort of kid. Well, until recently that was Max all the time. But things are definitely improving."

The rabbi interrupted, "How is school for him?"

"He goes to Harbor Country Day School, a private place, small classes with lots of kids with learning problems. I think Max is smart enough, but not strongly motivated to learn. The week after the funeral Max got into trouble and was suspended for a while. This resulted in some good changes and thanks to my sister-in-law we found a fabulous therapist who has helped both of us immensely. So now Max is back on track in school and things are a bit more relaxed at home. In fact, we now spend more time together than we ever did while Cathy was alive."

The rabbi asked, "Does he have friends?"

"I don't think so. I have the feeling that he's a loner."

"Have you guys talked much about Cathy?"

Marc answered, "Yes, but usually in therapy. Not much at home."

"What things do you guys do on weekends?"

"Before Cathy died every few months he and I would take our boat off-shore and fish. He loves fishing and becomes quite animated when we're out there. Now, thanks to our therapist, we play a bit of tennis, and sometimes go fishing. He is very good at both driving the boat and fishing. In fact, he likes every part of fishing even gutting and cleaning the fish."

The rabbi thought for a minute while stroking his beard and then asked about Max's involvement in Jewish youth groups and his interest in Judaism. To this Marc simply answered, "Zilch, nada." The rabbi then invited Max and Marc to join his family for dinner on the upcoming Friday night—an invitation that, to the surprise of both men, was readily accepted.

For the rabbi, Marc's agreeing to come to dinner was extremely gratifying. During the past several years he had extended several dinner and holiday invitations to Cathy who had always turned them down, citing her husband's lack of interest in anything Jewish other than bagels, lox and kasha knishes. *Perhaps*, he thought, *my personal diplomacy is working.*

"I am glad that you are getting help for Max. Cathy often talked to me about him and worried that he was quite isolated. In my line of work I sometimes see the consequences of this isolation such as teenage drinking, drugs, and so forth. Hard to believe, but this even goes on in Orthodox communities. Frankly, after the trauma you and Max experienced I think any of us would need some type of counseling. So *yasher koach* to you for taking care of this. Cathy would be pleased."

He then asked about Norman and his extended family. Friedman was curious as to how close the brothers were. Marc responded that they weren't particularly close, but there was no animosity between them. He then went on to say that in his experience geography played a crucial part in relationships and in light of the fact that both of them lead busy lives, and were thousands of miles apart, it was unrealistic to expect a great deal of closeness.

But Marc did note that the week after Cathy's death was the longest and most intense time that the brothers had spent together since their parents' died and it actually felt good. He went on to tell the rabbi that Max and he were going up to Alaska at the end of May for ten days to attend the his nieces' joint bat mitzvah. The signal that lunch was over came when the waitress brought the check and, looking at his watch, Marc announced that he had a patient scheduled in a few minutes. He then took the bill, paid it, and left a tip of fifteen percent—no more, no less, that was his firm policy.

Eighteen

FORT LAUDERDALE, FLORIDA

For Orthodox Jews, the Sabbath encompasses those twenty-six hours each week between sundown Friday evening and a cushion of time after sundown on Saturday night. During the Sabbath, rest is mandated and work is prohibited. Rest doesn't mean sleeping, but rather a period where one refrains from all manner of creative activities and focuses instead on spiritual and religious endeavors. At the Friedman home the preparation for the Shabbat began several days before Friday evening, when Mrs. Friedman planned her menu, invited her guests, shopped, and cooked. The rabbi's Shabbat preparations also involved helping with the menu and guest planning, as well as the shopping. Indeed, he was a well-known figure at the kosher markets and the local Publix. Additionally, the rabbi spent many hours preparing his remarks for his required presentations and discussions at the synagogue and home during the Sabbath.

On Friday evening, while the rabbi was leading services at the synagogue, Mrs. Friedman was at home marking the beginning of the holy Shabbat period by lighting candles, and reciting the blessings over the Sabbath candles. The rabbi had suggested to Marc that he should arrive at his home by 7:30 that evening, well before sundown, in order to not to begin the Sabbath by violating its prohibitions against driving.

The distance from the Cohn condo in Bal Harbour to the Friedman home in Fort Lauderdale was twenty-one miles and, without traffic, the drive took less than forty minutes. Marc and Max left their home at 6:30, but a not uncommon accident on Interstate 95 tied them up for an additional fifteen minutes. On the drive, Max had asked why they were going to Rabbi Friedman's house.

Marc responded, "I don't know. The rabbi invited us, he was a friend of Mom's, and it seemed like an interesting thing to do tonight."

"Who is he?" Max asked.

"Rabbi Friedman was the man who spoke at Mom's funeral. The tall guy with the red and gray beard. Do you remember him?"

"Not really."

"Well, he is a nice man and I think this should be fun."

Max being totally unfamiliar with any Shabbat observances asked, "What are they having for dinner?"

"I don't know. But if the food is anything like what my grandmother use to make, you will definitely not starve. In fact, you may not have to eat for the next two weeks."`

They arrived at the house a few minutes after Mrs. Friedman had lit her Shabbat candles. Marc immediately apologized for being late, and as he and Max were ushered into their cozy living room with its large windows overlooking the Cambridge Isle Boat Canal, Mrs. Friedman told Marc that an apology wasn't necessary. She explained that it wasn't a problem since the Shabbat did not technically start till sunset, but her tradition was to light candles eighteen minutes before sunset and accept the commencement of the Sabbath early. However, she noted that, "My bringing in the Sabbath early is not binding on anyone but me." This was all strange to Marc and Max but they both exercised discreet behavior and kept quiet.

Mrs. Friedman offered the visitors water and cut vegetables and told them, "My husband and the other guests would be coming to the house after services about 8:30." She then went on to mention that the other guests would include the Wolfsons, a young orthodox couple who had just moved to Fort Lauderdale in July and joined CCS. The woman was an occupational therapist who had grown up in Miami Beach and her husband was from New Haven and an independent computer systems consultant. The second group coming to dinner was the Goldman family. They were friends from Halifax who were visiting Florida for a week.

The last three people at the table would be Dr. and Mrs. Herman Berkovitz, Mrs. Friedman's elderly parents, who had recently moved to Florida full-time after decades of snow birding between Halifax and Hollywood Beach. The final guest was Rabbi Friedman's ninety-one year-old Aunt Ida who, despite her fragility, arthritis, and touch of dementia, would prove to be the most humorous and interesting person at the Shabbat table.

By the time the rabbi returned from synagogue at 8:30, Mrs. Friedman and Dr. Cohn were on a first name basis—Leah and Marc— and the conversation had focused on Canada. Like her husband, Leah was born in Newfoundland but when she was nine her father accepted a teaching post at the Dalhousie School of Medicine in Halifax. Leah explained that she loved Newfoundland, but Halifax proved to be a sig-nificant career opportunity for her father, who eventually became the dean of the school. Subsequent to the Berkovitz move, the remainder of the family left Newfoundland and settled in Halifax. They all eventually became active members of the Beth Israel Synagogue on Oxford Street, one of the oldest Orthodox shuls in Canada. She recalled that compared to St. John's, Newfoundland, Halifax was like living in Jerusalem.

Her story included the fact that the rabbi—who she called 'Yitz' — and she had been neighbors and classmates in St. John's where they both attended the same private school. Leah went on to explain, some-what shocking Marc, that because the public schools were quite a dis-tance from their homes, and not as good as the private schools, many of the Jewish parents sent their children to the Anglican school.

Leah explained, "The Anglican teachers and headmaster were perfectly respectful so we didn't have to sing the hymns and could be excused for our holidays. How many Orthodox rabbis do you think went to an Anglican Church elementary school?"

Marc asked, "How did you and Rabbi Friedman meet if you were living in Halifax and he was in Newfoundland?"

She answered with a huge smile on her face, "So, as I mentioned, we left Newfoundland when I was nine but Yitz's family stayed behind. Like us they were Orthodox, and most of the observant families in the Maritime Provinces sent their kids to Israel, Toronto, or New York for high school. Anyway, of all strange places we met again in New York on the IRT subway—I think they call it the number one train nowadays. We hadn't seen each other for six years. We were both fifteen and his parents had sent him to Yeshiva High School in Brooklyn, and my parents had sent me to a girl's Yeshiva in Manhattan. I was visiting a friend near Brooklyn College and he also was visiting a friend in the area. Anyway, we both were on the subway platform heading toward the city and I saw him standing there. I thought he looked familiar so I started walking toward him slowly. He was seemingly busy reading a Torah commentary and looked up at me and simply said, 'Hi Leah, what are you doing in New York?' Five years later when we were twenty, and both of us still in college—he was at Yeshiva University and I was at Stern College—we married. In August, we will be married thirty-four years and down here in Florida for twenty-six of those years. And our oldest daughter is now engaged to a lovely young man and in the second year of her residency in Toronto and our son is in law school at Cardozo in New York."

"Wow, what a story."

Leah then shifted the conversation and asked about their upcoming trip to Alaska. "Marc, have you ever been there before?"

"Yes, about six or seven years ago, when Max was in camp for a month, Cathy and I took an extended trip to Alaska. First, we went on a one-way cruise from Vancouver to Anchorage through the Inside Passage. Seeing the glaciers close up was very exciting. We spent a few days visiting my brother, his wife, and his wife's family who lived in Anchorage. And then one day we drove down to Seward to go fishing. That's the town where my brother and his family now live. We also went to Denali by train and spent about ten hours on a school bus driving through the park but didn't see much. But, all in all it was quite a nice trip. Have you been there?"

"No, but it is certainly on my bucket list. Yitz wants to go someday, maybe a cruise. I don't know," and then wistfully she said, "Someday. Anyway, I wanted to ask how did your sister-in-law's family wind up in Alaska?"

"The story I heard was that my sister-in-law was born in Anchorage. Her father went to Alaska as an Air Force doctor and decided to stay. Her mother's story is a bit more interesting. Her family was originally from Chicago and her grandfather went to Alaska with some friends to find gold. I think they wound up in Nome with some other Jewish guys and they panned and panned for about three years before finding enough gold to leave Nome and get to Anchorage. Blake also told me that her grandfather and his friends were part of the first Jewish congregation in Nome around 1900. After giving up on the gold, Blake's grandfather worked as a peddler in the towns around Anchorage. I gathered that he was successful enough to buy a movie theatre and basically he made a living owning a small movie theatre and some rental property. I'm not sure but I think her grandmother also came from Chicago but it was some kind of arranged marriage between very distant cousins. So the family stayed in Alaska and Blake's mother was an only child and was raised in Anchorage.

"Her mother then went to college in Fairbanks and during a summer break met her father through some family friends who had gotten to know 'The Jewish doctor at Elmendorf.' And the rest is history. Her parents stayed in Anchorage where her father was a surgeon at the regional hospital and her mother developed a career as a geologist and a very successful consultant to the oil and gas industry. Blake went to college at the University of Washington in Seattle and then decided to be a clinical social worker so she went to Miller in Massachusetts where she met my brother. And a few years later he found a job in Alaska and that was seventeen years ago. Go figure!" They all laughed.

A moment later Rabbi Friedman walked in along with his friends from Canada and the Wolfsons. The rabbi introduced everyone to each other, hugged Marc and Max, and asked the group to sit down while they waited for the last three guests. A few minutes passed and then they heard a car pull up and doors opening. Leah went outside to welcome her parents and Aunt Ida. The three elderly people were introduced and everyone was ushered to the dining room where the table that was set with a white tablecloth, silver trimmed white bone china, gleaming silverware, and crystal stemware.

Rabbi Friedman invited everyone to find a seat and then he took his place at the head of the table, sat down, and began to chant the Friday night blessing over the wine (in Hebrew): *"It was evening and it was morning, the sixth day. So the heavens and the earth were finished, with all their complement. On the seventh day God had completed all His work that He had undertaken and He rested on the seventh day from all His work He which He had been doing. Then God blessed the seventh day and made it holy, because on it He ceased from all His creative work, which God had brought into being to fulfill its purpose."*

He then poured several ounces of the wine into a separate glass, drank from the new glass, and poured the remainder of the wine into the top of a silver two-tiered Kiddush fountain. Max, and even Marc, watched attentively as the wine drained out the spouts of the fountain into the small silver Kiddush cups surrounding the fountain. The cups were then passed around and everyone drank. Rabbi Friedman spoke, "Sometimes new guests at our home wonder why we sit for the entire Kiddush. The answer is simple. There truly is no *halacha* rule about standing or sitting. Everything depends on your family custom. In my family in Newfoundland we always sat; who knows, maybe everyone was exhausted. But we sat, so I sit and our kids sit."

He then invited everyone into the kitchen to ritually wash and recite the blessing after washing before he cut the challah. Once that challah was blessed, cut, and passed, Rabbi Friedman spoke, "Leah and I are very happy to have all of you here tonight. For the first time visitors this is your chance for a short nap while I make a few comments about *Emor*, which is this week's parsha, and that section of the Torah that we read tomorrow morning in the synagogue. Emor literally means 'speak' and begins with the laws relating to the priestly clan of *Kohanim* including laws of purity and even the marriage restrictions that the Kohanim must follow. For example, they are only allowed to marry virgins or widows.

"Another section of Emor gives us the laws about the various holidays. Tomorrow in synagogue I will discuss that section. Tonight, a few comments on the rules about the purity of the Kohen. Why is this important? The simple answer is because God has decreed that the Kohanim shall be holy and as such should be a role model. Another view comes from the distinguished rabbi and psychiatrist Abraham Twerski who commenting on Emor notes that because God has sanctified the Kohanim they should be "respected and revered." However, in my opinion, Rabbi Twerski's most important message is that all of us are very important people because God has sanctified each of us. *Hashem* has given each and every one of us a very special gift, the gift of a *neshama* or soul. I urge us all to use that gift wisely. Shabbat Shalom."

And the dinner began with periodic singing, jokes, and stories many of which came from Aunt Ida. Marc and Max thoroughly enjoyed the food and camaraderie. After dinner they all sang the blessings after the meal although Marc and Max just hummed and read the words of the grace in English. As they were leaving Rabbi Friedman wished them a safe trip to Alaska.

On the Thursday before they were scheduled to leave, Marc received a call in his office from his brother. After a few pleasantries Norman went on, "Marc, I'm calling to see if you can help out a friend of mine,

Matt Atlas, who is the superintendent of the prison here in Seward. The facility has a very good health center and starting on Monday of the week you are visiting, another friend of mine Paul Polansky, who is the prison medical officer, will be on leave. Actually, he is getting married on Sunday and going on a cruise for five days. In fact, you and Max are invited to the wedding.

"Anyway, Matt was originally able to get coverage for Paul but today he learned that the physician scheduled for Tuesday and Wednesday canceled out of the deal and they haven't been able to find a replacement. So, in talking to Matt today I thought of you and floated the idea of you covering for Paul. Also, it should be pretty easy because Tuesday and Wednesday are usually the quietest days of the week in the health center. So, I know you don't need the money, but if you can help out and you're interested, the prison will pay you for your time and arrange a temporary license. They will also cover your hotel for those days. But the real point is that I would really appreciate it and it would be a huge favor for two of my friends."

For reasons that Marc never understood he immediately said, "That's fine, see you in about a week." That single decision was to change his life forever.

Nineteen

En Route to Alaska

E very evening at 6:30 PM, an Alaska Airlines 737-800 weighing close to 140,000 pounds backs away from its gate at Fort Lauderdale International Airport to begin its scheduled six hour and thirty minute flight to Seattle's Sea-Tac International Airport. During the course of the trip the plane flies at speeds in excess of 500 miles per hour as it traverses the second longest nonstop commercial route in the contiguous forty-eight states (the longest by seven miles is the flight between Miami and Seattle). On the Wednesday before the Memorial Day weekend, Marc and Max Cohn occupied two of the sixteen first class seats. Their plan was to fly to Seattle, stay overnight at the Radisson Hotel, just a short walk from the terminal, and take the 10:00 AM flight to Anchorage that would get them there at 1:40 PM. Norman was to meet them for the drive to Seward.

A few minutes after takeoff the aircraft reached 10,000 feet and the flight attendant made an announcement that the use of portable electronic devices was permitted. She then went on to say that for those interested the airline provided a digital entertainment device for a small fee (except it was free for those in first class). Within seconds of the announcement Max had his iPad out and was busily playing the latest version of Angry Birds. His tuning out included his simultaneously listening to some strange named music group that he had downloaded to his iPhone and was now experiencing through his Bose noise-canceling ear buds. For a moment Marc wondered why Bose didn't make a garbage-canceling earphone so that Max and other kids didn't pollute their systems with music that would certainly be history within a few weeks.

After the announcements one flight attendant passed through the first class cabin asking for drink orders while another one handed out the DigEcor in-flight entertainment devices. Marc began exploring the sleek portable audio-visual unit and soon learned that it contained seventy-five movies, ten hours of music, and games galore. He passed one to Max who looked at it and placed it in his seatback pocket.

After perusing the available movies, Marc put the DigEcor down, thought for a minute, and then tapped Max on the arm. "Max, we need to talk."

Max looked at him with a blank stare and a bit of annoyance for having had his game interrupted.

"About what?"

Mark responded simply that he wanted to talk with Max and a long flight was a perfect time. With that Max put down the iPad and pulled the buds from his ears.

"Okay, Dad, what do you want to talk about?"

"A few things, mostly about you and me."

"Like what?"

"What do you miss about Mom?"

"Just her. Her smile, her laugh, her cooking. Her hugs."

"You mean you don't like my cooking?"

"Come on, Dad, you don't cook; you order in and place stuff on dishes."

"You know, Max, Mom and I were a team. I was Mr. Outside and she was Mrs. Inside. My job was to make money and her job was taking care of the family, in particular you. Now that she isn't here anymore I have both jobs. And, to tell you the truth, I am very good at making the money but I'm not sure about being an inside guy."

"Dad in my civics class we studied some major cities and their governments. One city we talked about was New York. Back in the late seventies and eighties there was a very colorful mayor named Ed Koch who is now dead. Anyway, one of Koch's favorite sayings was 'How am I doing?' So, is that your question?"

"I guess so."

"My honest answer is fair. Dad, since Mom died we've gone fishing four times, played tennis three times, you haven't come to any of my hockey games, we've eaten out countless times, and five times we've gone to the movies. And, honestly, it often felt like you're simply completely one of Dr. White's assignments! I can't count the number of pizzas we've had delivered and the Chinese meals are probably in the hundreds."

This statement shocked Marc. Max had been keeping score and clearly Marc was way behind. He sat silently and then said, simply, "I'm sorry. I do love you, Max."

Max looked at his father and answered quietly, "Whatever." He then stuck his headphones back into his ears, picked-up his iPad, and went back to his game.

Marc reclined his seat and closed his eyes. Twenty minutes later he awoke with a startle when Max tapped him on the shoulder and pointed at the flight attendant who wanted to know if he was ready for dinner. The tap also ended Cohn's dream. Once again he had been walking in a snowy field but this time he was picking blueberries along with a woman and a toddler. He didn't know who they were but he felt relaxed and happy. Then the child reached up to him and the next thing that happened was the tap. Marc sat there quietly pondering the dream and wondering what it meant. While he often skied, he had never just gone for a walk in the snow to pick berries, and since neither Cathy or Max had come with him on his annual "guys only" ski trips, the dream made no sense. But it certainly did feel good. A few minutes later he recalled a vaguely similar dream he had had on the day of Cathy's funeral.

Dinner on the flight was a choice of steak, chicken, or salmon. Anticipating many days of salmon in the future, both Max and Marc opted for the steak. The food was in the acceptable category and after dessert Marc asked, "Max, about our earlier conversation, there is one more question I want to ask. Are you still mad at me about what happened to Mom?"

Max stared at his father and with tears starting to form in his eyes he looked down and said, "Yes."

"Why?"

"Look Dad, it's simple and I've said it before. You're a doctor and you should have seen it coming and you should have saved her. That's why!"

Marc felt he needed to clear the air and said, "Max, I've asked myself a thousand times if there was something I could have done or should have done to save Mom. Believe me, if I could have, I would have. But, I hope you are old enough to understand that most of the time a headache is a headache. Most people take a couple of Tylenols or Advils and it's over. I loved your mother and would do anything to have her here with us. Yes, I am a doctor, but I am not a miracle worker. I'm sorry, very sorry."

Max, head down, just said, "OK.".

The flight arrived on time. The Cohns and the other 139 passengers on the flight went through the usual hoops at Sea-Tac: long walks, escalators up and down different levels, and finally the baggage carousel where the luggage was ready for pick up. Another escalator up, over a land bridge to the garage, a down elevator, and then a wait for the shuttle bus to the Radisson. The room was ready and Marc and Max barely got undressed before they fell into bed. A wake up call at 7:15 AM jarred them from a deep sleep. They showered and dressed and went to the lobby for a buffet breakfast. By 8:30 AM they were again on the shuttle bus heading back to the airport for what they assumed was their last flight of the trip.

The plane landed at the Ted Stevens Anchorage International Airport ten minutes ahead of schedule. Max had spent at least half of the trip looking out the window and telling his father about the sites—primarily ice covered peaks so high it almost seemed as if the plane might scrape the mountaintops.

Twenty

ANCHORAGE, ALASKA

Being in the first class cabin had the advantage of an early exit from the plane but it did nothing to mitigate the long walk to the baggage claim area. As they approached the carousel they saw Norman standing there next to a police officer. Norman hurried over to his brother and nephew and embraced each of them in a bear hug. He then brought Marc and Max over to his friend, an Alaskan State Trooper named Jim Maclean. Within minutes the luggage arrived and the four of them walked out into cool but clear air. There was a patrol car at the curb and Norman motioned for them to get in. Max and Marc laughed and Marc asked, "What's this about? Am I being arrested?"

Norman chuckled, " No. Jim is a friend of mine who just went off duty and is stationed here. I ran into him when I arrived by cab from the other Anchorage airport. So, if you guys don't mind, we'll hitch a ride with Jim back through a bit of town. Be patient I have a surprise for you."

The fifteen minute ride took them from the international airport to the much smaller Merrill Field, the original airfield in Anchorage, and a mile east of the city's downtown. Along the way Norman pointed out some of the sights such as the Aviation Museum, the various hotels, the five-level 5th Avenue Mall, the Alaska Museum, and the Chugach Mountains hugging the eastern end of the city. Just as they were approaching their destination, Max looked out the window and ahead on the left he saw something, "Dad, look over there, it's just like home—a Bed, Bath and Beyond, a Michael's, and an Old Navy." They all turned to look and laugh.

Jim said, "Yup, Anchorage is becoming Anywhere, USA, but you won't have that problem in Seward."

The car pulled up next to a blue and white single-engine plane whose cockpit was empty. Jim helped Marc and Max out of the police car and said, "That's it gents. Have a good flight, and say hello to Chani for me."

Norman then said, "Here is the surprise: We are flying back to Seward in this plane."

Marc responded nervously, "Is this safe? You know I'm not really into small planes."

Norman smiled and answered, "Listen Marc, this is Alaska! You're probably safer flying to Seward than driving there on the mostly two-lane highway."

The three Cohns then loaded the luggage into the open hatch, after which Marc looked at Norman, and said, "I didn't know you had a plane."

"I don't, it isn't mine. It's my friend Chani's. It's such a nice day I thought it would be more fun for you guys to fly back to Seward than drive. Anyway, it's either a short flight or a three hour drive. As soon as Chani gets back from filing her flight plan we're off. You guys OK with that?"

In unison they answered, "Sure."

Five minutes later Chani Kahn walked over to the plane. Marc couldn't help staring at her face. He had over the years become a connoisseur of beauty. In fact, his business was making women beautiful. He thought to himself this woman was a natural. No plastic surgeon could possibly improve on what she possessed. She reached out to Marc, shook his hand, and welcomed him to Alaska. Then she did the same with Max. "Let's go," she said, as they climbed into the plane, fastened their seat belts, and put on earphones so they could communicate over the noise.

As the engine warmed up Chani focused on reviewing her checklist and the various cockpit gauges. Clearance was granted and they headed down the runway, gaining speed, and finally a few seconds later they were airborne.

The young woman pilot came on the intercom, "We are obviously airborne. You know what they say about flying, hours of boredom and seconds of sheer terror on takeoff and landing. So just relax for thirty-five minutes and we'll be home." As they flew down the Kenai Peninsula both Norman and Chani pointed out the sites, including the city of Anchorage and a few large cruise ships making their way up and down the coast. She also told them they were taking a slightly indirect route to Seward so that Norman could show them the Aleyeska Ski resort from the air as well as Portage Glacier and the Chugach National Forest.

When they were five minutes outside of Seward Chani came back on the intercom, "We will be landing shortly so check your seat belts and hang on. We're almost home." A chill ran through Marc's body, *Home*, he thought to himself, *never in a thousand years.*

The plane then began a slow descent to the runway. The landing was smooth, two or three bumps followed by taxiing to the operations office. Once the engine was off Norman opened the door, lowered the stairs, jumped out, and helped Marc and Max disembark and remove the luggage. They all thanked Chani for the ride and she waved back. Norman pulled out his phone and asked Blake to pick them up at the airport.

"Was that fun guys?" Norman asked.

Max answered for both, "Uncle Norm that was awesome."

Then it was Marc's turn to ask a question, "Who was that pilot?"

Norman answered, "Oh, Chani, you'll be seeing a lot of her over the next few days. She's our rabbi."

Blake arrived in ten minutes and, after a round of hugs, she drove them downtown to The Bayview Hotel where they were booked into an executive room with two queen beds and views of Resurrection Bay and Seward. Blake and Norman thought the hotel's downtown location and the short ride to their home made the most sense for Marc and Max's visit.

After the Cohns of Bal Harbour checked in, Blake and Norman drove them over to the Hertz office on Port Avenue to pick up a rental car that they could drop off the following week at the Anchorage airport. Marc showed his license and credit card, declined the various insurances, and was given the keys to a year old black Ford Fusion. As he and his son walked toward the car Max started laughing as if he had just heard the greatest joke in the world.

"What's so funny Max?"

Max struggled to gain composure and said, "Dad, it looks just like your Bentley! Enjoy." Even Marc laughed. In the parking lot it was decided that Norman and Max would go together to the house and Blake would drive with Marc and ensure that he had directions to get around town.

Seven minutes later they were at Norman and Blake's two-story timber frame home on Exeter Road with its views of Resurrection Bay and the mountains from the decks encircling the house. Greeting them as they got out of the car were Rachel and Rebecca, and Cookie and Cracker, their two gray Alaskan Malamutes. Both dogs, tails wagging, ran up to Marc and Norman, nosed around them, and accepted friendly pats. Max dropped to his knees and, remembering the lessons his mother had taught him about dogs, offered the back part of his hand to the dogs' noses. They both smelled Max's hand and then licked it. Next Max started stroking the dogs' necks—first Cookie, then Cracker. Before two minutes had past Max was completely involved with the dogs. Blake announced that they were barbequing fresh caught salmon for dinner and that Max and Marc should make themselves at home. Even though it was May, Norman brought some wood inside and carefully built a fire in the home's central fireplace.

The girls asked Max if he wanted to see their rooms and grabbed his hand to show them where they lived. The house was cozy with soft leather couches and chairs, Indian style throw blankets on the furniture, an oak dining room table and chairs, a grandfather clock ticking away in the hallway, and an ultramodern granite and stainless steel kitchen. What struck Marc though was the natural scenery visible through the home's large picture windows. Just to sit there was relaxing.

Norman told Marc how happy he was that the two of them had come up for the *B'not Mitzvah*. He then went on to share with Marc the plans for the next few days, "If it's all right with you, tomorrow morning I'd like to take you over to the prison, show you around, and we'll fill out the paperwork, get you an ID, and take care of the administrative stuff. In the afternoon I'm leaving work at two and will be happy to show you and Max the town. Also, when you are at the prison tomorrow, Max can come over to our house. Blake will be home and the girls will be back at noon from their volunteer work at a local kennel."

Norman then reviewed the weekend schedule for Marc, "On Friday evening we have services starting at 7:15 and the girls will be leading them. We have to do some setting up before the service and the synagogue is a bit hard to find so I'll plan to pick you up at 6:30 and then after services we'll have a community supper there. On Saturday morning, services start at 10:00 and that's the girls' actual bat mitzvah. So, I think we'll pick you up at 9:30 unless you decide to go to Torah study and then you're on your own. We have a catered lunch after the services and that should be fun. Then on Sunday, at noon, we are all invited to a wedding. As I mentioned on the phone, the groom is a local doctor, Paul Polansky, and he is marrying Akna Smith, a pediatric nurse practitioner who is also an Inuit Eskimo—and the first modern era Jewish convert in Seward. It should be fun and interesting, particularly since this is the first marriage for both of them; she's in her late thirties and Paul just turned sixty. By the way, the name Akna means goddess of fertility, so we shall see. I hope you guys will enjoy yourself up here with the frozen chosen. We're all a thrilled that you made the trip to share in our *simcha*."

Twenty-One

Seward, Alaska

Friday, 6:30 PM

Right on time, Norman pulled up in front of the Seward Hotel. Marc and Max got in the car. Max wanted to know where Rachel, Rebecca, and Aunt Blake where.

Norman answered, "They are already at shul getting ready for the service."

The trip from the hotel to the synagogue took less than five minutes. Marc and Max were not expecting a Cape Cod style house with a large and quite architecturally dramatic addition. Norman explained that the synagogue was actually attached to the rabbi's house. After parking the car in a field adjacent to a windowed building, they came in through French doors and were startled by the beauty of the "shul." It had floor-to-ceiling library shelves flanking a magnificent stone fireplace. As they walked in Blake and the girls were standing at the lectern practicing the evening service. Marc was pleasantly surprised when Max, without any prodding, went over to Blake and asked if there was anything he could do to help. She directed him to the cabinet with the prayer books and asked him to place one on each chair along with a Xeroxed sheet of the weekend's schedule.

Marc was intrigued by the room and slowly walked around it looking at the trusses, beams, and fireplace. As he was standing at the library shelf perusing the books, he felt a presence —he turned and was almost breathless. Chani, the pilot, was walking toward him in a pleated black skirt that ended just below her knees, a white silk blouse, and a long pearl necklace with matching pearl earrings. Marc thought to himself, *oh my, this woman is really beautiful.* She greeted him warmly with a handshake and a slight kiss to the cheek. Then she said, "Marc we really didn't have a moment to talk on the plane but I just wanted to express my condolences about the loss of your wife. Norm and Blake told me about her and she sounds like an amazing woman. I hope you and Max are doing well."

Suddenly Marc was tongue-tied and stammered out a reply, "Yes, thanks, OK, we're fine. Oh, and thanks again for the flight, it was great." She then excused herself in order to prepare for the service.

At that point a gray-haired man and woman walked over and greeted him, "Marc, we were so sorry to learn of Cathy's passing. We so much enjoyed meeting her when you came up to see Blake and Norm." Cohn recalled that they were Mort and Eve Richards, Blake's parents.

He replied, "Thanks. It's good to see you. Are you still living in Anchorage and practicing?"

Mort Richards answered, "Nope. I retired three years ago and sold the practice to my partners. We still live in Anchorage part of the year, but frankly we decided to head south because the winters were starting to get to us. I got tired of waiting till ten in the morning for sunrise and then by four in the afternoon it was dark. Also, the snow and ice were frightening me. The last thing either my wife or I need is a broken hip. So now we're up here from the beginning of May till after Rosh Hashanah or the end of September—whichever comes first. The rest of the year we have a condo near Lake Union in Seattle."

Marc then said, "May I ask why Seattle? Why not Arizona or Florida?"

Eve replied, "It's simple. Seattle is three hours away by plane and so one or twice a winter we get to see the kids. Also, lots of friends from Alaska come down to Seattle periodically so we get to see them in the winter. Finally, they have great physicians and hospitals in Seattle and for the past few years I've been followed by an oncologist at the Fred Hutchinson Cancer Research Center."

At seven o'clock Rabbi Chani Kahn walked through a door that connected the house to the synagogue. She was wrapped in an elegant pink and white tallit. She walked to the front of the *bima* and with a huge smile called out, "Shabbat Shalom everyone." There was a loud response of "Shabbat Shalom" along with laughter.

"Welcome. It's a delight to share with so many of you this wonderful Shabbat as well as the entire weekend. We look forward to meeting our guests from the cruise ship as well as all the visitors to our community. I want to extend a special greeting to both Esther Polansky, Paul's mom who flew here from Milwaukee, and Alasie Smith who flew down from Kotzebue, north of the Arctic Circle, to participate in the marriage of their children on Sunday. Finally, welcome to Uncle Marc and cousin Max who flew up from the 'promised land' of Miami Beach for Rachel and Rebecca's simcha. I should also note that they were brave enough to fly with me from Anchorage to Seward in my sturdy old plane.

" I shall begin as I usually do with announcements so that when the service is over I don't have to cause you increased *spilkus,* our Yiddish term for 'ants in your pants.' After services a beautiful Shabbat dinner is awaiting us thanks to the generosity of the Rachel and Rebecca's grandparents who are also our founding members Dr. Mort Richards and Eve Richards. Thanks!

"So, here is what is happening this glorious weekend. Tonight we will have our usual Kabbalat Shabbat service welcoming the Sabbath and Rachel and Rebecca will lead most of it. As I noted a minute ago, following services we will share a Shabbat meal together. And we have plenty of food so everyone is invited, including our all our visitors.

"Tomorrow morning Torah study is at 8:45 and services start at 10:00 AM. Our B'not Mitzvah, Rebecca and Rachel Cohn will lead the services, and after services Blake and Norman are inviting all of you to remain here for a Shabbat luncheon. Finally, on Sunday, at high noon exactly where I am standing, there will be a *chuppah* erected and I will have the great honor of officiating at the first ever wedding at B'nai Cheverim. In fact friends, this is an entire weekend of firsts. Tomorrow will be our very first b'not mitzvah with two of the most outstanding young women I have ever had the privilege of knowing.

"Announcements are over so let's welcome Shabbat by lighting the Sabbath candles together. On the table near the window there are candles and matches and I invite all the women and their daughters, as well as single men, to fulfill the mitzvah of lighting the candles. I urge you to remember that we do this in honor of God who, in creating the world, said on that very first day 'Let there be light.' I also suggest that the lighting of the candles reminds us of our obligation as Jews to be a light unto all the nations as well as our more immediate obligation to be a bright shining light unto our family and our community.

"For those of you who have never done this before, we will begin by using our hands to gather the light of the candles to ourselves, say the prayer in unison, and then have a moment for some private personal prayers. So friends, let's light up and bring Shabbat into our synagogue, our homes, and most importantly into our hearts!"

After the women, a few young girls, and a handful of single men lit the candles and had their time for private prayer, Rabbi Chani took her acoustic guitar from its stand, checked the tuning, and strummed. "Join me as we welcome the Sabbath with the song *Shalom Alechem*. If you know the words please sing, if not, just hum along." A few words into her singing many of the congregation joined in and by the time the final stanzas of the song were being sung the room was filled will happy voices welcoming the Sabbath.

Although the song was totally foreign to Marc, there was something about it that hit a chord deep in his soul, and in that place a tiny spark was ignited. Everyone moved to his or her seats. Blake waived Marc and her parents to front row seats next to her, Norman, and all three kids. After the song Rabbi Chani continued, "Shabbat Shalom, again. Our community here in Seward is named *Beit Cheverim* meaning House of Friends, so Shabbat Shalom Cheverim. And now it is my great honor to invite Rebecca and Rachel Cohn to the bima to lead our service."

With a poise that belied their thirteen years, the girls acted as a tag-team for the next forty-five minutes. They sang, read, and periodically explained the prayers. They told people what page to turn to, asked the congregation to stand and sit at the correct times, and finally they gave a short sermon on the significance of Shabbat in their young lives. The girls ended by thanking everyone for coming and particularly their grandparents for the dinner, their parents for their love, and Rabbi Kahn for teaching them and being their friend.

Rabbi Chani Kahn again stepped in front of the *bima* as the girls and Blake began passing out the wine and grape juice to everyone. The rabbi then asked the congregation to join her in the blessing over the wine. She next called Blake and Norman and Dr. and Mrs. Richards up to the bima. Rachel and Rebecca removed a cover from a table to reveal two homemade challahs that Chani had baked that afternoon. Rabbi Kahn had the girls place their hands on the challah while their parents and grandparents placed their hands on the girls' shoulders. She then said, "How beautiful, *l'dor v'dor*, from generation to generation. Everybody please join us in the blessing over the challah."

The challah was cut up, placed on several trays, and passed throughout the synagogue while the rabbi reminded everyone of Saturday's schedule. "Chevarim, please remember that tomorrow we will begin as usual at 8:45 with an hour of Torah study. Then we'll take a break at 9:45 to rearrange the room for the service beginning at 10:00. Tomorrow morning Rachel and Rebecca will once again lead our services. I look forward to sharing dinner with you tonight and seeing you tomorrow for study, services, and this wonderful Cohn family *simcha*. Good Shabbos everyone. Please enjoy the dinner."

The only table that was reserved had settings for eight people: the Norman Cohn family, the Richards Family, and Marc and Max Cohn. Everyone seemed to be starving so in short order the buffet line was quickly crowded. Chani used the time to walk around and greet the members of B'nai Cheverim, the guests from the cruise who were obviously delighted to enjoy a meal away from the ship, and a number of the Cohn family friends from the public defender's office, the prison, and the community. When everyone appeared settled Chani went up to buffet table and made a plate of some salads, a vegetarian curry, and a small piece of apple pie. As she glanced around looking for a seat, Blake waved to Chani and asked her to sit at their table. They brought a chair over, everybody squished a little closer, and Chani found herself seated between Blake and Marc.

Although Marc, who had not been inside a synagogue in decades, and was thus unfamiliar with the flow of the service as well as the Hebrew and English prayers, felt a need to make some conversation, "That was a lovely service."

"Thanks."

"How often do you have services?"

"About two to three times per month. Sometimes I'm out of town at one of the other communities I serve and I can't get back. I try to, but there are times when the weather doesn't cooperate."

"Where else do you go?"

"Four other towns on the peninsula: Homer, Kenai, Soldotna, and Stirling."

"You mean there are Jews in all those places"?

"Definitely, but not too many. But they really appreciate my working with them. In the better weather and for Rosh Hashanah and Yom Kippur many of our members from outside Seward will come here and the local families always provide home hospitality. Lots of friendships have grown out of our shul."

"Are most of your members transplants from what you call the lower forty-eight? Do you know what kind of work do they do?"

"My guess is that the vast majority of them came up to Alaska from the lower forty-eight. Workwise they do everything. Some have small businesses, a handful are in the tourist trades including guiding, and a few are fisherman. I know a couple of craftsmen like plumbers, carpenters, and electricians; there are some social workers and mental health workers; one dentist here in Seward; and a few government workers. There is one guy who breeds sled dogs here in Seward—Mike Pearl—who lives down the road. Mike is an interesting guy. He and his wife retired here to breed, raise, and sell sled dogs; run sled dog tours for tourists; and Mike has actually run the Iditarod twice. He's a retired Navy commander who served in Vietnam. He once told me he joined the Navy at age seventeen, became a hospital corpsman, and eventually got a commission. Somewhere along the line he managed to get a college degree and a master's degree. By the time he retired he was the administrator of a naval hospital. A real character!

"Also there is a woman who sometimes comes here but she hasn't joined yet. She's a pilot for Era Airlines and is based in Kenai. She flies prop planes—usually the Beechcrafts and the Dash-8s. I love to talk aviation stuff with her.

"What about you? Are you a member of any synagogue or temple or go anywhere?"

"No. We aren't members anywhere and I think this is the first time I've been in a synagogue in years."

Chani was a bit surprised by the response, but then Marc continued, "To change the subject, rabbi, where did you grow up?"

She laughed and said, "First of all I'm almost certain that I have yet to grow up. But, I was born not far from you. Actually, as strange as it may seem, the rabbi you see in front of you was born at Holy Cross Hospital in Fort Lauderdale and lived in a community off Las Olas Boulevard until college."

"You're kidding. I've lived in Bal Harbour for almost fifteen years."

"Marc, to be honest, I know who you are. I've seen your TV commercials at least a hundred times."

Marc Cohn's face reddened with embarrassment and then he almost choked out, "I'm sorry."

"Marc, no need to apologize. You made a choice to use your medical training to do what you wanted. It's a free country."

"I'm still embarrassed. But, let's get back to you. How did you wind up in Alaska?"

"I'll give you the short version. The long one takes days! After college I went to graduate school for an MSW and that's where I became friends with Blake and your brother. I didn't find social work to really be my cup of tea so I decided to become a rabbi and since Blake and Norman were probably my closest friends and they had already moved to Anchorage, I arranged a summer field experience placement in a synagogue in Anchorage. The weather that summer was great and Blake's folks kept a boat in Seward so I would often drive down there on Sundays and go fishing with them. I loved it. Anyway, by the time I was ordained and looking for a job, Blake and Norman and the girls had moved to Seward and they and some friends had a small *chavurah*, a kind of Jewish friendship group, and they wanted a real rabbi and they wanted to start a synagogue. So they approached me, and here I am."

Marc thanked Chani for sharing, but he had a sense that the story he had heard was not yet complete. The dinner went on for another hour or so with occasional breaks for energetic singing of Sabbath songs that most people knew. Virtually everyone came by their table to wish the family mazel tov and introduce themselves to Marc and Max. Marc was quite surprised to learn how many people both knew he was a doctor and also had some connection to South Florida ranging from grandparents to other friends and relatives.

The signal that the evening was over occurred when Rabbi Chani stood and simply said, "Let's *bench*," which meant 'let's say the grace after the meal.' The benching was a short version that only took a few minutes and then everyone helped clean up and straighten the room for the next morning.

As Marc was leaving Chani said, "I hope you and Max can make it tomorrow morning to our Torah study at 8:45. It's informal and interesting and you might enjoy it."

He answered, "Thanks for the invitation but I'm not sure we can make it."

He and Max walked out the door with Norman and his family and were driven back to the hotel. It was 10:00 PM and still light outside.

Twenty-Two

Saturday

The twins' bat mitzvah was three weeks before June 21st—the summer equinox and longest day of the year—when Alaska experiences more than eighteen hours of daylight. Marc and Max learned this firsthand when the sunlight streamed through their not entirely closed drapes just past 5:00 AM. Max seemed to be able to sleep through it but Marc, still dealing with jetlag, simply had to get out of bed. He didn't want to disturb Max so he got dressed and went outside for some exercise.

At the front desk he asked a slightly disheveled and exhausted looking clerk what the best route was for a jog. The man suggested a course that took him along a path in the waterfront park, past the boat harbor, out to the cruise terminal, and then a doubling back to the hotel. It was almost 6:00 AM when Marc began his workout. The sky was blue and cloudless with a temperature close to fifty degrees. Marc stood and stretched for a few minutes and took some deep breaths while admiring the views of the bay and mountains. He thought to himself, *this is certainly a wow place.*

A few minutes into his jog along the bayfront he noticed another runner coming toward him at a very fast pace. The person was wearing a purple hat and purple sweatshirt and warm-up pants. As the runner got

135

closer he saw that it was a woman and the outfit had Amherst written on it. Moments later she ran past him, waved, and called out, "Hi Marc." It took him another second to react and realize it was Rabbi Chani.

After finishing his run, cleaning up, and having breakfast with Max, they decided to go, for the first time in their lives, to a Torah study session. They were recognized and warmly greeted by many of the two-dozen attendees. At a table in the corner of the room there was a coffee urn, cups, sugar, sweetener, milk, and a plate of bagels and muffins plus cream cheese and butter. He laughingly thought to himself, *Bagels in Alaska, what has this world come to?*

Chani began, "Shabbat Shalom everyone and it's a delight to resume our Torah study after a two-week break. Today we start the fourth book of the Torah, Bamidbar—Numbers. Let me spend a few minutes introducing the parsha and then we'll have our discussion. This is the first of our readings in Numbers and appropriately enough it begins in the wilderness. The Israelites have escaped from Egypt and are now in the second year of what will be a forty-year trek. God tells Moses to take a census of all the men over the age of twenty and make sure that each tribe has a representative when the counting is being done. Then we go into a series of naming sections of the tribes and their sons. We also learn that the Levites won't be counted because they have special responsibilities in the new tabernacle. Next we read about the encampment where each tribe has a designated place in the formation. Following this section we have chapter three that begins with these somewhat mystical words— and keep them in mind because they are subject of today's D'var Torah. *'These are the offspring of Aaron and Moses on the day God spoke with Moses at Mount Sinai. These are the names of Aaron, the firstborn was Nadab, and Abihu, Elazar and Itamar.'* So, let's begin our discussion with the question: Why are only men counted in the census?"

Hands went up all over the place and the conversation was lively, kindly, and at times quite humorous. After fifteen minutes Rabbi Chani asked that they shift into a discussion of why the emphasis on numbers. Again there was an animated conversation including several people who doubted the reliability of the numbers and thought the Torah's enumeration of "six hundred and three thousand, five hundred and fifty" was merely a way of saying "a whole lot of people."

At 9:40, Rabbi Chani checked her watch and said, "A few final comments. The first is really restating Alison's observations. In this parsha we see one of several times when the Torah does counting and it's a way for the Torah to remind us that each of us is special, we are all different, and indeed from different tribes, but we all count. And, most importantly, together we find our strength as the people of Israel. If you ever are in doubt about that may I suggest you go to Israel and visit an Army base. There you'll see IDF soldiers from dozens of different countries, heritages, and skin colors. But in their souls they are all Israelis and Jews. And, they are all willing to lay down their lives for Israel and the Jewish people!

"My second observation has to do with names. Until a few hundred years ago Jews, and other people from Eastern and Southern Europe, did not have last names. Instead, their names were a function of paternal relationships such as Moshe ben Mendel, meaning Moshe son of Mendel. In fact many of our present surnames are like that—Mendelsohn, Jacobson, and so forth. Incidentally, I have yet to see in America Bessiesdaughter or Bessiesson as a surname, but maybe someday. Actually in Iceland and the Icelandic language they do have a way of saying someone's daughter with a mother or father. So, if I married an Icelandic man and had a daughter, her last name might be Hannahsdottir." This brought a roar of laughter from the group.

"My third and final observation is that, in my opinion, there is power in our Hebrew names, particularly for those of us who use our mother and father's name. For me it is always more moving to say my name is Channa bat Shimon and Leah, than Chani Kahn. Think about it. Thank you for learning with me and now let's get the room ready for the service."

Marc couldn't believe how quickly the time went and how much he enjoyed the learning. He walked over to Chani, extended his hand, and told her it was great to be in her class. Max had already gone over to Blake and Norman and was helping rearrange the room.

She then looked at him and said, "Thanks. Also, has Norman told you that you have the first *aliyah* and so when I call you to the Torah I know only the last part of your name. What is your Hebrew first name?"

Marc said he didn't know but it might be Moshe, the name of his grandfather who had died before he was born. Chani said that was a proud name worth remembering, so she would call him up with that name; Moshe ben Hershel, ha'Kohen. She also told him that there was a transliteration of the blessings over the Torah if reading the Hebrew was a problem. Marc nodded and then joined the other congregants setting up chairs and moving the food into a small kitchen.

By 10:00 AM, the large room was transformed and over seventy-five people had arrived and were ready for the service. Most people were casually dressed and seemed to know one another. The cruise ship, with its dozen visitors to the synagogue, had departed early in the morning, but those folks were replaced by several families who had driven over from Homer, Stirling and one family that had flown in from Kenai.

The rabbi walked around greeting everyone with a sincerity that Marc marveled at. His limited experience at Miami Beach social gatherings was that most greetings were air-kisses and too often superficial. Here he was finding a friendliness that he had rarely seen or experienced before in his life. He wondered whether it was the community or Chani. Marc did not realize that many of his observations and feelings emanated from his own sense of isolation.

The service began with the rabbi saying, "Shabbat Shalom Chevarim, and welcome back. This morning we have a number of firsts. To begin this is the first time that twins will be bat mitzvahed in our community. This is also the first time that we will be using our historic Torah. For those who were not at our dedication ceremony last month, let me briefly tell you that the Torah we are using today is on loan from the Memorial Scrolls Trust of London, England. This Torah is more than 300 years old and was used by a small synagogue in the central part of the Czech

Republic that was closed by the Nazis in 1941. Czech Jews from Prague undertook the task of saving Torahs from many synagogues throughout what was then Czechoslovakia and keeping them safe in what is now the Jewish Museum in Prague.

"In the year 1964 an art dealer from London was offered the opportunity to purchase 1,564 of these Torah scrolls. Through his efforts and those of an Oregon-born reform rabbi who had connections in London, plus the rabbi's administrator, and the generosity of one of the rabbi's board members who was a prominent attorney and philanthropist, all of these Torahs made it to London for subsequent restoration. Now the Torahs are managed by the Foundation and loaned to synagogues around the world. We, here on the last frontier of the United States, are fortunate to have one of the rescued Torahs thanks to the generosity of the Richard's family and the Moskowitz family of Kenai who flew in yesterday for the B'not Mitzvah. I also want to thank Rabbi Malka Kahn and Daniel Kahn for their generous gift of the new beautiful velvet and silk Torah cover that was given in memory of Rabbi Nathaniel Kahn.

"And now, the moment has arrived when Rebecca and Rachel will proudly breathe new life into this historic Torah, and this Torah will breathe new life into our congregation as we read from it as part of a regular service for the first time in more than half a century. So, let's get started. Rachel, Rebecca, lead on."

The girls ascended the bima and in clear strong voices began, "Shabbat shalom. Please turn to page 112 and join us...." And, with confidence and smoothness, the girls lead the congregation through the first part of the service up to the taking out of the Torah.

At that point Chani stood up and said, "I now invite Mort and Eve Richards as well as Blake and Norman to join us on the bima. In a moment Mort and Eve will open the Ark, I will remove the Torah and hand it to Mort, as the twins lead us in prayer. Next I will ask Mort to pass the Torah to Eve who will pass it to Blake, who will pass it to Norman, and finally Norman will pass the Torah to Rebecca, the oldest twin by two-minutes and nine-seconds, who will take it from her father and give it to Rachel. So, we shall be handing the Torah from generation to generation, and in a real sense entrusting its teachings, laws, and future to the two young women standing up here this morning.

"After a few more prayers Rachel and Rebecca will march the Torah through our synagogue and bring it back to the bima where they will read from the Torah and later read the teachings of the prophets. One additional thought. Centuries ago, before we had printed books that contained the words of Torah, our *Chumash*, it was essential that people read the Torah aloud in the synagogue and the Jewish community learned the Torah lessons by hearing the holy words on a regular basis. In a symbolic sense that is what our young women are doing this morning; as they read they are teaching, and as teachers they join the ranks of adults in the eyes of the community. So let's proceed with our service."

The Torah was passed and then there was the Torah procession. After the Torah was placed on the table near the ark Rabbi Kahn began the *aliyot,* the process of calling up people for the honor of chanting the blessing over the Torah before a section of Torah is read. Although the congregation was not affiliated with any of the Jewish movements, when it came to reading the Torah, Chani had decided to maintain the Orthodox tradition that she had grown up in of seven aliyot followed by a final aliyah for the person who would chant the haftorah. Marc Cohn was called up for the first blessing. He hesitatingly read the cumbersome transliteration but, in that forgiving community, no one cared. The girls' chanting of the Torah portion was flawless and done with obvious joy.

The second aliyah was for Mort and Eve who came up and handled the blessings with aplomb. Next the Moskowitz family was honored in gratitude for their contribution toward the sacred Torah that they had helped fund. Rabbi Chani next called the following day's bride and groom for their *auf ruf*—Paul Polansky and Akna Smith. As soon as they finished the blessings, the congregation jumped up and started singing to the couple "Siman Tov U'Mazel Tov," a spirited Hebrew song of rejoicing for the couple. The singing was accompanied with clapping and dancing in a circle around Paul and Akna.

The fifth aliyah was given to Norman and Blake. The sixth aliyah was given to Jody Pearl, the girls' closest friend who had been bat-mitzvahed a year earlier. At the twins' insistence the seventh aliyah was given to Rabbi Chani. Finally, the *maftir*, and last aliyah was reserved for Rachel and Rebecca who first chanted the blessing and then read from the Torah. Commander Mike Pearl was called up for the honor of lifting the Torah for all to see and offer a collective prayer. Mike then sat down while his wife Minnie wrapped the Torah and cinched it closed with a silk cloth. Next the Torah was covered with the new velvet-embroidered mantle. Finally, a silver breastplate with embedded colored stones symbolic of the twelve tribes of Israel was placed over the mantle. Mike then stood up, handed the Torah to Rebecca who along with Rachel returned the Torah to the Ark. The two young women closed the Ark, turned to face the congregation and Rebecca in a strong clear voice began,

"Our Haftorah today is from the prophet Hosea. The best piece of news I can give you about the Haftorah is that it's pretty short. This Haftorah is also PG-13 rated, so we'll be careful what we say. Fortunately, Rabbi Chani helped us through it."

Rachel then took over, "Our Haftorah is about an unfaithful woman and her long suffering husband who is quite angry at his spouse, but still in the ends takes his wife back and loves her. The story is really a metaphor in that God is also long suffering because of our lack of faith in Him. So God, like the husband, is willing to take us back despite our bad behavior. It connects up with the Torah portion because God keeps his end of the deal with us even though we don't always do our part."

Rebecca concluded their introduction saying, "So we think our responsibility is to always strive to do a better job as young Jewish women and members of this community as well as the broader communities that we are part of. Now we will read the Haftorah."

For the next several minutes the twins chanted the Haftorah together. The congregation was mesmerized by the beauty of the moment. When they finished people started shouting out mazel tov and clapping then the entire group broke out into the song of "Siman Tov U'Mazel Tov" one more time.

Rabbi Kahn stood up and suggested that the girls sit next to their parents and take a rest for a few minutes. She then began her sermon, "Friends, chevarim, Amazing! Are they great or what? We are truly blessed to have Rebecca and Rachel Cohn as part of our community. Girls, if you want to know the meaning of the word *kvell*, absolute unmitigated joy, just take a look at your parents and grandparents. And rest assured that your grandparents Henry and Eve Cohn are also at this moment smiling down on their granddaughters."

That last remark caught Marc by surprise and he was suddenly flooded with emotion over the loss of parents who had died almost two decades earlier.

Chani then continued, "All of us rabbis love to say that there are no coincidences. And so it is that today we read the parsha of Bamidbar on the special day of Rebecca and Rachel's bat mitzvah. One of the points of this parsha is simply that we all count. And these two young women are absolutely central to the community of our synagogue as well as Seward. In our synagogue they have been our babysitters and more recently our aides in teaching the younger children. Soon they will become the bar and bat mitzvah assistant tutors. In the community they are regulars serving food at the homeless shelter and they, without any prodding from their parents or me, decided to have a winter clothing drive for the less fortunate in the area. And to give you a preview of what they have up their sleeve, I have now been approved to tell you that before next Passover they are spearheading a food drive so that after all of you clean out your shelves of *chametz*, Rachel and Rebecca will be there to pick up sealed packages for distribution to our local food bank.

"Clearly, we are very proud of them. We are also proud of their parents whose own work in this community and in Alaska is so important. Similarly, I, as your rabbi, am proud of the contributions that each of you make to our congregation, community, and Israel through your purchase of Israeli bonds, contributions to Magen David Adom, Hadassah, and scores of other Israeli charities. And therein is the lesson of the parsha. Only by being together as a local, national, and international community is there strength. In the parsha we see the tribes assigned to different parts of the encampment each carrying their special banner. Each tribe had its strengths. For example, in his final blessings to his sons, Jacob identifies differing characteristics for each of those sons who will go on to lead tribes. Our patriarch Yaakov sees in Judah the strength of leadership, in Reuben he sees humility after he sincerely repents for his earlier impetuous behavior, and in Benjamin he sees the strength of a mighty and just warrior.

"But what is one tribe without the other? We have had too many examples in our society of wise people using their intelligence in destructive ways such as many folks on Wall Street or leaders of countries. We have seen wealthy people misuse their resources. We have seen talented people waste those God-given gifts and often their lives. Friends, the lesson of the parsha is we must work together for the common good. I absolutely believe that the common good of the Jewish people, our tribe, and the common good of our community are interwoven.

"And, like all tribes, just as we see with the Native Alaskans in our communities, we have our special clothing; our tallit and kippahs, our customs and obligations like the Kiddush, the challah, and most importantly the Shabbat. We also have our special ceremonies. In fact today we have been privileged to witness one of those beautiful ceremonies; the welcoming of our children into adulthood. Let us always remember it and cherish it.

"We should also take pride in our fellow tribesmen who have given so much to this world in terms of jurisprudence, the arts, medicine, and *chesed*, kindness. Yet I must offer a word of caution from the Torah. We must always remember that the glue that binds us comes from our shared values, traditions, and commitments. Thanks again Rachel and Rebecca for your wonderful reminders.

"Finally, while our personal investment must be on the basis of our own strengths we must always recognize and respect the strengths of other.

"I remember my first winter here when I went out on the dog sled with our member Mike Pearl. And after an exhilarating run of a few miles we tied up the dogs and went into his house for some warm coffee. Mike asked me a question, 'Chani,' he said, 'How can you be a rabbi? How can you study those texts and come up with sermons and stand in front of a room full of people and deliver a talk?' I answered, 'Mike how can you pick eight dogs out of fifty barking animals, tie them up to a sled, and take them out on a run, come back, feed them and love them, know every dog's names and habits—how do you do it?' The answer to both questions is always the same. That is the special drop of DNA each of has been given by God to be who we are, our own beautiful uniqueness.

"So, friends, we have in our midst two incredible young women. Mazel tov! And now I would like to invite the coordinator of our advisory board to say a few words to our B'not Mitzvah. Chevarim, you may not recognize him in a suit and tie. But I present to you Seward's nominee for GQ man of the year, the aforementioned Mike Pearl."

Everyone laughed as sixty-year-old Michael Pearl stepped up to the bima. "Folks as you all know I am not a public speaker, I just drive dog sleds, but for Rachel and Rebecca I make an exception. All of us who have seen you grow up here have come to love you girls as our own. We are exceptionally proud of you today, as we are every day. On behalf of the board we want to present you with three gifts. The first is a set of candlesticks so both of you can take your place amongst Jewish women all over the world as you light the Shabbat candles each week. And no matter where you are in the world, even the lower forty-eight, when you look on those silver candlesticks you'll remember your roots and a community that adores you. The second gift is a Tanach, a book that contains the Torah and other writings of the sages. Finally, I present each of you with a certificate that provides a $5,000 scholarship to go on the March of the Living when you are in the junior or senior year of high school. This is a gift from the Leah and Shimon Weissfogel Family Foundation of Florida and The Kahn Family Foundation of Dallas in memory of Rabbi Nathaniel Kahn. Mazel tov and God bless you."

Marc listened and although he had never heard of these foundations he was impressed with their generosity that extended to a small town in Alaska. Max sat there and wondered why he had never had a bar mitzvah. He was yet to realize that the answer to his question would be found in his father's adamant refusal to participate in any aspect of Jewish life, particularly synagogue membership, and his mother's unwillingness to quarrel with her husband over the issue.

Rabbi Chani, with a big smile on her face, looked at the twins and said, "Come on, let's wrap up this service."

The praying and singing lasted for another twenty minutes and was concluded with a final song that the rabbi accompanied with her guitar. Then, just as occurred Friday night, the girls led the Kiddush over the wine and the blessing of the challah.

For the next two hours the community ate, sang, kibitzed, and then cleaned up the room. It was closed to 3:30 PM when all the guests and congregants left except the two Cohn families and Rabbi Chani. Norman and Blake approached Chani and said, "That was amazing. Thank you so much"

She replied, "It was my honor and pleasure." Then she turned to Marc, "So, how was it for you?"

He thought for a minute and quietly answered, "Worth every second of the flight here and then some."'

She liked that response and she flashed him an enormous smile and said, "Thank you." Then she asked, "So, what's up for the rest of Shabbat? Anyone ready for a hike?"

Norman and Blake looked at each other and answered in unison, "No way, we believe in Shabbat naps, thank you!"

Max said, "No thanks, I'm hanging out at home with Rachel, Rebecca, and the dogs."

Marc, to his own surprise said, "Yeah, that sounds like a plan."

Chani responded, "How about meeting back here in an hour? Don't forget to bring a sweater; it'll be a little cooler on the trail."

An hour later Marc was knocking at her front door. Chani opened the door and asked him to come inside. She pulled out a map of the

Seward area and suggested two options. The easier hike was near down-town and known as the Two Lakes Trail around First and Second lakes. A dramatically more challenging hike she suggested would be up the Mount Marathon Jeep Trail. They chatted about the options and Marc finally suggested the lake hike and, if he felt up to it, maybe a bit of the Marathon Trail. He then asked, "What about hiking up to Exit Glacier?"

She smiled and answered, "Exit Glacier is a fabulous hike and if you're interested, maybe tomorrow after the wedding, we can all go there—I mean Blake, Norman, and all the kids. I prefer not to go there today because it's about a ten mile drive to the visitor's center and I try very hard not to drive on Shabbat. It's part of my way of observing the Sabbath."

Marc was quite surprised by her response. His thought was that she was some kind of 'new age' rabbi who did her job at the synagogue and then went totally off duty. He had much to learn about Chani.

Marc asked, "How long have you lived here?"

"Almost four years; ever since I graduated from rabbinical school and was ordained."

"Was I mistaken or did you say yesterday that you only do the rabbi thing part-time?"

She looked at Marc with a big smile and said with emphasis, "The rabbi thing!"

Marc stammered an embarrassed response, "Sorry, I meant to say, what else do you do besides being rabbi in the synagogue?"

"Oh, that's a better question. A couple of days a week I hunt moose and bear. Then on the alternate weeks I trap various furry animals, skin them, and sell their hides. Then I run an air taxi service throughout Alaska and when I have a few extra hours I fish for halibut."

Initially Marc was astounded at her reply but something in her eyes told him that she was jesting and he responded, "Are you serious?

"No, except for the halibut fishing. I sometimes do that. In addi-tion to my part-time pulpit rabbi work I also tutor kids for their bar and bat mitzvah in several other towns. A few times a year, I hold services elsewhere for special events, and twice a week I'm a chaplain at the prison on the other side of Resurrection Bay."

"Oh, you know I'm covering for Dr. Polansky two days next week?"

"Right, I heard about that. The superintendent sent a memo around concerning it. It's very kind of you. I don't think you'll have anything difficult to do."

"So, what does a Jewish prison chaplain do? Are there many Jews in that prison?"

"Marc, there are very few Jews in Alaska or in our prison. Just a handful. What do I do? That's a great question and we'd have to walk the ten miles to Exit Glacier for me to give you a complete answer. But the *Reader's Digest* condensed answer is that I do a bit of administration like coordinating the religious services. I also teach a weekly class on the Bible—I usually get about twenty-five inmates at each session. Some are regulars and others just drop in. I'm the mental health counselor for the fifty inmate women's unit. I also do individual spiritual counseling for both the inmates and staff. And, truthfully, my background as a social work therapist is invaluable because the place is crawling with mental health problems. And sometimes I work with families of inmates who are having problems and I also spend a bit of time with inmates who are about to be discharged. The fact is we have a lot of recidivism and lots of the inmates had problems before they got there and some develop more problems after they arrive. Alcoholism, drug addiction, lack of job skills, and a scarlet letter on their foreheads and souls reminds them and others what they've done. Hard time makes it tough once they're on the outside. Marc, I think I've answered your question and been a bit too preachy. Sorry."

Marc smiled, "Nothing to be sorry for. Sounds like you have a very busy and good life. So what if it's away from civilization."

They both laughed and for the remainder of the afternoon Marc and Chani engaged in pleasant conversation as they walked around the town lakes and the busy waterfront.

Twenty-Three

Sunday

Sunday was going to be beautiful in Seward. When the sun rose at 5:00 AM the morning temperature was fifty-two degrees—a regular heat wave on the Kenai Peninsula. The weather report from KIBH 91.7 FM was that the sky would be clear, no precipitation, light winds, and a high of sixty-one degrees. Paul Polansky thought it was perfect weather for a wedding. He and Akna had arranged with a local fish restaurant to barbeque fresh caught halibut and salmon in the yard outside B'nai Chevarim. Minnie Pearl, who was trained as a classical guitarist, volunteered to provide the music for the wedding procession while a local musician would play a synthesizer during the reception.

By 9:00 AM a florist was hard at work in the synagogue constructing a wedding canopy out of seasonal flowers. Also, Paul had asked Mike Pearl, Norm Cohn, and two other members of the congregation to hold up his father's prayer shawl under the canopy during the ceremony. By 10:00 AM the chairs were set up and everything was ready for the wedding. Minnie Pearl arrived at 11:15, moved a chair from the front, pushed it toward the side, and began rehearsing.

All the guests, most of whom had been to B'nai Chevarim twice that weekend, arrived early. At noon Minnie began playing Johann Sebastian

Bach's Air on G String, and the processional began. The first person walking down the aisle was Rabbi Kahn looking spectacular in a dark tailored suit and white silk tallit with a matching silk kippah. Next came the four men who would hold up Paul's father's tallit under the canopy. The group stepped up to the bima and unfolded the tallit, placed pole holders in each corner of the prayer shawl, and raised it under the canopy. Next Paul's best man, his brother from Boston, escorted their mother down the aisle. Finally, Paul walked down to the bima and stood facing the rabbi.

Minnie stopped for a moment and then began playing Johann Pachelbel's Canon in D major. After the first few measures Akna, holding a bouquet of white roses and accompanied by her mother, began walking down the aisle.

When Akna reached the bima, Paul stepped off, kissed Akna's mother, and escorted his bride to the wedding canopy. After she ascended the bima, Akna—followed by her mother and Mrs. Polansky—walked in a circle around Paul seven times and then the bride took her place on Paul's right and faced the rabbi.

Chani began, "Chevarim, friends, welcome to what is certainly the perfect conclusion to what has been for me, and I hope all of you, an extraordinary weekend. We have had the privilege of sharing in the bat mitzvahs of our dear Rachel and Rebecca and now we have the pleasure of witnessing the marriage of two of our founding members, Akna and Paul.

"We shall begin with the first of two blessings over the wine and the sharing of this first cup of wine." Rabbi Chani proceeded with the ceremony periodically interjecting a short explanation. After the ring was placed on Akna's finger, the traditional prayer was recited by Paul in Hebrew and English, "With this ring you are consecrated to me according to the law of Moses and Israel."

Akna then placed a ring on Paul's finger and then also in Hebrew and English she recited the same traditional prayer. And by these simple mirrored acts they had sealed their marriage.

Rabbi Chani said, "Akna, Paul, you are not only founders of the modern Jewish community of Seward, you are also wonderful friends to our community. Whenever there is a problem you are always there to help. If you lived in Washington, DC, you would be known as the 'power couple.' Here you are the '*Chesed* Couple'—the couple whose kindness is legendary. You are the folks who help the elderly and young anytime of the day or night. You are the go-to people at the prison. When there is an accident on one of the local fishing boats you are always part of the team helping out. Last winter when the roof of our shul started to leak on a Saturday afternoon you found a ladder, got up there, and patched it up until we could get a roofer.

"At wedding ceremonies one of the popular commentaries from rabbis is that it's harder to bring two people together than split the Red Sea. While that may oftentimes be true, clearly it is not the situation with the two of you. Having both of you as such an integral part of Seward and our synagogue honors all of us. God obviously had major plans when he brought a nurse from Kotzebue to Seward to meet a committed bachelor from Milwaukee. Finally, I'm thrilled to officiate at this first Jewish wedding in our shul, and perhaps the first in Seward in the 21st century. All of us love you and wish you many years together in happiness, health, and shalom, peace.

"In the next part of this wedding service we use a second cup of wine and chant the *Sheva B'rachot,* or seven blessings. The blessings are part of the mysticism of the number seven. In Torah we learn that God created the world in seven days, the seventh day is our Sabbath, and on the last day of *Sukkoth* in traditional synagogues, there are seven processions of the *luluv.* But for me the beauty of these seven blessings is their progression. They begin with a blessing that praises God for creating the world, then a blessing for creating humans, then a blessing for creating man and a woman to be mates and next the blessings rise to a crescendo with the sixth blessing which is so beautiful that I want to read to you from the translation of the Conservative Movement's Rabbinical Assembly:

"*Praised are you Lord our God, Sovereign of the universe, who created joy and gladness, bride and groom, mirth, song, delight and rejoicing, love and harmony, peace and companionship. Speedily, Lord our God, may there ever be heard in the cities of Judah and in the streets of Jerusalem voices of joy and gladness, voices of bride and groom, the jubilant voices of those joined in marriage under the bridal canopy, the voices of young people feasting and singing. Praised are You, Lord, who causes the groom to rejoice with his bride.*

"Then we have the traditional seventh blessing over wine. And, after I recite the seventh blessing I will ask Akna and Paul to drink from this second cup. For those of you counting, allow me to remind you that the ceremony began with Akna circling Paul seven times, and now comes to its completion with the seventh blessing. Why seven? The answer comes to us in Torah where the work of God is completed on the seventh day. And so, man and woman are completed with this mystical seventh blessing. Paul and Akna are married, and now and forevermore one and complete."

When the final Sheva B'rachot was finished Rabbi Chani took a glass, wrapped it in a cloth napkin, and placed in on the floor. Then looking at Paul she said, "Paul, this is the final symbol in a Jewish wedding, the breaking of the glass. There are many explanations for this custom from a reminder about destruction of the Holy Temple to the fragility of relationships. In light of the fact that this is a small community and we all know you and Akna well, I think the one explanation that makes the most sense is that this is the last time you are going to put your foot down."

With laughter echoing through the room, Paul brought his shoe down on the glass and everyone starting singing as the new husband and wife left the chuppah to shouts of mazel tov and much applause.

Marc and Max were sitting with the rest of the family. For Max it was just another confusing day in shul but for Marc it was the warmest, most engaging, and interesting wedding he had ever attended. A thought crossed his mind, *If I ever get married again, that's the way I want it done.*

Following the ceremony the congregation moved out of the building to a side yard, with its views of Resurrection Bay, for the fish barbeque and beer reception along with a wedding cake made up of one-hundred cupcakes set in a tiered holder. Paul's friend Denny Linden, a local fisherman and synthesizer musician, provided music. Chani had taught Denny the first song he would play, after which he would go on to play and sing the sounds of the 70s and 80s.

That first song, which lasted close to fifteen minutes, was a spirited traditional *hora*. Almost everyone joined in, even Marc and Max, who were pulled into the circle dance by Norman, Blake, and the twins. Periodically, the single large circle would break into two concentric circles going in opposite directions with Akna and Paul usually in the middle leading the dancing with totally uncoordinated steps. At one point Paul's and Akna's mothers were brought into the center of the circle and danced around with the continual singing of 'Siman Tov U'Mazel Tov' and clapping of hands. When the song was finally over the crowd needed the break for a drink and to pick up some food at the barbeque.

Once again, Marc found himself at a table with family as well as Chani. Unlike Friday night he didn't feel himself quite the stranger in the community. Max was sitting with his cousins and listening to them talk enthusiastically about their summer jobs volunteering at the kennel when Rachel turned to Max and asked, "What are you doing this summer?"

Max relied, "I dunno. My mother usually arranged everything. I guess I better ask my father."

Everyone was eating, drinking, and chatting away when Denny took the microphone and said, "Folks, it's time for Akna's and Paul's first dance and they've asked for the beautiful Julie Gold song, 'From A Distance,' that was made famous by Bette Midler." Denny started playing and Akna and Paul began their first dance as a married couple. Marc remembered how much he loved that song and its lyrics seem so applicable to his experiences in Alaska. A few moments later Denny asked everyone to join the bride and groom. Norm and Blake got up; the twins grabbed Max and pulled him on the dance floor as a threesome. Only Chani and Marc sat at the table and finally, with his heart beating at more than twice its regular pace he looked at Chani and said, "Would you like to dance?"

"Absolutely."

And they got up for their first dance. By 3:00 PM the wedding had wound down, people were leaving, the cupcakes were eaten, and the newlyweds were saying their goodbyes and heading to the Seward ship dock for their honeymoon cruise. The wait staff was cleaning up when Norman announced, "Are we all ready for a hike to Exit Glacier to work off lunch?" Everyone answered, "Yes."

Norman looked at Chani and asked, "Are you in?"

"I'm always up for a hike. Give me thirty minutes to change and I'll meet you guys at your house."

Norm replied, "Great, we can all go in one car."

An hour later the group consisting of Norman, Blake, Rachel, Rebecca, Marc, Max, and Chani had piled into the Suburban headed out for the ten-mile drive to Exit Glacier Nature Center. They parked the car and began a mile hike through a forest to 'Glacier View' where they could get a good look at the immensity of the Glacier, particularly the Toe. Next they agreed to hike the trail that would take them to the 'Edge of the Glacier.' The Seward hikers had made this trip numerous times but for Marc and Max seeing and touching the huge wall of blue ice was, as Max put it, "Awesome."

As they reached the 'Edge' and stood admiring the glacier Chani reached into her backpack and drew out a bag of cookies and small boxes of apple juice, "Energy for the return trip." The trip back down the trail to the nature center took over an hour as the group paused several times to admire wildflowers, spot birds, small animals, and share stories and jokes.

When they got back to the Cohn house, Max and the twins immediately ran inside to play with the dogs. Standing outside Chani declined an invitation to stay for a dinner of leftovers, said her goodbyes, and started to head for her car. Norman and Blake turned to go into the house and Marc simply stood there. As Chani was reaching for the door Marc called out, "Chani wait up a second," and he trotted over to her and said, "Can I take you out to dinner tomorrow night? Just the two of us?"

She responded with a big smile, "Like a date?"

His handsome face reddened and his stammered, "Yes, a date."

"Wonderful. I'd like that. It'll be my first date since moving to Alaska. I'll be home around six o'clock. Tomorrow I'm flying to Homer and Kenai to tutor a few kids and hold a short Torah class for the kids and any parents around. But I should be ready at seven. Does that work?" Marc smiled and nodded. As he walked back to his brother's house he suddenly felt like he was once again sixteen years old.

Norman asked, "Is everything OK?"

Marc's face turned red for the second time in less than five minutes and he stammered an answer, "Oh, yeah, fine, I'm going out to dinner with Chani tomorrow night." He then lowered his voice and asked, "Is that all right?"

Everyone in the room, except Max, grinned and nodded. Max simply stared straight ahead.

At dinner that night Blake asked Marc what he and Max had in mind for the rest of the week. Before Marc could respond Max answered, "I want to hang out with Rachel and Rebecca and go to Commander Pearl's kennels with them. Is that okay Dad?"

For the first time since Cathy's death Marc heard a joyful tone in Max's voice and saw it on his face. "Certainly," he replied.

"And what about you, Marc?" Norm asked and then added, "I'm sorry but tomorrow is a busy day for me. I'm taking a bunch of depositions and really can't take the day off. So, you're on your own."

"No problem," Marc replied, "I'm going to sleep late, wander around the waterfront, maybe hike into the mountains a bit, go over to the Sea Life Center—I'll be fine. And I'll pick Max up after Chani and I have had dinner."

Before he could finish Max again, chimed in, "No need, Dad, I'll just sleep here. OK, Uncle Norm?"

Once again, Marc was surprised because Max had never slept out or ever wanted to socialize with other kids.

Twenty-Four

Seward, Alaska

Monday

Morning couldn't come fast enough for Max. By the time the girls were waking up he was already in the family room playing with their two dogs. He loved to stroke their necks under the jaw and be licked in return. Cookie and Cracker had so adopted Max as family that within minutes of meeting him the dogs happily accepted his back and belly rubs. Max wished he had a dog in Florida but knew his father wouldn't go for it.

Max had been told by both Norm and Blake to make himself at home so after greeting the dogs he went into the kitchen to have breakfast. The girls had also shown Max the morning routine for the dogs and he volunteered to fill their water bowls and provide them with their morning meal which meant scooping dry dog food into a bowl and adding some water. Max enjoyed preparing breakfast for Cookie and Cracker, and couldn't help grinning and telling them to slow down as he watched the dogs rapidly devour their food.

As soon as the dogs were finished, Max sat down at the kitchen counter and poured himself a bowl of Cheerios and began his own meal. A few minutes later his cousins and aunt joined him. The girls thanked him for feeding the dogs and then opened the back door of the kitchen so the dogs could have a run on their large property and take care of their morning toileting needs in a designated part of the woods.

Blake asked Max, "Are you still planning to go with Rachel and Rebecca to Commander Pearl's kennel today?"

"Yes, definitely!"

"Then I'll drive you over there in a half hour and you guys can plan to walk home when you're finished. Max, it's hard work you are going to be doing, so my suggestion is that you have more protein than you get in a bowl of cereal. The girls are going to have scrambled eggs, toast, and milk. Do you want that too?

Max nodded. Then Blake said, "Girls please make some additional food for Max and I'll be back down in a jiffy."

Max watched in amazement as his cousins quickly organized themselves to prepare a hearty breakfast. In his fourteen years Max had rarely lifted a finger to provide for himself. A nanny or housekeeper had made his bed, washed and pressed his clothes, cleaned his room, prepared his food, and washed his dishes. In the few days he had been part of his uncle's household he had come to realize that he had been raised as a privileged prince and that he actually enjoyed the alternative.

The ride to the kennels took less than ten minutes and as they drove up Mike Pearl's driveway Max heard the sound of dogs barking. He looked at Rachel and asked, "What's going on? Is it like this all the time?"

Rachel answered, "No. The dogs are excited because Commander Pearl is taking some of them out on a run and they're barking because all of them want to go. They're saying, 'Take me, I wanta go.' Seriously!"

"No! Are you pulling my leg?"

"No, kidding, Max. You'll see. As soon as the Commander hooks up the team and the sled starts to pull out, the dogs will get so quiet you won't even know that they are here."

The teens headed toward the yard where each dog had its own small house that was a square box with a window-like opening. Next to each house was a metal tether pole and fastened to the pole was an eight foot long chain that attached to the dog's collar.

To Max, who was used to the pristine cleanliness of his condo building, the surrounding community of Bal Harbour, as well as his own school, the kennel was a shock. At first it appeared noisy, smelly, and disorganized. He was ready to leave. Then he closed his eyes for a count of ten, opened them again, and saw the neat rows of green flat-topped doghouses, the exercise merry-go-round, and the fenced yard with the sled dog puppies.

Seeing the three teens standing near the entrance, Mike Pearl walked over to say hello and reintroduced himself to Max, who immediately recognized him from the bat mitzvahs and wedding. It was hard to not recognize someone like Pearl who stood six foot six inches tall, weighed more than 250 pounds, and had white hair worn in a braided ponytail. Pearl lived in a large four-bedroom log cabin home next to the kennel that he shared with his wife; their son Ethan, a sophomore at the University of Washington who was spending the summer in Israel at a kibbutz to be followed by two semesters at Hebrew University; and Jody their fourteen year-old-daughter who was the Rachel and Rebecca's best friend.

When the Commander greeted the three volunteers, the dogs started to go wild. They were jumping up and down, barking, with a few leaping on the roofs of their houses and just as quickly bounding off. The girls were laughing heartily by the dogs' antics and Max was still frightened by all this noise and activity. Suddenly there was a loud, high-pitched, whistle that came from Mike Pearl. Instantly the kennel was quiet. Max thought, *No wonder they call him Commander.*

Pearl turned to the dogs and said, "Boys and girls this is your new friend Max and he came from Florida to work with you guys for a few days. Be nice to him." Mike Pearl then leaned down to Max and whispered, "Smile and wave. Now!"

Max followed the Commander's instruction and just as suddenly as they had come to attention moments earlier, they were now dismissed and back into their jumping and barking.

"Max, you just follow us and see what we do. Later you can team up with one of us or Jody and do the chores."

Max asked, "Who's Jody?"

Rebecca answered, "Jody Pearl. Mike's her father. Don't you remember her from our bat mitzvah? She's our friend who had the next to the last aliyah."

"I don't remember anyone named Jody."

Rachel jumped into the conversation: "She was the redhead, about your height, long hair, skinny with big boobs."

Rachel and Rebecca started laughing at their description of Jody, but it seemed to bother Max, who suddenly looked embarrassed.

Now it was Rachel's turn, "Max, you're red in the face because of Jody's boobs. Hey man, our father says your dad is the number one boob man in Florida. You shouldn't be bothered."

The girls became hysterical at their own joke and in a few seconds Max was infected by the laughter and he was bent over when Jody walked over and asked, "What's so funny?"

The kids started looking at each other and the waves of laughter seemed as if they were a jazz trio riffing off each other. Then the trio was a quartet with Jody also infected by the hilarity of the moment. Finally, someone started saying stop and the group calmed down.

Rebecca said, "Guys enough fun, let's get to work. Max, why don't you come with me and then Rach and Jody can team up. If it's OK with everyone Max and I will take the back five rows and you guys can take the front five."

Everyone agreed and the teens headed toward to shed to get tools. The next few hours passed quickly as the kids scooped poop, cleaned out and then replaced hay from the doghouses, provided water for the dogs, and did the morning dry food feedings.

Rebecca explained to Max that part of their job was to exercise the dogs and most importantly show them lots of affection. Initially Max was afraid of the dogs but Rebecca explained to him how to approach each dog and speak to it as a friend. By 11:30 AM Max was feeling comfortable enough around the dogs to pet and talk to them.

At noon Minnie rang a cowbell signaling a lunch break. All four teens and Mike came into the house to wash up and share a lunch of raw vegetables, fresh fruit, grilled cheese sandwiches, water and iced tea. Over lunch Mike announced that he had two groups of tourists coming at 12:45 PM for sled dog rides. The plan was that he would take one group out and Jody would take the second group. He asked if any of the other kids wanted to go on either ride. The girls said they still had chores to do so they would skip the runs. But Max said he'd love to go on a run. Mike decided to take Max in his cart.

As soon as everyone finished eating Max was about to get up when Mike said, "Hang on a second we like to have a quick blessing after eating to thank God, and in many senses our fellow human beings, for this bounty."

And, in unison the twins and the Pearls began a shortened version of the traditional Jewish blessing after the meal. Max was surprised and sat patiently through the three-minute prayer of thankfulness.

Twenty-Five

SEWARD, ALASKA

After helping Minnie clean up, the teens and Mike went back out to the kennel where the dogs once again greeted them with infectious energy. For the second time that day Max heard about canine behavior when Mike explained to him, "I know it may seem strange to you but they know that I'm soon going to pick some of these dogs to pull a cart out on our trails. And they all love to run. In many ways they are like kids yelling—'take me—take me.' And when I start to pick the dogs to run today, the barking will become almost unbearable. But you'll see, once I have my teams hitched up and as soon as we start to go then, BAM! It's all quiet."

Just as Mike was finishing explaining what was going to happen, two vans pulled up with the tourists who had signed up for the rides. Mike introduced himself as the owner of the kennel and the driver of one of the two sleds. With Mike's size and age it was clear to everyone that this man was an appropriate person to handle a team. Then he introduced Jody as the driver of the second team. Max could sense an immediate reluctance on the part of some of the tourists to even consider riding with her as the musher. Mike followed up his introduction of Jody by telling the group that she has been a dog musher since she was four, has a roomful of trophies from the many sprint dog mushing races she has won, and in February she would be competing in her first 150-mile race, the Junior Iditarod. Max could almost sense the collective "Wow!" from the group.

Mike then went on to explain to the group what all the noise was about and how it would suddenly quiet down as they got rolling. He also told everyone that he and Jody would explain more about the dogs once they were farther down the trail.

Mike reached into his shirt pocket and pulled out a sheet with the names of the six dogs that he wanted Jody and Rachel to hook up to one cart. He then told Rebecca and Max to come with him as he selected the other dogs and one by one tied them to into their harnesses and attached the dogs to the gang-line. Mike then invited the tourists to find seats in the two rubber wheeled carts. Mike also explained that the ride would be bumpy and that they should always wear the seat belts. The tourists were additionally urged to put on their helmets and keep the visors down in order to avoid scratches from low hanging bushes, flying pebbles, or dirt in the eyes.

Finally, it was time to take off and Jody's team leapt out onto the trail on her loud command of "HIKE." Once Jody's team was twenty yards down the trail Mike let out another whistle and his team was off. As advertised the kennel was suddenly quiet.

Ten minutes later the two mushers, with their carts full of tourists, slowed their teams with the loud and clear command "EASY" then pulled off the trail and halted their teams with a command of "WHOA." Max was impressed with the dogs' obedience to Mike and Jody. They both set the brakes on the cart and then Mike began a short lecture to the group about the dogs and mushing.

"Today we are running just twelve of our fifty dogs. Each day we try to make sure the dogs get enough exercise to stay in shape because they love to run. As you can see none of them are classic looking huskies. If fact, they're all mutts that have been bred for speed and endurance. A sled dog can typically run for a hundred miles a day over snow and ice in zero degree weather.

"Here in Alaska we have the Iditarod which is known as the last great race on earth. This race begins the first Monday in March and covers 1,049 miles from Anchorage to Nome—and goes through unbelievably rugged and isolated parts of Alaska. Historians say the race itself has two origins. One is the old Iditarod Trail that started a few miles away at the docks in Seward. Over there gold prospectors got off ships and headed out to search for gold in the north along the Iditarod trail that ended in Nome. At one time the races were shorter and followed that trail.

"More recently the race has morphed into what we do today. The 1,049-mile route we now use commemorates a run that saw scores of dogs, perhaps as many as 150 plus about fifty mushers, bringing diphtheria antitoxin to Nome. The problem was that Nome, a city just below the Arctic Circle, was both isolated and its population under siege because of a diphtheria epidemic. Put simply, the only way to get serum to the folks in Nome was via dog sled. Incidentally, for you New Yorkers, next time you go to the East Drive at 67th Street, right inside Central Park, you can see the statue of Balto the lead sled dog on the final relay into Nome. There are also several different films and books about Balto. Check it out!

"So, only the best-trained and greatest athletes can even complete in the Iditarod. You know who these athletes are? First, there are the sled dogs like those pulling these carts. Teams usually consisting of sixteen dogs begin the race with just one musher standing on the back of the sled. The second extraordinary athlete in this competition is the musher. He or she must be enormously strong of mind and body in order to endure the demands and punishment required to complete even a part of the Iditarod. And, usually eight or nine days after the start of the race some man or woman pulls into Nome and is declared the winner. Incidentally, some of the greatest mushers have been and are women—such as the late Susan Butcher, a four-time champion, and DeeDee Jonrowe, a breast cancer survivor, who has competed in twenty-two races and finished in second place three times!

"Lecture over—we're going to go down this trail for another ten or fifteen minutes then we'll take a break to give water to the dogs. Anyone who wants to help out certainly can. I should point out these dogs do their best work when it's very cold. This relatively warm weather today, meaning it isn't below freezing, is tough on the dogs and that's why we have to stop and make sure they're hydrated. Finally, listen for the commands. *GEE* means right turn and then *HAW* means left. Okay. Enough talk. Let's roll."

Jody again started her team with a "HIKE" and "STRAIGHT AHEAD." Mike followed. A mile up the road there was a fork and Jody called out "HAW" and the team smoothly took the left fork and continued racing along. Mike also called out "HAW" at the junction and his team maintained its position behind Jody's. Ten minutes later the teams were stopped, the carts secured, and the dogs knew it was break time. In the turnoff there were a dozen metal pails and a hand pump for drawing water from one of Mike's wells. Jody called for volunteers to carry a pail of water over to each dog. As the tourists lined up, Jody pumped the water from the well and filled the pails. The dogs greedily lapped the water and then settled down. Mike then provided each person with a plastic cup and suggested they too have some water. He assured them that the water had been tested and was safe to drink. He also handed each tourist a small protein bar. Then he said to the group, "So now you've learned another important lesson. When you're responsible for the dogs you take care of them first before indulging yourself. That's the way it is on the trail."

They rode for fifteen minutes and pulled off the trail for another dog water break. Mike then pointed toward a small structure about twenty yards up a path into the woods and said, "Folks, out here we only have outhouses so if you're desperate my suggestion is use the woods or the outhouse. But, be forewarned, it's really just a smelly hole in the ground with a wooden covering. We'll be back at the kennels in a few minutes. Also, this is what we use to call our official Kodak moment so Jody, Max, and I will be happy to take pictures of you with each other, the dogs, or whatever. Feel free to pull out your cameras and phones and shoot."

For the next few minutes photos were taken in countless configurations and a handful of desperate people ventured up to the outhouse and came out with the same response, "Gross."

Mike announced it was time to head home. He also told the tourists that on this last leg he would let the dogs run as hard as they wanted so they should be sure their belts and helmets were secure and the goggles in place. With that the two mushers pulled on the trail and yelled, "HIKE." The dogs knew they were heading home and ran with alacrity. Fifteen minutes later they were greeted with low barking of their many kennel mates.

The tourists stepped out of the carts, took a few more pictures, turned in their equipment, and thanked Jody and Mike for an exhilarating experience. When a few offered tips to Mike and Jody they both pulled out wooden boxes with a slit on the top and told the tippers that their money was being used for charity.

For Max, the ride, lecture, and taking care of the dogs were both exhausting and thrilling. And, he had a hard time keeping his eyes off Jody.

Mike asked Max to help him unhook the dogs from the gang-line and bring them over to their houses and secure them to their tethers. When that was finished Mike thanked Max for his help.

By the time the dogs were settled and the gear put away it was almost 2 PM and the girls told Max it was time to head home. They bid goodbye to the Pearl family and started the walk back to the Cohn house. Rachel looked at Max and asked, "So, what do you think? Was that fun?"

"It was amazing. Thanks. I had a great time. If it's OK with you guys I'm going to ask Commander Pearl if I can volunteer all week."

"Sure," the twins replied enthusiastically.

Max ran over to Mike Pearl and asked permission to volunteer. Mike looked straight into Max's eyes and said, "Absolutely. Max, you have a gift. The dogs seem to love you and you seem to love them. Am I right?"

Max nodded and smiled from ear to ear. He then ran back and high fived his cousins. They walked back to the Cohn home talking about the day, telling stories about the ride, the dogs, and the tourists. Rebecca and Rachel were overjoyed to have Max volunteering with them for the week. After they got home, washed up, and grabbed snacks of fresh fruit, Rebecca turned to Max and Rachel and asked, "What do you guys want to do this afternoon? Wanna go fishing?"

Max and Rachel answered together, "Sure."

They went to the garage, grabbed some gear, jumped on bicycles, and headed to the pier for a few hours of fishing. They only caught small baitfish that they threw back but had a rousing time telling jokes and stories. At six they went home and were greeted by Blake and Norman who were grilling hot dogs and hamburgers for dinner.

After filling his aunt and uncle in on his day at the kennel Max asked, "Is my Dad coming to supper?"

Almost shyly and carefully Norman answered, "No, remember he is having dinner with Rabbi Chani."

Max looked at Norman, slowly crossed his arms in front of him, lifted his right hand to his faced, stroked his cheek, and then said in mock seriousness, "Sounds like a date to me. Good for him." And everyone laughed. The sensitivity of the moment had been broken by Max's artful humor. Three hours later Max got into bed. As he was closing his eyes, he thought to himself, *This was the best day of my life.*

Twenty-Six

SEWARD, ALASKA

Monday

Marc Cohn awakened from the most unsettling dream he had had in years. In it he was having an argument with his late wife. She was saying, "Don't let Max play with those dogs because they're going to bite and scratch him." Max was screaming, "Leave me alone, let me grow up," and Marc was just standing there. In the dream Cathy said, "Marc, say something. Do something. Don't stand there like a rich moron." And then he woke up.

Marc also realized that despite the room being cold he was sweating. He thought to himself, *what was that all about?* He and Cathy had occasionally talked about her anxiety over Max. While Marc understood that Cathy's two miscarriages might have played a part in her being a "helicopter" mom, he also thought that Max needed more responsibility and independence if he were to mature into an adult. As it evolved over the past fourteen years, Cathy took almost total responsibility for Max's upbringing while Marc paid all the bills.

In thinking about all of that, plus his dream and Max's life up to that point, Marc realized that what he saw in Max was a scared and indulged kid, whose aggressive behavior at school the week after Cathy died may have masked a lack of confidence and a poor sense of self. For Max the consequence of this situation was remoteness from most kids at his school and the handful of kids who lived in their condo building.

Thanks to the months of therapy Marc also recognized that Cathy's death was an almost fatal blow to Max who sensed that his moorings in the world were in danger of being severed. In one of the earliest sessions with Dr. White, Max cried out that he hated everyone, and most particularly his father, whom he thought was busy chasing money and women. When White asked for elaboration on the statement Max relied, "I'm not stupid. I know we live in the most expensive building in the most expensive city in Florida. I can see all of my father's toys, the cars, the boat, and his collection of fancy watches. And I know he works with hot women all day long."

Dr. White responded, "Max, your father works hard and no doubt makes a good income. Doesn't that allow him to spend it on the family as well as himself? Why are you angry about it?"

Max answered that his father embarrassed him. He then told the therapist that ever since the sixth grade the guys at school would pester and tease him about his father feeling up women all day. They all wanted to know if Max worked in the office on weekends and snuck peaks at "butts and tits." Once Max was so mortified by Marc's work that he asked his mother to demand that his father stop the TV ads. Cathy defended her husband by saying, 'Your Dad is an ethical man helping people feel better about themselves. Max, you shouldn't be ashamed because of his work. It's all perfectly legal and honorable and frankly it pays the bills for our lifestyle.' Max never bought that line.

During another particularly troubling session Max admitted hating his father for not saving his mother's life. Max said, "What good is it to be a doctor if you can't even save someone who is sleeping next to you?" This sore subject had resurfaced once again on the flight to Alaska.

In one of their last therapy sessions Max asserted that all his problems in life stemmed from his father. When White questioned him about his plans to deal with this issue Max simply replied, "Leave him." He then told the therapist that the details had not yet been worked out but that he had already decided to join the Army when he turned eighteen. He went on to say that while he loved his mother, the further he got from Marc the happier he'd be. When Dr. White suggested that college might be another way of leaving home, Max shrugged his shoulders and simply said, "I can't wait."

The dream scared Marc. He knew that he wanted to be a better father, but wasn't sure how it was going to happen, particularly because of the bad blood between Max and himself.

While he initially thought of the trip to Alaska as primarily an obligation, he was now starting to feel that it was a fortuitous happening. For example, he reasoned, although they didn't talk much on the plane they were still next to each other, sharing a few words over the meals and laughing together at a film they both watched.

As he was reviewing the past few days everything seemed to start changing the moment they boarded a small five-seat aircraft in Anchorage and suddenly life was different. Initially both Marc and Max thought the woman pilot was also a tour guide as she pointed out the sights below. For example, the moment she spotted a humpback whale below the plane she circled and took the Cessna to a lower altitude to again catch the humpback breaching. And a minute later two humpbacks put on a show for them breaching and twisting. Marc and Max were thrilled.

Marc recalled how genuinely polite Max had been when he thanked the pilot, said hello to his Aunt Blake and greeted his cousins Rebecca and Rachel. In analyzing all of this he concluded that after arriving at his brother's home he had hardly spent any time alone with Max, and the times that he had seen him, particularly at the synagogue and the hike to Exit Glacier, Max had never looked happier.

Marc returned to thinking about his dream. He wondered if it had something to do with his date that night. Was he betraying Cathy by going out? How would Max feel? He didn't know.

He then looked at his watch. It was almost 11:00 AM. He hadn't slept that late in years. He decided to call the kennels and see how Max was doing, eat, and start exploring Seward. The conversation with Minnie

Pearl was brief and comforting as she assured him that Max was doing fine. Marc dressed and left the hotel. Although the fifty-seven degree overcast weather was balmy by Alaska standards, Marc felt chilled. He returned to his room, put on a North Face zippered ski jacket and stuffed a pair of gloves in his pockets. He was now ready to face Seward in the summer.

Marc's first stop was a nearby cafe where he had a cup of coffee and smoked salmon on a bagel with cream cheese and onion. He was amazed by the quality of the salmon as well as the international nature of the bagel. For a fleeting second he wondered if the bagel was Chani's doing—but he doubted it. Over breakfast he decided on two more stops. First he planned to walk to the Seward Library and Museum in order to see the film on the 1964 tsunami and earthquake that destroyed part of Seward's waterfront, started major fires at the oil storage farms, and resulted in twelve deaths. Then he wanted to spend time at the Alaska SeaLife Center.

The stroll to the museum and the film took several hours so it was close to 3:00 PM when he finally arrived at the Center. As an undergraduate he had taken one introductory course on marine biology and for a brief moment thought that being a marine biologist might be an interesting career choice. But, being a physician and making money easily won out for Marc Cohn. As he walked the few blocks toward the Center he recalled that the aspect of marine biology he found most interesting were the ecological connections between water, the environment, plants, and the various marine creatures. Perhaps it was his living in Florida, but he was particularly fascinated by coral reefs that he had heard were analogous to rainforests with their diverse ecosystems. He also liked to think about the cycle of life as seen underwater. A few years earlier, on one of their rare family trips, Cathy, Max, and Marc had gone on vacation to the Cayman Islands. While there they went out on the Atlantis, a commercially operated battery powered forty-eight passenger sightseeing submarine with large porthole type observation windows. Marc was totally engrossed watching the changes as the sub cruised past the continental shelf to a depth of 100 feet. After the excursion the entire family agreed that the trip beneath the ocean was extraordinary. All of them had been mesmerized by the teeming life on the coral reefs as well as the variety of tropical fish swimming through the sea, chasing and evading each other for nutrition and survival.

The SeaLife Center did not disappoint. Marc enjoyed watching the sea lions, the harbor seals, and, in particular, the puffins and other seabirds that were on view at the museum. He was also impressed about the size and scope of the Center, later learning it was built as part of the settlement between Exxon and the state of Alaska after the massive 1989 oil spill in Valdez. As he was staring at a group of puffins he checked his watch and realized it was almost 5:30 PM and he had to get ready for his date.

Marc walked back to the hotel, inquired at the front desk about getting some flowers, and was directed to the Safeway supermarket, a few miles north on the Seward Highway. He got into his rental car wondering why he was going through all this effort for a date with a woman he would probably never see again. And then he was inside Safeway looking for the floral department and buying a bouquet of roses.

On his way back to the hotel he stopped at his brother's house and watched the kids playing fetch with the dogs using Frisbees and tennis balls. Once more, he observed a cheerfulness in Max that he hadn't seen in years. He said hello to Rebecca and Rachel and asked Max how the day went at the kennels. Max answered, "Awesome. I'm going to work there every day on the vacation. OK?"

"Sure. Do you want me to pick you up after I go out to dinner?"

"Nope. I'll sleep here again. Actually, if it's OK with you I want to stay here all week."

"Did you ask Aunt Blake and Uncle Norman?"

The girls chimed in that they were certain it would be fine. Then they said something that startled Max and filled him with pride, "It's OK. Anyway, we love Max and he's like our big brother."

Marc was suddenly overcome with a feeling of warmth and he went over and hugged each kid. He then drove back to the hotel to get himself ready for his first date in decades.

Twenty-Six

SEWARD, ALASKA

Monday

For Chani the day had gone very smoothly. The weather was cooperative and there were no problems with her flights. Her Cessna performed admirably and at each of her stops the kids were ready and her classes went well. She had gotten home with plenty of time to shower and dress for her date. Although she also was wondering what the point was of going out with Marc, she thought he was an interesting person and quite unlike most of the folks she had been interacting with in recent years. Dinner with him, she reasoned, would be something like an anthropological trip down that materialistic dimension of Florida that she so despised.

She also wondered how one set of parents could have such a sweetheart of a son like Norman, whose generosity and commitment to both Judaism and social justice was so profound, and another son who seemed so committed to avariciousness and appeared spiritually apathetic.

Then it was 7:00 PM and Chani heard a knock on her door. She opened it to find Marc standing there in khaki pants, dark brown leather hiking shoes, a brown knit sweater, and black ski jacket. He had a broad smile on his face and said, "Hi, I picked some flowers for you."

She took them, smelled the sweet red roses, laughed, and said, "The only place to pick these beautiful roses is Safeway. Thanks. You're a regular adventurer."

"Are you ready for dinner as advertised?"

"You bet, let me get my jacket and we're off."

Chani was wearing black jeans, and a black cable knit sweater over a blue blouse that highlighted her creamy complexion. Marc had trouble keeping his eyes off her.

Chani then said, "Marc, would you like to come in for a minute while I finish getting ready?" He walked into her small living room and saw it decorated with an array of family photos. He was standing looking at them when she walked back into the room.

"These are very nice. Are those your parents and you when you were younger?"

She laughed and answered, "That's my folks and me in Florida and the Adirondacks—well before braces."

"And is this your sister in these wedding photos? She looks like you."

"I'm an only child. That's Nathaniel, my late husband, and me."

Marc was stunned. He didn't know Chani was widowed. Neither Blake nor Norman had mentioned it.

He said, "Oh, sorry, I didn't know."

"No problem. Nathaniel was a wonderful man who died suddenly almost ten years ago. Anyway, let's go."

They left for the restaurant and drove in an awkward silence. Just as they were parking the car Marc broke the quietness, "I must say I feel a bit weird. This is my first date since Cathy died and part of me feels like I'm fifteen years old and every pimple on my face is pulsating."

Chani suddenly began roaring at that remark and her laugher became contagious. They both sat in the car almost hysterical until tears filled their eyes.

"Marc," Chani said, "that pimple comment goes down as one of the best first date lines of all time." And, then once again they both cracked up.

"Stop." Marc called out, "My sides are splitting," and a final round of laughter began. Spent by all the levity, the couple got out of the car, went into the restaurant where they were escorted to an outside table overlooking Resurrection Bay. A tall propane heat lamp ensured their comfort in the cool night air.

They looked at the menu and ordered similar meals of salads and baked halibut. While waiting for the food, Chani asked, "How are you and Max enjoying the trip so far?"

"It's not what I expected. Actually, much better."

"How so?"

"Well, to begin, Max and I had a very nice flight up here. And thanks again for that bonus flight from Anchorage to Seward. In Max's words, it was amazing. Then the experiences in your synagogue were not what I had ever encountered before in services."

She interrupted, "Does that mean better or worse?"

He smiled, "Better, dramatically better. Makes me want to join your shul! And our two hikes, the barbeques. Everything. Even the museum today and the SeaLife Center– I like it here. And now, my first date. So, in short, I'm having a great time."

"And what about your son?"

"I think he enjoys hanging out with his cousins. I saw him this afternoon and he was having a wonderful time playing with Rachel and Rebecca and he loves volunteering at the kennels. It seems that he is going to spend this vacation under Commander Price's tutelage and also staying at Norman's house. I think he's as happy as I've ever seen him. Frankly, I wouldn't be surprised if he wanted to stay longer."

"When are you going back?"

"We're leaving Friday."

Chani smiled, "Well I'm glad you came. I know it has meant a great deal to your family. Your brother is a true pillar of this community and I don't just mean the Jewish community. He is a real *tzadik*, wise man. Everyone in town consults him on almost anything from repairing their boats to legal issues. We are really blessed to have the Cohn family here."

Marc had never heard anyone speak of his brother in such terms and it filled him with joy and pride. He loved Norman and respected him but to hear such praise from someone outside his family was special. Chani smiled at Marc and said, "Now that the food is here I have another question: May I ask why you became a cosmetic surgeon?"

"Sure, but do you disapprove?"

"No, not really; I guess I'm curious. It's the therapist in me—I'm always interested in what motivates people."

"The short answer is I wanted to make a lot of money and butt lifts, breast jobs, face lifts, and liposuction are not covered by most insurances and cosmetic surgery, probably, along with dermatology, are the best specialties for making money. The deeper answer I think relates to my going to a private school in Manhattan where I always felt like a second-class citizen. Most of my classmates were so rich that their last names ended in roman numerals. So, I wanted to make money and feel like a first class citizen."

"But was it simply money?"

"I think so. But, I guess, I always liked tinkering with stuff, taking things apart and putting them back together. For example, when I was a kid I found an old camera that wasn't working and I took it apart, figured out what was wrong, and fixed it. Amazingly enough, after I reassembled the camera, it worked. My mother said I had golden hands and I probably believed her. Also, at our school they had pottery and sculpture classes and I did well in both areas and even won some prizes for my work at the school fair."

"So that makes sense—you're like a body sculptor except you work on real people."

"I suppose. I actually think of it less like sculpting and more like surgery."

"Did you ever do reconstructive work?"

"Yes. During my residency I did a lot of reconstructive work on cleft palates and hands. At one point I thought of being a hand surgeon. Also, where I trained there was a burn unit, so I did a fair amount of burn work including skin grafts. To be honest, it was extremely difficult work although quite gratifying. But when my cosmetic business started to grow, I wanted total control of my practice, so I built my own clinic in Bal Harbour and as they say the rest is history. Now I have one partner and we stay quite busy. But, what about you? How come you became a social worker and then a rabbi?"

Chani was saved from answering that question when the waiter came for the dessert order. They both agreed the weekend had provided enough sugar for a month, skipped the sweets, and ordered café lattes. Marc, not having forgotten his question, and also curious, smiled at Chani and said, "I await your story, rabbi."

Chani began, "I'm happy to share it with you. Really, no big secrets. But, first let me finish my interrogation."

They both laughed and Chani said, "In social work school we always learned about the importance of family of origin. And obviously I know your brother well, and while he certainly hasn't taken the vow of poverty, he clearly could be making much more money in private practice in Anchorage or elsewhere in the country. And he is totally into Judaism while, correct me if I'm wrong, you are not interested in Judaism and let's say you are more financially oriented than your brother. I'm just curious, no judgments. Am I correct?"

Marc stared at Chani while he thought of his answer. Instantly, he realized that such a question from someone else might be considered rather rude but from her it seemed sincere and kind. He was about to answer when Chani interrupted.

"Marc, I'm sorry. I hardly know you, and you're not my patient, and I asked you a very personal question that I have no right to ask. I'm sorry. Forgive me. That was impolite of me."

"First, you're forgiven. But I think I can answer your question. Who knows, it might even help me sort out my life without paying a shrink.

"Our parents—I mean Norman and my parents, sorry. I'm getting tongue-tied I guess."

She smiled, nodded as if to say go ahead.

Marc smiled, "Anyway, I'm embarrassed to say this because you're a rabbi but our folks were not very religious so they sent us to a secular private school."

Chani interrupted, "Excuse me, Marc. I don't want to go too far off on a tangent, but do you mean religious or observant?"

"Aren't they the same?"

"Not the way I see it. In my opinion observant is when someone follows the rules, such as the *halacha* or *kashrut*. For many observant people halacha oriented Judaism is like skiing through slalom poles, making sure you go through each gate. Some see following the rules as their ticket to a happy present life or afterlife; others do it from fear or perhaps love, that is, they take the 613 commandments, and the rabbinical interpretations of those commandments, as God's word and then incorporate the commandments into their lives. I certainly have no problem with people being observant but, in my opinion, being religious is more difficult, perhaps transcendent. In the simplest terms a person who behaves in a religious way is the utmost mensch. Can I go rabbinical on you for a minute?"

"Sure, go for it."

"One of my favorite quotes about being religious comes from the prophet Micah who said: '*What does the Lord require of you: Only to do justice, And to love goodness, And then to walk modestly with your God.*' So, for me that is the grand test of being a religious person. End of sermonette."

Marc responded, "On that basis I guess I came from a religious family. My folks really did take care of the community. I remember one Sunday being really ticked off when my parents made Norman and me clean up the totally messy basement in my dad's pharmacy. The space was used for storage of all the nondrug-related items sold in the store. It took all day and part of the evening but by the time we finished our work, which included arranging everything on the new shelving my father had bought, the basement was not only neat and clean, but three-quarters empty. Then we found out my folks' real agenda. They had decided to provide a free meeting space in the basement for various small community groups that couldn't afford any rent elsewhere. Within a month of our clean up, the basement was being used five nights a week by groups ranging from AA to a sewing circle."

"Sounds like they were amazing people and in my book I would call them religious. But let's get back to your becoming a plastic surgeon."

"Sure. So, Norman and I went to this private school on the Upper West Side. It was pretty WASP-y and lots of the kids came from ultra-wealthy families. A number of them were picked up after school in limos, a few of them had famous parents including actors, actresses, and politicians. On breaks they would come back to school and speak of vacations in the Caribbean or Europe. Anyway, none of this bothered Norman but somehow I became very jealous of their money and lifestyle. I often complained to my parents who used to say, 'Marc you're there for the education. You are not 'Richie Rich' the ultrawealthy kid from the comic books.' They would urge me to do my best and then they said that if I worked hard maybe someday I'd be able to have some of the rich boy toys.

"They also told me that toys wouldn't bring me happiness—but making a difference in a positive way would be the best route to true happiness. To be perfectly honest, I never listened to their message beyond the way to get the toys. Anyhow, somewhere along the line I decided that being a doctor was my ticket to wealth. I did well in science and obviously became a doctor. And, after thinking about specialties, I decided that cosmetic surgery was the way I could be the most independent and make the most money."

Quietly, Chani responded, "Wow, that is an honest answer! Thank you for sharing that with me. Any second thoughts ever?"

Cohn became silent before answering. For a moment he wondered why he was sharing these intimate thoughts with Chani when he had never shared them with anyone else, including his late wife. He didn't know why he wanted to be so forthcoming with Chani but he decided to offer another honest response to her question. "A few times during my plastic surgery training I had to handle a tough burn or accident victim—cases that required reconstructive surgery. That work usually made me feel quite good. After those experiences I had second thoughts about cosmetic work but those feelings always passed pretty quickly. And more recently after Cathy died, and I was back doing the cosmetic work with some pretty vain self-centered people, I started wondering about my career and frankly its value to society. Also, I worry about whether I'll be wise enough to know when it's time to quit. Recently, I read a few articles about surgeons who insisted on continuing doing procedures while both their skills and practice volume were declining. I definitely do not want to be one of those guys. Anyway, in the short-term, I doubt if I'll be making any major changes in my life. So, when this trip is over, I'll go back to Florida and probably pick-up where I left off with my cosmetic surgery. On the other hand, to be perfectly honest, Cathy's death is causing me to do some very private rethinking of my life and frankly, I really am not really certain what I am going to be doing in the future. I'll have to figure it out."

They were both quiet for a moment and then Marc asked, "All right my turn to ask the tough questions?" Chani nodded her head.

Marc said, "The other day you gave me the abridged version of what brought you here and why you became a rabbi. I'm actually interested in the unabridged version."

"Do you have till sunset?"

"When's that in Alaska this time of year, 11:30 PM?"

"That's about right."

"That's fine with me. But before you go too far, I need to ask another question. You said you grew up in Fort Lauderdale off Las Olas. Was that Rabbi Friedman's community?"

She smiled after hearing the name of her old rabbi. "Yes, it was. He was my rabbi growing up. He's a wonderful man and a fabulous rabbi. How do you know him?"

"Well, I don't know him well. Cathy knew him and I asked him to conduct her funeral. He's a very nice and kind man. In fact, a few weeks ago, Max and I had dinner at his home."

"Great! If you see him or Mrs. Friedman again, please send them my regards," she responded.

Now confused, Marc asked a follow-up question. "So you grew up in his community. Does that mean you are or used to be Orthodox?"

"Well, I grew up in the Fort Lauderdale Modern Orthodox community but I don't consider myself Orthodox anymore. I had some personal issues with Orthodoxy, so for almost a decade, I've been on a journey of exploration. And that is also why I call myself a nondenominational rabbi."

Now Marc felt even more confused so he asked, "I don't mean to pry, but from my very limited experiences with Rabbi Friedman, and the people I met at his house, the community you came from seems quite hospitable and supportive."

Chani, taking her time to formulate her response, said, "Marc, you are exactly right about the hospitality and supportiveness. All of us lived within a mile of the synagogue and in many senses it was the center of our community. We prayed there, went to lectures and classes there, and celebrated with each other *simchas,* happy times. Then in our difficult or sad times we always came together to support one another.

"Additionally, there was a great deal of socializing in the community, particularly around holidays and Shabbat meals."

Marc asked, "Sounds beautiful, so why would you leave that?"

"I am going to answer your question, but please don't interpret what I have to say as criticizing my shul in Florida or even Modern Orthodoxy in general, which frankly is perhaps one of the great success stories in contemporary Judaism.

"But, in direct answer to your question, Orthodox Judaism didn't work for me. I wanted equal treatment with men and that meant I wanted to study the same subjects they studied and have the same rights, privileges, and responsibilities they do. For example, in the synagogue, I wanted to be called up to the Torah and read the blessings, I wanted to sit in the same part of the shul where the men sat so that I could at least hear the sermons or Torah commentaries, and I wanted to pray with a tallit wrapped around me.

"In Orthodoxy, roles are clearly defined. This is for men and this is for women. For example, women weren't supposed to wear pants because the Torah says a man shouldn't look like a woman and vice versa. Or men should not listen to a woman sing, this is called *Kol Isha*. The idea is that a woman singing, such as a female cantor, would sexually arouse a man. Sorry, but I love to sing and lead services—as I think you've found out. Do you want to hear more?" Marc nodded.

"However, there are many things about my experiences at the Cambridge Community Synagogue that I would love to replicate here in our Seward community."

He asked, "Such as?"

"Probably the most important is Torah study, which we are now doing pretty successfully on Saturday morning. A second is participation and engagement in the services. As I see it, services are a stepping stone toward a life of positive behavior that focuses on making this a better world. The time to pray is the time to rally our community to be better, stronger, and kinder people. Sorry, I'm being preachy."

"No, no. Please, go on. I'm very interested in your perspective."

"A third is the sense of community you find in Orthodoxy. As I said before, people really participate in each other's joyful and sad moments in a beautiful way. And, frankly, it's not limited to events like bar mitzvahs, weddings, and such, but I want to see it happening on the various holidays and even every Shabbat. As a kid growing up in that community, the vast majority of Friday nights we either had guests at our home or we went to a fellow congregant's house for dinner. And, that level of hospitality frequently happened after services on Friday evenings and Saturday afternoons. And when tragedy strikes, such as when my father died, and almost a year later when my mom passed away, the community was amazing. For example, during the Shiva period and for months afterward, my mom was invited for meals at other congregants' homes dozens of time.

"I was in college when my father died, and I found it very comforting to know that my mom was being looked after by the community. It was a truly awesome display of community *chesed*, kindness. My personal goal is to see that type of Jewish community here in our little corner of Alaska. But, your question deserves a more nuanced answer, so now I'll share with you my other issues with Orthodoxy.

"To begin with, there is something of a 'circle the wagon' mentality that I don't like or respect. By this I mean that I have found that many folks in the Orthodox community are more interested in the letter of the Jewish law, what is called halacha, than in the spirit. So, for instance, a few years back there was a problem with an Iowa based kosher meat processor who violated all kinds of federal laws. The Orthodox, particularly the ultra-Orthodox, circled the wagons around this company—defending him. It was the Conservative movement that said one element of kosher certification should be ethical behavior. The Orthodox were either quiet on this situation or they became outspoken supporters of the meat packer—who, by the way, eventually went to prison and is scheduled to be released in 2033.

"Another significant problem I have is with the *get*; do you know what that it?" Marc indicated that he had no idea what she was talking about.

"Under strict Jewish law a woman is only divorced if her husband gives her a document that releases her from the marriage. That document is called a *get*. Periodically, vindictive husbands refuse to give the document and some rabbinical courts have sided with the man, leaving the woman what is called an *agunah* or chained women. In an absurd situation in Las Vegas, a man refused to give his wife a *get* unless she gave him custody of their son, as well as a half a million dollars. Meanwhile, the couple had a civil divorce and the guy went ahead and got married again. But, the woman feels she can't marry again for fear of being ostracized from the Orthodox community. She also worries that if she went ahead and married without the *get*, any children from the new marriage might not be fully recognized under Jewish law.

"On this issue, Modern Orthodox shuls like mine in Ft. Lauderdale have been vocal in condemning men who keep women chained to them via the *get*. Many of the Modern Orthodox rabbis have even gone so far as to require that when couples marry they have a written marriage contract essentially guaranteeing that a *get* will be given if a couple divorces.

"And then you have my pet peeve. In my opinion, too many ultra-Orthodox men just want to study Torah in yeshivas all day and be supported by the government or wives with menial jobs. Recently, I was talking to a friend in Florida and she told me about one guy we grew up with who is now thirty-four and has yet to work one day in his life. He is always studying, or as he likes to say 'learning' in yeshiva. He is now married with two kids and when my friend asked him what he intended to do in the future he answered, 'continue learning.' She asked him if he was going to teach or be a pulpit rabbi and he said, 'no,' that he wanted to learn and maybe get some part-time work supervising the *kashrut* at the occasional wedding or bar mitzvah. So who supports him? Probably his parents, his wife and some people in the community.

"The funny thing about this attitude is that most of the giants in Jewish history like Maimonides who was known as the Rambam, and Nachmanides who was called the Ramban, both had day jobs as physicians. The famous Hillel was a woodchopper. Even in contemporary times many distinguished rabbis had secular jobs early in their careers. For example, the major leader in the *kiruv* outreach movement, Rabbi Schneerson, the Lubuvitcher Rebbe, had degrees in mechanical and electrical engineering. In fact, during World War II, this extraordinary man worked at the Brooklyn Navy Yard supervising some technical aspects of the construction of liberty ships. Another giant in contemporary Judaism was Rabbi Noach Weinberg who founded Aish Hatorah. He once worked as a clothing salesman for his brother. You would think that these pillars of Judaism would be the role models for the yeshiva boys!

"This business of full-time 'learners' is also a big issue in Israel, especially because many of these guys don't serve in the Army. In fact, some of these groups don't even recognize the state of Israel. Frankly, this is antithetical to my way of thinking on two levels. First, as I already mentioned, even the great rabbis who studied Torah also had regular jobs. And, the Modern Orthodox movements and shuls such as Rabbi Friedman's really lead the way for the Orthodoxy by saying, 'study Torah and have a *parnassa*,' a way to make a living. Heard enough yet?"

"You can keep going if you want. I'm a good listener."

"You asked for it. I also got tired of the community's attitude that it had all the answers and there was only one way to do things and it was their way. For example, too many of the people I knew at the Cambridge Community Synagogue looked down on the Reform, Conservative, and Reconstructionist Jews as if they weren't real Jews. Thankfully, Rabbi Friedman would often preach against those attitudes. Unfortunately, though, many people I knew in those days felt that they were indeed the 'real deal' and everyone else was wrong. One of my friends liked to jokingly say that anyone who was more observant than him was a fanatic and anyone less observant was a heretic.

"I think my final critique is really less about Orthodoxy and more about me. I'm a liberal and I want to be part of an active Jewish community that is egalitarian and open to the lesbian and gays as well as those people who are interested in nonorthodox conversions or merely being partners of Jewish individuals. So my approach to outreach is an open door policy and a very big tent. In my seminary I found a receptiveness to new ideas and different approaches that I now try to incorporate here in Resurrection Bay. Some might call it a new age blend of tradition and change. Clearly, it's a work in progress. That's it. Enough kvetching. Let's talk about something more interesting like bowling or curling."

Marc was taken aback by the strength of her opinions and impressed by her arguments. He then said, "So what about social work school?"

She nodded, he nodded, and they both laughed. Chani then began to relate the story of her experiences at Miller, and the need to reconnect with her Jewishness through the trip to Israel where she met Nathaniel. Then she shared with Marc the joy she found as a married woman living in Boston. She also told Marc about Nathaniel's plan to help develop a

Jewish community in rural Vermont where they could have a life that included their shared love of nature and the outdoors.

As she spoke of Nathaniel's tragic death, tears welled up in her eyes, and more than anything Marc wanted to hug her but felt that would be inappropriate. So, he reached across the table and simply placed his hands on hers. She looked at him and said, "Thanks."

They were quiet after that and finally Marc said, "I'm sorry if my curiosity has stirred up sad memories but it looks to me like this place, this community, and your friends are working for you." She nodded. They finished their meal and headed back to her house. Marc stood at her front door and thanked Chani for beautiful evening. In turn, Chani thanked him, and then leaned in and kissed Marc on the cheek and said goodnight.

As Marc drove back to the hotel he realized this was the best time he had had since Cathy's death.

Twenty-Eight

Seward, Alaska

Tuesday

Marc Cohn's shift ended at 5:00 PM and he was anxious to get back to the hotel after a boring day of upper respiratory infections, urinary tract infections, asthma issues, a few complaints of low back pain, and inmates trying to con him out of any drug from an ibuprofen to oxycodone. But, an hour before he was supposed to leave, everything started to change when the nurse told him of an inmate who had just sustained an injury to his finger. The patient's name was Mario Petrillo; he was tall, lean, with jet-black shoulder length hair, a chiseled face that was decorated with long sideburns and a Fu Manchu mustache. To Marc Cohn, he looked like a sinister guy.

The inmate walked in, and in a soft voice—almost a whisper—asked if he could sit down. Cohn nodded, and then the man said rather casually, "Sorry to bother you, but I'm afraid I have a tear in the extensor tendon of my right middle finger and despite not having an x-ray my best guess is that the distal interphalangeal joint needs to be immobilized in full extension."

An astounded Cohn could only grunt out, "What?"

Petrillo replied, "I said, I tore my extensor tendon in the laundry. You know what I mean? Mallet finger, I need a splint!"

"I get it, but first let me have a look." He held Petrillo's finger and then placed it flat on the table and asked, "Any pain?"

"No."

"How about when I touch it in these different places?"

"No."

"I think your diagnosis and plan of care is correct. Obviously an x-ray would be useful to rule out something more complicated."

"I know but I doubt if they'd send me to the hospital for an x-ray for this."

"Look Mr. Petrillo, I'm a fill-in physician for Dr. Polansky and he'll be back next week. I don't think we'll do any harm in just splinting it for the time being and letting Dr. Polansky handle this up the road."

"Fine by me."

"How do you know all the medical lingo—are you an EMT or paramedic?"

"No, I'm a plastic surgeon. Or, at least I was until I was convicted and lost my license."

"Where are you from?"

Petrillo laughed, "For the last three years the D cell block, which is the minimum security section of the medium security block of a maximum security prison . . . go figure! But before that Anchorage for eighteen years; Chicago is my hometown."

Curiosity overtook Cohn, "May I ask what you're doing here?" In Cohn's mind the guy probably killed his wife or girlfriend. Why else would he be in this prison? Cleary it was not a place for white-collar criminals.

Petrillo answered, "You're obviously not from here or you would have heard of me. It was all over the news in Alaska. I came up here to get away from the rat race of the lower forty-eight and set up practice in Anchorage. I'm in prison because I was convicted of conspiracy to harbor a fugitive and obstruction of justice. Frankly, I think I had an unethical lawyer who did a terrible job. I probably would have been better off with the public defender than the schmuck private attorney I used. And, for good measure, he also drained me of my last nickel."

Cohn's interest was piqued. "And?" This started a tirade from Petrillo.

"And? I'll tell what happened. First, the reason I didn't have much money and couldn't hire anyone but the clown I used was that the government brought this case against me right after a nasty divorce where I pretty much got wiped out.

"Anyway, the history of the case is simple. I set up practice in a poor section of Anchorage and was doing a lot of pro bono work or heavily discounted stuff like fingers, burns, and even some reconstruction. To subsidize this kind of financially thankless practice I also did some cosmetic stuff—the usual, breasts and ass implants, liposuction, and noses. My patients were generally not well off and they had their own reasons for this cosmetic work. The rich folks went to one of the other plastic surgeons in town. Some even flew down to Los Angeles.

"So one day I got a call from a woman who had been my patient for years. I'd taken care of a few of her broken fingers and sewed her up a couple of times from various accidents she had working in her restaurant. She called one day and asked me to see her twenty-six year-old son who had burned his fingers working the outside barbeque at her restaurant. Honestly, I didn't even know she had a son. I agreed and then her son, whose name was Frankie Olivera, came to see me. Google him when you get home.

"Now, I am not a reader of the local Anchorage papers, and I rarely watched TV, so the name Frankie Olivera meant nothing to me.

"I looked at his hands and all his fingertips were burned. I thought that was strange but they were clearly third-degree burns that were through the dermis. Honestly, it didn't look like they were barbeque fire burns. To me they looked more like acid burns. When I tried to question him about it he insisted that the burns weren't a problem, and that he only wanted me to re-bandage his fingers and give him a tetanus shot.

"A few weeks later he walks into my office just as I'm closing and asks if I could remove a bullet wound scar on his face. He told me he had gotten it in a training accident when he was with the Alaska National Guard on deployment to Iraq. I told him it might be better if he went to the VA and he said he would rather I do it. So, I did.

"A month after that he shows up again during office hours one evening and he wants liposuction to remove fat from his abdomen. I agreed to do it but I still required him to go through preop testing. Over the next few months I did the liposuction; always as the last patient of the day. He walked into my office one evening to ask whether I could fix his nose that absolutely looked like he had lost a dozen boxing matches. I agreed to do that also. All this time he paid me in cash and never haggled about money . . . Still interested?"

Cohn answered, "Definitely, keep going. This is fascinating."

"A year goes by, I never see Frankie again and then suddenly one day a couple of Anchorage detectives and two FBI agents are at my door and they want to ask me about Olivera. I said there is not much I can say because of doctor–patient confidentiality. Then they want to know about my relationship with him. And I tell them I know his mother. And that's when the shit hit the fan. It turns out that Frankie is a big-time Anchorage drug dealer. How was I to know? And, for close to two years, he had been eluding capture traveling all over the state including Nome, Skagway, Bethel, even Juneau. And once the cops captured him they claimed that the reason they couldn't find him sooner had nothing to do with their own efforts or competency, but rather because of his changed appearance thanks to *moi*.

"So, Frankie cuts a deal to get twenty years in prison if he'll flip on those who helped him evade capture. And guess who he rolls over on? First, his mother and that gets him nothing because she is already convicted of other drug charges and doing fifteen years. Then he rolls on his mistress and then his wife. They cut nothing on his sentence for these women. Still no deal for Frankie! Finally, he rolls on me claiming that I'm the one who helped him evade capture by changing his appearance through plastic surgery. Sure, I did the surgery. But I didn't know he was a fugitive. And you know what really frosted my ass? At my trial Frankie couldn't even identify me in the court room and my lawyer did nothing with that!"

Cohn thought about this and asked, "What about your expert witness; what did he say?"

"Expert witness? My lawyer said I didn't need one. He would handle everything. So now he's got all my money and I have 777 days left in this place and after that I'll be lucky to get a job at Burger King."

"Wow, some story. I'm sorry. What happened on appeal?"

"What appeal? I'm broke. The guy won't do an appeal unless I have another fifteen grand."

"Thanks for sharing this story. I've got to get going so let's get a splint on your finger and I'll leave a note for Dr. Polansky to check next week. Remember, don't take the splint off until you see Polansky, but you already know the drill. Just do it."

Marc's drive back to the hotel took him on a scenic two-lane road that skirted Resurrection Bay on one side, and wide-open spaces on the other that abutted glacier-topped mountains. It was a peaceful drive and he had decided to turn off the radio so that he could mull over what Petrillo had told him. He wasn't a lawyer and had been warned ahead of time by the prison staff to be skeptical of anything said to him by the prisoners, but something that the inmate had said did not sit right.

In general, Marc saw himself as a right wing conservative, not as far to the right as the Tea Party, but clearly approaching many of their positions. Part of his thinking was that criminals were getting off with light sentences, and that anyone who was arrested was probably guilty.

As he was thinking about that he also recalled the time he was stopped one evening in Aventura, Florida, for a lane change violation, and the cop treated him like a serial killer. The police officer barked commands demanding his license and registration. A high-powered flashlight was shone into the passenger compartment of his Bentley. When he went to open the glove box to pull out his registration, the officer yelled at him to stop and place his hands on the steering wheel. In a gruff voice he was then asked if he had any weapons. When he replied "no," the cop then let him open the glove box and take out the registration. Marc recalled that while he was rummaging through the glove box the officer also had his hand on his gun.

Next the cop looked at the license and registration and then lit up Marc's face with the flashlight. The cop smiled and asked Cohn if he was, "Marc Cohn the plastic surgeon." When Cohn said "yes," suddenly the entire tone of the traffic stop changed. The officer returned the license and registration and proceeded to ask Cohn a dozen questions concerning a boob job for his girlfriend. He ended the encounter by saying, "Be careful. Have a good evening."

As Marc now thought about it, he, for the first time in his life, started to wonder about the fairness of the criminal justice system. Indeed, he thought, maybe his brother was onto something when he often said that as a public defender he was both defending specific individuals as well as constitutional rights. Tonight over dinner he planned to discuss Petrillo's case with Norman.

At 7:00 PM Marc was sitting at an outside table at the Seward waterfront when Blake and Norman approached and sat down.

Marc asked, "Where are the kids?"

Blake answered, "They decided to stay home, order in a pizza, and watch TV. They're all tired from the day at the kennel."

Marc was disappointed that he wasn't going to see Max that evening but he decided he would call him right after dinner. He then turned to Norman and said, "Norm, I don't want to talk business, but I met an inmate today and I'm wondering if you've dealt with him. He might even have a good case for an appeal."

"Go ahead, I'm listening."

Marc then began explaining the case as best he could to his older brother. When he finished Norman said, "Sounds interesting. I'm going to be in the prison tomorrow to interview a few of my clients and I'll make it a point to meet this guy. And, if you want, we can have lunch there."

Twenty-Nine

KENAI PRISON

Wednesday

Wednesday was proving to be more boring than Tuesday. The duty nurse easily treated the inmates who had shown up at sick call. Marc was spending the day in the medical office watching the clock, skimming through Polansky's collection of *The New England Journal of Medicine*, *The Journal of Correctional Health Care*, *The Journal of Emergency Medicine*, the *Journal of Ambulatory Care Management*, and looking forward to meeting Norman for lunch.

At 11:30 AM Norman called Marc and suggested they meet in the staff cafeteria in ten minutes. Marc told the nurse he'd be back at 1:00 PM and he left for the three-minute walk to the dining hall. Norman was waiting; they each took a tray and made their way down the serving line, found a table, sat down, and were discussing Petrillo's case when Chani came by with a tray and asked if she could join them. They stood up and invited her to sit down.

"Chani, you should know that my brother's been in town less than a week and he's already drumming up business for me." She looked at him quizzically and then Norman asked, "Do you know Petrillo from cellblock D—the guy who was a plastic surgeon?"

She nodded, "I heard he was here because he altered some drug dealer's appearance so the guy could evade the police. Something like that."

"Right. Well, anyway, he came to see Marc yesterday and shared his story. And, I think he has a good case for appeal on several matters, most significantly inadequate representation. I'm going to look into the case transcript tomorrow and I might have a solid appeal of his conviction."

The conversation then turned to Marc's experiences at the prison that he summarized in one word: tedious. He then went on to say that he wondered how Paul managed to do the job day in and day out. Chani explained that Polansky's work was far more than sick call. It involved every aspect of health and safety at the prison including some psychological counseling and occasional minor surgery. Additionally, she noted that many of the staff guards require initial and periodic update training in first aid and Paul was the lead trainer, while she functioned as the assistant lead trainer. Marc was surprised by this last remark and asked how she came to be involved in training for first aid.

"The rabbi you see before you is also an EMT and an active member of the Seward Fire Rescue Department. Seward is a small town and our department has a handful of full-time staff so we are basically a volunteer operation. In this town we all watch each other's back."

Chani went on to explain that she had been an EMT since her student days at Amherst College where the local fire rescue squad had Engine 3—a student manned brigade comprised of undergraduates from Amherst College, The University of Massachusetts, and Hampshire College. Marc sat and listened in silence as he thought this woman he was sitting next to was truly impressive.

Just as they were finishing lunch Norman received a text message from Blake asking him about dinner. He replied that he'd call her as soon as he got back to his office and that he was at the prison finishing up lunch with Marc and Chani. She instantly replied: "OHHHHHH. Ask them both for dinner!!!!!!! LOL B."

Norm looked at the two of them amicably chatting and said, "Excuse me folks. But, if you don't have other plans Blake and I would love to have you both join us for dinner."

Marc said, "Count me in."

Chani replied, "Me, too."

Norman excused himself and left for his Seward office. Chani and Marc picked up the trays, dumped their garbage, and left their dishes on the conveyor as they walked out of the dining hall; Chani heading to the chaplain's office to prepare for the 2:30 Bible class and Marc walking back to the infirmary for hours more of reading.

At 3:30 PM, the nurse left. She had arranged with the deputy super-intendent to depart early on Wednesday so that she could catch a flight to Anchorage to visit her mother who had recently been hospitalized. The plan was for her to return that evening and work on Thursday along with the locum physician who had agreed to provide coverage for the remainder of the week.

It was almost 4:15 PM and Marc Cohn, MD, was getting restless. He looked out of the barred window to see that the parking lots were less crowded than when he had arrived that morning because of the shift change—the more numerous day staff reduced to a smaller staff com-plement for the evening and overnight shifts. He expected a quiet forty-five minutes and then it would be time to head to the hotel, change clothes, and perhaps walk to Norman's house. The job at the infirmary had resulted in as monotonous a day as he had experienced in years. As part of his orientation he had been told to limit his dispensing of virtu-ally everything from Band-Aids to over-the-counter medications. Word had spread quickly through the prison that seeing the "temp doc" was going to be a waste of time.

About the only two aspects of the day that were interesting were his lunch with Chani and Norman, as well as a guard who came to see him concerning a finger that had become infected as a result of a dirty fishing hook. The finger was swollen and it had progressed to the point where it could be lanced. Marc drained the pus-filled finger and gave the guard a week's worth of antibiotics. He also assured the guard that he would survive. As Cohn watched the wall clock he remembered thinking, *just thirty more minutes and I can leave.* Charlie, the infirmary guard, was sitting outside the office/exam door reading a paperback crime novel. Cohn later recalled wondering at that moment whether such reading counted toward the guard's continuing education requirements. That's when all hell broke loose.

At exactly 4:35, sirens and alarm bells began ringing. Cohn's adrenaline started pumping. He assumed it was a prison break. Outside the door he heard Charlie's two-way radio come to life and then he suddenly heard over loud speakers repeatedly, "Signal 25 in the laundry. Code three. Signal 25 in the laundry. Code three." Charlie opened the door and yelled, "Doc, we have a fire in the laundry and it needs to be evacuated. Standby."

Guards materialized from every corner of the prison as inmates were rushed back to their cells for a lockdown. Less than a minute later another message blared over the loud speaker: "All emergency personnel report to the laundry. Fire in progress."

Simultaneously, the alarm went out across Resurrection Bay to the Seward Fire Department that sent out the message to its volunteer firefighters and EMTs.

Seventeen inmates and one civilian manager were inside the laundry when a gas-fired large capacity dryer malfunctioned, overheated, caught fire, and ignited the lint and nearby linen. Thick white smoke enveloped much of the laundry within seconds. Fortunately, the automatic alarm system as well as the sprinkler system activated and started dousing the facility.

As soon as the fire began, four inmate laundry workers, responding instinctively, rushed to the dryer in order to aid two fellow inmates who had been unloading the machine when it burst into flames. Seconds later six inmates were severely burned on the hands and face. At the same time as the fire and smoke were visible the civilian manager, an overweight man in his sixties, ran into his office, unlocked the protective case where the fire extinguishers were kept, and started carrying them into the laundry room with the intent of using them to suppress the fire. As he exited his office he suddenly let go of the extinguishers and fell on his face.

Maintaining security at the laundry was the responsibility of one of the prison guards. When the guard heard the code notification he immediately opened the laundry's locked door and ordered the inmates out of the building and told them to lie down on the grass outside and away from the burning structure. Most of the inmates staggered out of the building puking and gagging with tears in their eyes. One inmate, a man about 50 years old, was, with the help of a second inmate, carrying the laundry manager out of the building. As soon as he was clear of the laundry the older inmate began CPR on the manager, alternately providing mouth-to-mouth resuscitation and chest compressions.

At the infirmary Charlie raced back into the exam space, opened the locked emergency cabinet, and grabbed the two large emergency backpacks. He handled one to Cohn, took the other bag, and yelled, "Let's roll."

Cohn followed the guard, jogging the 200 yards down the road toward the laundry. By the time they got there, he saw a familiar looking car with red and blue pulsating strobe lights on its dashboard still flashing. He also saw the back of the person wearing yellow protective gear and a respirator racing into the laundry. As he approached the mass of people lying on the ground he wondered how that Seward-based fire-rescue EMT had gotten there so quickly. Then he remembered that most of the staff lived in Seward and some were probably part of the volunteer fire and rescue squad

Cohn immediately went over to the inmate who was providing CPR and saw that it was Petrillo. He handed him an oxygen canister from his emergency bag and just tapped him on the shoulder and gave him a thumbs up. He then went to look at the burn victims and realized that they all needed immediate help. Marc called over to Charlie and asked him to go back to the infirmary and bring all the IV bags and kits he could find as well as all the Ambo resuscitation bags he could locate. Finally, he asked Charlie to see if they could bring as many large containers of water they could find so they could wash down the fire victims.

He was kneeling looking at one of the burn victims when the EMT emerged from the building and called out, "All clear," and headed toward Cohn, pulled off the respirator mask, and said, "OK Doc, what do we do about these burn victims?" He started to answer, never looking at the EMT, and then turned looked over his shoulder and suddenly realized that the EMT was Chani.

"What are you doing here?"

"I told you before. I'm a fire-rescue EMT, been one for ten years, and always carry my gear. You never know. So what do you want me to do? You're in charge."

Suddenly, and for the first time in years, Dr. Marc Cohn felt like a real, indeed, an important physician. Working the front lines.

"Chani, get one of the guards to watch the laundry manager, get Petrillo over here, and let's start evaluating and triaging the inmates. Some of them look like they have bad burns."

A moment later Chani and Petrillo were standing in front of Cohn when he said, "Guys, this is a mess. I'm certain we have some serious burns and a few of these people no doubt have inhalation injuries. Let's start by cutting away any clothes that might be covering the burns and as soon as the water arrives we'll start cleaning. Also, with the worst cases, make sure to do a quick check of mouths and throats and see if anyone needs intubation. This can always be a problem with smoke inhalation. As soon as Charlie gets back with the IV kits cases we'll start them on the worst cases as well as the laundry manager. Chani, can the hospital handle these cases?"

"Most, but a few may need to be moved to Anchorage."

"Let's get started. Minutes count."

Just then two prison trucks arrived with seven guards, linens, blankets, and water. The prison disaster plan was working smoothly.

Nine minutes later the ambulances and trucks of the Seward Fire Department arrived on the scene. The firefighters got busy putting out the blaze while the teams of EMTs worked with Marc, Petrillo, and their colleague Rabbi Kahn to stabilize the inmates and decide who could stay in the prison's medical support unit and who was to be transported to the hospital's emergency room.

An hour later the entire area was secured with yellow tape. The fire was out, six inmates were in the local emergency room, two were at the hospital awaiting transport to Anchorage, the laundry manager was doing fine but being observed in the hospital's ICU, five of the inmates were in the medical support unit, and Petrillo was escorted to the superintendent's office where he was sitting in the waiting area under a guard's watchful eye.

Marc and Chani were exhausted and inside the superintendent's office debriefing him about the incident. When the questioning was completed the superintendent stood up and said, "Dr. Cohn, Rabbi Kahn, your actions today saved lives and averted a disaster. You're a great team and we owe both of you a huge debt of gratitude. If I can ever help you, please let me know."

They shook hands all around and as they were leaving Marc stopped, turned around, and said, "Just one thing. We don't deserve all that much credit. We had help. Two people in particular were really important. First, Charlie, I don't know his last name, the infirmary guard. He swung me into action and raced for the supplies we needed. The second is the inmate Petrillo. I think he's sitting outside your door. You probably know he is—or was—a plastic surgeon. He's the guy who saved the manager's life, not me. And, he probably saved other people when the three of us triaged the patients. He's a good guy. Give him a break if you can."

As they walked out the building, hot, dirty, and sweaty, Chani said to Marc, "Come closer." He did and she placed a big kiss on his dirty face then said, "Marc, some people may think you're a prick, but I know better, you're a mensch. I'm proud to know you."

They got into their cars and left the prison. As Marc was driving back to the hotel he felt proud of himself for the work he had just done during the accident. *Perhaps,* he was beginning to realize, *doing good can also make you feel good.*

Without planning it, an hour later, they both arrived at Norman's house at the same time. They smiled at each other and Chani said, "You clean up nicely."

"You, too." They laughed and headed up the steps toward the front door. They knocked and when the door opened Blake, Norman, Rebecca, Rachel, Max, Cookie, and Cracker were all in the foyer and Max was holding a sign that read, "Welcome, Our Heroes." They then started applauding and kissing all around. Even Max got into it with a big hugs for both his father and Chani.

Norman announced, "In your honor we have pizza, soda, beer, and an ice cream cake for dessert. Let's go."

By 9 o'clock both Chani and Marc announced they were exhausted and needed to get some rest. Norman asked them both about their plans for Thursday. Marc replied that he hoped to sleep late in the morning, go shopping for gifts for his office staff, and then workout before joining everyone for a last dinner prior to Max and he leaving for Florida. Chani responded that Thursday was her day to get ready for services on Friday night and Saturday.

Blake, an incurable romantic, was disappointed to hear the recitation of the plans. Despite the fact that she had some misgivings about Marc, she had hoped that the week might be the beginning of a relationship for her best friend Chani, who she thought was ready to have a man in her life.

As Chani and Marc walked down the steps Blake was sad as she anticipated the loss of Max, Marc, and perhaps the romance of Chani and Marc. In the few days that Max had stayed at their house both Norman and she had become enormously fond of their nephew. Also, the twins and even the dogs seemed to love Max. She knew it would be hard on all of them when Max and Marc left.

Marc and Chani said good night to each other without a hug or kiss and headed to their cars. Marc regretted not saying anything more intimate than good night and at some visceral level Chani was already missing this plastic surgeon who had materialized from out of the blue. Just as Marc was closing the car door he heard a call, "Hey, Marc, I have a question."

Chani walked over to the side window of Marc's car and said, "How about hanging out tomorrow? I'm free till four."

A broad smile crossed his face and he enthusiastically said, "Absolutely!"

"I'll meet you at your hotel at 9:15, we'll walk over to the boat harbor and catch the 10 o'clock tour boat to the fjords. I think the trip lasts four or five hours or so and we might be able to do a little hiking on Fox Island and maybe get something to eat there."

"It's a plan." Then Marc got out of the car stood next to Chani, wrapped his arms around her, and drew her into a tender hug that she responded to by melding herself into his strong body. He then pulled back from her ever so slightly, looked into her eyes, and said, "You are a truly beautiful and amazing woman."

Moving toward her Marc gently cradled her face between his hands and their eyes slowly closed as, in a soft tender kiss, their lips touched. Their kisses continued each time growing in intensity as Marc and Chani tightly embraced one another. A few minutes passed and then their faces parted slightly as they gazed in each other's eyes and once again they came together for a long and tender hug.

Witnessing all of this from behind a window shutter that she had been in the process of closing was Blake Cohn. Her breath was taken away by the beauty and tenderness she had just observed. *Maybe I was wrong,* she thought.

Thirty

Seward, Alaska

Thursday

At 9:15 AM Marc was standing outside the front door of the hotel carrying a backpack and holding two cups of coffee. When Chani walked up, he offered her a cup, "Two sugars and light, if I remembered correctly."

"Yes, thanks. And for you, one kiss for your kindness," which she planted on his lips. "What's in the backpack?"

"Did you see the morning paper?"

"No. Why?"

"In my backpack I have my camera, a small tripod, some extra batteries and storage chips, two bagels with cream cheese, and two bottles of water in case we're shipwrecked. Plus, I have a big surprise that I'll show you on the boat."

They walked briskly along the waterfront to the boat tour kiosk where Marc purchased two tickets for the 10 o'clock trip. They boarded the boat, went to the upper deck, and sat there snuggling close in the cool morning air with the light northerly breeze.

"Marc, am I nuts or something? I get the feeling that people are staring at us."

He started laughing and then said, "Aha, and that's the surprise." He then opened the backpack and took out two copies of the *Seward Daily*

Gazette. And there, on the front page was a story that was headlined: ***VISITING MD AND LOCAL RABBI SAVE 17 LIVES AT PRISON.***

Chani read the story, put the paper down, kissed Marc, and started laughing. "They think we're heroes. We were just doing our job. I'm glad they mentioned Charlie and Petrillo. They were so important to the work. Anyway, now you know that in a small town everyone knows your business—for better or worse."

A few minutes later a foghorn blasted and the catamaran started slowly moving away from the dock. Over the loudspeaker the tour guide made a series of safety announcements and then outlined the trip which would be an hour and half cruise through Resurrection Bay with a close up look at the Kenai Fjords followed by an hour and half stop on Fox Island where a salmon buffet would be provided and time would be available for short hikes. The final part of the trip was a ninety-minute cruise back to the dock. The announcer then introduced a National Park Service ranger who was the naturalist on the trip and would point out the sites along the way that might likely include puffins, whales, and sea otters.

All of these words were meaningless to Chani and Marc who were wrapped up in their own thoughts and world. Marc was lost in the warmth of being so close to someone who he felt was an extraordinary and somewhat mysterious woman. Chani was also enjoying the physical closeness of Marc but wondering what kind of person he truly was. She thought that there was so much more to learn and she wondered how that was even going to be possible.

As the catamaran headed into the fjords the naturalist started pointing out the sea otters in the Bay along with the harbor seals that were sunning themselves on the coastal rocks. Then suddenly he pointed out the fin of a humpback of the starboard bow. Marc jumped up, moved toward the rail, and readied himself to get a shot of the giant whale. Right on time the whale breached, elevating almost three-quarters of its body out of the water, and then it was back in the Bay with a final slap of its tail. Marc was thrilled to have taken the shot and immediately looked into his camera's digital displays to be certain he had caught the breach.

He then turned the camera toward Chani and shot a dozen pictures of her. She looked at him and asked about his interest in photography.

"I love photography. I've been a photographer since my parents gave me a 35-millimeter camera when I was ten. I even was the photo editor of my high school yearbook. When I was in residency we had a small apartment with a bath and a half. Cathy almost killed me when I turned the half bath into a dark room. Thank God we don't need those dark rooms anymore. Over the last few years I haven't done much photography but when we decided to visit Alaska I thought it might be fun to try to get some good nature shots. Who knows, maybe I'll start to redecorate my office with Alaska pictures?"

Chani thought, *this guy gets more interesting by the minute.*

They kept cruising for another hour and then pulled up to the dock on Fox Island. The passengers were briefed about the buffet, the island, the gift shop, and the departure time that would be preceded by a ten-minute warning blast from the boat's foghorn.

Chani and Marc walked through the long food line picking up the salmon, corn, and other vegetables as well as a roll and some hot tea. They carried their trays over to a picnic table near the water's edge.

Marc said, "Thanks for suggesting this. It's just great. I am totally and completely enjoying my time here—in large measure due to you. Want to move to Florida?"

Chani laughed. "No. I've already done my time in South Florida and been paroled to Alaska. I just love it up here and I truly feel that this community is my home."

Just then the boat's captain, the park ranger naturalist, and the head tour guide walked over to the table and the ranger said, "Sorry for interrupting, but are you Rabbi Kahn and Dr. Cohn?"

Marc answered, "Yes, we are. Is there a problem?"

Speaking for the group the captain said, "Problem? Hell no, we just wanted to say thanks for your work yesterday and refund your ticket price. You two are our guests today and forever, for that matter. What you did was truly heroic and we are very appreciative."

Then the ranger added, "By the way, the laundry manager is doing well and he's my brother-in-law, so I'm doubly appreciative."

Once again, Marc refused to take the credit, "Thanks so much, but your brother-in-law really owes the thanks to an inmate, Dr. Mario Petrillo. But, thanks so much for your kindness."

By the time Chani and Marc finished their leisurely lunch there was little time left for a hike. They decided to stroll back to the boat and enjoy sitting next to each other while looking out at the Bay from the upper deck.

The boat returned to the dock in Seward at 2:30 and Marc and Chani walked back to the hotel where her car was parked.

"Do you want to split my last bottle of Alaskan summer ale before you leave?"

She smiled and nodded. They went up to Marc's room, he got out two clean glasses, poured the beer, and they went outside to sit on the balcony overlooking the harbor.

Marc looked at Chani and asked, "Do you have time for some serious conversation?"

"I think so."

"I sort of asked you this before, but I feel like you didn't give me a total answer, so I'm going to try again. Chani, you are a smart, kind, beautiful, funny, super educated, and talented woman, why are you up here in the middle of nowhere? What are you running away from?"

Chani pondered the question for a minute, her face slackened and drained of some color as tears formed around her eyes and she choked out a response, "You're very perceptive. I am running away from some very painful memories and experiences. But right now is not the time or place to talk about them. All I can say is that I'm trying to deal with them and Seward, as well as Alaska, is an extraordinary venue for my healing. You know what I'd really appreciate now is, if we went inside, and just hugged for a while. Can we do that?"

And that is exactly what happened. They went inside, got on top of the bed and just hugged without even kissing. At 4 o'clock Chani said she had to leave to meet her bar and bat mitzvah class. She got up and thanked Marc for a wonderful time and said that she hoped to see him sooner than later. They hugged and kissed for a minute and then Marc walked Chani to her car and shared one final embrace. She got into her SUV and drove home. Marc went back to his room and cried.

⸙

By the time Marc arrived at his brother's home everyone was there. Norman and Blake were busy in the kitchen, and Max and the twins were out back playing with the dogs. As soon as Marc arrived Norman asked if he and Blake could sit down in the family room and have a little talk with him. *Something's wrong,* Marc thought. *What has Max done?*

Norman began, "Marc, let me be frank, I wasn't sure how this week was going to turn out, but Blake and I have thoroughly enjoyed having you and Max around. The girls adore Max and so do we. So, here goes. Max is a bit afraid of you, and certainly doesn't want to hurt you, but he wants to spend the summer up here rather than going to camp. And if you're comfortable with that we can guarantee that he'll be busy, probably volunteering at the kennels and hanging out with us. We would love to have him, and we will take good care of him. And in August we'll take him to Anchorage and put him on the nonstop back to Ft. Lauderdale. Or, if you're ready for another break, you can come up here, stay with us, and take another vacation. What do you say?"

"Wow. I'm speechless. Let me talk to Max. If he really wants to do this, and you guys are sure about this, I'm OK also. It'll be good for him."

Marc and Max spoke privately, and when Marc gave his approval Max threw his arms around his father, gave him a hug, and said, "Thanks." Max ran out to tell Rachel and Rebecca who responded with cheers and hugs as the dogs jumped around and barked. The plan was settled. Max would stay. Marc was being picked up by a car service at 2:30 AM the next morning for the ride to Anchorage where he would take the a 7:00 AM flight to Seattle then on to Atlanta and home to Ft. Lauderdale—not getting home until 2:00 AM Saturday.

Part Four
Changing Winds

Thirty-One

Bal Harbour, Florida

When it came to surgery, Marc Cohn was a perfectionist. During his residency he witnessed what happened when a surgeon had the dual demons of arrogance and a superman complex—specifically, an incident involving a surgeon who had just flown in on an overnight flight from Tokyo and scheduled a 7:00 AM procedure. Not recognizing the lack of control he had over the circadian rhythms of his body, the doctor started making bad choices during the initial phases of the surgery.

As the operation progressed, the anesthesiologist attempted to slow things down by asking questions to which the surgeon growled answers. Finally, the chief resident intervened and demanded that the doctor stop immediately. At that point the surgeon started screaming at everyone, threw a handful of sterile instruments on the floor, and stormed out of the operating room. Fortunately, the patient was still under anesthesia and unaware of what was happening. The chief resident went on to successfully complete the surgery. The surgeon was disciplined and a hospital policy established to prevent such incidents in the future.

Cohn had been a second year resident in the operating room when this had occurred and the experience had a profound impact on him.

Although he and his partner only operated within the space of their own facility, and functioned without the oversight of a hospital's medical staff or administration, they had agreed on a policy that neither of them would operate during the first seventy-two hours after any trip that took them three or more time zones away from the East Coast.

In accord with the Institute's policy, Cohn's first week back was planned to be very light—his schedule included only initial consultations and evaluations. Traditionally, these appointments served to sell prospective patients on the value of the Institute's services. A typical dialog often ended with, "Yes, we're expensive, but I can assure you that we provide outstanding care." That was usually the deciding pitch and at that point almost all of the prospective patients asked to be scheduled for surgery.

When Cohn arrived in the office on Monday morning, he learned that he did not have any appointments scheduled on Wednesday or Thursday afternoon. He decided to keep those days free for meetings he needed to arrange. During a break on Monday, Marc made two critical phone calls. First, he scheduled a telephone conference on Wednesday at 2:00 PM, and then he arranged a different meeting near Las Olas Boulevard at 2:00 PM Thursday.

All day Monday and Tuesday and again on Wednesday morning he met with potential patients. He wasn't sure why, but he was starting to get annoyed with many of the people he saw in those first few days. As he thought about it, he recognized that none of these individuals had done anything wrong and their desire to change their appearance wasn't a crime. In fact, he recognized that people have every right to look younger, appear more glamorous, or try to be sexier. This was their business not his. If a woman wanted to go from an A cup to a C cup, was that his concern? *After all*, he reasoned, *it's not my life.*

But, after years of doing cosmetic surgery, Cohn was suddenly tired. Several times on Tuesday of that first week back he tried to discourage different patients from undertaking the expense and pain of breast augmentation surgery. He even remembered saying to one woman, "Your breasts are fine, why mess with God's gift?" After that interaction he went back to his office, closed the door, and said out loud, "What? Am I losing my mind?"

That Tuesday evening, as soon as Cohn got home, he went into his study and turned on the computer. He started logging into his various financial portfolios—his IRAs with several insurance companies, his stock holdings with Wells Fargo, and finally his broad and deep range of mutual funds with Vanguard—and totaled up his net worth: $5.9 million in his IRA, $6.5 million in various stocks, and $12.3 million in mutual funds. He also knew that the proceeds from Cathy's $2 million dollar life insurance policy had gone directly into a trust for Max and that if he sold both his condos he could probably get another $4.5 million. The Institute building and equipment, his boat, and car he thought would bring in another $4 million. As he thought about all of this, his decision to talk the next day with Andy Cagnetta made even more sense than ever.

He had met Cagnetta several years earlier when a prominent Miami Beach cosmetic surgeon decided to move to Philadelphia and offered to sell his practice to Cohn. Marc, acting on the advice of his stockbroker, contacted Cagnetta, the president of Transworld Business Advisors in Fort Lauderdale. The plan was to hire Andy and his company to do a valuation of the practice that was for sale. In the course of their first telephone conversation Cohn remembered that there was once a rock and roll guitarist with the same last name and asked if he was a relation. Andy answered that he was that guitar player and that he left the field because of the travel demands, financial insecurity, and his desire to have a more normal family life. A bond had been established.

After that first conversation Andy examined the proposal, undertook an evaluation, and concluded that the asking price was dramatically out of line and recommended that Marc take a pass. Cagnetta also refused to accept any money for the evaluation. Instead, he surprised Marc by asking him to make a donation to a program that feeds the homeless in Broward County, a charity that Andy was passionate about. That year Cohn donated $250, an amount that he thought was fair in light of the time he believed Cagnetta put into the evaluation.

Thereafter, every year Andy would call Marc and ask for another donation for a program known as Andy's Family Pasta Dinner. Cohn learned that Cagnetta organized and sponsored (along with many others) a pasta night as a fundraiser for the local homeless. And, like clockwork, Cohn, in his uncharitable way, would give twenty-five dollars per year. The following afternoon Cohn and Cagnetta connected by phone.

"Andy, this is Marc Cohn. How are you?"

"Marc, how are you and your son doing? I was so sorry to hear about your wife."

"Yeah, it was awful."

"I can't imagine. Also, thanks again for the donation to the homeless feeding program in Cathy's honor. I'm certain she would have appreciated that. So, what's up?"

"Two things, first I know it's June and I usually don't hear from you till Thanksgiving or so, but I thought that this year I'd just jump the gun and tell you I'm not giving my usual twenty-five dollars."

"Oh, Okay."

"How about $2,500 instead? Will that help?"

"Is this really Marc Cohn?"

"Yes." And they both laughed.

"Thanks so much. It really will help. And, please this year do me a big favor and come to the dinner. Bring your son, bring anyone you want."

"I'll try. Ready for number two? I'm thinking of selling my practice. What do you figure it's worth?"

"Look Marc, I don't have to do a big study to answer that. What's your net each year, say for the past five years?"

"Around a million or so, take or give a couple of hundred thousand."

"Is that for just you, or for you and your partner?"

"That's just me."

"Wow, I should have listened to my mother and become a surgeon!"

They both laughed and then Andy continued, "I would estimate your side of the practice, exclusive of the real estate and equipment, is worth somewhere in the range of $2.5 to $3 million. The real estate and equipment will need to be appraised, but a ballpark figure is that it's worth about $4 million. Overall a deal could go in the $7 million range. In these situations, the buyer typically gets a ten-year bank loan to pay for the practice or alternatively you could finance it and that's usually a five-year payout. From your perspective, the decision of what's best is simply based on tax consequences and your needs. More importantly, may I ask why are you considering this?"

"Between you and me, I'm not sure. I think I'm burned out by cosmetic surgery. I have plenty of money and maybe, just maybe, I'm in love with a woman from a small town in Alaska."

"What does she do up there?

"Believe it or not, she's a rabbi. How about if I call you when I figure this thing out?"

"It's a deal. But remember if you are serious about selling you can't slack off on the practice now. A buyer will want to see that it is consistently a busy practice. Also, I would offer it to your partner first—he might be the best person to buy the total package of the building, equipment, and the practice. Let me know what you want to do."

Thirty-Two

On Thursday promptly at 2:00 o'clock, Marc Cohn walked into the office of Rabbi Yitzchak Friedman. The rabbi stood up and greeted him with a hug and a kiss on the cheek.

"So, how was Alaska? Cold? Did Max have a good time?"

"Rabbi, Max is fine. He had a great time and decided to spend the summer in Seward living with my brother and his family and working in a sled dog kennel owned by a Jewish guy."

"Is it Jake Berkowitz's kennel?"

"No. It's a guy name Mike Pearl. Who's Jake Berkowitz?"

"A Jewish guy from Minneapolis who moved to Alaska and raced in several Iditarods. I read about him in some Jewish newspaper. Sounds like a nice guy. Anyway, how are you doing?"

"Rabbi, I have a problem. I want to be more Jewish."

"What? Marc, you're either Jewish or not Jewish. Fortunately your mother was Jewish, your grandmother was Jewish, and so forth so that makes you Jewish. In the Orthodox and Conservative movements we only recognize matrilineal descent, so poof, you're Jewish. In the Reform movement, they added patrilineal descent.

"Let me make an analogy. My two children were born here in the United States. They are citizens by birth. That's it. They get to vote, become president, and so forth. Leah and I are naturalized citizens. We had to fill out a twenty-one page application form that asked everything from soup to nuts including where we had volunteered from the time we were 15 years old. Then we had to take an exam. Point being, we make it easy for those born to a Jewish mother. On the other hand, an Orthodox conversion is like a citizenship process that we usually make difficult and time consuming. Sometimes I think we actively try to keep people out who want to get in. We then also go on to spend a huge amount of energy trying to get people in who want to stay out. Go figure! So you're already in, now where do you want to go, and why?"

"Where I don't know. Other than I feel totally dumb about Judaism. Why, I'm not sure, but I may be in love and the woman is heavy into Judaism."

"Seriously?"

"Seriously! In fact, she's a rabbi."

"Then she's certainly not Orthodox."

"That's correct, but she grew up Orthodox; in fact, I think right here."

"What's her name?

"Chani Kahn. She's widowed. I think Kahn is her married name."

"Her name was Weissfogel. She was one of my congregants and she is an outstanding person. If fact, I remember meeting her on my first day here in Florida. I knew her parents very well and I officiated at their funerals. Tragic, very tragic. Anyhow, now I understand. So, would you like to learn with me? It would be an honor to be your teacher, and *beez-rat Hashem*, perhaps there will be a *shidach* between you two."

"So, how do I start?"

"Here is what I suggest. Let's meet every two weeks for a few hours and we'll discuss various readings I provide you as well as any questions you might have. We'll do it like an Oxford University tutorial. Will that work for you?"

Marc Cohn, although not certain as to what he was getting himself into, nodded his head and asked, "When and how much is tuition?"

Rabbi Friedman laughed and said, "For you I'm providing a full scholarship, but I'd like fifteen pounds of liposuction and maybe a butt lift," then he started roaring with laughter and almost fell off the chair at his own joke. "Seriously, no tuition but a commitment to do this up to Rosh Hashanah which this year is the middle of September. Every two weeks, three hours. Does Thursday afternoon, say from two to five, work?"

"Absolutely. I'm all in."

"Wait a second. There's another part to the deal. I want you to have a *chavrusa,* a study buddy, to learn some Torah with. The man I have in mind is Reb Avrum Dov-Baer, and like you he is a physician, retired though, and a widower. I met Reb Avrum about five years ago shortly after his wife passed away."

"Excuse me, but is he a rabbi?"

"No, I call him Reb as an honorary title just because he is learned and loves to study Torah. He was an interventional cardiologist in Miami Beach and after his wife died he moved near you to a condo in Surfside. Anyway, he had a solid background in Judaism from the Prozdor program in Boston during his teen years, but more recently he has made studying and learning Torah his greatest priority next to fishing. I think he has a house in the Keys. Anyway, I want you two to meet and start reading the Torah together. Your questions will be challenging for him and his insights will be helpful for you. By the way, he recently finished a master's degree in Jewish education, primarily online, from Hebrew College in Boston, and last I talked with him he was going to try to find a place to get ordination as a rabbi. I should also mention that, unlike me, he isn't Orthodox. He's kind of eclectic. He prays everywhere from Chabad shuls to Reform temples and everything in between."

"Sounds good. I really appreciate your willingness to help me."

"Let's start. Here is your first assignment." Friedman got up, found a tattered paperback copy of *This Is My God* and handed it to Cohn. "This book by Herman Wouk, the Pulitzer Prize author of the *Caine Mutiny,* is an excellent introduction to Judaism. Also, this particular slightly worn paperback has an interesting history. Look inside the front cover and read the beautiful inscription." Cohn opened the book and read, *To My Good Friends Mary and George who forced me to get them this book by their continuing probing questions on a subject about which I should know more—but don't. With hope that in the future you will use this book as a reference and thus avoid embarrassing me by my show of ignorance. Ron Klein*

The rabbi explained, "Ron Klein was a West Point graduate, the son of a founder of our congregation. Unfortunately Ron was killed in Vietnam in 1966. His parents were wonderful people and several years ago they received this book in the mail from George O'Connor who was Ron's first battalion commander and a friend. George was cleaning out his house in preparation for a move to an assisted living center. He found the book on a shelf, tracked down the Kleins, and sent the book to them with a note of appreciation about their son. I later learned that Ron Klein was a true American hero who was awarded the Silver Star for his actions during the Battle of LaDrang Valley. When the Kleins moved up to Boca they gave me this book and asked me to pass it on to a special person who might benefit from its wisdom. Marc, you are that special person."

Hearing this story, Marc Cohn held back tears. He stood and hugged the rabbi and left with a plan to read the book and see the rabbi in two weeks.

By five o'clock he was back in his condo reading the book and making notes. The four-hour time difference between Seward and Bal Harbour meant he would have to wait hours before calling Max as well as Chani.

Finally, at 10:00 PM he called Max who picked up on the first ring and began speaking with an enthusiasm that Marc never had heard before.

"Hi, Dad. Guess what happened today? Commander Mike let me take a dog sled out on my own. I was able to pick the dogs, tie them to the gang-line, and run them for several miles. All by myself. It was awesome!"

Marc was astonished by this, "Wow, that's great. How fast did you go?"

"Not too fast, maybe eight or ten miles an hour? But the dogs listened to my commands and everything. The commander said I'm a natural musher. He even said that if I work at this for a few weeks he might even let me take some tourists out."

"That's great, Max; I'm proud of you." Marc thought to himself that this was the first time in years he had said those words of praise to Max. He realized he needed to do that more often. Just then he heard a lot of laughing and background noise.

"Dad, Uncle Norman just came in and he wants to talk with you. Bye."

Norman came on the line. "Hi, Marc how are you doing? Are you back in the groove of making Miami the center of the universe for beautiful women?"

"To tell you the truth, I'm getting a little sick and tired of these vain women and now my practice is starting to fill up with vain men. I think Viagra has solved one set of problems and a lot of these guys are looking for the quick fix for their flab and wrinkles. How is Max doing?"

"Great. We love having him with us and he's having a fabulous time at the kennels. He may be a natural for the Iditarod races. Look Marc, I wanted to thank you for putting me in touch with Dr. Petrillo. After reviewing his case file I thought he had a good shot at getting a new trial because of the poor quality, truly inadequate defense that his so-called lawyer presented. But that is not really the good news. Petrillo's role in the fire wound up putting his case squarely on the desk of the governor who just announced this afternoon that Petrillo's sentence has been commuted. Tomorrow morning I'm going to the prison to take care of all the paperwork and escort him out the front gate where his children will be waiting for him. Marc, I'm proud of you. Your advocacy for Petrillo is giving this man back his life. Marc, you did a great mitzvah! Mazel tov!"

While Marc was thrilled to learn of Petrillo's impending release it was his brother's words of praise that were emotionally overwhelming.

Marc choked back tears as he thanked Norman for his own contribution to freeing Petrillo. At that moment he once again came to the realization how important his own earlier words of praise were to his son.

The conversation lasted for another few minutes and then Marc signed off and told his brother that he'd call again in a few days.

The next call was to Rabbi Chani Kahn. She picked up the phone, "Hello, this is Rabbi Kahn."

"My, that's rather formal."

"Oh, Marc. Hi. I forgot this wasn't the office phone. How are you doing? Enjoying being back in sunny Florida?"

"Chani, you forget that this is hurricane season so it's partially sunny, partially rainy, and always humid and warm in Florida."

"Good thing you don't work for the chamber of commerce."

"Anyway, I'm OK. Just busy trying to figure out my life. And, frankly, I sure miss you."

"Marc, I miss you, too. I wish you could have spent more time here so that we could have gotten to know each other better."

"Me, too. But, I'll be up there in mid-August to pick up Max and maybe we can make some plans to be together?"

"Sounds good. You must be busy backlogged with a bevy of beauties."

"Nice alliteration. Actually, after a big trip I schedule very little surgery. Jet lag gets to me and I don't like taking chances when it comes to using my trusty scalpel. So it's mostly follow-ups and consultations. And this afternoon I had a meeting with an old friend of yours."

"Who?"

"Rabbi Yitzhak Friedman."

"Am I intruding if I ask why you were meeting with him and how I came up in the conversation?"

"I went to see him because I find him an easy guy to talk to and I wanted to ask him how I could learn more about being Jewish. So he asked me why I was interested. I told him that I had met a beautiful woman in Alaska and Judaism was central to her life and I needed to get more into being a Jew if I was ever to have a chance with her. So Rabbi

Friedman asked a few more questions and I told him that you were a rabbi. He stroked his beard for a minute and then asked for a name. Almost instantly he made the connection that Chani Kahn was the infamous Chani Weissfogel. So, that's the story."

Chani was quiet for a minute and then responded, "Marc, I think Rabbi Friedman is a great man. And if there is anyone you can learn from it's him. And Marc, I am very attracted to you. I really think you are an exceptional person. But please, I beg you, learn about Judaism and your being Jewish for yourself, not for me. You're already Jewish; you don't have to become Jewish. But, maybe, as you learn more it might change your perspective on some things." She then stopped, took a deep breath, and said, "Marc, look, this conversation is getting too heavy. I'm glad you met him, and let's take this rather long-distance relationship one step at a time."

"Sure. Well, it's actually late and dark here so I better turn in. Have a good evening."

"Thanks. I look forward to our next call. Have a good Shabbos."

"You, too."

As Marc Cohn disconnected from the call he suddenly felt very lonely.

Thirty-Three

Seward, Alaska

The call from Marc Cohn was disconcerting. For the past several years Chani had successfully built her life around friends in Alaska, her own Jewish learning, her chaplaincy duties, and her outdoor adventures.

After Nathaniel's death she had consciously and subconsciously avoided any romantic entanglements. She felt that her life with Nathaniel had been perfect. They loved living in Boston, they both enjoyed the rhythms of the week and the Jewish calendar, and they were both loved the outdoors. Someone once called them clones of one another, and she felt it was true. Then suddenly it was over. And now she was thrown back to those awful and depressing days after Nathaniel's death.

She suddenly was recalling how her apartment was constantly packed with seminary and work friends during the Shiva week. She remembered that Nathaniel's family came for the funeral, stayed a few days, and went back home to Texas. The only constant was Blake, who had arrived that same evening the rabbi had come with the sad news of her husband's death. Although Norman was busy tending to the twins he drove in for the funeral and again brought the twins in one afternoon to try and cheer up Chani. After the Shiva week Blake decided to spend a few more days with Chani and together they cried, reminisced, looked at photos, and talked. It was clear to Blake that Chani was totally lost.

The conversation that changed everything for Chani began simply enough with Blake asking, "Sweetheart, what are you going to do? You can't sit here all day. Do you want to come home with me? You can stay a while and Norm and I will help you sort this all out."

"Thanks, but that's running away. Nathaniel wouldn't want me to do that. I keep asking myself, *what would he want me to do?*"

"Come on, Chani, you know the answer to that. He'd want you to live your life."

"I know that. But, I don't know what that means. Should I be a social worker the rest of my life or what?"

"How about being a pole dancer?"

That remark startled Chani, her eyes opened, and for the first time since the accident she started laughing and then the laughter turned to tears and her whole body began to shake. Blake held her tightly while tears poured from her soul through her eyes for what seemed like an eternity.

"Oh, my God, Blake. I think I just had a catharsis or maybe an orgasm." And then the two women laughed, but this time without tears.

Chani continued, "Nathaniel was the best. I'll miss him every day of my life. We had such great plans. Go to a small town, start a shul and a family, and live happily ever after with a community, friends, children, and God. And now it's all gone."

For the next two days the friends talked about the dream. On the third day they cleaned the apartment; threw out trays of rotting turkey, corned beef, rye bread, cookies, and cake; put on their winter clothes; and walked to the Charles River, which was covered with a thin layer of snow, and talked. Two hours later they were back in the apartment. After removing their winter boots and coats Chani stood silently looking at her friend, took a few steps toward Blake then threw her arms around her and said, "Thanks. You are a truly amazing friend. I think I know what I want to do."

"Don't keep me in suspense. I think it isn't social work or pole danc-ing, so what is it?"

Finally, Chani declared, "I'm going to be a rabbi. Nathaniel's dream was not just his, it was also mine. I want the dream; so I am going to make it happen. Tomorrow I'm going to his seminary and see if I can start this summer."

Now, almost a decade later, Chani's dream was a reality. But as she thought about that reality it felt like it was being threatened by Marc Cohn. Her sleep that night was the most troubled she had had in years.

In the morning she knew what she had to do. This 'romance' needed to be stopped before it went too far. At first she thought she would call Marc and tell him that a long distance relationship was simply impos-sible. But she needed to think this through. Blake was her closest friend, and Norman was like a brother. She couldn't hurt them and she really didn't want to hurt Marc. She decided to wait a while.

Waiting and not thinking about Marc was difficult, particularly since during the month of June he telephoned several times a week. She handled the calls by being friendly although she made a point of not responding to his periodic attempts to move their conversations into more intimate areas. Although Chani recognized her considerable attraction to Marc, she also concluded that the relationship needed to end before it became disruptive to the carefully designed life she was living. But she wasn't sure how and when to bring it to an end. However Chani did know that the best prescription for her own emotional health, particularly her ambivalence about Marc, was to keep busy. This was an option that was relatively easy in Seward during the summer when the town's population swelled with tourists. She also had three scheduled bar or bat mitzvahs in Seward and one each in Homer and Stirling.

Additionally, Chani—along with six other runners—was busy train-ing four times a week for that year's Mount Marathon Fourth of July run. Two times a weeks she did a strenuous workout at home on a treadmill that she elevated well beyond its maximum fifteen percent incline by placing wooden blocks under its front legs. On Mondays and Thursdays the group would work out together on Mount Marathon itself. This was Chani's third race. In the previous two years Chani had already established herself as one of Seward's top female runners, finishing the grueling course in less than one hour and twenty minutes.

The least demanding part of the race was the first half-mile on a road from Fourth and Adams Street past the crowds of cheering people to the base of the mountain. The run up the mountain was more of an ascent on a steep slippery rock, thick brush, and a tree rooted narrow path. It was demanding and, if not careful, dangerous. After jumping on a timing mat at the top of the mountain Chani learned that the "fun" really began with the descent which involved less running and more mountaineering skills such as slip-sliding, crab walking, and careful bracing against the slope down another group of trails. Even on the best of days the ascent and descent were difficult.

The evening before the race Chani's phone rang. It was Marc on the other end wishing her well on the upcoming race and talking about seeing her in August when he was scheduled to take Max back to Florida. She was anticipating the call and had already decided that the time had come to end the relationship. Chani began, "Marc, I need to clear the air. I really enjoyed our time together and getting to know you. I think you're a great guy, but for now, I'm very busy with my work and various commitments and frankly I'm not ready for any sort of relationship."

Cohn was shaken by her words and remained speechless for a minute then said in a subdued voice, "Is it something I said or did?"

"No, it's not about you. It's about me. But look Marc, I really don't want to discuss this. I've made up my mind. And, I've got to go and get ready for tomorrow. I appreciate your calling and I hope everything goes well for you and Max. Take care of yourself."

The conversation was over. At opposite ends of the country Chani and Marc hung up their phones, stared out their windows, and tears ran down their cheeks.

Race day the town was packed with over 20,000 people who lined the sidewalks and watched the various groups of runners, women, kids, and men take off for the demanding 3.1-mile trail run. The men were always the most colorful, many of them stripped to their running shorts often showing off their buff torsos. One woman called it the "running of the bulls."

Norman, Blake, Rachel, Rebecca, and Max arrived downtown early and stationed themselves in front of the Chinese restaurant so they could cheer on Chani. The weather that Fourth of July was cold and drizzly. While they waited the Cohn family warmed themselves with endless cups of hot chocolate topped with plenty of whipped cream. Finally, the race began at 9:30 AM with the kids' division taking off. They had to wait till 11:15 for the women's division and they knew that Chani's bib had a low number so she would be in the first wave of runners. Then the women were off. The Cohns knew many of the runners and cheered them on and waved as they passed. As hard as they looked though, they did not see Chani in the first wave—or the second wave.

"Did we miss her?" Blake asked.

Norman responded, "I doubt it. We were all looking. Maybe something is wrong. Why don't you call her?"

Blake dialed both of her numbers, "No answer. I'm going over there."

"We'll all go."

"No. Norm, you stay here with the kids. If I need help I'll call."

Blake left downtown and drove over to Chani's house where she saw her car in the driveway. She rang the bell and there was no answer. She then went to the front window and saw Chani sitting in front of the fireplace wrapped in a blanket. Blake knocked on the window for seconds that seemed like minutes. Finally, Chani turned and Blake could see that she was crying. She unlocked the door, opened it, and fell into Blake's arms.

Minutes passed before Blake guided Chani to a couch. They both sat, still holding hands, and then Blake looked directly at Chani and asked, "What's happening? What's going on?"

"I'm a mess. And I think I'm just messing up everyone's life."

"What do you mean?

"Everything was fine until Marc appeared."

"Did something happen between you two? Did he hurt you in some way?"

"No, nothing like that. It's me, not him. I basically haven't been nice to him. He calls, wants to talk, and I am always pushing him away. Last night he called to wish me luck with the race and urge me to be careful and I told him thanks, but I'll be fine and then I said some other stuff and I told him not to call me anymore. Just like that, I said it."

"Is that what you meant? You don't want to see or speak to him again?"

"I don't know what I meant. I am totally screwed up."

"Chani. I love you. And trust me when I tell you that you're more important to me than Marc. But I also want you to be happy. The week you were together was the first time I saw the old Chani since Nathaniel's death. I don't understand."

"Neither do I. I keep thinking about Nathaniel dying because of me. If I went with him to Vermont he wouldn't have been in such a rush to come home. We would have just enjoyed another day up there and he would still be alive."

"Chani, you can't blame yourself. I've treated scores of widows and widowers and unfortunately many of them spend lots of time beating on themselves. Marc has told us that he feels guilty that he didn't recognize Cathy's problem sooner, and that if he had, he might have been able to save her life. Honey, give it up. It is what it is. And, is this what Nathaniel would have wanted for you? To be a nun, hiding out in Alaska?"

"I'm not hiding out here. I love it here and I love the people. But, I'm not ready for a romantic relationship."

"Well, maybe it's time."

"The other thing is I'm worried that I might fall in love with Marc and he and I are not on the same page. I'm totally into my Judaism. He's a first grader just starting and maybe thinking of quitting."

"And?"

"And, he is obviously totally into money and making money. That's not my thing. We are simply on different paths."

"Honey, stop kidding yourself. You're not into money because you already have it. You grew up with it. He and Norman didn't have money. Their parents were hard working but never accumulated much. And what they had they used for their sons' educations. If you didn't have a few dollars you definitely would not have built this building, or fly that plane, or have a shul with next to nothing in dues and give scholarships to Israel for every bar and bat mitzvah. Marc didn't get his money that way. He earned every nickel of it, honestly. And frankly, neither Marc nor Norman had it easy. A drug addict murdered their parents in the store when Marc was twenty and Norman was in law school. Holy crap, I'm defending the guy!"

Suddenly the tension was broken and the two women started smiling followed by hugs.

Chani then continued, "And, there is one more thing. He does this stupid cosmetic surgery. What a waste of talent!"

"I'm not going to defend much of cosmetic surgery but truth be told you are not someone to judge. You're beautiful. When God made you he must have been thinking of the *Sports Illustrated* swimsuit issue. Not all of us are so lucky."

"Get serious Blake. Since the day I met you you've always been a knockout."

"Really? Let me tell you a family secret. When I was a junior in high school my nickname was Woody. You know why? The boys called me the carpenter's delight because I was flat as a board. And you know my father's bulbous nose? That's what I also inherited. Although I was a star student and athlete I really did not like the way I looked. My self-esteem was heading toward the ground. So, during the summer before I started college my parents took me to Seattle, and thanks to the miracle of plastic surgery, I picked up some wind for my sails and said goodbye to my Jimmy Durante nose. So, sweetie, life isn't so black and white."

Chani was suddenly deflated and embarrassed. "I'm sorry. I hear you. Thanks for the swift kick in the butt. Maybe I now need one of those Brazilian butt lifts."

Blake looked at her friend and said, "No, what you need to do is stop feeling sorry for yourself and start feeling again—whether it's with Marc or some other man. But for now let's wrap up this pity party. Time to clean up, put on some warm clothes, and let's go back and watch the end of the race. We can solve all these other problems later."

Chani smiled, went to her bedroom, changed, and the two women, arm in arm, went downtown. When she got home that evening Chani decided that the day had finally arrived when she needed to open the letter that she had found in her backpack more than a decade earlier but never read.

She opened her top dresser draw and under her clothes she fished out the envelope that simply said: *For Chani, My Ethical Will, Dad.*

My Dearest Chani,

I am writing this ethical will to you a week after I accepted a plea in the Federal District Court. Lest there be any doubt in your mind about my behavior, I am ashamed to acknowledge it was absolutely wrong. I had no right to take the money I was entrusted with from the patients who were residents in my nursing homes. In my defense I did keep careful records of this money and intended to repay every penny once the financial situation of my businesses improved.

When you read this will I shall have perished from this earth and where and what Hashem chooses to do with me is a mystery. I leave behind to you some material possessions and hopefully a few dollars to smooth your way in life. Unfortunately, I will also leave behind a tarnished name for which I apologize profusely.

Please know that while my attorneys may have argued strenuously that my acts failed to have the requisite intent to deprive the residents of their money based on my plan to repay the money (why else keep a record?), I do not share that view. After much soul searching it is clear to me that I did not behave in a manner befitting a God-fearing man. Simply, I was wrong.

And from this inappropriate behavior that has brought dishonor on me I have learned important lessons that I feel I must share with you. First and foremost try very hard to live a life that uses Torah as it guiding light. If I had been more observant (and thoughtful) I think none of this would have happened. While the 613 commandments may not always make sense, they are all worth taking seriously. Clearly, my dear Chani you have a lifelong task of studying these commandments and learning how they can make sense for you in your life. Someday, I hope you will have the privilege of teaching them to your own children.

If possible try to work and live a life within the Jewish community. As an observant woman you will find it easiest if your work and personal life can be in synch with the Jewish calendar.

Next, avoid the temptations of living beyond your means. Similarly, do not fear economic failure. It is nothing compared to personal failure. I was simply so afraid of the economic consequences of losing my business that I started to do things that I should have not done. Never, ever follow in my footsteps—it will only lead you to quicksand.

Chani, when it comes time to marry my only advice is find someone who shares your values but don't trust creeds. Only trust deeds! In my experience too many guys only talk the talk but don't walk the walk! Secondly, make certain that the lucky young man loves you like crazy and you love him like crazy.

I know you love nature and the beautiful world that God created. Continue to enjoy your time on this planet and do what you can to make it a better place for yourself and everyone else.

Please take good care of your mother. She is a true gem and I know I have hurt her and you and for this I am deeply sorry.

Always be charitable with your money and, most importantly, your time. You are a very special person and you have the rare ability to bring joy to anyone you meet.

Finally, as I noted earlier, if you are reading this it means that I have passed on. I only hope that I can live long enough for you to again be proud of me and perhaps I can even be blessed to see you bring the next generation into the world.

My blessings to you, my darling daughter. I am enormously proud of you. You have been the greatest blessing of my life and I am sorry for disappointing and embarrassing you in any way. I shall always be looking out for you.

Love,
Dad

Tears were streaming from Chani's eyes as she refolded the letter, taped up the envelope, and replaced it in her drawer. She crawled into bed and fell asleep to the sounds of her own weeping.

Thirty-Four

BAL HARBOUR, FLORIDA

The early summer was a difficult time for Marc Cohn, with the exception of his hours with Rabbi Friedman and Reb Avrum Dov-Baer.

Cohn was busy doing the type of surgery that earned him a fortune. He still was interested in selling the practice but not for the reasons of love that had initially motivated him. Rather, he decided it was time to do something else, maybe even somewhere else. He also felt that the romance with Chani was fizzling—perhaps had already fizzled. He had called her on the third of July to wish her luck with the race and she thanked him and then said that she felt uncomfortable with their relationship. She went on and suggested that it would be simpler to end it now and just be friends. Marc was upset but not surprised since their previous several conversations had been neither warm nor friendly.

He decided to mention none of this to Rabbi Friedman who actually showed little apparent interest in his love life, but a far greater concern about his learning. The second session focused on the concept of the chosen people skirting the deeper question of God. Friedman's take was that the Jews were chosen not as a superior people, but rather as a people who had a mission to spread the word of Torah through their actions. And the Rabbi went on to raise the question of how were the actions of the Jewish people any different than those people who followed the seven Noahide Laws; the six negative laws and the single positive law. The negative laws forbade idolatry and thus required a belief in one God. Other forbidden actions were incestuous and adulteress relations, murder, cursing, theft, and eating the flesh of living animals. The one positive law was to establish courts of justice. Rabbi Friedman explained these seven laws were the basis whereby all the children of Noah, not just the Jewish people, could live a decent and kind life.

For the next few hours Rabbi Friedman and Marc Cohn considered these laws, discussed the Ten Commandments and their relationship to the Laws of Noah, and finally Rabbi Friedman said, "Marc, I'm afraid that's it for today. Let's meet again in two weeks and we'll begin talking about the holiday cycle. Since Rosh Hashanah and Yom Kippur are coming up why don't you skip over to that section in Wouk's book and we'll discuss them at our next meeting. By the way, how is your time with Avrum?"

"Great, I love that guy."

"That's wonderful. I'll see you in two weeks."

And, indeed, in a very short time Marc and Reb Avrum had bonded. It almost seemed that, despite their twenty-five year age difference, they had known each other for their entire lives. At their first meeting they both learned that they had gone to the same medical school decades apart, both were widowers, and each had one son. Reb Avrum's son was thirty-seven, lived in Boston, and was a lawyer and a professor at Boston University Law School where his specialty was intellectual property. Reb Avrum was very proud of his family as evidenced by the pictures of his son, daughter-in-law, and three grandchildren that decorated much of his two-bedroom condo.

Initially, Marc thought that Avrum's only career had been at the University of Miami Medical School from which he had recently retired as an associate dean and professor of cardiology. But what he also learned on his first visit was that Reb Avrum Dov-Baer was also General Abraham Dov-Baer, U.S. Army (retired). Prior to moving to Miami Avrum had served in the Army for 23 years, including postings as chief of cardiology at Walter Reed, commander of a medical brigade during the first Gulf War, with a final military tour as professor of Interventional Cardiology at the Uniformed Services University of the Health Sciences in Bethesda, Maryland; the U.S. government's medical school.

Although Cohn had never served in the military he was familiar with many of the military awards and medals. On his first visit to Dov-Baer's condo he was startled to see a picture of Avrum standing straight to his full height of six feet with the two stars on his shoulders, the gold on his sleeves, and several rows of ribbons and other badges. Surrounding this picture was a host of medals but the ones that Cohn recognized were the silver star and the bronze star with a combat V. Cohn's curiosity got the best of him when he asked Reb Avrum about his medals. Avrum answered, "Another life, another time. The short answer is Desert Storm. Enough about me. I want to hear about you."

And so began a friendship that grew deeper every week. Their plan to meet for two hours often lasted till midnight. The talked about everything: Torah, Israeli politics, widowhood, kids, the Marlins, the politics of South Florida, the weather, and, on the Fourth of July, Chani. "Avrum, I think I'm being dumped."

"Sounds like you're in high school when you say 'being dumped.' I thought you and the rabbi were becoming an item. What happened?"

"Well, I called her yesterday to wish her well in a race she was doing today and she basically dusted me off. Amongst other things she suggested that if I was coming up to Alaska to pick up my son in August she really had no intention of seeing me. Truth be told, Max is old enough to fly home by himself. I really was planning on seeing her then. So, I guess it's over."

"Marco, my boy, I'm much older than you and have been around the block a few times. If there is one thing I've learned it's the truism that was spoken by none other than the great American philosopher Yogi Berra, 'It ain't over till it's over.' And, my friend, that is the truth! Now let's study Torah."

After the July conversation Marc stopped calling Chani, but every few days he spoke with Norman and Max getting updates on his son's progress as a musher. By the beginning of August Mike Pearl had promoted him to overflow musher. He loved working with the dogs and they loved him too. He had by that point in the summer developed a close relationship with his cousins and Jody. Marc also learned that Max had started joining the Cohns every Shabbat at the synagogue and had even learned some of the prayers and songs. In his call at the beginning of August Max asked his father's permission to fly with Chani to Homer for a bar mitzvah weekend. The bar mitzvah boy and Max had become friendly at shul, and the plan was for Max to spend the weekend at the boy's home. Marc discussed the arrangement with Norman, and then told Max it was fine with him. Marc was also careful to avoid asking anything about Chani.

And, it hurt him to remain silent. In that phone call Marc explained to Max that he was extremely busy in the office and he wondered if Max would be willing to fly back home at the end of August by himself. Max agreed in such a subdued manner that Marc had to ask him to repeat his answer.

On the second Sunday in August Norman called and said, "Marc, we have to talk about Max."

"Is something wrong?"

"Not really. To be perfectly honest I wish you could come up here next week but I know you're busy and, frankly, I'm sorry about the Chani business. I simply don't understand women. Maybe that's why I'm a lawyer not a therapist. Anyway, Max is doing great here. He is very much part of our family. The girls all love him, Blake and I love him, and he's developed a bunch of friends all over town. He's afraid to tell you this, but he wants to stay here for next year of high school."

"Huh? I'm stunned. He wants to stay there? This is a Florida kid. Does he know how dark and cold it is up there for six months of the year?"

"We've told him. He says he doesn't care. He wants to be up here. What do you think?"

"I don't know. Give me a few days."

Immediately after getting off the call with Norman, Marc dialed Avrum's cell phone and asked if they could meet in an hour. Avrum agreed, and Marc decided to walk over to his friend's condo in Surfside. The air and breeze might help him sort out his feeling.

"What's up Marc? Another crisis?"

"No kidding, General! Now Chani doesn't want to talk to me and my son doesn't want to come home. He wants to stay in Alaska for the next year of high school. What do I do?"

"First of all my good friend you should understand that if he stays in Seward for another year he'll probably want to finish high school there. The good news is no more private school tuition. The bad news is you won't see much of him and then he's off to college and you'll see him even less, and who knows after that. I can tell you I see my son three or four times a year up in Boston and once a year down here. But, my friend, that's the way of the world and I thank the Lord for Skype and FaceTime because I'm forever yakking with my grandkids.

"Look, Marc, I suspect you miss the life you had with Cathy, and the possible life you might have had with Chani, but that's not a reason to hold back Max. My vote is to let him stay. My second vote is that you get on with your life."

"I think you're right on all accounts. I owe you!"

"Yes, you do. So tell me, what are you doing for Rosh Hashanah?"

"I don't know. Frankly, I don't think I've gone to shul for the high holidays since I was a kid."

Avrum chuckled. "Time to see what you're missing. I go to a very interesting place that's quite unusual. For me it works. For you, I don't know. Want to join me?"

"Sure, where is it?"

"Jerusalem."

"Are you serious? Go to Israel for two days? That's crazy."

"Marc, you've never been there before. Come with me. We'll stay a week. We'll go to shul. We'll wander through Jerusalem, eat some great food, and there are some very interesting people I want you to meet at Hadassah Hospital and elsewhere. Please come."

After a moment's hesitation to ponder the proposal Marc surprised Avrum by his response. "Let me talk to Alfredo. He'll have to cover for me. I'll get back to you tomorrow."

Alfredo Nussbaum, his associate partner and the person he had in mind as a potential purchaser of his practice, was an active member of a primarily Latin speaking Conservative synagogue in North Miami Beach. Nussbaum always took off for Rosh Hashanah and Yom Kippur and the first days of other holidays. The practice was closed on weekends, and from casual conversations Marc Cohn knew that Nussbaum, his wife and young son were regular Shabbat shul goers. The following day he left a message on Alfredo's voicemail that he needed a few minutes with him after they had both completed surgery.

Marc began by apologizing for the short notice and then he went on to tell Nussbaum that he needed to reschedule his patients for the time around Rosh Hashanah because he would be going to Israel for a week. Alfredo was astounded to hear about the trip to Israel. In the years they had worked together the subject of Israel, or for that matter Judaism, was never discussed. Nussbaum, a graduate of one of Miami's community Hebrew day schools, was an ardent supporter of Israel. On more than one occasion he had even thought of moving there. He was thrilled to hear of Marc's plans and told him that everything would be covered and if there were any particular patients that Marc wanted to pass on to him, he would handle them.

It was settled. Cohn was going to Israel. He called Avrum to confirm the trip and then later that evening, he called Max with his decision to allow him stay for the next academic year. His son wanted to know when he was next coming up to visit. Marc answered that his schedule was tight and suggested maybe sometime around Thanksgiving might be an option. Max responded in a voice that registered as disappointment in Marc's gut. So, almost instinctually, Marc changed his mind and said,

"On second thought, I'm going to try to get up there sooner maybe around the Columbus Day weekend."

"Great, Dad. I'm going to take you out on a sled dog ride. Thanks, Dad. I love you." And the conversation ended with Marc saying, "Max, I'm proud of you and I love you, too!" Nothing was mentioned about the trip to Israel.

In the morning Marc called Avrum's travel agent and had himself booked on the same flight with his friend.

Part Five
Days of Awe

Thirty-Five

Jerusalem, Israel

E L AL flight # 2 leaving from John F. Kennedy Airport in New York arrived at Ben Gurion at 12:30 PM on Friday afternoon, hours before the start of Shabbat and several days before the beginning of the Rosh Hashanah holiday. After getting their luggage and clearing passport control, Marc and Avrum took a cab to the David Citadel Hotel, the former Hilton, located on King David Street. Avrum liked the hotel primarily because it was close to the Old City of Jerusalem as well as the synagogue where they were planning to *daven* on Rosh Hashanah. Once they checked in Avrum said, "Let's take a little rest, clean up, and then leave for the Western Wall around six o'clock. It's an extraordinary scene on Friday night."

Forty-five minutes before sundown they left the hotel and headed toward the Jaffa Gate, through the Armenian Quarter into the Jewish Quarter, past the imposing edifice of the Aish HaTorah Center, and down the steps to the Western Wall. Cohn was astonished to see the crowds of people and the energy throughout the Old City. As they walked Avrum pointed out and explained the sites along the way. He also told Marc that they would be back later in their trip for a more in-depth look.

As they stood in the Western Wall Plaza Avrum asked Marc if he wanted to approach the *Kotel* (The Western Wall) and say some prayers. Marc wasn't certain why but he agreed. The two friends weaved their way through thousands of men and boys, most of whom were praying in small groups, some standing around, and others talking in animated conversations. Cohn noticed the range of ages, dresses, *kippahs,* hats, and colors.

He and Avrum approached the Kotel and Marc watched while Avrum touched it, closed his eyes, and seemed to go into a trance while his lips moved soundlessly. Self-conscious and embarrassed by his own lack of skills, Marc slowly drew near the 105 foot high holy Wall, touched it, and stood there feeling nothing. Avrum turned his head slightly and said to Marc, "*Boychik*, pour your heart out to God. This is a good place to talk to Him. Ask Him for anything. You've got nothing to lose."

Marc touched the Wall again and kept his hand on it. His heart suddenly broke and tears flowed from his eyes as he talked to God about his pain over losing Cathy, his own inadequacy as a father, and his screwing up the relationship with Chani. He kept saying, perhaps hundreds of times, in barely a whisper "I'm sorry . . . I'm sorry . . . I'm sorry," until Avrum tapped him on the shoulder and told him it was time to go.

Avrum and Marc turned around and started heading back from Wall into the Plaza when they saw a handsome college aged young man wearing a black beret and large, white haired man in a gray suit, white shirt, and blue tie walking toward them. The four men stood there looking at each other for a second, when Avrum—almost as a question—said one word, "Mikey."

The instant response was, "Abie," and they threw their arms around each other—two old military buddies reuniting in front of the Western Wall.

Avrum then looked at the college student and said, "Don't tell me this is Ethan. Oh my God. Come here son, give me a hug. You use to sit on my lap." Standing slightly out of the circle and feeling a bit awkward was Marc Cohn. Then Avrum said, "Mikey, Ethan, this is my friend Marc

Cohn," at which point Mike broke into a huge grin, grabbed Cohn, and hugged him.

"It's my turn to be an idiot. Of course, I knew you looked familiar, Dr. Cohn from Miami. It great to see you again." Marc was a little unclear who this man was although something about him was familiar. Then it all came back when Mike Pearl said, "I was just telling Ethan about Max and what a natural musher he is." He turned to Avrum and said, "Abie, you always said that it's a small world, particularly for Jews, and if this doesn't prove it, nothing will. I'm good friends with Marc's family in Alaska and his son works for me at my kennels." Turning to Marc he said, "Max is one great kid. You should be mighty proud of him."

Avrum was amused by this turn of events and then he asked, "Mike, where are you and Ethan staying?"

"We've borrowed a small apartment a few blocks from here near the Great Synagogue. It belongs to a member of our shul in Alaska who is an Israeli. Marc, do you remember meeting Alvin Goldberg, the guy who owns the fish restaurants in Homer and Kenai? He was at your nieces' bat-mitzvah."

Marc chuckled, "I think half the Jews in Alaska were there. Sorry, I don't recall him."

"Well, anyway, he's been in Alaska for decades but he grew up in Jerusalem and when his parents died he and his brothers inherited the place. So they keep it, occasionally visit, rent it out, and sometimes let friends use it. We don't have too much food but do you guys want to come over for supper?"

Avrum suggested an alternative—that they go back to dining room at the David Citadel Hotel. They agreed and started the walk back.

For the next several hours the group sat around enjoying dinner and the conversation. For the most part Mike and Avrum spent the time catching up with one another. Mike's move to Alaska and his becoming the owner of a kennel particularly intrigued Avrum. While the two friends were talking,, Marc asked Ethan about growing up in Alaska, and his more recent experiences in Seattle and Jerusalem.

Marc found Ethan to be an unusually thoughtful and articulate young man. At one point in the conversation Marc started asking about Ethan's relationship with the rabbi in Seward. Ethan replied that he was a high school sophomore when she arrived in town totally disinterested in Judaism. But he said, "Chani wanted to get to know me although I had already told her of how indifferently I felt toward Judaism, even though it was important for my folks." He then smiled as he shared with Marc the exact words he had spoken to Chani, "I couldn't care less about being a Jew."

Ethan went on to explain that the change in him occurred one morning when he went out with the Cohn family salmon fishing and she was part of the group. He recalled that when they were out on Resurrection Bay in Norman and Blake's 26-foot Hewescraft Alaskan aluminum fishing boat he saw, for the first time, the rabbi as a human being and not some stiff member of the clergy. He remembered her as an expert fisherman who was confident, had a great sense of humor, and obviously loved the outdoors.

Somehow that nonreligious experience with Chani broke down a barrier for him and that night at the Cohn's house, where his family joined in a barbeque, he started asking her questions about Judaism that had been nagging at him for years. He then went on to study with Chani for the following two years, had a bar-mitzvah a month before he graduated from high school, and has been active in Hillel since he arrived in Seattle. Ethan also said that the summer in Israel, as well as well as the next two semesters in Israel, was thanks to Chani's encouragement and her help in getting a partial scholarship from some Florida-based foundation. Marc listened and said nothing. Once again, his heart was breaking for what he may have lost and likely never had.

As they were getting ready to break up after an unexpected and delightful evening, Avrum asked Mike and Ethan what their plans were for Rosh Hashanah. They answered probably the Great Synagogue, a shul that they had heard about but had never visited. Avrum pointed out that the traditionally Orthodox Great Synagogue was an incredible place—huge, beautiful, with a fabulous chazzan and a world famous choir. He also told them that there was hardly any English in the service or sermon, plus there was a good chance they would wind up standing for the entire time if they didn't have tickets and an assigned seat.

When Mike indicated that they had neither tickets nor seats Avrum suggested that the Pearls join Marc and him at the Yosef Yehuda Shul, a relatively small synagogue that was fairly close to their apartment. He went on to explain that a wealthy American Jew from Baltimore established the shul. "Almost thirty years ago this guy invented a tiny component for antilock braking systems. This part is now used on almost every plane, truck, and car manufactured in the world. Do the math! He makes twenty-seven cents for every one of the sixty million vehicles annually manufactured worldwide. That's about $16 million a year, year in and year out. Not bad!"

He then went on to say, "Amongst his various charities was this shul named in honor of his father. He gave it a hefty endowment with the only requirements that the services be in English and Hebrew and that they be conservative egalitarian. It's a place with lots of *ruach* and a very nice group of people. Do you want to meet there Sunday night?"

Mike replied, "I think we'll skip the evening service and meet you there on Monday morning."

Avrum told them the address and directions. The friends parted and Marc and Avrum went up to their rooms to sleep, agreeing to meet for breakfast.

Saturday morning, Avrum, already on his third cup of coffee, had been waiting more than a half-hour when Marc walked into the dining room. Avrum asked, "Are you OK?"

"Sorry for being so late. I'm fine but my brother called me on my cellphone at three in the morning and woke me from a deep sleep. Then I had trouble getting back to sleep. I'm sorry. I hope I haven't screwed up any plans."

"No, we're fine. Take your time. Enjoy the breakfast. When you're finished I'll go to the Kotel for a Shabbat service. It's like CNN over there, you know praying 24/7. Do you want to come with me?"

"For sure."

"Marc, you said your brother called, any problems in Alaska?"

Norman had tried calling to wish him a Happy New Year and had made numerous attempts. But no one answered at home and the office was closed. Then Marc explained he forgot to tell Norman or Max that he was going to Israel with his "study buddy." So, Norman, thinking that it was 8 o'clock in the evening in Florida, called again, but it was actually 3 o'clock in the morning in Israel.

When Marc finally finished his first experience with a hearty, perhaps overwhelming, Israeli buffet breakfast of breads, eggs, fishes, pancakes, and assorted baked goods, he looked at Avrum and said, "If I don't watch myself I'll put on two pounds a day here."

Once they arrived back at the Kotel, the whole scene again overwhelmed Marc. He stayed close to Avrum, put on the extra prayer shawl that his friend had brought with him, and Marc tried to blend in, although he felt like a total outsider and fraud. Avrum sensing Marc's discomfort whispered to him, "Try this, put the *tallit* over your head like I'll show you, and use this time to think about life, talk to God, and make it your own personal service of the heart."

Marc whispered, "I'll try." He pulled the *tallit* over his head and close to his face blocking out the sounds and sights around him. He started silently humming to himself and his mind filled with an image of standing beside his grandfather on one of the rare times his went to services with him.

Then he remembered his father humming a Yiddish song while filling prescriptions in the back of the pharmacy. His mind wandered to the last days of his parents and then the awful moments of Cathy's death. His thinking then shifted to the joy he felt when he held Max for the first time and when his son was a little boy and they would walk on the beach holding hands. He found himself whispering, "Hey God, why is this so hard? What happened between Max and me? How do I make it better?" Then he started thinking of Chani and wondering what he had done to alienate her. He liked her a great deal, maybe even loved her, but he didn't understand what went wrong. Once again, he quietly besieged God to show him the way.

An hour had past but it seemed like a minute when he felt a light tap on his shoulder and the voice of Avrum, "Marc, are you finished? Let's go for a long walk."

And for the remainder of the day Avrum took Marc on a walking tour of the Old City, through the Yemin Moshe neighborhood, past the Montefiore Windmill, then over to the German Colony neighborhood, and finally a stroll through Liberty Bell Park. A short distance away from the park they stopped for a rest in the lobby of the Inbal Hotel where, once again, Avrum ran into some old friends. As evening fell they headed back to their hotel for another break and then walked through the glitzy Mamilla Mall and finally up to BenYehuda Street. Marc and Avrum found a table at an outdoor restaurant and celebrated the end of Shabbat with pizza and a couple of bottles of Gold Star beer. Marc was amazed by both the mass of young people hanging out Saturday night on Ben Yehuda, and the lively spirit of the place. Any fears he had about safety and security vanished. At 10:30 PM they walked the short distance back to the hotel.

The plan for Sunday was a trip to Yad Vashem, the major Holocaust Memorial, a visit to the City of David where they could tour the archaeological digs, and the last stop on their schedule was a tour through the tunnels adjacent to and under the Western Wall.

By 5 o'clock they had visited all three sites. Marc was moved, overwhelmed, and exhausted. He told Avrum he was ordering food from room service that evening and then hoping for a long night's sleep. Avrum went to synagogue for the evening service to mark the beginning of the Rosh Hashanah holiday.

Thirty-Six

JERUSALEM, ISRAEL

After a good night's sleep Marc felt much better Monday morning when he came down for breakfast at 7:45 AM. He was ready to eat and leave for shul. Avrum was already busily working his way through the buffet line. When they arrived at the synagogue a few minutes after 9:00, Mike and Ethan were already waiting out front. They shook hands all around and exchanged the traditional Jewish New Year's greeting offered before the end of the first day's morning service, *Leshana tovah tikatev v'tichaten* (May you be written and sealed for a good year). Additionally, Marc had learned from Avrum that after the morning service, the proper greeting is changed to *Gemar chatim tovah* (a good final sealing). His mentor had also written out these words in transliteration for Marc, who proceeded to practice them a dozen times, but still stumbled a bit delivering the 'message.' He soon found out that regardless of his poor Hebrew pronunciation the recipients always accepted his kind wishes graciously.

Once inside the shul's small lobby another couple rushed up to welcome Avrum. He introduced them to Marc, Mike and Ethan as Sam and Audrey, close friends from Hollywood, Florida, and the U.S. Army where Sam and Avrum had once been stationed in Texas together as young officers. Nowadays Sam, a retired orthodontist, was active in all manner of Jewish charities in the United States and Israel, and he and Audrey had an apartment in Jerusalem where they stayed several months a year. Audrey asked Mike where he was from, and when he said Alaska, another round of Jewish geography began. But this round was over in a minute when Sam said that they knew a young woman rabbi in Seward. Mike simply said, "Chani." It turned out that Sam and Audrey had been friends with her parents and Sam had done some orthodontia on Chani years earlier. Overhearing this conversation was Marc Cohn.

Services were about to begin when Audrey said, "Look, why don't you all come to our house after *Shacharit* for a nice dairy lunch. It's about a twenty-minute walk and I guarantee you the best view in town. We are next to the Tayelet Haas Promenade and we overlook the Old City." They all agreed on the luncheon plans about which Ethan wasn't too eager. That too changed when a beautiful young woman approached Sam and Audrey, kissed them, and was introduced as Dani, their twenty-year-old granddaughter, a sophomore at Yale doing her junior year at Bar-Ilan University in Jerusalem. Suddenly, Ethan was looking forward to lunch.

The Rosh Hashanah morning service began when a young couple stepped onto the bima and the woman said, "Hag Sameach, Gut Yontiff. Zev and I are so delighted to see all of you and we look forward to our davening together this Rosh Hashanah. We are happy to have our regulars from Yerushalayim, our out of town members from New York, Boston, Toronto, Atlanta, Miami, and LA. Did I miss anyone?" Someone called out New Orleans, and another Dallas. The woman rabbi apologized to those people by their first names and said, "Either my eyesight is going or my memory. This definitely is not good at thirty-seven." The laughter immediately relaxed the congregation.

"For all the newcomers, I am Rabbi Talia Liebowitz and I share the pulpit with my husband Rabbi Zev Katz. We also double as the *chazzans.*

"I like to begin these lengthy services by quoting Rabbi Louis Finkelstein who served as the Chancellor of the Jewish Theological Seminary in New York for more than thirty years. Rabbi Finkelstein said that 'when we pray, we speak to God; and when we study Torah, God speaks to us.' These services are a time for two-way conversations. I hope that all of us make the most of this special time.

"The rabbis of past generations and some contemporary rabbis have written prayers to help facilitate our conversations. I urge you to use these prayers not in a rote and unthinking manner, but as a guide to the service from your own heart. Remember God does not need our prayers; we are the ones who need to pray. God needs to merely hear our thoughts whether they are in Hebrew, English, Aramaic, Spanish, Chinese, Tagalog, or whatever. So the first challenge for all of us is praying from our hearts, and the second challenge is learning with our brains. Then we have the most important challenge, which is allowing that learning and praying to be turned into action by our feet and hands. My dear husband Zev will now begin this morning's service. We pray that this day is meaningful to each of you."

The rabbi and congregation began singing the opening prayers while Marc, who was sitting next to Mike on one side and Avrum on the other, opened the English-Hebrew *Mahzor* and attempted to follow the service. Although Marc had gone to Hebrew School and attended junior congregation services for three years, he remembered very little. The only remnants that endured surfaced the few times the *Shema* (Hear on Israel, The Lord Our God, The Lord is One) was chanted. So Marc listened, periodically closing his eyes and meditating. At other times he read the English commentaries about the prayers, many of which he found quite interesting. Toward the end of the first part of the service the congregation began singing the *Avinu Malkeinu* (Our Father, Our King) prayer and for some unknown reason he recalled parts of it, which he sang and hummed, almost as if he were being lifted by a giant wave.

The rabbi then announced that they were now beginning the Torah service. Two Torahs were removed from the ark, prayers were recited, and then the Torahs were marched around the synagogue and congregants had the opportunity to kiss each of the Torahs. They were then brought back to a table where they were unwrapped in preparation for reading. The holiday Mahzor they were using had the Torah readings in it. So, during that portion of the service, Marc was able to read the translations of the Torah readings.

With the completion of the Torah readings a woman from the congregation chanted the Haftorah from the First Book of Samuel followed by the Torahs being returned to the ark.

Next Rabbi Katz approached the lectern looked over the congregation making eye contact with virtually every person and then he began his sermon. "Hag Sameach. I hope that our services prove to be meaningful, perhaps inspiring to each and every one of you. The board of our synagogue, my wife, and I thank all of you for sharing these very special holidays with us. Today I want to talk about Channah."

Suddenly Marc's faced reddened and he turned to look at Reb Avrum who smiled and whispered in Marc's ear, "Not your Channah, the Channah from today's Haftorah."

The rabbi continued his talk. "As most of you know the Haftorah is a later addition to our services, dating from around 200 BCE. This was a time when the Greeks banned the public reading in the synagogues of the Five Books of Moses; Genesis, Exodus, Leviticus, Numbers, and Deuteronomy. The rabbis devised a way around the ban by teaching the Torah through readings from the Book of Prophets that were related to the weekly Torah section. These readings are the Haftorah. And in our time we still honor this tradition by the reading the Haftorah after completing the Torah section readings. Interestingly enough in some congregations before the Haftorah section of the service begins many men will step out and return at the completion of the Torah service. It would be nice to say it was in order to protest the unnecessary additional of time added to the service by the Haftorah reading, but the truth is that it's a time for the weekly meeting of the Kiddush club, and an opportunity to have some high quality scotch." The congregation responded to this remark with joyful amusement.

"But let's get back to the Haftorah that tells the story of a woman who was the favored but childless wife of Elkanah, a minor prophet. As was common in those times men often had multiple wives. Elkanah's other wife Penina was quite fertile and had numerous children. Every year Elkanah would go with his wives to Shiloh to offer sacrifices to the Lord. As a manifestation of his special love for Channah he would give her double portions for the sacrifice and only a single portion to Penina. In today's Haftorah Channah is seen so fervently praying that Eli, the high priest, mistakes her for a drunken woman. Channah, perhaps an early archetype of a modern assertive woman, doesn't simply accept the rebuke from the priest, but counters that she is very upset and explains that she is praying for a child who, if a son, will be given to God's service. The priest apologizes for his reproach and says, 'May God grant your petition.'

"What lessons do we learn from this Haftorah? The most popular rabbinical response is that Channah is a model of how we should pray. Specifically, she teaches us to pray from the heart—that is, talk to God about your most important needs and speak with passion. The proof text the rabbis offer is found in the lines from the Haftorah where we learn that Channah was weeping bitterly and her lips moved, but she uttered no sound. More importantly, Channah teaches us that God can be prayed to from the heart. She approaches God in love and awe.

"These are the lessons we must remember as we begin the next part of the service, that section which is essentially the substitute for the sacrifices that our ancestors offered. Approach God, speak to the Lord from your heart, put your entire being into your prayers, and move your lips, but be silent so you can hear your prayers, while allowing your neighbors to hear their own prayers.

"One final thought. In the Haftorah we learn an invaluable lesson from Eli the priest. Eli, who you will recall, apologizes to Channah for his misunderstanding of her behavior in the Temple. All of us, at one time or another, misunderstand someone; usually someone we love. This holiday, which as we all know is part of the Days of Awe culminates in Yom Kippur, the Day of Atonement. Before that final judgment day each of us is required to clean our slates. We do this on Kol Nidre with God. But before Kol Nidre, we need to do it with our family and friends. I urge you to make it a practice this year to do just that. And while I am talking to all of you, may I apologize to each of you who I may have offended in the past year. May I be forgiven."

Marc was startled when in unison the congregation called out, "You are forgiven."

The rabbi smiled, thanked the congregation, and asked everyone to stand as they prepared for the first blowing of the *shofar*, the ram's horn. The rabbi waited a minute while parents rushed into the courtyard to bring young children in to hear Rabbi Zev blow a dramatic looking three-foot long twisted Kudu Yemenite Shofar. The introductory prayers were chanted and then Rabbi Talia called out the notes as Rabbi Zev expertly blew the shofar. Marc's face had an expression of awe, not dissimilar from that on many of the children.

The service went on for another hour and a half with periodic breaks for the blowing of the shofar and short explanations by one of the rabbis on the section of the service that they were reading. One prayer that Marc couldn't stop thinking about was the *Unetanah Tokef* and its haunting words. "*On Rosh Hashanah it is written and on Yom Kippur it is sealed: How many shall leave this world and how many shall be born into it, who shall live and who shall die..*" and the prayer then stated of how people will die, concluding with questions of wealth and poverty and humility and honor. In that prayer there was a line that read, "*But repentance, prayer, and righteousness avert the severe decree.*" Cohn pondered if those words were written especially for him.

By 1:15 PM Marc was tiring and about ready to go when the rabbi announced the final shofar blowing. This was followed by a song lead by all the children, another prayer, and then Rabbi Talia asked everyone to sit for a moment. She thanked everyone for being there and praying with such spirit. She then announced the timing of the afternoon and evening services as well as the next day's services. Rabbi Zev took over and again thanked everyone for their participation and told them that the courtyard would be opened all afternoon for those who wanted to do a *Tashlich* service at the synagogue's screened well but he reminded everyone, "Please, small crumbs." Marc had no idea what he was talking about.

Rabbi Zev then asked everyone who had a yahrzeit or was in mourning to please stand. Reb Avrum leaned over to Marc and said, "That's you, stand up." Marc looked back at Avrum and followed his orders. Next the rabbi asked everyone else in the congregation to stand up in order to demonstrate their support to those saying Kaddish." The mourner's Kaddish was recited with Marc participating in this prayer for the first time in months. The service was completed with a final song, the rabbis wished everyone a "Hag Sameach," happy holiday, and there were the sounds of old friends and the newly acquainted shaking hands, laughing, exchanging hugs, kisses, and greetings.

Fifteen minutes later Sam suggested they leave. The group of seven started their walk up to the Tayelet. Ethan was talking with Dani who was intrigued by the handsome Jewish young man who grew up in Alaska on a dog kennel. Sam, Avrum, and Mike were engaged in a spirited discussion about Israeli politics. Marc found himself walking with Audrey, an intelligent and charming woman, who was asking him questions ranging from plastic surgery to his relationship with Reb Avrum. When she learned about his wife's passing she could see a great sadness in his face that only changed when she asked whether they had children. "Yes, one son, Max. He's fourteen and living for a year in Seward with my brother and his family. That's how I know Mike, my son works in his dog kennel."

Audrey was fascinated and asked Marc about his experiences in Alaska. Marc laughed, "Well it's a beautiful place and there seems to be a great community of people. And you know the rabbi and I think she is doing a fine job. She is a . . ."

"What?"

"Never mind; just a fine rabbi."

As they approached Sam and Audrey's home, Audrey thought that Marc, the celebrity plastic surgeon, was far less interesting than the Marc Cohn she had just met who was about to have lunch at their home in

Jerusalem. After getting comfortable they approached the table, made the blessings, and then dipped apples in honey as a symbolic way of wishing everyone a sweet New Year.

By 5 o'clock the entire group had bonded as friends and they were also satiated from the salads, fish, desserts, and wine that Audrey and Sam served. Avrum stood up with his glass and said: "I propose a toast to Audrey and Sam, good friends and the best hosts in town. May this coming year be a great one for you and your family. *L'Chaim.*"

Everyone joined in with an "Amen." Avrum continued, "Thanks again, this was great. I think it's time Marc and I went back down the hill for Tashlich."

Mike stood and said, "Thanks so much. We'll go with Avrum, he can lead the way. If you guys ever come up to Alaska, please visit."

Audrey replied, "Sam and I might just do that."

Dani interjected, "Hey, Granny, don't forget me. I want to see the kennel and hang with the dogs."

And then Marc said, "I want to thank all of you for the most enjoyable and meaningful Rosh Hashanah in my life. And Sam, Avrum, and Mike, you three guys are the most amusing people with the most interesting stories I've ever heard. Were they all true?" That comment lead to another final round of laughter. Thanks and hugs were exchanged and everyone said they hoped to see each other at services the next day.

As they walked back toward the Old City, Cohn asked about Tashlich. It was Ethan who quickly chimed in by saying that a week earlier he had been studying this tradition with a local rabbi.

"Tachlich is a custom that dates from the late 14th or early 15th century and has various explanations. Some rabbis suggest it comes from the story of the binding of Isaac and an attempt by Satan to slow down or prevent Abraham from fulfilling God's order to sacrifice Isaac. Satan did this by putting a stream along Abraham's route that would have to be crossed before reaching the place of sacrifice on Mount Moriah. Other explanations, which most of us don't like, are that we were mimicking other non-Jewish traditions. Regardless, what we do is go to a flowing body of water and toss breadcrumbs into the water and say a couple prayers.

"To be honest Tashlich is my absolutely favorite part of Rosh Hashanah. When I was a kid we didn't have a rabbi in Seward, so every year some of the Jewish locals hired a rabbinical student who came up for the holidays. Some services were good, others kind of boring. But Tashlich was always the best. We would go to Resurrection Bay around five or six in the afternoon, toss our crumbs in the water, say prayers, sing a song or two, and then go to the Bloomberg's home. They moved away a few years ago, but they had a beautiful house with incredible views of the mountains and the Bay. And after Tashlich we would go up there for cookies, cake, and hot drinks. It was usually cold by then, the service was quick and the kiddush hit the spot. Who knows maybe we felt good because we had dumped our sins. Anyway, some rabbis in Israel say the rules here are different and actually we don't have to do Tashlich in the Holy Land. So that's the story."

Reb Avrum spoke, "Wow, thanks Ethan. Now the question is where do we do it? My vote, even if it's a little out of the way, is the Shiloah Spring at the City of David. Does that work for everyone?"

They all agreed and with a piece of bread in their pockets, given to them as a parting gift from Audrey, they headed to the City of David and the springs to ritually rid themselves of their sins. After performing the Tashlich ritual in the ancient City of David, they walked backed to the David Citadel Hotel via the Old City.

Once back at the hotel Marc excused himself, telling his friends that he was exhausted and that he would see Avrum in the morning.

Thirty-Seven

JERUSALEM, ISRAEL

The next morning Avrum walked into the dining room and found Marc sitting at a table working his way through a sumptuous breakfast of pancakes, fruits, tuna fish, croissants, vegetables, and various sweet rolls as well as a pot of coffee.

"Sleep well?"

"Avrum, I went to bed at 8:00 PM and got up 12 hours later. I feel great! What about you?"

"I should have gone back to the hotel when you did. Instead, I walked with Mike and Ethan to their place, had some pasta for dinner, and Mike and I sat around catching up while killing a bottle of vodka. I got back here at 1:00 AM and feel like crap today!"

"Eat something, have some coffee, you'll feel better. Drink a lot of water, you're probably also dehydrated."

"Doctor's order?"

"Sure, why not. Could I have your Medicare card so I can properly bill you?"

They both laughed. Avrum went to get some food and when he returned he asked Marc if he was coming to shul with him. Marc told him he needed some time to chill and would be hanging around the hotel, reading, and perhaps taking a walk. But, he would be back at the hotel by one o'clock in case Avrum wanted to get together for lunch and discuss their plans for Wednesday and Thursday. Tentatively they had agreed that on Wednesday the two of them would be going to the Hadassah Medical Center in Jerusalem and to the offices of the IIGRS in Ma'ale Adumim, a newly developed town about fifteen minutes away from Hadassah. The Thursday plan was focused on touring in the Tel Aviv area including a few museums, the Port of Jaffa, and the beaches on the Mediterranean.

Avrum's initial schedule was to stay in Israel through the Yom Kippur holiday but he wanted to remain flexible and perhaps stay for several additional weeks. After they chatted about the general plan for the rest of the week they agreed to meet for lunch, Marc excused himself, picked up a cup of coffee to go, and headed back to his room to sort out his feelings while Avrum went to second day services.

Once back in the room Marc opened the French doors, walked onto his small balcony, and stood there looking across the pool to the ramparts of the Old City. Several minutes passed before he sat down, closed his eyes, and began thinking. Within an hour his mind was made up. He walked back inside, opened his computer, and made a new plan for Thursday.

When they met for lunch at 1:30, Avrum began reviewing the details of their schedule for Wednesday as well as Thursday. Marc interrupted him, "Avrum, sorry but I've switched my flights. I'm leaving on a 5:00 AM flight Thursday morning."

"Oh. When does that flight get back to Miami? Is there something wrong? I thought you were staying through Saturday night."

"I know this may sound crazy but I'm not going to Florida. I'm going to Alaska and spending Yom Kippur up there."

"Really? What made you decide to do that?"

"There are a lot of people I have to see there and I need to have them forgive me for the ways I've hurt them this past year—or maybe in the last decade."

"Can't you do it by phone? It's going to take you days to get there."

"I think I need to do this in person. It is a long schlep, almost a full day of traveling and layovers, but I have to do it."

"Marc, you are a good man. I hope this works for you."

Thirty-Eight

JERUSALEM, ISRAEL

On Wednesday morning right after breakfast the two friends headed out to the Ein Kerem campus of Hadassah Medical Center. Although their first meeting was with the British-born cardiologist Mordechai Maxwell, a decades old colleague of Avrum's, they decided to begin their visit at the hospital's Abbell Synagogue. Avrum wanted Marc to see the sanctuary's twelve Chagall windows, each one telling a different aspect of the biblical story. Avrum, always moved by the sight of the windows, particularly in the bright morning sun, explained to Marc the art and stories of the windows with a passion and love that was simply infectious. Marc regretted not knowing Avrum at an earlier point in his life and sharing this experience with Cathy, Max, and his parents.

The next stop was Maxwell's office but en route Avrum spotted two clowns walking down the hallway toward him. Almost simultaneously the clowns spotted the retired American general and started pointing and jabbering in a language that Marc couldn't understand. When they were about ten feet from Avrum they stopped talking and started pointing and shaking their heads. Then suddenly they came to a military-like attention and spoke out, "Attencion, El Jefe, El General Avrum. Attencion."

Suddenly there was laughter all around and bear hugs between Avrum and the clowns who were introduced to Marc as two of the most famous hospital clowns in the world. They spoke in Hebrew and French for a minute and then proceeded on their daily rounds of patients. Avrum looked at Marc and said, "These guys and the other clown doctors at Hadassah and throughout the hospitals in Israel are amazing. The best. They bring joy in the darkest places.

As they walked down the crowded hallway to Maxwell's office, Avrum related a story from the Talmud. He told Marc how Elijah the prophet had been walking through a marketplace when someone stopped him and asked who went to Olam Haba, meaning the afterlife, but in many senses the Western concept of heaven. Elijah pointed to two men sitting in the corner. The questioners were puzzled because the men weren't rabbis or scholars but Elijah offered an explanation. He said that the men he had pointed to made other people smile. Avrum concluded his comments just as they got to Dr. Maxwell's office by saying, "If anyone in the world is going to Olam Haba it certainly will be those two guys and their troupe of clowns as well as all the other hospital clowns in the world."

Dr. Mordechai Maxwell was a short, red haired, barrel chested 50-year-old man whose white coat almost touched the floor, and would likely not close around his waist. On a coat rack in the corner of his office Marc noticed his military uniform on a hanger with three oak leaves on his shoulder insignia, indicating he was a brigade commander similar to a U.S. Army colonel. He wasn't surprised because Avrum had told Marc that Maxwell was a strong Zionist who served on active duty during the Second Intifada, the 2006 Lebanon War (where he was wounded), and the Gaza War.

These days, though, his efforts were focused on treating patients at Hadassah as well as overseeing a series of new training programs that the medical center was developing in cardiac care and preventive medicine for several African nations. In their hour together Mordechai briefly outlined the programs for Marc, and then turned to Avrum for some review and comment. Before the meeting broke up Mordechai Maxwell pulled out a calendar to check some dates at the beginning of the following year when Avrum could be available to train African health workers on cardiac interventions. Also he wanted to check Avrum's availability to travel to Africa with a team from Hadassah to do on-site training. By 12:30 PM all the business was concluded, and despite an invitation for lunch, Avrum and Marc departed.

Marc asked, "How come we didn't stay for lunch?"

"Come on Marc, haven't you had enough hospital food in your life? I know a great little restaurant in Ma'ale Adumim, that's where we'll go."

They got into a cab and in fifteen minutes they were in front of a small restaurant with about ten outside tables shaded with multicolored umbrellas. Avrum explained that they would go inside to place their order, and when it was ready someone would deliver it to their table. Avrum selected a grilled lamb shwarma on laffa bread with Israeli salad and tahini. Marc settled for a falafel on pita bread with tahini, hummus, Israeli salad, and cole slaw. They both ordered iced lemonade. When they had finished eating Marc said, "Buddy, I need a nap! That was the best falafel I've ever had. Glad we skipped the cafeteria!" Avrum answered with a giant burp, followed by an apology and more laughter.

"Only one more stop and then you get to head up to Ben Yehuda Street for some gifts. I'm going to miss hanging around with you, Marc. And, I really hope everything works out in Alaska. Do they know you're coming?"

"Not yet."

They walked up the block to a small office building and on the second floor found a door with the sign International Institute for Global Reconstructive Surgery (IIGRS). Inside the door was one large room with several desks, bookcases, and a wall map of Africa that had numerous colored pins stuck in different locations throughout as many as a dozen African countries. There was a second space behind the large room that Marc would later see was a huge conference area that included a full-scale mock operating suite.

Welcoming them when they arrived was a tiny elfin looking woman with wisps of white hair. Marc instantly knew who she was even before she spryly stepped forward to offer her hand. It was Dr. Hattie Ferguson, a legend in the specialties of orthopedic and plastic surgery. Dr. Ferguson had held professorships in her native Edinburgh, as well as Oxford. Many of the most important reconstructive procedures used throughout the world bore her name. In fact, Marc, like many others, assumed she had been dead for decades. And there she was in front of him and at age ninety-one, clearly not retired and very much in the center of the action.

After greeting Marc she approached Avrum who encircled her with his huge arms. She then stepped away from Avrum looked up at him and said, "Abraham, my love, I am so happy to see you. I assume you are here to rescue me from the desert, make me your bride, and bring me to Florida so I can get my green card." They all roared with laughter. Hattie then turned serious.

"Marc, thanks to an article a few years ago about your clinic in the Hebrew language edition of *Cosmopolitan*, as well as your 'touching up' two of our best known Israeli fashion models that made our tabloids, you are fairly well known here as an excellent surgeon. Now although I realize that your focus is all those folks we read about in *People Magazine*, you and I are in similar businesses. I run this NGO—what you in the States typically call a nonprofit—and our mission is to help victims of torture and conflict in Africa. Unfortunately, that continent is still in the midst of many wars and the victims, who range in age from infants to the elderly, are numerous and everywhere.

"Although we classify all our work as reconstructive, some of it is cosmetic. But as you well know, such work is often reconstructive of the soul. When Avrum told me you were going to be in Israel I pleaded with him to bring you here so that I could use my Scottish charm to enlist your help with our projects. May I continue?"

Marc nodded and Dr. Hattie Ferguson, a woman who seventeen years earlier had been honored by Queen Elizabeth as a Dame Commander, began her presentation. Marc couldn't help thinking what a humble person she was. *Here she was, despite her being entitled to be called either 'Dame' she was known to simply prefer Hattie.*

She opened her computer and began a comprehensive PowerPoint presentation on the clinical conditions that her Institute addressed. This included everything from cleft palates and lips to burns, breast and facial reconstructions, to the simplest of problems such as the mallet finger that Marc had seen in the Alaskan prison. She then went on to discuss the medical resources to deal with these overwhelming problems. Finally, she paused, looked Marc deeply in the eyes, and said, "I need your help. These people, patients, and medical personnel need your help. And Marc, I love to quote the Talmud, even though I'm a Scottish Presbyterian, that 'whoever saves one life, saves the world.' Can you help us?"

"Hattie, this is very moving and I think you do great work. And I would definitely like to contribute money but I'm not sure what else I can do."

Hattie chuckled and said, "Marc, I never, ever, turn down contributions and the more the better. But I need you and your skills! Specifically, at the beginning of December I shall have ten African doctors from three different countries coming here for five days of intensive training. Then the following week I need to send a reconstructive surgeon to Africa to mentor these physicians. To be perfectly blunt I need you on our team for two weeks in December. Can you do it?"

Marc remained silent for a minute, his eyes closed, and when he opened his eyes he simply said, "Yes."

Hattie, who barely came up to his waist walked over and embraced him, saying "This is a dream come true. Thank you so much."

Avrum came over and patted him on the shoulder and whispered in his ear, "Marc, I'm so proud of you."

It was time for them to leave and as they were walking out the door Marc looked over at Hattie and said, "Thanks. And, as soon as I get back to Florida I'll send you a check for $5,000." Both Hattie and Avrum were overwhelmed by Marc's generosity.

On the return trip to the hotel Avrum filled Cohn in on Hattie's back-story. "She moved to Israel twenty-five years ago after she got married at the age of sixty-six to Isidore Fuchs an American academician in the field of dermatology. Dr. Fuchs, a widower with grown kids, was one of the world leaders in the treatment of parasitic related skin diseases. After he retired from Harvard he made *aliya* to Israel and became the nation's guru of dermatology. Hattie and Izzy had known each other for years but started dating when they were working together on a World Health Organization (WHO) project a year before they married. So Hattie left Britain and came here, developed the Institute and began the final chapter of her remarkable career. Izzy was a sweet guy who I truly loved. Unfortunately, he died two years ago after a short battle with pancreatic cancer."

Because of the evening rush hour traffic, the cab ride back to the hotel took close to thirty minutes. Avrum suggested that Marc get off at Ben Yehuda Street pedestrian mall and look for his gifts there and then walk back to the hotel where they could meet for dinner in the lobby at 7:30. Marc had in mind buying a *tallit* for himself, one for Max, and another for his brother. For his nieces, he wanted to get sterling silver *hamsas* and for Blake he was thinking of a silk scarf and matching head covering. He also wanted to bring them something special for their home and when he saw a beautiful modern silver *havdalah* set he knew he had found the right gift.

Finally, he thought about something for Chani, but he was certain that their relationship was on either over, or at best on thin ice, so the idea of something personal made little sense. Then he thought perhaps something for her synagogue and, as he looked through options, he found an elegant silver Torah *yad* (pointer) decorated in a floral pattern. His shopping complete, Marc returned to the hotel to pack, and then met Avrum for a final meal.

Before going down for dinner he returned to his room and sent out three email messages. The first to Max was to offer his son the New Year's greeting he had learned, and to share the words of praise about him that he had heard from Mike Pearl. He told Max that he loved him, and wanted to spend Yom Kippur with him. He then told Max of his revised flight schedule and that he anticipated arriving in Seward late Thursday evening.

The second email was to his brother with whom he shared his new schedule. Marc ended his communication by saying that he looked forward to seeing the family on Friday.

The third email was to Alfredo. In that email he apologized for the late notice of his change and asked his partner to cover for him. He also wished Alfredo and his family a traditional Happy New Year and, finally, he asked Alfredo to forgive him for any offenses that he may have committed against him in the past year.

Having completed these critical emails, Marc booked a hotel in Seward (absolutely no problem in late September), placed an order for a car service to take him from Anchorage to Seward, arranged for a 2:00 AM checkout from the hotel, and, lastly, he called the concierge for a cab to the airport at 2:00 AM for his 5:00 AM flight to Frankfurt. With everything completed, Marc took a shower and went downstairs to meet Avrum at the hotel's Lobby Lounge and Terrace dining room.

The evening was clear with a temperature in the mid-60s and a slight breeze. A hostess ushered them to an outside table with a view of the illuminated sandstone walls surrounding Jerusalem's Old City. Then for the next two hours Marc and Avrum reviewed their previous several days in Israel. Marc told his friend how grateful he was for inviting him on the trip. As they were parting Marc looked directly at Avrum and said, "I know I've said it before but I truly can't thank you enough. This has been the most interesting, spiritually uplifting, and incredibly thought provoking Jewish experience of my life. Right now I've got to get some sleep and then I've got many relationships to fix and a great deal of *teshuvah* to do."

At 1:45 AM, his alarm started ringing and within minutes he was taking the first steps on his 6,129-mile journey.

Meanwhile, back in Seward, Norman read his email and called Blake to relay the information that Marc was coming in the following evening. Blake wanted to know why he was traveling from Jerusalem all the way to Seward. Norman replied that his brother's email was vague. The only two things he knew for certain were that Marc wanted to see Norman for lunch on Friday and anticipated seeing Max Friday afternoon. He told Blake that there was no mention whatsoever of Chani.

The imminent arrival of Marc Cohn presented a quandary for Blake. As a friend she felt she should alert Chani of Marc's unplanned visit so that she was not taken by surprise if their paths crossed. On the other hand, since Marc didn't mention her, and there was obviously a problem between them, she thought it might be disloyal to Marc if she spoke to Chani about him. She realized her concern was less about compromising her relationship with Marc than she was about potentially alienating Norman and Max by being a *yenta*. In the end, she decided to say nothing to anyone.

The trip to Anchorage was long and tiring. The Lufthansa flight left Israel on time and arrived five hours later in Frankfurt. Flying business class had the advantage of some good food, comfortable seating, and decent legroom. Marc managed to get a short nap on this first leg. The airport was a busy place with a range of shops. He walked past many of them and thought about buying some perfume for Chani, but once again decided against getting her anything, particularly an intimate gift such as perfume.

The first and business class lounge was quite pleasant and relatively empty. Marc sat down, had a café latte from a machine, along with a German crusty roll that an attendant identified as a *brotchen*. He then read a local English language paper until he heard his next flight announced—an almost ten-hour flight to Seattle. Thankfully, it had the advantage of particularly comfortable fully reclining seats, great food, and movies that he had not before seen. A few times during the flight he sensed that he had dozed off.

Once in Seattle there was another two-hour layover and finally the last leg—a three-hour flight to Anchorage. The plane was an older Alaskan Airline jet with a packed business class section and not a great deal of room between seats. Each passenger received the usual hand-held video screen that was preloaded with dozens of movies. Marc was exhausted but couldn't sleep. He tried reading his Wouk book but that didn't hold his interest. At the Seattle airport he did buy a novel by Daniel Silva about the Israeli spy and assassin Gabriel Allon. By page five, Marc was hooked. He easily connected with Allon because of the past week and his new found familiarity with Jerusalem. He was halfway through the book when the plane began its descent into Anchorage. As the aircraft was taxiing toward the terminal, Marc sent a text message to Max and Norman telling them he had landed, was exhausted, and would see them Friday.

As he exited the secure area a young man named Kyle stood with a sign that read, Dr. Marc Cohn. Cohn walked over to Kyle, introduced himself, and followed the driver to the baggage carousel. Marc's luggage, with its priority tags as a business class customer, was one of the first to arrive. The driver put it on a cart, walked to the parking space, loaded it up, and they were off to Seward.

The driver asked, "Business or pleasure, sir?"

"Please, call me Marc. I have family here."

"You were coming from Seattle, do you live there?"

"No, I live in Miami but I was coming from Israel."

"Israel, wow—that is one long trip. How was it?"

"Yup, it's a long trip, and it is a great place and I'm going back in December."

"May I ask what kind of doctor are you?"

"I'm a plastic surgeon."

The driver was quiet for a minute, he looked in the rearview mirror, looked again, and then said, "You're the doctor who saved the inmates in Seward! I thought I knew who you were; I saw your face all over the news. Wow. It's an honor to have you in my car."

Part Six
Teshuvah

Thirty-Nine

SEWARD, ALASKA

The drive from the Anchorage airport to Seward was covered in just under three hours. At times Marc and the young driver talked and then there were many quiet moments when Marc rehearsed what he would say to Max, Norman, and Chani, if he got the opportunity.

He arrived at the hotel at 9:00 PM, having been traveling for almost thirty hours. Marc immediately checked in, showered, and a half-hour later was sound asleep. When he woke up shortly after 8:00 AM he saw it was a cloudy day with a light drizzle. By the time he dressed, went to the hotel's breakfast room for some coffee and a bagel, it was well past 9:00. His first stop was the car rental agency, a five-minute walk from the hotel. He checked in and was able to obtain another Ford Focus for the several days he would be in Seward.

An hour later, he left for the short drive to the home of Rabbi Chani Kahn. Marc anticipated hostility from her for reasons he did not quite understand. He decided that this was likely a pro forma visit but he still needed to do it because he felt that he had somehow offended her, and in Israel he had learned that before Yom Kippur he needed to clean his slate by asking for her forgiveness. He also told himself that he did not want to appear to be begging for her attention or approval. As he walked up to her front door his heart was pounding so loudly he thought she would hear it right into her living room.

Chani was working on a sermon for the Shabbat morning service on the topic of seeking atonement from family and friends by asking their forgiveness for behaviors that may have been hurtful. In preparation for her D'var Torah she reread her master's thesis, as well as a dozen articles on this often-neglected pre-Yom Kippur practice that was designed to clear up troubled personal relationships before the end of the High Holiday period. An issue that preoccupied Chani had to do with the obligations of an 'offender' who asks a 'victim' for forgiveness but the request is denied. Although Chani knew that there were varying rabbinical opinions on this subject dating from as far back as Maimonides in the 12th century, she decided to stick with what she called the three strikes approach—ask for forgiveness three times and if it isn't granted you've met your obligation. Having completed her thinking about her forthcoming talk Chani started to type it out when she heard a knock on the door. Initially she thought it might be an animal in the yard and then she heard a second knock. Chani was not expecting anyone and the white Ford she saw in her driveway was unfamiliar.

She opened the door and there standing in front of her was Marc Cohn. He wasn't smiling and didn't ask to come in. All he said was, "Hi Chani, if I have offended you in any way, I ask for your forgiveness."

She was startled to see him. She stood there expressionless, wide-eyed, and rigidly straight.

Marc said for a second time, "If I have offended you in any way, please forgive me." Chani's expression did not change.

Then for third time, looking directly in her eyes, he said, "If I have offended you, please forgive me."

Chani was stunned. As still as a statue she stood silently in the doorway while her eyes started to fill with tears. Marc had concluded that Chani was not going to forgive him. He turned and started heading toward the car when he heard his name shouted, "Marc, come back."

Chani, choking back tears said, "Marc, you're forgiven, but you didn't do anything. I'm the one who needs to be forgiven. I am the one who offended you and I had no call to offend you. Please come in. It's cold and I want to explain."

Marc walked into Chani's house closed the door, turned around, and felt Chani wrapping her arms around him and sobbing.

Chani moved her papers from the sofa, sat down, and asked Marc to sit near her. "Marc, I'm the one who needs to be forgiven. You are a wonderful man with a fabulous son. You and Cathy did something very right with that boy. Frankly, he may have been a bit lost in Florida but up here he has certainly found himself. I also need to tell you about me and why I am begging for your forgiveness."

Choking back tears she said, "As you know I became a widow almost ten years ago. Since then I've thrown myself into a dream that Nathaniel and I had. Truth be told, it was initially more Nathaniel's dream than mine. When he died I felt it was my mission to actualize that dream. And, as you know, I work hard to make it happen every day. It is also a dream I don't want to abandon because it's now totally mine and I am proud of it and what it has become."

With tears streaming down her face Chani continued, "And like all dreams I've made sacrifices and decisions about my life that were shaken when you came on the scene. Until I met you, I decided that romance was not part of my life. I had a beautiful love with Nathaniel and I figured that was to be it. My requirements for men were so idealized and high that only a Nathaniel clone could meet them. And here in Seward, even Alaska, there was nobody. Then you appeared. And you're you, not Nathaniel. And, to be frank, I fell in love with you and it scared the holy crap out of me. And honestly, I'm still scared . . . But Marc, if you're ready for round two, I'm ready!"

Marc Cohn was stunned. He was, for one of the few times in his life, totally dumbfounded. Then finally he said, "Chani, I think I love you too. And I want to definitely try to make this work. But truthfully, right now, there are so many logistic problems. For example, I'm trying to sell my practice in Florida and it will take months, maybe more. And, I just made a commitment to work in December with a NGO in Israel training African physicians in reconstructive surgery both in Israel and Africa— I'm not sure what my own future holds."

Chani smiled through her tears, "Don't worry, I have a good job. Seriously though, we do need time to be with each other and we'll figure it out. Meanwhile, for this year, you can take care of your business knowing I'm here for you and Max is being well looked after."

It was 11:00 in the morning when Chani invited Marc into her bedroom and said, "Let's get close, but don't expect much, I'm way out of practice."

Marc replied, "Chani, every second we are in each other's arms is the best second of my life."

They undressed, held each other, and then made slow and passionate love. When they had each been satisfied, Chani looked at Marc and said, "I think I'm falling deeper and deeper in love with you every minute."

And he replied, "And those are my exact sentiments, rabbi."

A few more minutes of lying in bed wrapped in each other's arms passed when Chani said, "Marc, darling, I have to get up and get ready for services tonight. I will see you later, yes?"

He replied, "Later, forever, in person, via Skype, via Face Time . . . until we are always together. I need to call Norman and see if I can have lunch with him. After that I'm picking Max and the girls up at school."

They got up, dressed, and shared one more lingering kiss before Marc left for Norman's office.

Forty

SEWARD, ALASKA

At precisely 12:30 PM Marc arrived at Norman's office carrying two tuna fish salad sandwiches, a large order of French fries, and two diet Cokes. When Norman got up from his desk he was surprised to see Marc approach him, give him a hug, and kiss his cheek.

He then said, "I'm happy to see you, big bro."

Norman was pleased by Marc's affection and the fact that Marc was there in the first place. "Thanks, Marc, but what's going on? I didn't know you were in Israel and next thing I know you're in Seward. What's up?"

"Nothing's up. I wanted to spend part of the holiday with my son and my family."

"And Chani? I gather that's over. Sorry."

"Don't be sorry. It's not over. In fact, it is just beginning and I hope and pray it goes on for a very long time."

"Wow! That's great. You both are very special people. But anyway what was this Israel trip all about?"

"I'll answer that in a minute, but tell me how Max is doing?"

"He's fabulous. He is a great kid, the girls love him, he helps around the house, and he is totally into Mike's sled dogs. Frankly, at the beginning, I wasn't so sure about him. Let's face it he was a bit spoiled and used to having everything done for him. But now he's great! He's up early every morning, takes care of the dogs, makes his own breakfast, keeps his room neat, does his own laundry, and the girls are teaching him to cook. No problem at all. And do you know that Mike has hired him to help at the kennel a few hours a day?

"Also, don't worry about school—we see his teachers around town and he is a serious and star student. You probably won't even recognize him. He's grown a few inches but he's also put on a lot of muscle. You'll be surprised."

Marc was pleased to get the report. He also told him about being with Mike and Ethan in Jerusalem and how Mike had also sung Max's praises. He then related his experiences in Israel with Avrum and told Norman of his forthcoming work with the African doctors in December.

After Marc finished sharing stories about his time in Israel Norman updated his brother about the Petrillo case. Subsequent to the pardon the attorney general decided that the state wouldn't pursue any other possible charges against the doctor. Marc was also pleased to hear that Petrillo got back his license to practice medicine. "Good job, Marc, that guy owes his freedom and bright future to you."

As they were finishing eating and talking Marc stood up to leave, then turned to face Norman and said, "One more thing, Norman. If I have offended you in this past year, or in fact over the last forty-three years, please forgive me."

Norman was stunned by Marc's sincerity and the fact that he even knew about this tradition. He answered, "Of course, I forgive you. And please forgive me for my various and sundry offenses."

"Yes, you are forgiven."

Marc extended his hand to Norman who said, "Cut that handshake crap out. Give me another hug."

Marc's next stop was the Seward High School where he stood outside the main entrance. At two o'clock the teenagers started walking out in groups of three or four kids. In one of the first groups out there was a tall young man wearing a Mariners baseball cap who he didn't initially recognize. Then Max saw his father and yelled out, "Dad!" They embraced, totally unselfconsciously. Max turned to the others and said, "Guys, Jody, this is my Dad." They all seemed to know who he was, perhaps from the papers, and they all greeted him with a handshake and a, "Glad to meet you doc."

Marc asked if Rachel and Rebecca were coming out and Max said they had biked to school because they had a club meeting after class. Max then told Marc that he had to work for two extra hours at the kennel because Commander Pearl was in Israel. In reply Marc said he knew because he had just spent time with Mike and Ethan. Max suggested that they head to the kennel.

Once there it was evident that Max was comfortable and confident in the environment. He immediately got to work fetching water for the dogs, providing them an afternoon snack, and cleaning up. He went about checking each doghouse to see if hay was needed inside. On his rounds he made it a point to pet each dog and talk to them. Marc followed him around and was impressed with how well Max handled himself and how he knew each dog and even told his father something about them. "Dad, it's getting too late to take you out for a ride and we have to get home and clean up for Shabbat, so can you take me home? Tonight we have to be at shul by six and then there is a potluck."

Before they left the kennel Marc stopped in to say hello to Minnie who was quite interested in Marc's first hand and glowing report about Ethan. Meanwhile Jody had pulled Max to the back of the kitchen, whispered something in his ear to which they both laughed. A few minutes later they all said their goodbyes, at least for the next hour.

Arriving at Norman's, Marc hugged Blake and the twins and then said he would meet them at shul. Blake wasn't sure how Marc's appearance would affect Chani. She felt a sudden need to forewarn her closest friend.

As soon as Marc left and the kids had gone upstairs to shower and get dressed, Blake dialed Chani's number. She answered on the first ring.

"Hi Blake, are you calling to tell me Marc is in town?"

"Yes, how did you know?"

"I've already talked to him and everything is cool. Don't worry." Chani smiled to herself, *much better than cool, I wasn't looking for anyone but I think God has sent me a mensch.* "I'll see you in a little bit. Don't forget it's potluck vegetarian Shabbat and you had better have made the vegetable lasagna."

Forty-One

Seward, Alaska

The Cohn family arrived at the synagogue early Friday night to help set up for the potluck. Later that night when Blake and Norman were comparing notes about the evening they sensed that something was different about Chani. They also agreed that it was an inner joy and radiance that they hadn't seen in years.

Chani greeted them warmly and a few minutes later when Marc entered the building, Norman and Blake were surprised at how Marc was met with an extended embrace and kiss. They all proceeded to set up the buffet table for the after-service dinner and then move the chairs into rows facing the bima for the Friday night service.

At 6:30 PM the service began when Chani stood up on the bima and started singing a round of the song "Shalom Aleichem," which was picked up quickly by the fifty congregants. She then welcomed everyone. "We are particularly delighted to see our members and friends from the other side of the Kenai Peninsula who are joining us for Shabbat and then again on Sunday night for the beginning of Yom Kippur. By the way, all the out-of-towners can come to my house on Yom Kippur for a wonderful pancake breakfast." This elicited laughter from the group since everyone knew that Yom Kippur is a twenty-six hour fast day beginning at sunset with the Kol Nidre Service and ending the following evening with the Neila service.

"And a special welcome back to Dr. Marc Cohn, Max's dad, who just flew in from Israel to spend this holiday with us. We'll have a surprise for him and the rest of you at the end of tonight's service. So, let's begin."

The service proceeded as a typical one on Friday night in Seward with a combination of joy and enthusiasm. Right before the conclusion Chani stepped to the front of the bima and said, "Friends this is the beginning of a very special Shabbat. It is the Shabbat between Rosh Hashanah and Yom Kippur and known as Shabbat Shuvah. In traditional synagogues this was one of two Sabbaths when the rabbi would give a long sermon, usually on return or repentance. Don't worry; my sermon tomorrow will be my usual fifteen minutes in length. What is particularly important for us to remember is the message from tomorrow's Haftorah—that we need to repent—that is, ask forgiveness from each other for our deeds that have offended others, whether knowingly or not, and on Yom Kippur we'll deal with God. So, dear friends, and I say friends because in the years I have been here you have become my friends, indeed, my family, I offer my sincere apologies to any and all of you for anything I may have done to offend you and I request forgiveness."

The congregation, hardly in unison, some loudly and others quietly said, "You are forgiven."

"Thank you. And now for a special treat, I mentioned earlier. The service will conclude with Adon Olam, followed by Aleinu and then Yigdal. This final part of the service will be led by a new vocal group called The Yiddisher Dogmushers. Our singers are the three Cohns and Jody Pearl."

The four teenagers came forward and Max stepped to the front and said, "Please join us in Adon Olom to the tune of 'America The Beautiful.'"

Marc was astounded. He was thrilled to both see Max's poise and to watch him having fun and interacting with the girls. When the song was completed to rousing applause the teens transitioned into the serious

Aleinu prayer and then Chani took over again and asked the mourners and those observing a Yahrzeit to please stand. Nodding in the direction of each person she asked the six people standing if they wished to mention the name of their lost loved one. The first three mentioned the names of deceased mothers or fathers. Then the fourth and fifth, an elderly couple from Homer, mentioned a man's name and identified him as their son. It seemed that most people there knew him, or knew of him. Norman later explained that the man was a commercial fisherman who had died at sea almost a decade ago. He had left a wife and three children who were now living in Anchorage.

Chani next looked directly at Marc and he said, "I am saying Kaddish for my late wife, Cathy Feldman Cohn."

When he said that Max stood up and said, "Excuse me, rabbi, I am saying Kaddish for my mother, Cathy Cohn."

Those words from Max struck a chord in Chani and she needed to suddenly take a few deep breaths to prevent herself from crying. Seconds passed, she regained her composure, and continued, "Please everyone stand and join our friends by saying Kaddish in support of them and their families." They then began the traditional Kaddish prayer.

When the prayer was completed Chani, said, "The Yiddisher Dogmushers will now lead us in the closing song Yigdal. After that they will chant the blessing over the wine; for those who would like to wash, please head to the sinks. And Max, backed by his Dogmusher partners will lead us in the Hamotzi. Then we'll enjoy this wonderful food that I thank all of you for preparing."

When the blessing of the bread was finished Chani gave each of the teens a long hug and kiss. Max had, in the several months he had been in Seward, become very fond of Chani and especially enjoyed her warmth. After that she stepped off the bima and walked around the room hugging and kissing each person and wishing him or her a Shabbat Shalom. When she came to Marc there was an especially long hug, followed by a short kiss, not on the cheek but the mouth. Blake observed this, nudged Norman, and said; "Now that's what I call forgiveness."

The conclusion of the potluck came when Chani stood up and said, "Friends, just a reminder. Because of the long weekend of services there will be no Torah study tomorrow morning and our regular services will begin at 10:00 AM. The Kol Nidre service will begin promptly at 6:30 on Sunday night. Let's bench and tonight Norman Cohn will act as our leader." And so they began. When that was over the cleanup started and a half hour later the garbage was in the bear-proof containers away from the building on a well-lit path, the aluminum dining tables were folded up and put in a cabinet, a table was set up along the wall for Saturday's after-service Kiddush, and the chairs were once again arranged in rows facing the bima for Saturday's service.

Everyone was leaving when Chani called to Marc and said quietly, "Can you stay the night? It will feel like a real Shabbat with you next to me." He said yes, but he would first go to his hotel and get clean clothes for Saturday and his toiletries.

An hour later Marc arrived at Chani's home where he found that she had started a fire in her fireplace. She beckoned him to sit next to her on the couch facing the glowing and crackling logs. Chani put her arms around Marc's neck, kissed him gently, and said, "I think I could spend the rest of my life just like this."

Marc laughed and simply replied, "Me, too."

She then pulled back a few inches looked into his blue eyes and said, "So much has happened so quickly and I feel a need to talk for a while."

Marc nodded.

Chani resumed, "Well, to begin with, I think I love you. But I'm scared about going too far, too fast. I don't want to hurt you and I also don't want to get hurt. So, there are a couple of things I want you to know about my background that few people know, in fact I think only Blake knows and perhaps Norman."

Marc again nodded his head and held Chani's hand even tighter than before while she went on to talk about her feelings of betrayal and abandonment by her father, whom she had once loved without reservation. For close to two hours Chani described what she characterized as her father's flawed character based on what she thought were his greed-focused investments with Ozzie Wolfe and his theft of money from the nursing home residents whose trust he had broken. She concluded by saying that she blamed her mother's death on her father's behavior, and her own occasional feelings of abandonment on her father and Nathaniel, although she acknowledged that in her husband's case it was an accident.

Marc quietly listened and then with a few words he said to Chani precisely what she needed to hear, "Sweetheart, I understand. You have had a more difficult time than you or anyone deserves. But, in this season of forgiveness and renewal I think we have to not only forgive the living but also the dead. And sometimes we even need to forgive ourselves for our own feelings. But please remember just one thing. I love you and even if I'm not next to you or around the corner, I will always be there for you."

Chani listened and then smiling through tears said, "Thank you. I love you Marc Cohn. Maybe you should be a rabbi."

They laughed, hugged for a few minutes, checked to make sure that the fire was out, turned off the lights, walked into the bedroom arm in arm, and went to sleep.

Over breakfast the next morning Chani pushed a few typewritten pages across the table to Marc and said, "I would appreciate it if you read my D'var Torah for today and share with me any thoughts. In particular, please read the last paragraph and tell me what you think."

After completing the reading Marc looked directly into Chani's eyes and said, "My God, you are beautiful. But that wasn't the question. I think your sermon is both outstanding and inspiring. It truly captures the essence of teshuvah. Thank you for giving me this preview. I love you!"

A broad smile crossed Chani's face, she got up and kissed Marc and said, "Thanks, my love."

When Blake and Norman arrived they were surprised to find Marc already at the synagogue taking care of the final arrangements for the services. They were also quite pleased by the unexpected gifts from

Marc. Chani was showing them the beautiful Yad that Marc had brought for the shul from Israel. He had explained to Chani that he had been afraid to bring her a more intimate gift and she replied, "You are my intimate gift from Israel."

Max and Norman loved their new prayer shawls and for the first time Marc was wearing his own new one. The girls liked their hamsa necklaces and Blake was quite pleased with her silk scarf and head covering. When Marc asked Max if he wanted to wear the new prayer shawl, Max replied that he wanted to talk privately about it with his father.

Max then said, "Dad, I hope it's OK with you but I want to study with Chani and have a bar-mitzvah around my next birthday. Is that OK?"

A huge smile crossed Marc's face and as he hugged Max he said, "Yes, absolutely, that would be great."

"So, I'd like to wait for my bar-mitzvah to wear the tallit. OK?"

"Absolutely."

As the other three-dozen people arrived for the service the shul became full of joyful conversation and fellowship. The services began once Chani mounted the bima and welcomed everyone. After the Torah was read, the Haftorah chanted, and the Torah returned to the ark, Chani began her sermon.

"As I promised last night my sermon this morning is related to our Haftorah readings from Hosea, Michah, and Joel. All three of these readings have the common theme of seeking God's forgiveness and our returning to God. My focus will be on Hosea, the fourth line of which begins the essential theme of today: 'And return to the Lord, Say to Him: Forgive all guilt.' The next part of that section basically points out the benefits of return and the words of Hosea conclude, 'For the paths of the Lord are smooth; The righteous can walk on them, while sinners stumble.'"

"So here is my question: How do we seek forgiveness? And part of my question is also how do we forgive? A related question is, do we always have to forgive? Whenever I think of forgiveness I am reminded of a controversy that happened when President Ronald Reagan planned a visit to Bitburg Military Cemetery in Germany. The visit, scheduled for May 1985, was somehow related to a ceremony celebrating Germany's relationship with the United States forty years after the end of World War II. Reagan's handlers had decided it was reasonable to visit this cemetery with German Chancellor Kohl despite the fact that approximately forty-nine German SS troops were buried there. Once this trip was announced in April an uproar ensued with many politicians—and even Reagan's wife—objecting to his visit to Bitburg. Fueling the uproar was the claim that President Reagan's schedule was so crowded that he did not have time to visit a former concentration camp.

"A month before the scheduled trip to Germany, President Reagan presided over a White House ceremony where Holocaust survivor Elie Weisel was presented with the Congressional Gold Medal of Achievement. In his speech after accepting the medal he urged President Reagan not to go to Bitburg and Weisel said, 'That place, Mr. President, is not your place. Your place is with the victims of the SS.' Indeed, the hue and cry in this country over his itinerary was so great that President Reagan's handlers finally added a stop at the nearby Bergen-Belsen concentration camp where the President paid homage to more than 50,000 victims of Nazi terror who were buried there.

"Friends, there are simply some things that we do to one another that are beyond reconciliation. Such things must be avoided at all costs. I must admit that these questions of forgiveness and reconciliation have been on my mind for years. In the past I have mentioned that when I was a graduate student in social work I wrote my thesis on forgiveness. For those of you who are new, and those who have forgotten, the essential finding was that for us the Jewish holidays provide a naturally reoccurring time each year when we can reconcile with one another as well as God. And, this particular season is when we are expected to effect that reconciliation. Now, although we have a formulaic way of asking forgiveness, is that enough? And what is it that we can forgive?

"Recently I read *Sunflower*, a short memoir by the famed Nazi hunter Simon Wiesenthal. In this book he writes about the time when he was a prisoner in a concentration camp and he is sent on on a work detail to a hospital. At the hospital a nurse takes him into the room of a twenty-one year-old heavily bandaged Nazi soldier who was mortally wounded and dying. The soldier, who had participated in horrendous and savage acts, requested that a Jew be brought into his room. Once Wiesenthal entered the room the Nazi soldier began a detailed description of the terrible things he did as a SS soldier. Then after his lengthy confession, the Nazi asked Wiesenthal for forgiveness. Simon Wiesenthal listened, said nothing, and walked out of the room. The question that is often asked is, what would we do under the same circumstances? There is a Jewish answer and I will discuss it in a few minutes.

"Last night I offered those of you who were here the formulaic request for forgiveness. You forgave me and I in turn forgave you. Let's face it: such an approach is pretty wimpy! If I really offended any of you in some particular way you are not likely to just blow it off with last night's request!

"On the other hand, if I approach you personally and genuinely ask for forgiveness, and we both know what it is about, or we discuss it, then I would hope I would be forgiven. But, what is the real test? The test will come when I am again faced with the same situation and then act in the appropriate manner. Remember, whether I am the forgiver or—excuse my botching the English language—the forgivee, I become unburdened. As the one asking for forgiveness I can recognize my error, acknowledge it, and thus unburden myself. As the person granting the forgiveness I cannot carry that hurt around and thus also unburden myself. This is all spelled out for us in the Mishnah from which we learn that Yom Kippur is our day to confess our sins against God and seek atonement. But for our sins against each other, we need to seek forgiveness directly from the other person.

"The question in the case of Simon Wiesenthal is whether he can forgive someone for misdeeds against others. Virtually all Talmudic scholars answer the question in the same way and that is, that someone cannot forgive another for offenses against a third party. Thus, a murderer can never be forgiven despite all the penance in the world. Only the dead person has the power to forgive.

"Friends, when we begin Kol Nidre on Sunday night we shall be entering a holy time when we need to return to God and ask for forgiveness at that level. But we still have a small window of opportunity left to clear the books with our families, friends, and, yes, even people we don't like very much.

"Finally, allow me to share a very personal experience and insight. Recently I offended someone who did absolutely nothing to deserve my extremely unkind words. The result of my behavior ended an important friendship. For months I was unhappy about what I did, but frankly I didn't know what to do about it. And, as so often happens in these situations, I went through my days and nights with a pebble in my shoe. My friend was also unhappy that our friendship had turned sour. This friend simply didn't, and I daresay couldn't, understand what occurred to garner my unkind words because at that point I failed to have the insight to understand the situation myself.

"But fortunately for me, this friend was a more religious person than I am, and knowing that Yom Kippur was upon us, came halfway across the world to see me and ask for forgiveness for offending me. That moment caused me to wake up, confront myself, and realize that I was really the person who needed to ask for forgiveness. Fortunately, I was forgiven and we are good friends again and I hope forever.

"I share this very personal experience with you, my friends and community, because I want this to be a season of healing for all of us, followed by seasons of joy and love. Shabbat Shalom."

Chani sat down, wiped tears from her eyes as the congregation sat in silence, many of them also blotting their eyes. Then Chani stood and said, "Let's begin the conclusion of the service with the silent Amidah."

A few minutes later services were over and everyone moved to the Kiddush table where the kids blessed the wine and challah and people stood around enjoying each other's company. Marc was busy talking with Max, his nieces, Norman, and Blake. Minnie came over to inquire some more about Ethan and Mike. After an hour most of the people had left. Marc was sitting with Paul Polansky discussing prison healthcare when Chani walked over and put her arm through his. When Paul and Akna departed, Chani looked at Marc in mock seriousness and said, "So Marc, how do you like being a *rebbetzin*?" They both laughed and then started to the help the others prepare the room for Kol Nidre.

During the cleanup Chani asked Marc about his schedule for the next few days. He told her he would be leaving early on Wednesday morning for Florida. It pleased her that they would be spending this important holiday together. By the time the cleanup was finished, and the room set up for Kol Nidre, only the Cohn family and Chani were left. She asked all of them to come into her home for some leftover food. The kids demurred saying they were heading over to the kennel to do some work. The two couples had a light lunch and then Blake and Norman went home. Chani suggested that she and Marc go for a hike before all of them met for dinner at the waterfront. Marc's clothes were at the hotel so he drove back downtown, changed, and met Chani at her house for a hike that took them on the lower segments of the Mount Marathon trails.

They walked and talked for most of the afternoon discussing everything from Marc's experiences in Israel to Chani's travels, her work at the prison, and the synagogue. At one point they were taking a rest by sitting on a log and drinking some coconut water. Marc asked a question that was still bothering him, "Why of all places in the world are you in Seward?"

"Marc, it's a complicated answer and I think I've been dodging that question from you for a while. But I'll try to be honest with you. Some of the reasons I'm here are no longer important. But, for me, the reasons I am staying have become very important. To begin with, like a lot of people I meet up here in Alaska, I was initially escaping some serious pains. There was obviously the pain of my late husband's death, but frankly by the time I was ordained that had pretty well abated.

"Then there were the pains I mentioned last night of embarrassment and shame I felt about my father. As you probably know Cambridge Isles was a pretty affluent community and while observance was important, so was money.

"After his death, I felt that I couldn't walk around my home community without people whispering behind my back or even to my face. I needed to start somewhere fresh. So, as you know right after I got my MSW I took off for Israel looking for a break or something and *voila!* I found Nathaniel. Together we shared the dream and then he died. I was lost for a while and Blake kicked me in the butt; I became a rabbi and here I am with my best friends in the world."

At the next rest stop, Marc posed another question that intrigued him, "So, why be a rabbi?"

"Wow, you're really digging! I'm going to answer but then I have a question for you, lover boy. My simple answer is I want to be Godly, in the best sense of the word. When I was about ten years old I remember once walking home from shul on a Saturday after a rainstorm. I was with my parents and Rabbi and Mrs. Friedman. The rabbi saw a beautiful rainbow that he pointed out to us, and then he quite unpretentiously and naturally recited a Hebrew prayer. When I asked him about the prayer he explained it way of thanking God for remembering his covenant with us after the great flood. I was totally astounded how he enjoyed the world around him with such ease and gratitude.

"So I'm a person who also searches for God everywhere, in prayer, in nature, but mostly in people. My absolute favorite musical is *Les Miserables*. I've seen it five times and listened to the music countless times. And, the line that resonates most with me is, 'To love another person is to see the face of God.' Marc, I think I really love you and God's face sure is handsome."

"Chani, my love, ditto for you!"

"And what about you Marc? Ever want to be anything other than a plastic surgeon?"

"Sometimes when I was a kid I would hang around my father's drugstore and two things fascinated me. First, there was the back part of the store, behind the counter, where my father had what seemed to me to be thousands of bottles of pills and powders. I would watch him read the prescriptions and pick and choose drugs, count, and bottle and label them. Frequently he would be compounding the medications, mixing stuff, making liquid drugs. I didn't understand it all but I was loved watching the production in this little factory that my father owned. The other part of the store that I liked was the cash register, which my mother usually operated. She seemed to know every item that they sold and the price. My mom was truly able to help every person who came into the store.

"When I think back on all of that, as well as my medical school experience, I realize what I was looking to do was, for lack of a better term, short cycled. I wanted to do some type of quick fix mechanical medicine. See a problem, fix it, and move on. So, surgery appealed to me; someone had a problem, I fixed it. Frankly, I couldn't do the more long-term cerebral parts of medicine such as neurology, nephrology, or oncology. Don't get me wrong. I have the greatest respect for the people in those specialties, but I frankly like the action of the operating room, and when I went into cosmetic surgery and built my own center, I liked the clientele, the money, and the control of my own space.

"So I really didn't answer your question but told you more than you probably wanted to know about me. But, I want you to know that over the last few months I've done a lot of thinking about my life, and frankly, I don't know what I'd do if I gave up cosmetic surgery. I'm at a crossroads. I'm planning on selling my practice. I really don't know where I'm going or what I'm doing or who I'm doing it with—but I certainly hope it's you!"

"Could you imagine living here in Alaska?"

"Chani, if a year ago someone had said to me that a day before Yom Kippur I'd be hiking in the mountains near Seward, Alaska, with a beautiful woman rabbi who I love, that the week before that I would be in Israel, that in December I'd be working pro bono for an Israeli charity training African doctors, and, in fact, I would also be somewhere in Africa supervising those same doctors, that my son would be mushing sled dogs in Alaska, and that I would be contemplating selling my practice, I would call 9-1-1 and tell them to pick me up and bring a straitjacket. My answer is what my mother used to say and about the only Yiddish expression I remember: *Mann trakht und Gott lakht* (man plans and God laughs).”

Marc and Chani starting laughing and when the laughter died down they turned and held each other tightly, grateful that fate had brought them together.

Sunset that evening was scheduled for 7:31 PM and the plan was to meet at the Cohn house for Havdalah—the closing ceremony of Shabbat—at 7:00, and after a short service head out to a waterfront restaurant.

Marc dropped Chani off with a plan to pick her up a few minutes before seven. He then went to the hotel to shower and change. As he was getting dressed for the evening he looked at himself in the mirror and realized that he was, at that moment, extraordinarily happy about his life.

When Chani and Marc arrived at the Cohn house they were in for a surprise. What they found as they walked in were three teenagers busy in the kitchen cutting and chopping vegetables and a slightly thawed salmon. Max announced, “Dad, in your honor we have decided to eat at home. The three master chefs, Madams Rachel and Rebecca and Monsieur Max, will prepare your dinner. Please sit down and enjoy the munchies while we slave away preparing a feast.”

The adults did as they were told, and Marc’s smile of gratitude and happiness once more appeared on his face. As the teens worked through the preparations for their surprise meal, the adults were working their way through bowls of popcorn, chips, hummus, and nuts all the while talking about Marc’s trip to Israel. He shared with them his experiences with people and places and the coincidental meeting with Mike and Ethan, as well as the long-term relationship that Mike had with Reb Avrum. Marc suddenly remembered something and he looked at Chani and asked her for a big smile. She said: “Huh, why do you want a big smile?”

"Come on indulge me for a minute, just one beautiful smile." So, Chani smiled and Marc said, "You know who else I met, and he said he did a great job and he was right—Sam and his wife Audrey."

Chani broke out in laughter, "They're some of my favorite people." She looked at Blake and Norman and barely controlling herself said, "He was my orthodontist in Florida."

Marc turned serious when he spoke of Hattie Ferguson and her International Institute's work in Africa on reconstructive surgery. "Hattie is an extraordinary person and after talking to her I had no choice but to get involved." Chani suddenly felt such a deep emotional connection to Marc she leaned over and kissed him and squeezed his hand. Blake and Norman just watched feeling both joy and befuddlement.

At 7:30 Blake got up and brought out her new sterling silver Havdalah set. She said, "Chani, this is a new set that Marc brought us from Israel. Would you do us the honor of leading our first Havdalah service with it?"

The kids came in from the kitchen, dimmed the lights as Blake filled the Kiddush cup with grape juice and lit the multicolored braided Havdalah candle. Next the group began the short service that separated the Sabbath from the remainder of the week. After saying the prayers and engaging in the simple rituals, the group held hands and sang a final song together followed by kisses all around. Even though all of these rituals were new to him, Marc felt close to everyone, and was overjoyed as he looked as his son and saw contentment in his face—the contentment of someone who was an integral part of a family unit.

Rachel then said, "Friends and family please amuse yourselves for another half-hour and then we shall begin this pre-pre-Kol Nidre feast that is being prepared by the RR&M Group, Seward's newly established, finest and only kosher caterer."

Thirty minutes later they were called to the table where Max and Rebecca took turns announcing the menu of stir fried salmon and vegetables seasoned with Paul Prudhomme's Blackened Redfish Magic, brown rice, and garden salad. The food was delicious and Marc again was thrilled at his son's engagement with everyone as well as his cooking skills. Dessert was a homemade carrot cake and a tub of vanilla ice cream. When the supper was over, the adults sent the kids off to watch TV while they cleaned up. By 11:00 the dining room and kitchen were straightened up and the dishwasher was humming through its cycles.

As Chani and Marc were getting ready to leave Max came out of the family room, gave his father and Chani a hug, and thanked them for coming. He then told his father that he was working half a day at the kennel and he would like to take him out on a sled dog ride around 10:30 AM. Without a second's hesitation Marc said yes and then asked if Chani could come along. But before Max could answer, Chani declined, saying she had too much work to do in preparation for Kol Nidre. The plans made, Marc and Chani went home.

Forty-Two

Seward, Alaska

By the time Marc arrived at Commander Pearl's kennel, Max had been there more than two hours. It was a Sunday morning in October and no tour groups had booked rides but the kennels still needed cleaning, the dogs needed food and water as well as attention, and, finally, they needed exercise. Working that morning were Max, Minnie, and Joe and Judy McGee—the couple from whom the Pearls' had purchased the business. The McGees worked part-time at the kennel where Joe was Mike's right-hand man about everything. Judy, a social worker turned Iditarod musher, used Mike's kennel as a site for training local teenagers, particularly troubled ones, to work with the dogs as a form of animal-assisted therapy. When Judy heard that Marc was Max's dad she simply said, "Max is fabulous. A totally natural dog man and musher."

With an obvious pride of ownership Max once again led his dad around the kennel and introduced him to all the dogs and described some of the operations of the place. After the short tour Max asked his father if he was ready to go for a ride. Marc was enthusiastic in his affirmative reply.

Max then explained to his father that the kennel had several different types of sleds for the snowless runs and all of them had been designed and built by the Commander to accommodate different size teams and numbers of tourists. "The one we are going to use today was constructed to hold two people on a bench seat in front of the musher. You'll sit on the bench and I'll stand behind you on a platform built over the rear axle that is attached to two 12-inch diameter wheels. The front of the cart has one smaller wheel and the whole mechanism is steered by ropes that I use, somewhat like reins.

"Also, as you'll see, the dogs are well trained and they instantly respond to my vocal commands. When we stop, or in case of emergency, I also have a basic braking system that consists of a metal plate on a spring, and when I step on the plate, it jams against the rear wheels. Once we've stopped, I can lock the brakes. Also, all of us mushers carry some kind of an anchor system. Right now we obviously can't use the snow hook so I have a single prong hook that I'll use to secure the sled and dogs when we stop. Dad, are you ready to roll?" Marc nodded.

Lastly, Max explained that they were taking a small team of five dogs out that morning, but that the dogs he selected were strong enough to pull them. He also noted that he had decided to pick older and gentler dogs that wouldn't be running too fast. Marc liked the idea of older, gentler dogs and appreciated Max's thoughtfulness.

As soon as the dogs saw that Max was going to start the selection process an incredible ruckus of barking and jumping began. For a moment Marc got scared. He looked at Max and anxiously asked, "What's going on?"

Once again, Max went through the spiel he used with tourists: "Nothing. This is their natural behavior. What they are doing and saying is 'pick me, pick me.' It's actually kind of amusing. You'll see as soon as we harness them up and start to move the kennel will become absolutely quiet."

Max went around and selected his dogs one by one and tied them onto the gang-line all the while talking and petting them. When the team was tied in and ready to go Marc sat down on the sled's bench, Max released the brakes, and called out "HIKE." Immediately, the dogs took off. As they raced down the trail Max explained that his lead dog was getting on in years but had all the important characteristics of a leader, including an innate desire to run and an ability to listen to commands and react quickly as well. Perhaps most importantly, the lead dog was not intimated by the other dogs. Marc listened to his son's observations and thought they were as applicable to people as animals.

"Dad, are you okay—do you want to go faster?"

"Thanks, I'm fine. This pace is good for me."

"Hang on, we're going to make a few turns."

Max started calling out the commands of "HAW" to turn left, then two minutes later he shouted "GEE" and the dogs executed a smooth right turn. A few minutes after that Max shouted

"EASY" and the dogs started to slow down, then "WHOA" and they stopped as Max smoothly stepped on the brake.

"Dad, you want to stand and stretch? In a few minutes we'll head back."

Marc stood up, stepped off the sled and watched as Max tied the sled down and walked over to each dog, talked to the animal, petted them, and checked their legs and feet for any injuries. He then said, "Dad, if you're ready, let's head back. If it's all right with you I'll let them run a little faster." Marc nodded ascent.

Max freed the secondary safety brake, stood on the platform, released the foot brake, and called out "HIKE." A few times during the run he called out "GET UP," urging the dogs to have some fun and run faster. As they approached the kennel he slowed them down and stopped the sled.

Marc got off the sled and said; "Max that was great and now I know why everyone tells me that you're a natural musher. This was amazing. I am so proud of you." And he then moved toward Max and gave him a huge kiss on the cheek.

Max asked if Marc could stay around for another half-hour so that he could complete his chores and then be driven home. Marc agreed but also suggested that before going back they first have lunch. Max liked that idea. They decided to go back to Marc's hotel room, clean up, and eat in the hotel restaurant.

An hour later when they were sitting in the dining room ordering lunch, Marc began, "You seem to like it here."

"I love it. I like this town, I love Aunt Blake and Uncle Norman, the girls are awesome, and I like the shul and Rabbi Chani. School's great and the kennel is amazing."

"Would you want to come back to Florida"?

"Honestly, Dad, I don't want to hurt your feelings but, no! In fact, if you'd let me, I want to finish high school here."

"You know it gets very cold and snowy as well as dark here all winter?"

"I don't care. Do you think Aunt Blake and Uncle Norman would let me stay with them? Maybe you can pay them?"

"I'll think about that. Give me some time."

"Speaking of time, I think we better hustle back and get ready for Kol Nidre."

Forty-Three

SEWARD, ALASKA

By the time Chani walked into the synagogue, the place was packed with people standing along the side of the room and sitting on the ledge surrounding the fireplace. Chani began: "Welcome friends to what I hope will be a meaningful period of prayer, meditation, learning, and communication. I wish each of you an easy and meaningful fast.

"I would like to now introduce Professor Shlomo Fishson, Mike Pearl's brother-in-law, and our cantor for the Kol Nidre and Yom Kippur services. As I am certain you will come to agree, it is a blessing that we were able to cajole Shlomo into leading our services. In real life, besides his occasional chazzan gigs, he is professor of engineering at a university near Boston.

"As the regulars know, I always introduce this service with a poem written by Sandra Brooks, a friend of mine from social work school who fought a long battle with ovarian cancer and died just a few months after we both graduated from Miller. It's a touching poem from her book of poetry, *Presence of Absence*, and it was written a day before Yom Kippur. It is aptly titled Kol Nidre.

> I walked out of the
> Sunlight

And into a room
Where slept a
Young black woman
Painfully twisted
On a blue plastic
Lounger
A still, smiling lady
With a halo of
Grey and
A very small
Very old man
Grey and frail
Beside her.

I walked out of the sunlight and
Into a room
Where I heard sobbing
And the
Senseless blare
Of daytime TV.

I walked out of the
Sunlight and into
A room where I
Took my place
With all of the
Others and hooked
Up to dripping
Poisons and waited my turn, this time
Just for a prick and
A flush and then
Back out into the
Sunlight,

Transformed by the room
And a code blue
In the
Pain clinic.

I walked out of
The twilight
And into a room
Crowded and bright and full
Of chanting and
Prayer, "Shana
Tova" and
"Gut Yor."

From lightness
To dark from
Darkness to light
The circle of
My day is complete.

"This Kol Nidre service itself begins when we open the ark, take out our two Torahs and the chazzan chants the Kol Nidre statement, in what is conceptually a formal court-like setting. The actual statement made by the chazzan on behalf of the congregation is that all vows and promises we make to God between this time and next Yom Kippur, we repent or retract, if we forget them. In other words, we are asking God for absolution for those promises to Him that we can't keep.

"As a young girl this service was unbelievably dramatic. In our synagogue in Florida all nine Torahs with all their beautiful white velvet covers, silver breastplates, and finials would be removed from the ark and ten men, usually past presidents, would be given the great honor of holding a Torah while the prayer and its responses were chanted.

"As most of you know we do it slightly differently in our community. Every year a committee comprised of our past presidents meets on the morning before Kol Nidre and selects two people to hold our Torahs. The criteria for selection are extraordinary service to our synagogue and/or the area or some activity that has reflected particularly well on our Jewish community. This is our version of the Academy Awards. Norman, the envelope please."

Rabbi Chani took the first envelope and a broad smile crossed her face when she read, "The past presidents give the honor of holding the first Torah to Dr. Marc Cohn who brought credit to our Jewish community by his heroic and selfless actions in saving lives at the Kenai prison during a disastrous fire." She asked Marc to join her on the bima as she went to the ark and handed him what was now known at the Czech Torah.

Chani then took the second envelope, opened it, and her face turned crimson and tears filled her eyes. The congregation wondered what was happening and then it became clear as she haltingly read, "The past presidents give the honor of holding the second Torah to Rabbi Chani Kahn who brought credit to our Jewish community by her heroic and selfless actions in saving lives, at great personal risk to herself, at the Kenai prison during a disastrous fire." She moved over to the ark, took out the second Torah, and stood next to the chazzan as he began the Kol Nidre service.

The next twenty-six hours passed relatively smoothly as the service proceeded through many prayers, meditations, responsive readings, confessional prayers, and countless stories and explanations by Chani and Cantor Shlomo. Many people fasted as they tried to get into the rhythm and feeling of the holy day. As the sun was setting on Monday, and Yom Kippur was drawing to a close, Chani was pleased to see so many of the congregation and visitors finding a renewed strength to stand through the final Neilah service.

Rabbi Chani explained to the congregation that this was meta-phorically the closing of the heavenly gates after each congregant had professed to God, and themselves, their repentance and plans for a good year to come. The sections that Chani emphasized were the *Vidui* where she said, "We confess our sins individually and collectively and ask God for forgiveness." She told her congregation: "Chevra, please work hard, feel this prayer in your heart and your *kishkes*. By engaging with this prayer we connect with our higher selves and God. Try it. It works!"

One of the concluding prayers brought out every last ounce of energy in the congregation when they sang the Avinu Malkeinu, a haunting plead that she explained, "Acknowledges our sins and asks God to forgive us, ignore our past sins, and annul evil degrees and plots against us as well as various bad things that could happen to us. Finally, the prayer has its request section where we ask God to seal us in the Books of Happiness, Deliverance, Prosperity, Merit, and Forgiveness."

The Yom Kippur service ended with the three traditional prayers proclaiming the oneness of God and a final blowing of the shofar.

Chani thanked the congregation for their participation, Chazzan Shlomo for leading a beautiful service, and wished everyone a healthy and happy new year. "Hopefully all our prayers will be answered affirmatively and the coming year will see many simchas and good things in our lives. Now, give the caterers a few minutes to set up and we will share in a lovely community break-fast."

This was the first time in his life that Marc had participated in an entire Yom Kippur service. The day was simply perfect from the first moment of Kol Nidre to the final shofar blast. Sitting next to Max, Norman, and the rest of his family he experienced a contentment and connection that he had never felt before. Watching Chani on the pulpit, her intelligence, grace, and charisma were mesmerizing for Marc. As his mind wandered at one point he realized that his love for Chani was growing by the second.

He was also totally appreciative of the honor of being asked to hold the Torah during Kol Nidre. This was another first—he had never held a Torah before. A few weeks later, in a conversation back in Florida, Reb Avrum asked him how it felt holding this Torah that was hundreds of years old and rescued from the Holocaust. Marc replied, "Magical, thrilling, almost as if the Torah was totally part of me."

It took a few minutes for Chani to work her way through all the well-wishers and come to the Cohns for whom she had the most effusive greetings, especially Marc. She was starting to feel like all the Cohns were not only her closest friends but also her family.

The caterers worked swiftly in setting up the tables, chairs, and a buffet that was laden with juices, fruit, bagels, salmon, salads, sweet rolls, and hot drinks. Before long everyone was busy eating and enjoying one another's company.

For most people the following day meant back to work. For Marc it meant a late afternoon and evening drive to Anchorage to take the 1:35 AM flight to Seattle so that he could connect with the 8:40 AM nonstop flight to Fort Lauderdale. Although he was very much enjoying the break-fast and he knew he would be back for Thanksgiving, he was already missing Chani, Max, and the rest of his family.

By 10:00 PM the synagogue was cleaned up and the food put away for the following Shabbat's Kiddush. Only Chani and Marc remained. He looked into her eyes and said, "You are not only beautiful but brilliant and inspirational. This Yom Kippur was totally awesome! I thank you. And, I love you. And worst of all I already miss you and I'm not leaving till 3 PM tomorrow."

"Thank you, my love. Having you here meant a great deal to me. And, I want you to know I love you and your family, and I already miss you. And, I'm sorry I couldn't sleep with you last night. But in many ways I'm very traditional, and Yom Kippur rules are no nooky. But tonight is different. I hope you're staying."

"I am."

"Great. But let's talk about tomorrow. You said you're leaving at 3 o'clock. When are you seeing Max?"

"I told him I'd meet him at 11:00. He has a forty-five minute break for lunch and we'll grab something and say our goodbyes then. Can we spend part of the afternoon together before I go?"

"I've got another idea. The weather for the next two days is fore-casted to be clear. So how about returning the rental car here in Seward, and we'll fly up to Anchorage around noon and spend the whole day up there? We can stay near the airport and you can get some rest before the flight, maybe—or maybe not—and then I'll fly back the next morning. We can look around Anchorage; go to the Jewish Heritage Museum, and maybe the new museum downtown, it'll be a vacation and fun. Are you game?"

"It's a deal."

The following morning Chani and Marc were up before sunrise and both were privately thinking to themselves that they were as happy and content as they had ever been in their lives. Chani got out of bed first and insisted on making Marc a "proper post Yom Kippur breakfast" of French toast with some leftover frozen challah—"the best food in the world." They sat at her kitchen table with a view of the mountains in the background. Chani told Marc that after they cleaned up she needed to do some paper work, and then go to the airport to check out her plane. Marc's plan was to return to his hotel, pack, check out, pick up some sandwiches for lunch, stop in and say goodbye to Norman, visit with Max, return the car, and get a ride from the auto rental agency to the airport.

At 10:15 AM he was sitting in Norman's waiting room while his brother completed a phone call. A few moments later he was ushered into the office where Norman greeted him with what had become the customary bear hug. Marc said, "I wanted to stop by and thank you and your family for taking such good care of Max. I've never seen him happier."

"It's not just us. It's everything. The community is right for him and it's obvious that he has found his niche with Mike's dogs. Who knows, maybe he'll be the first Floridian to run the Iditarod?"

"We'll see. But, really Norm, I can't thank you enough. Anyway, I'm leaving for Anchorage around noon. Chani's flying me up there and I should be back in Miami by tomorrow evening. So, three things. First, I'll be back for Thanksgiving week, if that works for you?"

"Of course, that's great. You are family and don't need an invitation. As you guys say down in Miami, mi casa es su casa." And they both laughed.

"Number two, right after Thanksgiving, I'm heading to Boston for some refresher training and then Israel for a weeks where I'm giving the course at the International Institute to the African doctors. Then I'm spending four days in Africa for some hands-on mentoring of the physicians. After that, I'll be back in Florida. Number three: before we came here in May, Max and I had picked out a headstone for Cathy that will be ready at the beginning of December. So I am going to arrange for the unveiling of the stone the day after Christmas. I know you guys like to take a ski trip to Alyeska then, but I would really appreciate it if all of you came with Max to Florida for the unveiling."

"Done. We'll make our reservations."

"Norm, I'll take care of everything—it's the least I can do for you guys. Just let me know what flights you want and my secretary will make all the arrangements. Also, please stay in our condo. We have plenty of room and it will be more fun than a hotel."

"Thanks, we'd like that."

One more bear hug and Marc was out the door walking down the street to pick up the sandwiches and drinks and head to the high school. As 11:00 o'clock approached, groups of kids started exiting the main doors of the school. Some were heading to their part-time jobs; others heading home, and a few were on lunch break. Marc spotted Max and his heart sank.

"Why the long face Max?"

"You're leaving and I already miss you."

"Max. I feel the same way, but I have to go. There are a bunch of things I have to do at home."

"Dad, I love you, but I'm also very confused and conflicted because this feels more like home to me than our condo."

"Yeah, I understand. Let's just see. For the time being just enjoy every single day that you're here. We can talk on the phone or over the

Internet as much as you want and we'll figure this out. You're my main
man and I've got your back all the way. You understand?"

"Yeah."

"Good. I love you Max. Trust me, it will all work out well."

"Thanks, Dad, I love you too. When are you leaving and when will I
see you next?"

"Let's find a picnic bench, eat, and I'll answer your questions and
share some plans with you."

They headed over to an outside eating area twenty yards from where
they had been standing, sat down, unwrapped the sandwiches, opened
the drinks, and started eating. A few minutes passed when Marc said,
"Max, I'm leaving right after we finish eating. Chani's flying me to
Anchorage and I'm getting a red-eye to Seattle and an early morning
flight home. I'll be back here for the Thanksgiving week, and then I'm
going to Israel and Africa for two weeks."

"Huh. What's with Israel and Africa? Is that a vacation?"

"No. I'm helping out there as a volunteer. I'll be training African
doctors on certain aspects of plastic surgery."

"Are you kidding me? They want to do boob jobs and butt lifts in
Africa?"

"Truthfully, I don't know. I hope not. Maybe some of the rich people
want that. But, I'm working with the poorer people who need to have
their cleft lips and palates repaired. Or fingers fixed or maybe learn how
to deal with burns. I'm not really certain but it won't be the kind of cosmetic work I do in Florida."

"Do you know how to do that other stuff?"

"I use to and over the next few weeks I'm going to do a lot of refresher
studying."

"OK, good for you. And what else?"

"Max, this is the tough part. The day after Christmas we are having
the unveiling of the monument we picked out for Mom's grave. It's a
short ceremony but it also marks for us the end of our mourning. I want
you to be there?"

"Sure, but how do I get to Florida?"

"That's simple. I talked to Uncle Norman this morning and everyone is coming to the unveiling so you'll travel with them. After that we'll all be on vacation in Florida for the Christmas break."

Suddenly Max brightened up knowing he would be with his family and not alone. He then said, "I'll have to clear it with the Commander but I'm sure he'll give me the time off. Maybe Rachel and Rebecca would want to go to Disney for a couple of days? Would that be okay?"

"It's really up to Uncle Norman and Aunt Blake, but if they want to do it I'm certainly game." Smiles and hugs all around and then Marc departed for the rental car agency.

The flight to Anchorage was short and the scenery spectacular. Marc sat in the copilot's seat and marveled at the ease and expertise Chani displayed as she flew her Cessna. *What a person,* he kept thinking to himself.

They landed at Merrill Field, the same place he had met Chani for the first time six months earlier. A cab was waiting for them and Chani suggested that their first stop should be the Captain Cook Hotel where she had booked a room with a view of Cook Inlet. On the ten-minute cab ride to the hotel Chani whispered, "I feel like I'm on vacation with my lover."

"You are. And, I love you. I'm only sorry it's such a short vacation. What do you want to do?"

"Let's check in, drop the bags, and head out. I think we should make two stops. First, I want to show you the Alaskan Jewish Museum. It's now a few years old—it's expanded a bit and they have some interesting stuff about Jewish history here in Alaska. After that we'll come back downtown, spend a little time wandering around, and then maybe dinner and finally some preflight cuddling. How does that sound?"

"Perfect."

They followed their plan and enjoyed roaming the city, holding hands, laughing, and just being together. Their last evening together was playful and passionate. Finally, at 9:00 PM, they fell asleep in each other's arms. At midnight Marc's cell phone started chirping. He was up in a flash, turned the alarm off, and began dressing for his flight. Chani was sound asleep. He wrote her a short note that said, '*Chani, my darling. I already miss you. I love you. Take good care of yourself. Safe travels home and I'll call you tomorrow. I love you very much. Marc.*'

Part Seven
A New Beginning

Forty-Four

BAL HARBOUR, FLORIDA

The flight between Anchorage and Seattle left promptly at 1:35 AM and arrived in Seattle three hours and fifteen minutes later, right on schedule. Marc had a two-hour layover before boarding the daily non-stop between Seattle and Fort Lauderdale. The plane landed on time in Florida and by 6:30 that evening Marc was walking into his condo along with a cart full of mail and packages. The apartment suddenly felt lonely. Marc was exhausted but he texted messages to Max and Chani that he was back home, the flights were fine, but he hadn't slept on the plane. At 5:30 the following morning Marc was up and on his way down to the fitness center for a workout with plans to be in his office by 8 o'clock.

On the long flight home Marc spent hours ruminating about his future. For the first time since her death he was mad at Cathy for upending what he had thought was the perfect life. He asked himself whether he was ready to change. Was Chani really the one? Did he want to change his lifestyle? After all, he thought, *I'm an honest and honorable guy. I'm not doing anything illegal or immoral. Do I want to live in a small town in Alaska? And, if I did, what would I do?* The more he thought about his future the more uncertain he became. Finally, he concluded that he needed to talk this out with someone he could trust.

When he arrived at his office on Thursday morning he found a backlog of more than forty phone calls as well as appointments with patients starting at 10:00 AM and ending at 5:30 PM. He also saw that Friday was no better with patients booked back-to-back from 9:00 through 5:00 PM.

The first thing he did was sort through the messages and set aside the most important ones—a call from Reb Avrum and another from Rabbi Friedman. There were calls from salespeople that he discarded, a call from the Bentley dealer that he put into a return call pile, and one from the marina about some problem with a leak on his boat. That he also needed to deal with. All the rest were general inquiries about procedures and the local TV network had called asking for an interview. He also received a call from Andy Cagnetta to follow-up on the discussions concerning the sale of his practice.

By the time of his first appointment he had called the marina, authorized the repair on his boat, and asked them to do a thorough inspection of the boat and routine maintenance on the engine because he was planning on putting the boat up for sale. Next he called the Bentley dealer who was calling to see if Marc would be interested in trading in his convertible for a newer model. Marc responded by advising the salesman that he actually wanted to sell the car. An appointment was set up for the car to be appraised and sold. Next, Marc call Reb Avrum and Rabbi Friedman and left messages with both of them that he was back from Israel and Alaska and urgently needed to meet with each of them as soon as possible. Avrum called him back minutes later and a plan was made to have dinner that night at Marc's condo. He didn't hear from Rabbi Friedman until the afternoon and they agreed to meet Sunday at the Rabbi's house.

The remainder of Thursday was devoted to patients. By mid-afternoon Marc was utterly bored and wishing he was back in Seward with his family and Chani. He was also exhausted from a day filled with more discussions about plastic surgery.

By six o'clock Marc finished up his notes from the last patient and was headed out the door when he ran into Alfredo leaving for the day.

"How was your trip?"

"Fabulous and exhausting. By the way, *gamar tov* to you and your family. I hope all of you have been sealed in the book for a very sweet year. You guys deserve it!"

Alfredo was once again astonished. This was the first time that Marc Cohn ever acknowledged a Jewish holiday much less said anything in Hebrew. Alfredo's shocked reply was, "Huh?"

"A happy and healthy new year! Look I have to run, let's have lunch tomorrow—there are a few things we need to discuss."

"Sure."

With that Marc was out the door and Alfredo simply stood there wondering what in the world was going on. As soon as Cohn got home he went on the Internet to find the closest kosher pizza restaurant and ordered two kosher pizzas, one with mushrooms and pepper, and the other plain cheese, as well as two large green salads.

Avrum arrived a half hour later. The two friends sat around sharing their differing flight experiences home when Avrum looked directly at Marc and said: "You asked me over for pizza and beer to talk about flights and movies? What's really on your mind? What happened when you apologized to Chani? Did she slap you on the face or knee you in the groin?"

A smile quickly spread across Marc's face and then he related the story concluding with, "I think I'm in love with a rabbi! What do I do?"

"Oh my lord! I take you to Israel for a week, leave you out of my sight for five minutes, and next thing I know you're diving off the twenty-meter high board, in love, going to Africa, and saving the world. Am I missing anything?"

"Yeah, I'm thinking about selling my practice and moving to Alaska. Want to come with me?"

"No thanks, but I'll visit. Anyway, what will you do there? Be the *gabbai* of the shul?"

"I don't know. I haven't gotten that far. But, am I crazy or what?"

"Look Marc, I don't know Chani but Mike Pearl tells me she's a gem. I trust your judgment and our mutual friend Rabbi Friedman tells me she is a lovely woman who, like you, has suffered a great loss. So, my only advice is be fair to her. Don't get serious unless you are truly serious. Are you?"

"I think so."

"Maybe you need to be more certain than that before proceeding. Anyway, the second issue is leaving Florida and relocating to the boondocks. My friend, it's a huge adjustment. No fancy restaurants, no clubs, no big performing arts centers, and her shul is the only game in town. Face it, as Sarah Palin would say, you'll be closer to Russia than the rest of the U.S. Finally, how would this sit with Max? Is this how you see your life playing out?"

"I don't know. I really don't know. For me, though, when I was with Chani I didn't want to be anywhere else. I know I love her, but I'm scared."

"Of what?"

"Of hurting her; as you just said, she has been through enough. Of hurting Max and of being unhappy myself in Alaska."

"What were the most important words the old Jedi master Obi Wan Kenobi's said to Luke Skywalker?"

"Trust the force."

"That's it! Marc, trust that God is leading you in the right direction. It will be all right."

"I get it," and after a moment's hesitation he added, "I think."

"Great, let's eat before this pizza starts getting moldy!"

Forty-Five

BAL HARBOUR, FLORIDA

By the next morning Marc was back at his routine including gym time and in the office before 7:30 AM. The hours in the condo were hard. For the first time since Cathy died he was truly alone. The son he loved and woman he loved were four time zones and more than 4,100 miles away.

His office schedule that Friday morning included numerous follow-up visits and some new patient consultations. At noon he met Alfredo in a small conference room where tuna sandwiches, French fries, and diet cokes had been ordered. Alfredo was very curious about what was on Marc's mind. He was actually somewhat fearful that Marc was meeting in order to dissolve their practice or perhaps ask him to leave.

Marc began, "Alfredo we've been at this cosmetic practice for years, we've made a good bit of money, and I think we've actually helped some people who may have been down on themselves over their looks, and now feel better after the surgery. No doubt we've also helped some exotic dancers and other show business types. But frankly, we run an honest practice and that's what counts. And, Alfredo you do beautiful work and certainly earn your income. Your patients love you."

As Marc spoke Alfredo started to get anxious. He was waiting for the axe to fall when Marc said, "But I think the time has come when I am going to leave the practice and turn it over to you."

"What?" Alfredo almost screamed. "Are you ill? What's going on?"

"Relax my friend. Here is what is happening. I am thinking of marrying a woman who lives in Seward, Alaska, and moving there."

"A woman from Alaska? Are you kidding me?"

"Actually, Alfredo, my partner, she is a woman from Fort Lauderdale who lives in Alaska. And, she is a rabbi."

"What about Max?"

"He is already there living with my brother and his family and he wants to stay there. I think he wants to grow up to be a dog musher and run the Iditarod."

"But, Marc, how would this happen? You are essential to this practice. You're the big name. I may be your partner, but most people are coming for you. How would I handle this without you?"

"Look, Alfredo, I know this is a lot to think about but here is what I'm contemplating. Presently, we are partners. For the last few years each of us has been keeping all the money we generate minus the fifty percent of your gross for overhead since I own the building, equipment and theoretically the staff works for my professional corporation. So, what I'm looking for is simply a way to sell or rent you the building and equipment for a fair price. After that you're on your own.

"Give me a few days to figure this out. Do I keep the Institute name?"

"Yes, if you want it."

"Do I pay you for goodwill?"

"Sure, does a $1.00 sound like too much?"

"I can handle a dollar. But, would you be willing to stay as a named partner in the practice coming down here periodically to operate or consult so that there is continuity of your being part of it?"

"We could probably work something out."

"Would you be willing to consult with some patients and me via Skype or some kind of a telemedicine?"

"Very interesting idea, Alfredo. Let me look into that. In fact, that may solve a few other problems."

"How certain are you about this? I mean, getting married and leaving this practice?"

"I'd say, fairly certain, not 100% but definitely serious about both."

"Mazel tov!"

O n Sunday afternoon Marc drove to Rabbi Friedman's home where Leah warmly greeted him.

"You're staying for dinner, yes?"

"Thank you, yes, I'd be happy to."

A minute later the rabbi appeared looking relaxed in khaki pants and a short sleeved shirt, "Marc, welcome back. How was the trip?"

"It was extraordinary. Reb Avrum is a fabulous man and we have become good friends. I love being with him and every conversation is a true learning experience. Rosh Hashanah was simply amazing. In fact, I'm heading back in a few weeks to do some work with a woman named Hattie Ferguson and her international medical group."

"Hattie! Wow, she is a saint. I've known her for years and supported her organization since she started it. What are you going to do?"

"As best as I can figure out I'll be training some doctors from Africa on basic reconstructive plastic surgery techniques at the Institute's Jerusalem facility. After that I'll be accompanying the physicians back to Africa to assist them in actually doing the surgery in their own facilities. Truthfully, I'm excited and scared!"

"How is your son doing?"

"Great. I think he's found himself in Alaska. He wants to stay."

"Is that acceptable with you?"

"Well, rabbi, that brings me to another issue. You see when I was in Israel I learned a few things about Judaism, Torah, tradition, and myself and I decided to fly to Alaska and ask this woman I had met there for forgiveness. And one thing led to another and I'm thinking of marrying her and maybe moving to Alaska."

Rabbi Friedman and his wife were startled by this news. Finally, the rabbi asked the question that was on his mind as well as his wife's, "Is she Jewish?"

Marc laughed and answered, "I hope so. She's a rabbi."

Leah and the rabbi looked at each other and with tears in her eyes Leah almost tentatively asked in a quiet and uncertain way, "Is it Chani Kahn?"

"Yes."

"Baruch Hashem," they both said with the greatest of joys. "She is precious. You both deserve the joy of one another. Mazel tov!"

"Wait guys, I haven't asked her."

The rabbi replied, "Don't worry, you will. And you certainly will have my blessing. If you get married down here I would love to do the ceremony."

"It's a deal."

Then Leah chimed in, "Let's eat and celebrate." And they did.

That night Marc made the usual two phone calls, first to Max then Chani. Max and he talked about school, the dogs, and the kennels. He told his father about the recent snows and how enjoyable it was to drive the regular sleds over the snow-covered trails. He also warned his father to bring some warm clothes for his Thanksgiving week visit.

The conversation with Chani lasted over an hour. They shared their day's experiences and he told of his visit with Rabbi and Mrs. Friedman— leaving out the part about marriage.

Forty-Six

BAL HARBOUR, FLORIDA

For Marc the next few weeks seemed to fly by. He was busy seeing patients during the day and three nights a week he met with Avrum to study Torah and prayer book Hebrew. They often talked till midnight about Jewish laws, customs, and the inevitable subject of God Himself, Herself, Itself, or Whatever. They solved nothing but enjoyed themselves in the process. The other nights Marc devoted himself to studying the surgical techniques that he was going to teach the doctors when he got to Israel. Each evening he would call Chani and they would talk for hours. He loved to hearing about her work with the upcoming bar and bat-mitzvah kids and the activities at the congregation. Sometimes Chani would also talk about problems she was having at the prison and Marc would then usually serve as her sounding board. On Thursday night they began having late night study sessions about the following week's Torah session. Both Marc and Chani thoroughly enjoyed this time of learning together.

Marc was also particularly pleased about her developing relationship with Max. One day Chani told Marc that Max, the twins, and she had gone out cross-country skiing and on another occasion Max and Jody Pearl had taken Rebecca, Rachel, Norman, Blake, and her on a two-hour sled dog ride in the snow. Despite their physical distance and their temporary separation, for Marc everything about the relationship felt right. He hoped that Chani felt the same way.

Marc's plan was to fly to Seward the Sunday before Thanksgiving, spend the week in Alaska, and then fly to Boston. In Boston an old friend from his residency days had arranged for Marc to observe and perhaps scrub in on a range of reconstructive plastic surgery procedures. Cohn felt this would be a great refresher course prior to his trip to Israel.

Before he left for Anchorage he had one important stop to make in downtown Miami. Although Marc Cohn had lived in Florida for more than fifteen years he had never visited the historic Seybold Building, the epicenter of Miami's jewelry business. He went to the eleventh floor and spent two hours with Saul Glassman, a friend of Reb Avrum's.

Twelve hours after leaving Fort Lauderdale and two plane changes later Marc arrived in Anchorage at 2:50 PM. To his great surprise, Chani was waiting in the baggage area and holding a small sign that said, "Welcome to Alaska." After greeting each other with affectionate hugs and kisses, she said, "I was hoping the weather would be clearer and I could fly up and bring you back. But anyway, I missed you so much that I decided to drive up. The roads are clear so we can head back as soon as you get your luggage."

By 3:30 it was close to dusk and they were on the road back to Seward. When they were approaching the town of Girdwood it started to snow and Chani suggested that they should stop for the night and drive during the daylight. Fortunately, the Alyeska Resort was only a few miles away and they had plenty of availability.

Neither Marc nor Chani had ever been there before but from the moment they walked in they were impressed by its charm and elegance. The reception area had leather topped counters and a silk fabric ceiling. Their room was equally beautiful with dark wood walls, a well-appointed bathroom, and large windows overlooking a snow-covered forest. After checking in they called Norman and told him that a storm had blown in and they would be back in Seward late the next morning.

Chani and Marc then took showers, crawled into bed, and made love. They decided to order room service, had dinner, made love again, and fell asleep holding hands. Marc knew he was almost there. He needed to speak with one more person.

The next morning they were up early, dressed, and on the road by nine o'clock. The weather had cleared and the road had been well ploughed. As they drove Marc asked about the strange sounds coming from her tires. Chani explained, "Marc, my love, we are in Alaska in the winter; the sound you hear is the music of the studded snow tires. That's the only way to travel here."

For the next two hours they talked about his trip the following week to Boston, his subsequent trip to Israel, and his plans to sell the practice. They both carefully skirted the issues of their deepening relationship.

"Where are you staying in Seward?"

"I hope with you, but I have a room at the hotel for the sake of propriety."

"That's sweet of you. I appreciate that. Do you want me to drop you anywhere?"

"Actually, I have a car reserved so how about taking me there? Then I need to see Max and can we have dinner tonight?"

"As we say up here, 'you betcha'."

They both laughed, kissed, and Marc walked into the rental agency where they had an all-wheel drive Toyota 4Runner ready for him. He checked into the hotel and called his brother's house, and when Max answered, Marc said, "Hi, sweetheart. How are you?"

"Great, Dad. Where are you?"

"I'm at the hotel downtown. Are you working this afternoon?"

"No. We're off from school this week so I worked this morning and the Commander said I could have the afternoon off. He also sent his regards and said he'd like to see you while you're here. "

"Great. So, if I pick you up can we have lunch down here? I need to discuss something with you."

"OK, I'll be ready in ten minutes."

When he saw his son Marc was simply filled with joy. It seemed that even in the two months since he had last seen him Max was walking taller. In fact, to Marc it looked like Max had put on twenty pounds and grown six inches. No longer did he appear to be a frail teenager but rather he was a sturdy young man. They greeted each other with hugs and kisses on the cheek. Marc suggested they eat at the hotel where the food was decent and it was usually quiet.

Max asked, "So what's up, Dad? Are you really going from here to Boston and then Israel? Did you join the CIA or something?"

"No, as I mentioned before, I'm doing volunteer teaching in Israel and Africa and I'm stopping in Boston to brush up on some techniques. Max, there is something serious I need to talk with you about. And, frankly, this is very hard to do. But, here goes. You and I loved your mother very much. Both of us are very sorry she died. But she did die, and we have to move on. Right?"

"Right, so?"

"So here's the hard part. You are almost fifteen, a young man, and someday I'm sure you'll fall in love and get married and I as you father will certainly be supportive."

"Dad, where is this going? Are you trying to tell me you got married again or are going to get married again?"

"Yes, that's it. How'd you know?"

"Dad, this is the twenty-first century. Like you said, I'm almost fifteen and know what's what."

"Max, you'll always be my son and I will always love you but I do want to get married again, if it's okay with you."

Max smirked and asked, "Is it one of those hot Brazilian women you worked on?"

Marc's face turned red and he said, "No."

Max laughed, "I'm only kidding, Dad. I hope its Chani."

Marc was startled, "Holy crap, how'd you know?"

"Dad, like I said, thank God we see what's up around here. She's great and I'm very happy for you. Are you moving here?"

"If she agrees."

"This is the best news I've gotten all year!"

They talked about this for another hour when Marc said, "It's time for me to take you back and time for me to see Chani. Wish me luck."

A half hour later Marc was knocking at Chani's door. She greeted him affectionately. "So how was lunch with Max?"

"Better than I could have imagined."

"I hope you realize that Max is a bright and spectacular kid. I have been teaching him for his bar mitzvah next spring and he's picked up everything quite quickly, he's eager to learn, and he works very hard. I also gather he has lots of school friends. I said it before, but I'll say it again, you and Cathy did a great job with him."

"Not me, Cathy. I'm really just getting started with him nowadays. And, I've got a way to go. I hope you realize that he likes you quite a lot; I guess you guys have a mutual admiration society going. Anyway, I need to change the subject and get serious for a minute."

Suddenly Chani worried that something was wrong, especially when Marc asked her to please sit down. She did, he reached into his pocket, got down on one knee, and said, "Chani Weissfogel Kahn, will you marry me?"

Chani was startled as Marc opened the tiny velvet covered box and showed her the two-carat ring that he had carried with him from Miami. With tears slowly trickling down her cheeks she nodded and choked out a yes. Marc placed the ring on her finger; she looked at it, at him, and threw her arms around his neck and hugged her fiancé.

A little while later Marc called his brother and suggested they all meet at Miss Gene's Restaurant on Fifth Avenue for dinner. He said that it was important.

At 5:15 PM everyone was seated except for Chani and Marc. When they arrived a few minutes later there were warm greetings all around, Chani and Marc took off their coats and jackets, and sat down to look at the menus. Suddenly Blake spotted the engagement ring yelled out, "Oh my God!" She jumped up and hugged Chani and Marc and within seconds the dinner had turned into a joyful party as the Cohn family realized what had just happened.

It was indeed a wonderful celebration. Norman and Blake were thrilled that Marc was moving to Seward, Max was happy that he was staying there and getting Chani as a new member of the family, the twins were ecstatic that their favorite and only cousin was not moving back to Florida, and seemingly the two happiest people on earth were Chani and Marc.

The remainder of the Thanksgiving week proceeded with the same joy and good spirits of that evening in the restaurant. Despite the cold weather and light snow, Friday night and Saturday services were well attended and particularly spirited as the word spread about Chani and Marc's engagement.

On Saturday afternoon Norman asked to speak with his brother for a minute. "Marc we have a problem. Blake and I and the kids will probably have to go to Seattle within the next week or two. It seems that Blake's mother may start chemotherapy shortly and we need to be there to help her and my father-in-law. Max can come with us if he wants or he can stay in the house. What do you think?"

"If you're comfortable with it, I'm impressed that he can make up his own mind. So let's ask him."

They did ask Max who answered that he would rather stay behind in Seward, take care of Cookie and Cracker, and just look after things. Marc asked, "What would you do in case of emergency?"

"Dad, I'll call Chani, she's practically family." Marc liked that answer.

Norman then suggested that, just in case of emergency, Marc prepare a written authorization for Chani to consent to any treatment for Max if Marc or Norman are unavailable, "Like you're in Africa and we're in Seattle." Marc thought that was a good idea. Norman found a standard power of attorney form focused on consent to medical care for a minor on the Internet and printed it out. Marc signed it and gave it to Chani who read it over and nodded. She thought to herself, *this is for real.*

The last thing for Marc had to do before he left was to talk privately with Chani about their forthcoming marriage and future together. They spoke quietly in Norman's study and came out smiling. Chani had agreed to come to Florida in December with the rest of the Cohns.

On the Saturday night after Thanksgiving, a car service picked up Marc Cohn from his hotel for the drive to the Anchorage airport where he boarded the 1:45 flight to Seattle and then a nonstop flight to Boston.

Forty-Seven

JERUSALEM, ISRAEL

On his flight to Israel, Marc reviewed his week in Boston and realized going there for refresher training was a very good decision. He definitely felt better about his skills and knowledge, particularly when it came to pediatric work. Through his friends and their colleagues he was able to assist on some cleft palate and lip repairs, a skin transplant, some basic hand surgery, ear deformities, and a few trauma cases. He was ready and eager to teach and mentor. Despite his engagement and his love of Chani, he still wondered if he was honestly prepared to marry again as well as change his life. *Stop practicing cosmetic surgery? Move to Alaska? Was it really going to work? Was it too soon?*

Marc spent his first day in Israel getting a comprehensive orientation to the Institute. He was thoroughly fascinated by the state of the art teaching technology that they utilized. Of particular interest were the patient simulators that had been designed to imitate specific complications experienced in common plastic surgery procedures that were done on patients ranging in age from newborns to adults. Hattie explained the mechanics of the high-tech teaching devices and introduced Marc to the various staff that would help him during his week at the Institute. Next Hattie and Marc reviewed the curriculum and then the resumes of the physicians from Africa with whom he would be working for the following two weeks.

That first evening Hattie, Marc, the three technical staff, the program administrator, and the African doctors all went to a private room in a nearby restaurant for a "meet-and-greet." Marc was impressed by the intelligence and seriousness of purpose displayed by the African physicians. At one point during the dinner his mind drifted back to other small medical staff dinners that he had previously attended. He recalled that they often felt more like parties paid for by drug companies or equipment manufacturers. *These folks,* he thought, *are really serious about their work and totally into it for humanitarian purposes.*

The week was extremely intense. Marc was lecturing or demonstrating from eight to ten hours a day. Every evening back in his hotel room he spent hours reviewing the material, making certain that nothing he said was incorrect, and preparing for the next day. The last classroom session was over on Friday afternoon and Marc was totally exhausted. He sent an email to Max and one to Chani telling them of his experiences and his exhaustion. For the first time in his life he couldn't wait for Shabbat so he could rest and recover.

The hotel had a Shabbat meal that he finished in record time and then he went up to sleep. The next morning he went out for a walk in the tranquility that is Jerusalem on Shabbat. It was actually cool as Marc, almost on automatic pilot, headed to the Western Wall where he found hundreds of people praying the morning service. He put on his kippah, found a prayer book in Hebrew and English, and made his way to the Kotel. For the next forty-five minutes he read prayers and then leaned into the wall and spoke from his heart thanking God for the blessings of his life including two good women, his parents, his brother and his brother's family, and most importantly Max. He asked God to bless the souls of his parents and Cathy, and then he thought about it and asked for the soul of Rabbi Nathaniel Kahn to also be blessed.

As he was about to leave he turned back and said one more prayer. "I'm so in love but so conflicted. I feel Chani is a great person but I also feel, maybe in marrying her I'm betraying Cathy, and not helping Max. How about a sign? Is that asking too much?"

On Sunday morning, Marc and his new colleagues left Israel for two different stops in Africa. The plan was for Marc to split his time between each team of physicians in their home environments. Marc was alternatively pleasantly surprised and shocked by the situations in which his new friends found themselves. Sometimes surgical instruments weren't available, occasionally supplies were limited, and often those aspects of first world medicine that most American surgeons take for granted were simply absent in the third world. Improvising became the watchword.

While language was not a problem because all the local physicians and many of their nurses spoke English, Marc had to learn to be patient in dealing with the government dominated hospitals and clinic bureaucracies. By the end of the week Marc was thoroughly impressed with how well his students did under rather difficult conditions as well as how kind and appreciative the patients were for their surgical care. He also felt an enormous sense of accomplishment being part of Hattie's program that was providing much needed assistance to an underserved population. The mission was over on Thursday evening. The following morning he boarded a plane for the three-hour flight to Israel. Marc intended to use the remainder of Friday to prepare a mission report that he would present to Hattie and the staff on Sunday.

Marc Cohn was quite pleased and surprised to see Hattie waiting at the arrivals gate. Then she said, "I've been trying to get a hold of you since late yesterday but I was unsuccessful." Her next words made his heart stop, "Your son had an accident."

Marc suddenly felt dizzy. He sat down, took a few deep breaths, and looked up at Hattie who proceeded to explain. "Basically, Max is OK. Your friend Rabbi Kahn called. She said Max was in the hospital in Anchorage and is doing fine. It seems he was out dog sledding when a large snow-laden tree branch snapped and caused a freak accident. The EMTs took him to the ER in the town where he was stabilized, and the

Rabbi drove him to a hospital in Anchorage where another one of your friends, a Dr. Petrillo, did the surgery on his fingers and arm.

"Anyway, he's in Anchorage Memorial Medical Center, recovering from the surgery. Rabbi Kahn said she's staying with him and your brother was notified and he'll be back in Alaska by Sunday. The rabbi said you have her cell number and she's staying in the room with Max till he's ready to leave."

Marc was stunned and knew he would be forever grateful to Chani for saving the day. He also again realized how isolated Seward could be in these situations. He looked at Hattie and told her that he needed to get to Anchorage as soon as possible.

Hattie replied, "I thought that might happen so I took the liberty of booking you on flight to Los Angeles that is being held for you. In LA you'll be met by a friend of mine who will fly you on a private jet straight to Anchorage. You'll be there before you know it."

"Thank you so much. How can I repay you?"

"You already have and I'm certain we'll be working together for many years."

⸺⸺

Twenty-two hours later Marc walked into Max's room. Max was sound asleep in his hospital bed, and Chani was sleeping in a reclining chair.

Marc sat down on a second recliner and promptly fell asleep. A short time later he was awakened by the sound of someone walking into the room. It was a tall older man in a white coat looking at Max's chart. He placed his fingers to his lips and beckoned for Marc to come out into the hallway. Once out in the light Marc recognized the man as Dr. Petrillo.

"Dr. Cohn, how are you doing?"

"I'm fine. How's Max?

"In a few months he'll be good as new. Thanks to that Rabbi Kahn your son probably won't have any residual problems. As an EMT she knew about the accident right away and found Max in the ER. The local hospital did an excellent job of stabilizing your son but he needed surgery right away. Everything happened to his left arm and fingers that he used to deflect the tree limb. Two of his fingers were fractured; the ring finger was stabilized by 'buddy-taping' it to the middle finger. The index finger had an unstable fracture pattern with malrotation so it required treatment with plates and screws. He also had a displaced compound fracture of the ulna and radius and that surgery required two plates and nine screws. Overall, I would say he is in pretty good shape and there doesn't appear to be any neurovascular damage. If you want to read my notes or see the CT scan, they are all available for you at the nurse's station.

"Unfortunately, when the accident happened the weather wasn't very good for air evacuation—never mind the fact that the fixed wing plane and the helicopters were already busy elsewhere. So they needed to call for an ambulance to come down from Anchorage to take him because the Seward ambulances don't leave the local area. Anyway, the rabbi said that it would be faster if she'd take him to Anchorage but they wouldn't let her until she showed the letter from you giving her authorization in case of emergency. Good thing that letter was there because nobody could find you. Were you really teaching in Israel and Africa?"

"Yes."

"Doc, you really get around—Florida, Kenai prison, Africa, Israel. Any plans for settling down?"

"Actually, this just about convinced me. I think I'm going to open a surgical practice in Seward so there's at least some emergency and basic coverage. What do you think?"

"I think it's a great idea but you won't make much of a living."

"That's okay, the woman I'm marrying has a good job."

"Anyway, don't worry about Max, after he gets up and gets dressed, I'll come by and check him out one more time, write the discharge orders, and you'll be good to go. By the way, they have excellent rehab in Seward so no need for him to come up here.

"One more thing: because of you and your brother, I'm a free man again and doing what I love doing. So, thanks, and I'm totally serious when I say that you and Norman gave me back my life! Also, I checked you out on the Internet and it's clear you're a top-drawer surgeon. If you ever have a need to do some cosmetic work or even make some extra money you'll always be welcome to use my facilities. Thanks, again. See you later."

Marc walked back into the room and found Chani with her eyes slightly opened and she said, "Am I dreaming? Is that you?"

"Yes, my love. Thank you for taking care of Max. You are a treasure. I love you so much. Go back to sleep. We'll talk in a few hours."

Marc found a couch in the hallway, stretched out, and immediately fell asleep. Two hours later the sun shining through a window onto his face awakened him. He stirred and heard talking in Max's room. When he walked into he found a nurse, Dr. Petrillo, as well as Chani standing at the bedside. He heard Petrillo ask Max, "You ready to go home?"

"Yeah, I feel fine. But did anyone tell my Dad?"

Marc moved closer to the bed, touched Max's head, and said, "Hi sweetheart, I'm here. And I know what happened and glad that you're going to be fine."

Max smiled, "Hi, Dad. I'm sorry about this."

"Don't be. Things happen, particularly when you're a dog musher. But thank God that the EMTs responded quickly and Chani was there to bring you here and Dr. Petrillo fixed you up."

"Dad, where'd you come from?"

"I'm really not sure what today is, but I arrived here a few hours ago after leaving Africa about thirty hours ago. When I stepped off the plane in Israel they told me what happened and they already had me booked me on a flight to Los Angeles. From there a friend of a friend arranged for a private jet to fly me here. Very glamorous but exhausting."

After a family meeting it was decided that they would all stay in Anchorage for two more days at the Hilton downtown. Marc wanted to be certain Max was stable before his son traveled back to Seward. And,

Norman was due in shortly and then Max and Chani could travel back to Seward together with Norman and his family. However, Marc had to get back to Florida to finalize arrangements for selling his practice and arranging the unveiling.

Two days later everything fell into place. Max was feeling much better and anxious to get back to school in order to take final exams. Chani was ready to go home so she could take care of some end of the year work at the prison and the shul before the December trip to Miami. Blake had decided to stay in Seattle with her mother until it was time to go to Florida, and Norman came back with the twins. Everyone was happy with Max's progress and after what seemed like endless goodbyes, the Seward group set out in two cars for home. Once again, feeling quite lonely, Marc took a cab to the airport to wait for his flights to Florida.

Forty-Eight

BAL HARBOUR, FLORIDA

By the time Marc arrived in his office it was already the end of the second week of December and he had missed numerous days of surgery and consultations. While in Anchorage he had had several long conversations with Andy about the terms of the sale of his practice and Alfredo had been thrilled with the deal. As part of their agreement Marc asked that he be the person to announce to the staff the changes that were going to happen.

On Wednesday Marc came to work early fully energized for the day. The minor procedures that he did went smoothly and the missed surgeries on Monday and Tuesday had been rescheduled for Sunday. Alfredo handled a few of the patients who would have been canceled, and as Marc had expected they were quite pleased with their experience. All those inconvenienced were given a twenty percent discount on their procedure. Alfredo was astonished at Marc who in the past had never given anyone any discount for any reason whatsoever.

On Wednesday evening Andy came to the office and reviewed the terms of the sale with Marc and Alfredo. He suggested they each have their lawyers review it independently before signing papers the following week. The terms were simple. The name of the practice would

Seth B Goldsmith

become Alfredo's property. The facility, equipment, furniture, and all operating theatres would be leased with an option to buy after five years at a fixed rent and purchase price. The practice itself would remain as a partnership with Alfredo owning ninety-five percent and Marc the rest. Marc would be free to consult in person or via telecommunications as much or little as he wanted and would contribute fifty percent of his gross earnings from the Florida practice to the office's overhead. The terms of the deal allowed Alfredo total discretion with regard to bringing in new associates or partners.

The final part of the deal involved the staff. Marc viewed the staff as dedicated people who, while not physicians, had been central in building the practice. Marc insisted that they all be guaranteed employment at their current salaries for a period of at least six months after the deal was signed. Alfredo also recognized the significance of his staff and readily agreed to this provision. Once again, he was surprised at Marc's thoughtfulness toward these people.

That evening when Alfredo was discussing the sale with his wife he said, "It's astonishing. Marc has always been a superb surgeon. Until last year he was also one of the biggest 'you know what's' I had ever met. It was almost embarrassing to be his partner. Then his wife died, he went to Alaska, met a rabbi, and now he has become one of the kindest and most thoughtful guys in the world. Unbelievable!"

The next day Marc started surgery an hour early because he had much to accomplish, including a staff luncheon. Unlike other times when the staff brown-bagged it, Marc had called the kosher pizza place and had five pies delivered along with salads and drinks. To the staff it felt like the "old days" when the drug detail folks were bringing in "goodies." With Alfredo standing in the corner, Marc began.

"Friends, this past year has been a challenging one for Alfredo and me as well as all of you in a variety of ways. Regardless you have stuck by us and it turned out to be a good year for the practice. As I look around this table I see folks who have been with me since the first week I opened the Institute, and only a handful who are rookies. Each of you has contributed in a significant way toward our success. Both of us thank you from the bottom of our hearts."

Most of the staff were now glancing at one another wondering what shoe was about to drop. Rumors had been flying ever since the call from Israel when Marc told his office manager not to book any patients after the 25th of December.

Marc continued, "I know that there must be some confusion about what's going on so allow me to clarify the situation. Effective the first of January, I will become the junior partner in this practice and Alfredo is taking over. In order to keep the practice operating at its current level, he will be hiring one or two additional surgeons who may or may not become his partners. That remains to be seen and is entirely up to Alfredo. I will be transitioning to a more consultative practice and my own schedule will evolve over the next year. Frankly, I don't want to be mysterious but I am truly uncertain about the amount of time I'll be working in Florida because I am planning on opening a practice in Alaska.

"With regard to your employment, Alfredo has assured me that there will be no staff changes during this transition period so no one has to worry about losing their jobs just because I'm not here. Finally, since it's so close to Christmas, I want to announce this year's bonus will not be the one week's pay that we have been providing since the inception of the practice. This year, and this year only, to ease the transition into the new practice, we will provide a bonus of one month's pay. Thanks. I hope this clarifies what is going on."

The group sat silent for a minute and then one person began clapping and in a few seconds there was rousing applause, smiles, kisses, and well wishes for Marc.

Alfredo stood in the corner, proud of his new junior partner.

Forty-Nine

BAL HARBOUR, FLORIDA

Two days before Christmas a group of six weary travelers who had left Anchorage early in the morning arrived in Fort Lauderdale airport at 5:23 PM. A very happy man greeted them. Marc had rented a van for their visit so that they could all be together. He had also set up the condo in a way for everyone to be comfortable. Max's room was as he had left it before the bat-mitzvah trip.

In the master bedroom Marc had a bought a new mattress, cleaned out the closet that Cathy had used, donated her clothes to a Jewish charity's thrift shop, and put some photos in storage. The largest guest room was ready for Blake and Norman, Cathy's study had been converted into a temporary guest room with beds for Rachel and Rebecca, and finally Marc's study, which already had a high end convertible sofa bed, had been set up for Chani. The refrigerators and freezers were stocked, and his housekeeper had agreed to stay that evening for a dinner that he had planned for everyone.

The weather in Alaska during the week prior to their departure had turned cold, dark, and wet. By the time the travelers arrived they were ready for the Florida sunshine. Max was particularly happy to be home. He hadn't seen his room since May and looked forward to reacquainting himself with his 'stuff.' When Marc asked him about the arm and fingers that were still in a cast and bandaged he laughed and said, "OK, I'll survive. You know the doctor told me I'll never be a surgeon, but if my rehab goes well there was a good chance that I could still be an Iditarod champion." And then they both smiled.

Chani was overjoyed to see her fiancé. They enthusiastically hugged and kissed and hand in hand went to get the luggage. By 7:00 PM they were all at the condo and greeted by the smells of warm and tasty food. Marc suggested they drop the luggage and eat. The evening went smoothly and after dinner everyone wandered around the condo but the best part was sitting on the balcony watching the fading colors of the day. Marc helped Chani move her bags into the study. They closed the door and she said, "I love you, but this is a bit frustrating and awkward."

A minute later there was a knock on the door and they heard Max say, "Dad can I talk to you for a minute in my room?"

"Sure. I'll be right there." Then Marc whispered to Chani, "I hope I didn't start something here."

"You mean with my staying here? Maybe I should check into the hotel. It's a short walk away. I don't want Max to be uncomfortable about us."

"Let me see what's up."

Marc walked into Max's room and was asked by Max to shut the door. Then Max began speaking in a rushed manner: "Dad, please sit down. Look, I know this is a little awkward with this having been our family's condo for so many years and this being your house and mom's house and now you're engaged to Chani and she's here and staying in your study and I saw that you made some changes in your bedroom and I sat on the bed and I can tell it's a different mattress than you and mom had and I see it's a different cover and . . ."

Max started to sniffle and tears came to his eyes. "Dad, you know that mom's dying has been really hard for me. But I'm fine now. I still miss her, but I'm fine, and I want you to be happy. And I know mom would want you to be happy and not alone." At this point Max was crying and

Marc and he were holding each other. "And we both need each other and we both need Chani."

Max stopped, wiped his eyes, as did Marc. Then Max said, "So, Dad, like I told you in Alaska, this is the 21st century. I love you; I love Chani, stop pretending for my sake and please share a room with her. She shouldn't be alone here." Marc thought, *Wow, my son has become a man.*

———— ✖ ————

At breakfast the next morning the group started scheduling their day. Marc suggested a boat ride into the Everglades, "Maybe we'll see some alligators?" Everyone liked the idea and then Max asked, "What will we do after that?"

Blake said, "Well, I don't think this is a guy's thing, but we girls have been talking. Since we are so far out west near the Sawgrass Mills Mall we'd like to do a bit of shopping, and maybe have our nails done. You guys want to join us?"

A male chorus answered, "No way!"

So the plan became that they would take Marc's car and the van to the Everglades and then leave Blake, Chani, Rebecca, and Rachel at the mall while Norman, Max, and Marc would hang out in the afternoon probably seeing the latest adolescent thriller movie in Aventura. They agreed to meet back at the condo around 6 PM and then walk over to a new kosher restaurant for dinner on nearby Harding Avenue.

On Christmas day the weather was beautiful and everything was closed. Marc's boat had not yet been sold so the group decided that they would pack a picnic of leftovers and take a leisurely cruise down the Intracoastal Waterway and into Biscayne Bay. Marc suggested they dock at a tiny cay known as Shmot Island. He explained that the place was named by a local young Jewish couple that lived in one of the nearby high rises and regularly kayaked out to the island on Shabbat and camped there. The legend was that they also studied the Torah while on their camping excursions, and the first time they made the trip they were reading the parsha Shmot, thus the name. Although Marc claimed that his information was reliable; everyone laughed and thought the story was bogus until they set foot on the island and found a sign nailed to a tree that said Shmot in English and Hebrew.

The following morning was the unveiling that was scheduled for 10:30 AM at the cemetery. Chani felt awkward about going despite Marc's urging her to be there. Chani's ambivalence ended when Max approached her and simply said, "You're part of the family. We need you there."

Marc did not expect many people. He was surprised though to see Reb Avrum and Alfredo and his wife. The arrival of Rabbi Friedman and Mrs. Friedman led to a quiet and sweet reunion with Chani, whom they had not seen in more than a decade.

The short service commenced when Rabbi Friedman began speaking. "This morning we are gathered here at the grave of Catherine Feldman Cohn who passed away a year ago. Our purpose today is to dedicate this monument as a marker of Cathy's final resting place. This custom of dedicating a monument comes from the Torah where we learn that our Patriarch Jacob dedicated a stone, or as the Torah says, a pillar, to mark the grave of his beloved wife Rachel who died during the birth of their son Benjamin. Let's begin with a reading of the 23rd Psalm." Together the group began reading from the sheets Leah Friedman had passed out, "The Lord is my shepherd; I shall not want. . ."

When that was completed Rabbi Friedman said, "Please join me in reading one version of a beautiful poem written by Rabbi Jack Reimer and Rabbi Sylvan Kamens titled, 'We Remember Them.'" Together the group read:

In the rising of the sun and its going down,
We remember them.
In the blowing of the wind and in the chill of winter,
We remember them.

337

In the opening of the buds and rebirth of spring,
We remember them.
In the blueness of the sky and in the warmth of summer,
We remember them.

In the rustling of leaves and in the beauty of autumn,
We remember them.
In the beginning of the year and when it ends,
We remember them.

When we are weary and in need of strength,
We remember them.
When we are weary and sick at heart,
We remember them.

When we have joys we want to share,
We remember them.
As long as we live, they too shall forever in
Our hearts and souls,
We remember them.

"As I mentioned earlier this is a ceremony that traditionally occurs at the end of the period of mourning which on the regular calendar is now a year, and interestingly enough is a week after Cathy's yahrzeit. Before we conclude with the *El Malei Rachamim* memorial prayer and Kaddish I want to invite any of you to share your thoughts about Cathy." Nobody moved or said anything and Rabbi Friedman said, "Now no doubt we all have private thoughts about this extraordinary person who I'm certain is in Olam Haba. Let's conclude with the …"

Just then Max spoke up. "One second, rabbi; may I speak?"

"Absolutely."

"Everyone, thanks for being here. I know my mom would have appreciated it." Then he turned to the gravestone and said, "Mom, you are a very special person. Thank you for loving me all the time whether I did what you wanted or not. Thank you for being there for me whether I was screwing up or not. Thank you for always helping me and loving me. I miss you every day and I'll love you every day. Don't worry about Dad, or me we're finding our way. Please keep looking out for me, for Dad, for the rest of our family and also for Chani. I love you Mom."

Everyone at the gravesite, including the man from the funeral home, was in tears. Finally, Rabbi Friedman, who was also choked up by Max's words said, "Thank you Max. That was the kindest and most moving tribute I have ever heard. Rest assured your mom will be smiling down at you and your family for eternity. I shall now chant the memorial prayer in Hebrew and then Marc will read it in English."

When that was completed the group together chanted a final Kaddish. The rabbi urged the group to linger for a few minutes in silence and then leave quietly after placing a stone on the monument to mark their presence there.

As the group was starting to leave Chani pulled Marc aside and quietly said something to him. He then looked at his family and asked if they could wait in the van for a few minutes while Chani and he visited the graves of Devora and Shimon Weissfogel. They easily found the tombstones, stood there for a moment looking at them, and Chani began to cry. Marc placed his arm on her shoulder. She turned and continued crying while he held her. Once Chani regained her composure she moved away from Marc and approached her father's stone and whispered, "Daddy, please forgive me for being so angry with you and not being there for you when things were difficult and I forgive you for any offenses against me. I need you to look out for me as I start my new journey with this remarkable man." She turned and reached out to Marc then continued whispering to the stone, "Watch over us." They stood there for a minute holding hands, then bent down, picked up stones, and placed them on the monuments.

The unveiling drained everyone and once they got back to the condo they had lunch and decided that the day would best be spent walking on the beach, reading, or napping.

Fifty

FORT LAUDERDALE, FLORIDA

On December 30th, the Alaska Airlines nonstop flight from Seattle landed in sunny South Florida on schedule at 5:25 PM. Waiting in the baggage claim area to welcome a group of twenty-three people flying from Anchorage was a distinguished man with white hair and beard, Bermuda shorts, and a khaki T-shirt that said "Army." He was holding a sign that said "Commander Pearl's Vacation Club." Standing next to him was a handsome young man with a deep tan, also wearing Bermuda shorts and a khaki T-shirt, but this one was the shirt of the Israel Defense Forces, Zahal.

As Mike Pearl, the leader of the group got off the escalator and saw the man holding the official looking sign, he burst out laughing. But, Pearl was in for one more surprise: the handsome young man standing next to his pal Reb Avrum was his son Ethan. He hugged Ethan and quickly learned that Marc had also flown him in from Israel for the wedding.

"Good trip?" Avrum asked.

"Great, it's like the old days of stealth operations."

"Yeah, I can't wait. Get your folks together and then I'll call the bus to pick us up."

The Alaskans, including Mike, Minnie, Jody, Ethan, as well as the Polanskys and others from Seward's Jewish community, picked up their bags and headed to the curb where a large executive coach arrived for their trip to the Riverside Hotel on Las Olas Boulevard, in the heart of Fort Lauderdale. The group was exhausted. Anticipating their needs, Avrum had made arrangements for a buffet dinner at 6:30 PM in a private dining room on the hotel's rooftop. After everyone finished eating Avrum and Mike reviewed the schedule and logistics for the following day.

R abbi Friedman's normal routine during the weekday mornings, including Sundays, was to pray the morning service with his congregation as early as possible. After *davening* he typically went into his office to read and work on his correspondence, phone calls, and mail. On this particular Sunday morning he wanted to review his thoughts in preparation for the wedding. As he was doing this he suddenly recalled something. Frantically he searched the shelves behind his desk and there it was just where he had placed it many years earlier. He then called the synagogue's maintenance man, handed him the velvet bag, and gave him the instructions.

That same morning, a short distance east of where Rabbi Friedman was working on his comments, the group from Alaska was up early for breakfast. At 10:15 AM, they assembled in the hotel's lobby. The bus was outside at 10:30 for the five-minute ride to the next venue. Most of the people said they would rather walk the mile to the building and enjoy the Florida sunshine. They were given directions and strict instructions to be there by 11 o'clock. Everyone followed Mike's orders and they were at the appointed place and in their seats on time. Many of the Alaskans had never been inside such a large and elegant synagogue.

At precisely 11:15 AM a gray-haired woman walked into the sanctuary and said, "Hi, I'm Leah Friedman, the wife of Rabbi Yitzchak Friedman

and we are thrilled that all of you made this long schlep to be here today.
Today all of us are privileged to share in one of the best simchas I've ever
experienced. Your being here will be a surprise for Chani, and I know it
will be a great joy for her. You are her family, and I know that she loves
each of you and thanks to Marc's generosity you're in the Sunshine State
for a few days. He wanted to do this for her and you too. In a few minutes
the wedding will begin. So, just relax."

By 11:30 a classical guitarist had begun playing music from Haydn. A
minute after that Rabbi Friedman walked in, smiled at everyone, headed
to the bima, and stood under a chuppah that was covered in white roses.
He then checked a notecard, looked at the group and asked that Ethan
and Mike Pearl, Paul Polansky, and Reb Avrum to join him for instructions concerning a last minute detail.

A few minutes later the music stopped for a moment, and then began
again as Marc and his brother walked down the aisle and up the stairs of
the bima. Marc was thrilled that the Seward group had made it on time.
Next, Marc's best man walked down the aisle. Max, with his new suit,
white cast, and bandage, looked handsome and rugged. Marc noticed
that Jody couldn't keep her eyes off him.

The rear doors of the sanctuary opened once more and escorting
Chani down the aisle was her best friend and soon to be sister-in-law Blake
Cohn. Chani was wearing an elegantly tailored white linen suit. Initially
she looked straight ahead then halfway down the aisle she glanced to the
left, and for the first time since walking into the synagogue, she saw her
congregation from Alaska. Tears filled her eyes as she started to cry with
great joy. Spontaneously tears and smiles spread across the entire room.
Even Rabbi Friedman had to wipe his eyes.

Finally, Chani made it up the steps to the bima and stood next to
Marc. She looked up at the chuppah and saw Mike, Ethan, Paul, and
Avrum holding four poles that had a large tallit stretched between them.
She carefully looked at the tallit, then at the Rabbi, and mouthed the
words, "My Dad's?" He nodded and she again started tearing up as she
mouthed, "Thank you." The tallit had been found in her father's locker

two years after he had passed away—it had been put in the rabbi's office and forgotten about until that morning.

Rabbi Friedman began, "Wow! This is unbelievable. Friends this is a first for me—a wedding of a woman rabbi from Alaska." Then he focused on the couple, "Chani, Marc, I am thrilled and honored to officiate at your wedding. Chani, I remember you as a young girl, as the best athlete who ever grew up in this synagogue, and as the wonderful daughter of our dear friends of blessed memory, your mother Leah Weissfogel and your father Shimon Weissfogel, whose tallit you and Marc stand beneath today. You were always a bright and energetic person with a challenging intellect. I still remember our conversation so many years ago when you told me that you wanted to be a rabbi and I suggested social work. I guess we both got our way. And Leah and I remember that day in Israel when you met Nathaniel of blessed memory. We have been through so much together and now today a new beginning.

"Marc it has only been a year since we first met under the most difficult of circumstances. Since then our friendship has grown and I have kvelled, been thrilled, as I have watched you move in new directions and do truly amazing things in Israel and Africa. You are a mensch to be emulated! When you told Leah and me about your developing relationship with Chani I knew for certain that God was very busy working His mysterious ways. At weddings many rabbis like to say that it's more difficult to bring two people together than to split the Red Sea. In your case 4,000 miles is a pretty good chunk of land over which to bring two people together. This may be a record for a long distance romance.

"Chani, you've studied Talmud and you probably know or perhaps have even used this teaching at wedding ceremonies where you joined two people. So I hope that at least for you this isn't new information. In the Talmud we learn that the first marriage is *bashert*—essentially preordained by God—but the person you marry in a second marriage is based on your merits. What brings both of you here is not a bad first marriage but rather two beautiful first marriages that ended prematurely in tragedy. But both of you have not been glued to your sadness but rather have moved to a different and truly meritorious level.

"You, Chani, from all reports are doing fabulous work bringing yiddishkeit to the last frontier of the last frontier. Your congregation's presence here today is an extraordinary tribute. You, Marc, are a distinguished physician who is now moving to bring your talents to new populations around the world. The two of you are truly an extraordinary couple who together will bring God's blessings to each other and the world. It is really a privilege to be standing here with you. So let's get to work and make this official."

Rabbi Friedman continued the ceremony by picking up a cup of wine, chanting two blessings—the first was the traditional blessing over the over the wine and the second focused on those Torah commandments about the sanctity of marriage that ended with the words, "Blessed are You Lord, who sanctified His people Israel through chuppah [the wedding canopy] and kiddushin [holiness]." The rabbi then passed the cup of wine to Chani for a sip and then Marc. Next he asked Max for the ring, which he produced, and then asked Marc to place it on Chani's finger and recite in Hebrew, "With this ring you are consecrated to me according to the law of Moses and Israel."

Rabbi Friedman next read their artistically beautiful *ketubah*, wedding contract, in Hebrew and English rolled it up and handed it to Chani who passed it to Blake. The rabbi then explained the next part of the ceremony is called *nisuin:* seven blessing are recited over wine essentially in honor of the new union with each of these blessings celebrating God and His gifts, including the joy that is brought to a new bride and groom. The honor of reciting the first blessing was given to Max, followed by Norman, Reb Avrum, Mike Pearl, Paul Polansky, Alfredo Nussbaum, with the final one being chanted by Rabbi Friedman. The newly married couple then drank from the cup.

As the concluding part of the ceremony Rabbi Friedman placed a small glass wrapped in a cloth napkin on the ground and explained, "As you both know there are many interpretations to this final act where I ask Marc to stomp on the glass and break it. Today, I believe that the mystical explanation is the most appropriate. This view suggests that while the marriage ceremony is one where we bring two halves together, the breaking of the glass is a reminder of the fragmentation that preceded the unity and how hard it is to move from fragmentation to wholeness. Marc, do the honors!"

Marc lifted his right foot and brought his heel down on the glass. Immediately there was applause, calls of mazel tov, and singing of "Siman tov, mazel tov."

And then their lives began anew.